PASSION'S WILLING STUDENT

Wyatt pulled her closer, fitting her willowy slenderness against him. Incredibly, Cassandra did not pull away, but instead wrapped her arms around his shoulders and parted her lips, letting their breaths mingle with sweet heat. Wyatt couldn't get enough of the heady wine she offered, and he lifted her from the ground to bring her even closer. Cassandra could feel his need, his desire, for they matched her own churning excitement. She thought nothing would ever equal the rapture of Wyatt's kisses. Maybe this time he would teach her where these kisses led. . . . Maybe this time he would fill the hunger of her heart with love's dazzling lesson. . . .

TOUCHED BY MAGIC

TOUCHED BY MAGIC

PATRICIA RICE

AN ONYX BOOK

ONYX
Published by the Penguin Group
Penguin Books USA Inc., 375 Hudson Street,
New York, New York 10014, U.S.A.
Penguin Books Ltd, 27 Wrights Lane,
London W8 5TZ, England
Penguin Books Australia Ltd, Ringwood,
Victoria, Australia
Penguin Books Canada Ltd, 10 Alcorn Ave.,
Toronto, Ontario, Canada M4V 3B2
Penguin Books (N.Z.) Ltd, 182-190 Wairau Road,
Auckland 10, New Zealand

Penguin Books Ltd, Registered Offices:
Harmondsworth, Middlesex, England

First published by Onyx, an imprint of New American Library,
a division of Penguin Books USA Inc.

First Printing, March, 1992
10 9 8 7 6 5 4 3 2 1

Chapter 1

March 1816

Soaring marble columns bearing gilded sculptures depicting the Graces carried the gaze upward to a staggering arched ceiling embellished with murals of the Greek gods and accented with exquisitely carved gilded moldings bearing the certain stamp of Robert Adam. Beneath the canopy of tinkling crystal chandeliers and between the brocade- and velvet-covered walls and windows milled the procession of soberly black-clad gentlemen and extravagantly arrayed ladies in the silks and flounces of the current Season. None of the distinguished guests raised their voices above a civil level to make themselves heard over the hubbub of orchestra and hundreds of people speaking at once. The guests moved with well-trained precision as they balanced punch cups and napkins, fans and quizzing glasses, dance cards, and other necessities suiting their particular station and occupation of the moment.

The couples in the center of the gleaming waxed ballroom floor swayed with stately grace to an old tune, not the rackety waltz the Regent had accepted at court two years before. Harmony prevailed among sedately wigged musicians and modishly styled dancers alike. In the perfection of this scene at the London home of the distinguished Duke of Roxbury, not a whisper nor a hair was out of place, as befitted the occasion and the genteel society.

Only a few noble guests stared visibly at the sudden

whirlwind swirling from behind an elaborate sculpture
of a draped Diana, to rush headlong through the towering open doorway of the ballroom entrance to the
crowded hall beyond. Those few gasped in surprise
and hastily stood aside. They waved their fans and
raised their quizzing glances. They caught sight of only
a glorious mass of sunset-gold hair and a tall, slender
figure garbed in daring primrose disappearing through
the doorway. Cassandra! They shook their heads and
whispered behind their hands and turned away.

The fleeing figure exploded through the doorway
into the mass of still-arriving guests. Top hats and fur-
trimmed pelisses discarded, the latecomers lingered to
greet old friends and smile politely at new acquain-
tances. Black swallowtail coats and silk breeches
swung in startlement as the fiery explosion catapulted
past. The occupants of this sober garb swiftly stifled
admiring looks as feminine eyes caught their gazes
with disapproval. The golden figure didn't stop to inquire why.

A tall striking-looking gentleman stopped to help
his lady adjust her yards of Kashmir shawl. His stern
features held a formally imperturbable expression as
he listened to his petite companion's comments on the
successful squeeze and the evening ahead. The lady
herself was little more than plain, but she carried her
looks with the arrogance of wealth and nobility. Even
a stranger would know she was someone of consequence, at least to herself.

When the spectacular trail of flame came to a
breathless halt before this pair—indeed, she needed to
grab the gentleman's arm to stop her headlong flight—
both gentleman and lady stared in obvious confusion
and surprise.

"Wyatt! Thank goodness! You have to help me. Tell
him you've already claimed my next set. I'll escape
somehow afterward, but he's right behind me. Dash it
all, Wyatt, don't stand there like a looby! Look pleased
to see me. He'll never believe you elsewise.''

The tall gentleman looked even more confused as he gazed down into the magical features of the fiery-haired creature on his arm. Had the goddess Diana come down from her pedestal in the other room he could not have been more surprised. Not unintelligent, nor inexperienced in what society requires of a gentleman, he gallantly covered gracefully gloved fingers with his own awkwardly large ones and managed an uncertain smile.

"I do beg your pardon, miss. Are we acquainted?"

"Wyatt! It is Cassandra! Have you completely lost your wits?" The short lady on his other arm hissed and tugged impatiently in a futile attempt to free him.

"Cassandra! By Jove, little Cassandra?" Eyes of a deep rich coffee brown continued to gape with bemusement at the outrageous sun goddess clinging to his arm. "It's been how long? You weren't above—"

His words were rudely cut off by the goddess's less-than-heavenly answer. "Since last Wednesday. I promised you this set then. Smile, curse you, Merrick! Do not play the prim and honest with me now." Her own gloriously lovely smile spread across her face as she spoke, so none watching from a distance would have any knowledge of the biting tones with which she addressed the noble guest.

"Lady Cassandra, there you are! I have been searching this age for you. Lord Eddings said I might have this dance." A slender gentleman sartorially correct in tight black silk breeches and white satin waistcoat but heavily festooned with more gold than the ceiling came to a graceful halt in front of them. Although immaculately turned out, he wore the certain signs of dissipation, and the glass in his hand smelled of spirits stronger than punch.

Cassandra turned a blazing smile of condolence upon the newcomer. "Sir Rupert! What a pleasant surprise. I am so sorry, but this set is taken by an old neighbor of ours. Wyatt, Catherine, are you acquainted with Sir Rupert?"

Proper politeness disguised the disdain on Lord
Merrick's mobile features, but his stiffened stance at
this introduction gave evidence of his opinion of the
rake. "We're acquainted, Lady Cassandra. Rupert, I
was just taking Lady Catherine to a friend of mine.
Here he comes now." Over the heads of the crowd he
signaled a young gentleman of muscular build who
delightedly broke off in their direction. "Lady Cassandra and I previously arranged this set."

Merrick could scarcely be indifferent to the angry
intake of breath on one arm and the joyful exhalation
of relief on the other, but he maintained his balance
with incredible equanimity. Rupert appeared ready to
exert a vehement protest, but the arrival of the stocky
blond gentleman intruded.

"Scheffing, if you will, Catherine has requested a
glass of punch while Cass and I carry out this next set.
Would you be so kind. . . ?"

Smoothly Lord Merrick maneuvered the short lady
onto his friend's arm and carried the much younger
miss past Rupert. He glared his disapproval, but there
was little he could do to prevent his prize from being
carried off. A mere baronet did not face down an earl,
especially not an earl like Wyatt Mannering, Lord
Merrick. Even Cassandra would not be so bold as to
confront a lord of his rank, although her father's title
was far older and more noble than Merrick's. Disgruntled, Rupert watched as the two walked gracefully
through the parting throng. Heaven and Hell, he
dubbed them to himself as they disappeared into the
ballroom. And one could be certain that daughter of
Satan wasn't Heaven.

The earl's distinguished features didn't exactly por-
tray an angelic demeanor either as he gazed down at
his unexpected dance partner. The weathered lines
about his mouth deepened but reflected neither approval nor disapproval as he guided the young lady
onto the floor. The dance they joined was not a lively
one, and he used the opportunity to quiz his compan-

ion thoroughly. "You will explain what that was all about?" The words were more demand than question as he caught Cassandra's hand and led her through the pattern of the dance.

"That's quite plainly obvious, Wyatt," she replied disparagingly, with a trace of fire still flashing in her eyes. "Duncan promised that libertine I would dance with him and I took exception to it. There simply wasn't time to find my pelisse and summon a carriage. If you will be so kind as to dance me to the far staircase when the music's over, I shall pretend to go to the powder room and make my escape that way. It's quite kind of you to rescue me. I always knew you were the kind of man that white knights are made of."

"That's doing it a trifle too brown, my lady." Aside from the fact that there was a decade difference in their ages and he was due the respect of his rank, Merrick had not seen this chit in a half-dozen years, since she was practically in leading strings. Her airy familiarity now rankled his pride and dignity, and he determined to put her in her place. "Since your brother is your guardian, you're obliged to obey his wishes. And I cannot remember giving you leave to call me by name, much less molest me in public places. I require a more thorough explanation than that."

Cassandra gave a great sigh and turned a pair of meltingly blue eyes up to him. "You haven't forgiven me for stealing your apples yet, have you? I did not think you so petty."

"The apples in question were the result of years of experimentation lost to me because of your childish prank. There were only three on the tree. You did not need pick all of them. That is not to the point."

Merrick's air of injury returned the smile to Cassandra's face. "Any tree that bears only three apples cannot be worth much. And there is always the next year. Presumably it bore a great many more then. How did the experiment work out?"

"The tree bore a great deal too many while I was

away, and the gardener failed to prune it adequately. The tree split in half and died."

Cassandra laughed as he whirled her around in the pattern of the dance and brought her back to him. Despite his awkward size, Lord Merrick danced quite well, she noted.

"All those apples wasted! That's a terrible pity. Now, had I been there, I would have taken enough that the tree might be standing still. The Widow Jones always thought your apples were the best in the county."

"Is that what you did with them? I always thought there were far too many missing for one little girl to eat. You could have told me who they were for. I would gladly have helped you pick them. She always sent me the most excellent pies."

"Telling you wouldn't have been nearly as much fun." Cassandra's radiant smile would have affected a blind man. The earl merely raised an eyebrow at her lack of character. She made a slight moue of resignation. "Besides, she died that next year and we moved away."

Pages of explanation could have disappeared into the gulf created by that simple statement. Six years ago she had been a child pulling a foolish prank on her neighbor, who happened to be a happily married man at the time. A year later her home was gone and so was his wife, not to mention the Widow Jones. A momentous year, indeed. Wyatt carefully bridged the gap with a more innocuous topic.

"Where is your chaperone? If you mean to leave just to spite Rupert, she could be fetching your carriage."

Cassandra blithely waved away such niceties. "Do not concern yourself, my lord." She added a sharp emphasis to this last, showing she had quite acknowledged his earlier cut. "You have been more than kind. Simply see me to the stairs and I will fend for myself."

It may have been six years since he had seen her

last, but Wyatt was beginning to remember the rash little brat with more than foreboding. The reckless and awkward limbs and skinny child's frame might be replaced with creamy skin and a woman's grace and form, but he rather suspected her character had not undergone any such radical changes. None of the Howards were known for their retiring character or circumspect behavior. He frowned fiercely.

"You surely do not mean to go home alone?"

Since Cassandra had no chaperone other than her brother and had no intention of consulting her obnoxious sibling over the matter of leaving, she diverted the topic. "Have you and Lady Catherine set the date yet? She and your friend Scheffing seem to be getting along quite famously."

Merrick's head instantly turned in the direction of her gaze. While he had scarcely been able to elicit a smile from his fiancée during the entire length of their courtship, Scheffing always managed to bring her to animation. Since his friend had the wits of an overgrown puppy, he could only assume Catherine responded to his blond good looks. Well aware of his own lack of such charm, Merrick turned his gaze back to the slender young lovely on his arm. Time had certainly wrought changes in the skinny twelve-year-old he remembered. Dragging his gaze reluctantly from the barest hint of primrose silk over full young breasts, Merrick gave her a shrewd look.

"Catherine and Bertie are old friends, as surely you must remember. You have not been away from Kent so long that you have forgotten that. Where is your brother? I think it might be best if I make myself known to him before you spirit yourself off."

"Honestly, must you treat me as a child too? Duncan is off in the card room as usual. The set is almost ended, and Rupert is waiting by the entrance. The stairs it must be. Hurry, please, my lord, before he guesses where I am going."

He had little choice in the matter, actually. She

tugged his arm as soon as the music ended, and without creating a battle in the midst of this proper company, Wyatt could do naught but follow her to the stairs in the anteroom at the far side of the ballroom from the entrance.

"I am much obliged my lord." Cassandra smiled prettily as she gained the bottom steps. Then, without warning, she leaned from her perch to place a quick peck on the upturned face of the man frowning up at her. "Cathy doesn't deserve you," she whispered wickedly before fleeing up the stairway and out of sight.

Shocked at this unexpected tribute, Merrick hesitated like some inexperienced schoolboy besottedly staring after his first love. Recovering his senses, he schooled his frown into his normal indifferent expression and swung on his heel to regain the ballroom. Beyond any question of a doubt he knew what the little minx meant to do, and as neighbor and gentleman, he could not let her do it.

He would go search out the new Lord Eddings and confront him with his sister's waywardness, but he knew Duncan Howard of old. The man had as few scruples as Rupert, or less. Only a father as insane as the late marquess could have left an innocent young female in the guardianship of Duncan Howard. Provided Cassandra Howard could be termed an innocent.

Not wishing to question the morals or character of a female he had not known since her childhood, he acted out of the gallantry of a gentleman toward a lady. Merrick proceeded hastily across the crowded ballroom, gesturing toward Scheffing to follow.

They met at the entrance on the far side of the room. Catherine did not look at all pleased to be dragged around like a puppet on a string, but the earl had already decided time was of the essence and ignored the signs of an impending set-down. That was one of the advantages of being affianced to a woman he had known all his life. He knew her every mood, and experienced none of the uncertainties of gauging her reaction as he must with any other woman.

"I am forced to rescue a lady in distress, Bertie. Catherine, I hate to take you away before you have a chance to enjoy yourself, but I feel obligated to escort Cassandra home. You know what Duncan is . . ." He let his voice trail off without mentioning the indiscreet topics that immediately came to mind when the Marquess of Eddings was mentioned.

"And I know what Cassandra is," Catherine snapped. "How do you think she has managed all these years without you? Don't make a cake of yourself, Wyatt. I have no intention of leaving early. She will find her own way home."

Merrick stiffened haughtily. "She is just a young girl. I could not live with my conscience should anything happen to her because I neglected my duty. Scheffing, perhaps if you would look after Catherine, I will be back shortly."

As he stalked off, Bertie murmured reassuringly in the lady's ear, "You know how he is about duty, Cathy. You have to learn not to twit him when he's on the ropes. You knew he was a high stickler when you accepted his suit."

The lady's reply went unheard as the earl pushed his way through the upper hall and toward the staircase descending to the foyer. Perhaps had he been a foot shorter his aristocratic appearance would have been less noticeable and his progress more impeded by the crowd. As it was, people saw the dark-haired lord coming and hastily moved out of his way. Merrick had no difficulty in reaching the foyer in good time, but he didn't trust his prey to dawdle overlong either. After casting a glance upward to assure himself she was not above him on the stairs, Merrick stepped out onto the high stone steps and glanced down at the carriage drive.

He saw the slim figure in lined pelisse and hood

hurrying away almost at once. Throwing a curt order
to a footman, Merrick strode swiftly after her. One
advantage to having these damned long legs, he cursed
to himself, was that very few people could outstride
him. Though Cassandra was of above average height,
she was hampered by narrow skirts and thin slippers.

He caught her arm and swung her around with less
gentleness than he normally would accord a lady. If
she behaved like a wayward child, then he deemed it
best to treat her as one. "I will see you home," he
announced curtly, marching her back toward the stairs.

Cassandra stared up at the earl in astonishment. For
the first time that evening she saw him as more than a
means to an end, and she wasn't entirely certain she
liked what she saw. She remembered Wyatt Mannering as a quiet man who seldom raised his voice even
when giving a scold to a rambunctious child. She had
taken that quiet politeness as a sign of weakness to be
exploited with ease. The strength of his hand now and
the force of his will compelling her into his waiting
carriage told an entirely different story. She hastily
revised her opinion of his character.

"This is not necessary, my lord," she protested
stiffly as she halted before the open carriage door.

"It is entirely necessary for my peace of mind, Cassandra. Now, get in or I will carry you in."

She was not entirely unacquainted with harsh words.
Although she had had no governess since they moved
to London, her father and brother had often spoken to
her in just such tones when she had crossed them. The
difference was that they never carried through on their
threats. She concealed the overpowering certainty that
the Earl of Merrick would not be as lenient. She
climbed into the carriage.

Once inside, she oohed in delight at all the modern
conveniences revealed by the lamplight inside the expensive landau. The velvet squabs, cushioned by
springs, sank as she sat down. Behind the matching
curtains, clear glass allowed her to gaze out upon the

street. Beside each seat a vase held a single carnation, and she triumphantly lifted one and tucked it in her hair. She reached up and found the lamp-wick knob and dimmed the light, then turned it up brighter.

Merrick sat with arms crossed over his chest in the seat beside her, watching this performance with amusement. She truly was an innocent. What was Eddings thinking to allow her out in public with no chaperone in sight?

Cassandra's reply neatly ended that train of thought. "You should have let me find a hackney, Merrick. Catherine will not speak to you for a week. I'm scarcely worth the trouble."

She had a definite knack for startling him out of complacency. He gave her a starched look, but she had turned the lamp down again and wasn't paying attention to him. "A hackney? In the middle of the night? Have you completely lost your wits?"

"Oh, no." She turned to him with that brilliant smile. "I do it all the time. My only problem tonight was that I had no coin to pay the fare. It's devilishly difficult to carry coins in a ball gown, particularly one as daring as this. Any extra weight and . . . whoop!" She made a laughing gesture downward to indicate the effect on her daring décolletage.

Merrick could well imagine the effect of a tug on the frail bodice, and he turned searching eyes heavenward. It was quite obvious that Cassandra Howard's upbringing had suffered severe neglect for years. He wasn't out to correct it in a single night. He bit his tongue and made a muffled noise of assent.

Cassandra surveyed his pained expression with practiced care. "I should not have said that to you. Duncan said you were a high stickler, but I didn't imagine he meant humorless. Forgive me, I'll not offend your sensibilities again. It was most kind of you to see me home."

She settled back against the velvet cushions with grave dignity, primly crossing her hands on her lap and staring at the empty seat across from them. The carnation slipped from her disheveled tresses and slid down her cheek.

Wyatt rescued it, his hand brushing her satin cheek as he retrieved the flower from its entanglement. "I am not entirely humorless, but someone needs to teach you proper behavior with gentlemen with whom you are scarcely acquainted." He laid the carnation over her crossed hands.

"Fustian. I daresay I know you as well as Catherine does. You just won't admit that someone you think is a mere child can know anything. You've grown top-lofty, Merrick, puffed up with your own consequence. I can mind my manners when I choose. I just didn't think it necessary between neighbors."

The carriage came to a halt before the narrow town house of the Marquess of Eddings that Merrick remembered from his youth. It was in the less-fashionable district on the wrong side of St. James's and many of its neighbors had been converted to flats, but Merrick was not a believer in new being better. The old Georgian building looked pleasantly weathered by time. He waited for his driver to open the door as he gazed down upon the pert strawberry blond at his side.

"We have scarcely been neighbors for a number of years, Lady Cassandra, and you were much too young to know me even then. Duncan and I are barely on speaking terms as it is, but if I find you taking off on your own again, I will be forced to report your behavior to him. Now, come, it's time you went inside." He stepped down from the carriage and held out a hand to help her down.

Arching her wrist to gently rest her hand upon his, sweeping up her skirts and pelisse to make the step from the carriage, Cassandra descended with all the grace and dignity of an offended queen. She cast him a scathing glance as he offered his arm to see her inside.

"You had better return to Roxbury's with all due haste, my lord, or your fiancée will teach you the truth of her name. I bid you farewell." Without waiting for any servant to open the door, she threw it open and marched in, slamming it shut in his face.

It wasn't until he was back in the carriage that Merrick deciphered the remark about Catherine's name. In typical Howard fashion, the noble name of Catherine would be shortened to the epithet of "Cat." Well aware of his intended's claws beneath velvet gloves, he leaned back against the cushions and sighed. Women!

Chapter 2

The thick stench of cigars and the smoking table lamp did not irritate Cassandra's nose so much as the sharp odor of spirits as her brother poured another glass of port. She forced the frown back from her face as she idly bent over Duncan's shoulder to better examine his hand of cards. The numbers were a blur to her in this light, but she had learned the placement of the symbols at an early age. He was losing, and this hand would not turn the odds. She scratched a warning against his coat, but he ignored her, as he was increasingly wont to do these days. He had some illusion that his recklessness served him better than her cheating. She shrugged and wandered to the curtain partitioning his alcove from the main room of the gambling hell.

She was no stranger to these rooms. Early on her father had conceived the notion that she was his good-luck charm. It had only been the card tables at home at first, but as the marquess's luck away from home had dwindled, he had insisted on bringing her along to his more important games. In time, that had become every game he played.

Knowing her father's fortunes at the table determined the mood of the entire household that day, Cassandra had quickly learned the ways to ensure a happy outcome. She had not considered it cheating so much as love and filial duty. If her father won, her mother didn't cry. After a while, she also realized that if her father won, the servants didn't quit, she might have meat instead of cheese for dinner, and the bottle of port in the cabinet didn't dwindle as fast, all excellent reasons to develop her talents. She had cultivated them carefully for years.

Now that she was eighteen and more aware of society's strictures, she knew what she was doing was wrong. The quick glance at another player's hand, the warning signal indicating the wrong card to be played, the sudden smile to tip off a right card, all the innocuous games she had learned over the years would be considered cheating in the eyes of men like the Earl of Merrick. When her father had died last year, she had thought the game safely ended. Duncan had quickly disabused her of the notion.

Not wishing to entertain dismal thoughts of her brother's selfish pursuits, Cassandra contemplated the room outside the alcove. Most of the men out there were familiar to her, though few were of the class of gentlemen. Occasionally a band of young swells would invade this place, or a lone gambler bent on destruction like her brother, but this particular den of iniquity had an unsavory reputation. Duncan didn't always gamble here, but the same men frequented the same places eventually.

She generally moved with impunity through these hells, protected by her father's rank and reputation and a certain camaraderie of acquaintance. Lately she had become less sure of herself around these people. They were always inclined to testiness when losing or overt jocularity when winning, but their treatment of her at these times had changed of late. Whereas before they might have tweaked her hair or cuffed her ear, now they tended to pull her onto their laps or give her sloppy kisses or worse. She laughed it off as she always had before, but she no longer laughed inside. Had she given herself time to think of it, she would have been afraid.

Her attention caught on the movement of a tall man at the door. The way he moved seemed vaguely familiar, although his beaver hat and long cloak effectively disguised most of his shape from this distance. He wielded the walking stick in his hand more like a weapon than an ornament, and he made his way through the smoky, stale fog with less than assurance. His stiff reaction to someone's jostling elbow brought sudden recognition, and Cassandra smiled benevolently. Here was entertainment for the evening, indeed.

Duncan scarcely noticed as she slipped through the curtains into the room beyond. The emerald velvet of the gown she wore tonight was less daring than her primrose ball gown, but in these surroundings it beckoned like a gleam in the darkness. Heads turned as she maneuvered between tables. Eyes savored the sight of creamy round breasts barely disguised beneath a high-waisted bodice. Gazes followed the flame of red-gold curls piled high and loose and bouncing tantalizingly about a youthful face of ivory perfection. But the coolness of an icy blue stare as any hand reached for her stopped all but the most daring.

Fortunately, none were daring this night. A prize-fight outside the city had drawn the crowds away, leaving only the most inveterate card and dice players at the tables. Even so, Cassandra could hear the comments on the fight and its potential outcome from every corner of the room. These were diehard gamblers willing to bet on every activity in the country, including the date of their grandmother's death if necessary.

She lifted a hand to one of Duncan's friends calling to her for some advice as to which way to place his bet. She turned her hand in a gesture of a wheel to indicate her preference for ''Millstone'' Wright. A hoot of disbelief came from onlookers who favored his opponent, but a number of wagers were hastily laid on the basis of the lady's suggestion. The odds went up against Millstone's opponent. Cassandra smiled and looked quickly toward the fat man tending the ale keg. He made an approving gesture with thumb and forefinger. The wager Duncan had made earlier just went up another point in his favor. He had assured her Millstone was a certain loser.

Without any seeming effort on her part, she floated to a halt just behind the out-of-place gentleman in top hat and cloak. "Looking for someone, my lord?" she whispered suggestively.

Lord Merrick turned to lift an eyebrow in disbelief at the jewel glittering amidst the ashes of this hell. "Cassandra? What the d . . ." He stopped and rephrased. "What are you doing here?"

"I think the question is more of your presence than mine, my lord. As you can see, you're the stranger here, not I." She lifted another hand in greeting at a salute from the nearest table when she took the earl's arm.

Horrified at the implications of finding Cassandra rubbing shoulders familiarly with the rakes and scoundrels of this dismal gambling hell, where no lady was wont to go, Merrick stumbled over some reply. He would not believe the obvious. She could not be as familiar with these men as their lewd winks and foul grins seemed to indicate. She was the daughter of a marquess, by Jove. Even a debauched marquess would not . . . Merrick refused to think further of it.

"I'm looking for the younger brother of a friend of mine. I had promised to look out for him this evening, but the young devil . . . demon slipped away. You wouldn't happen to know Bertie's youngest brother, would you? I should think he was just about your age."

He was looking mightily uncomfortable, Cassandra observed with amusement. He had finally remembered to remove his hat in her presence, and he kept darting scandalized glances at the men accosting her with overfamiliarity. He rigidly kept his own gaze from falling lower than her face, which made her very aware of her new, more mature figure. None of the men she was familiar with made her pleasantly aware that she was a woman, but this courtly gentleman did. She tried a provocative smile and was gratified to notice he colored slightly but didn't look away.

"I don't know any young gentlemen my age, my lord. They can scarcely be expected to occupy places such as this, can they? But if he's here, I daresay I know where to find him. Come with me."

Delighted at being able to show off her superior knowledge to the haughty earl, Cassandra led the way across the room to a corner not easily observed from the door. A round table of rickety construction held a foursome of players. Drink rings stained the cheap wood, but the players took little notice of their moist mugs, although they were promptly refilled by a slatternly barmaid as soon as they were emptied.

"I don't suppose the young blond fellow with his back to us would be the one you seek?"

Merrick didn't have to look closely to identify the youngest Scheffing. All the males of the family were built like young bulls. It was a pity their dispositions weren't more like the animals they resembled. Suspicion, stubbornness, and anger would serve them better in this city than their amiable and generous natures. Merrick stared suspiciously at the large stack of markers before the pompously garbed gambler in the corner. Cassandra answered his question before he could phrase it.

"Norton fleeces every youngster who comes through that door. He takes pride in it. He thinks he is teaching them a valuable lesson," she whispered from somewhere near his left shoulder.

"Since Thomas has only just received his quarterly allowance, it will be a rather expensive lesson. With five boys, his parents do not have much extra to spare."

His tart words had scarcely left his mouth before Merrick realized Cassandra was slipping away from his side and toward the table. In horror, he watched as the gambler called Norton looked up with a paternal smile and gallantly stood and gestured her toward a chair. The earl developed a sudden leaden feeling in his stomach as he approached to stand behind her.

"Cassandra, I cannot approve of this," he murmured, bending near her ear as she reached for the cards she was dealt.

"Fustian, Merrick. I've been playing with Norton since I was naught but a schoolgirl. He doesn't mind at all, do you?" She sent a sunny smile in the portly man's direction.

"Of course not, Lady Cassie. You are an astute student of Lady Luck. Have a seat, my lord. We're all friends here."

Merrick caught Thomas' bleak gaze and shook his head. "I'm no hand at cards. I'll just watch if you don't mind." He gave the lad a warning frown and then posed to wait for the final fiasco. It was a hard way for the boy to learn, but he couldn't pull him out of the fire now. Merrick knew the rules of the game but little more. He would just watch and make certain nothing more was wagered than the few coins left upon the table.

Cassandra began an idle chatter about the prizefight as she nonchalantly held her cards. When she wished to place a wager, she held her palm up and wiggled her fingers at the towering man behind her. Bemused, Merrick obligingly placed a gold guinea there. She gave him a suspicious glance at the sum, but carelessly threw it in the pot as if it wouldn't pay a half year's wages for the lady's maid she didn't have.

Young Thomas seemed to sink even lower in his seat as Cassandra's casual aplomb took over the table. She laughed. She teased. She scolded and folded her cards and held out her hand for another coin from the earl. All attention focused on her and away from the boy, whose entire quarterly allowance had dwindled to a single silver coin.

To his amazement, Thomas saw his fortune begin to change as soon as Cassandra won the deal. The coins came slowly at first, somehow disappearing one at a time from the other men at the table. None noticed his small change of fortune in the shadow of the more spectacular winnings of the amazed lady. She laughed with incredulity as the huge pot came her way, and generously offered to split it with everyone. The men at the table grumbled good-naturedly. One dropped out. Norton gave her a wary look, but comfortable behind his still-considerable winnings, he shook his head.

"Your brother should have your luck, my lady. I'm glad you don't play often."

A dimple appeared at the corner of her mouth as she gave him a bewitching smile. "You're just jealous because I'm prettier than you are tonight. Shall I let you have the cards back?"

Ruffled at the insinuation that she was manipulating the deck better than he, the older man made a negative grumble. "Nay, child, let the boy try his hand. He has a few coins yet to share."

Merrick listened in amazement to the nuances of this exchange. He was nearing thirty years of age, had come into his title almost a score of years ago, and had considerable experience with the fashionable world. True, his tastes had never run to the seamier side of London. He seldom had time to indulge himself in the various vices available, but that wasn't to say he hadn't tried them. He knew perfectly well that somehow Cassandra was cheating. What he didn't understand was the fact that the gambler knew it too and didn't complain.

Of course, if he delved into it further, he'd have to question why and how a gently bred lady knew how to cheat, or what she was doing here in the first place. But these were questions better left to another time. She would scarcely appreciate being questioned on the matter in front of others, particularly since the others didn't seem to be at all surprised to have her company.

Even with Thomas dealing, the coins in front of Cassandra continued to grow. She laughed with the guilelessness of a child, made gold coin houses with the stacks in front of her, and generously lent Thomas what he needed to make his wager against the rapidly climbing odds she and Norton were constructing. Another player dropped out, but under the sharp eye of the earl, Thomas rebelliously stayed in the game.

Deciding Cassandra had quite aptly proved her point, although his friend's younger brother hadn't seen it yet, Merrick brought an authoritative hand down on the shoulders of both youngsters when it became Cass's turn to deal again. "I'm quite bored with this pastime, my lady, Thomas. Bid your friends farewell and let us find more amusement elsewhere."

Norton looked decidedly relieved and hastily retrieved the deck from Cassandra's grasping fingers. Cass gave his lordship a sharp look of annoyance and disgust, and Thomas appeared wary as he rose obediently at the command of the earl.

Polite murmurs of farewell were made, and conscious of Cassandra's pantomime of what happened when she added coins to her pocket, Merrick hastily scooped up her winnings in his handkerchief, knotting it securely. Her triumph hadn't exactly made her happy, the earl noted as he caught a glimpse of shadowed blue eyes before she turned away from him, but a wild shout near the door kept him from pondering this discovery.

"Millstone won! A knockout in three rounds! Hand it over, my boys, I'm going to be a rich man!"

Merrick couldn't see the bearer of these tidings, but he could see Cassandra's creamy complexion pale another shade whiter. He fingered the bundle of coins in his hand thoughtfully but pretended he hadn't observed her distraction when she pasted a lovely smile on her lips and took his arm.

"Well, my lord, I trust you wagered on the right man. Millstone has become quite a favorite, hasn't he?" She gaily acknowledged the triumphant wave of several men holding wads of paper in their raised fists to show her their winnings. Mugs clanked throughout the room as the winners raised their elbows in tribute to the favorite.

One penguin-shaped old gent waddled up and bussed Cassandra neatly on the cheek and pressed a coin in her hand. "Here's for yer tip, lass. Ye're a good gel." He gave Merrick a leery look. "Ye take care o' the lass or ye'll be hearin' from the likes of Timothy O'Leary."

Merrick hid his pained expression at this confrontation with the whiskey-soaked old reprobate and hurried to usher the two youngsters through the riotous scene. Men jumped on tables and waved bottles while others cursed and flung empty mugs at the walls or the winners. A fistfight broke out in a far corner, and Merrick felt Cassandra step a little more quickly toward the door. He caught her shoulder and pushed her in front of him and gestured Thomas to protect her with his back. In a narrow phalanx they hastened through the growing tumult toward the door.

They had to hurry down the narrow back alley to the wider street, where the carriage waited. The riot inside the gambling hell hadn't reached these dark streets yet, but the thick silence was almost as unnerving. Merrick cursed at finding himself shepherd to two lambs in this wolf den, but grimly he told himself they had found their way here on their own and deserved a good fright.

Unfortunately, fear didn't seem to be uppermost in their minds as they climbed into the gleaming landau waiting for them. Cassandra again bounced joyfully on the cushioned seat and Thomas grinned unabashedly at her.

"I say, you were bang up to all the tricks back there. You must teach me how to play like that. Did you really know Millstone was going to win? Dash it all, if I'd only met you earlier, I wouldn't be looking down the River Tick now."

"Thomas, you're a rag-mannered young slowtop and when you're done rusticating the next quarter you

won't be so eager to repeat tonight's performance.''
Merrick threw himself down beside Cassandra in a
decidedly dampening manner. Both youngsters gave
him wary looks. ''I'm taking you both home and
washing my hands of the two of you. If your families
can't teach you common sense, I don't intend to try.''

Abashed, Thomas sank into silence under the earl's
toplofty set-down. Cassandra coolly held out her palm.
''My winnings, my lord.''

He bent a curious gaze to the nearly translucent illumination of her face in the dim interior, but blue
eyes behind gilded lashes gave no hint of thought or
emotion. He drew the bundle from his pocket and
placed it on her palm. ''I don't believe my young friend
here realizes how you won it,'' he admonished.

Merrick thought he detected a slight flinch at his
words but she immediately responded with one of
those brilliant smiles he had learned not to trust.

''I am certain you will explain it to him with time.''
She turned her taunting gaze to Thomas. ''How much
did you lose to Norton tonight?''

The young man turned a puzzled look from bene-
factor to enchantress. As the carriage rattled over cobblestones through darkened city streets, he found no
oddity in sharing this space with such a disparate couple. Merrick could look forbidding enough when he
pulled a straight mouth like that, but he knew the earl's
retiring nature well enough. His father might deal him
a bear-garden jaw, but he would suffer only a look of
disappointment from Merrick's honest brown eyes.
That the aristocratic nobleman came accompanied by
a young fire goddess was exceedingly strange, but one
couldn't question such loveliness attaching to the older
man's side. Merrick might be plain in looks, but
Thomas was well aware of his gentle nature. Any lady
would feel safe with him. His puzzlement stemmed
from the air of disapproval and defiance between these
two who had rescued him.

He turned a solicitous glance to the lady. ''You need

not concern yourself over my losses, my lady. I shall scrape along well enough. I congratulate you on how well you played.''

To Merrick's amazement, a thundercloud formed across the sun of Cassandra's smile. She ripped open the handkerchief in her lap and spilled open the mountain of coins.

''Merrick, how much did I steal from him? Name a fair sum. I would not take candy from babes.''

Young Thomas looked astounded, then wounded, but Merrick calmly named a sum that emptied nearly half the coins from her lap when she leaned over and poured them across the lad's thighs. Merrick was hard pressed to keep a straight face at the boy's reaction to that.

Instead, he held out his gloved palm. ''I believe you owe me a small sum, also, my lady.''

Cassandra gazed at his palm with contempt, then began to bundle what remained of her winnings into the linen again. ''That's my finder's fee. I'll have the handkerchief laundered and returned to you on the morrow.''

The grin began to force the corners of his mouth upward as Wyatt read the defiance of a cornered fox in her eyes. ''Very well, my lady, I'll remember that. Do you have a schedule of fees for your other services?''

He should not have said that. It really was quite wicked of him to taunt her, but she raised the pale ghosts of long-gone childhood emotions, and he could not resist responding in kind. It worked. The thundercloud immediately disappeared, and she grinned at him with quick understanding before adopting a sultry expression and leaning provocatively closer.

''Of course, my lord. Shall you come in while I show them to you? Bring your young friend. I'm certain he would profit from further lessons this night.''

The jest had gone entirely too far. Ignoring the shock on Thomas' face, Merrick caught the young chit by the nape and held her firmly at a proper distance. "Cassandra, you ever were in serious want of a sound thrashing. I'll be round to see your brother in the morning."

Faint mockery laced her voice as she leaned back comfortably, forcing Wyatt to release her or caress her shoulder. "I fear you just left Duncan behind. He won't be home until morning, and I can promise you he won't be in a humor to hear of my shortcomings. But you're certainly welcome to try. I might sell tickets of admission."

"You really are an undisciplined brat, aren't you?" he asked calmly, removing his hand to the safety of his cane.

"And you really are a stuffy old stick. That makes us even."

Thomas could scarcely believe his eyes or ears as he watched the dignified earl and the golden miss rip up at each other as if they were cat and dog. What was worse, they did it with such control that he couldn't be at all certain that he could believe what they were saying, particularly when they looked at each other as they were doing now. It ought to be daggers they were drawing, but instead, Thomas felt decidedly *de trop*. He had the sudden feeling that the earl's hands would not have remained long on the walking stick had a third party not been present.

That was an irrational thought. He was feeling a little fuzzy from all the strong ale he had drunk. Merrick was the last one to be accused of molesting a lady. The fellow didn't even keep a mistress. He had mockingly been called St. Wyatt behind his back for years for his views on the weaker sex. Not only did he hold the radical notion that women were not meant to be used by men except for bearing their children within the confines of marriage, he included all women in that notion, not just ladies. Had the earl not been reticent about speaking his opinions in the company of others, he would have been blackballed by every club in town.

As the landau came to a rattling halt before the lady's residence, Thomas lifted the curtains to investigate their surroundings. He had every intention of continuing the lady's acquaintance despite her insult. She looked like she needed a friend, and Merrick obviously didn't mean to be one. He frowned at the sight of another closed carriage waiting across the street, but he didn't speak up. Perhaps it was the habit of the neighborhood to come and go at all hours.

Thomas gallantly took the lady's hand, murmured all the polite phrases he knew, but remained behind as Merrick escorted her to the door. He didn't want to know what was between those two. His head was already beginning to ache just thinking about it.

When the earl quickly returned to the carriage, Thomas gave a sigh of relief and commented idly, "I say, Wyatt, ain't that Rupert's carriage across the street? I thought he had enough barrels of gold to live in a more fashionable district."

With a soft curse, Merrick glanced out the window to the carriage indicated. Rupert's, of a certainty. Well remembering the theatrics that had driven Cassandra into his arms not many nights ago, he could imagine that the baronet's equipage here at this hour of night did not bode well. Before Thomas had time to register the pithiness of his curse, the earl was out of the carriage again.

The faint sound of a woman's scream echoed through the open landau door, and Thomas blanched. Hastily he scrambled after Merrick.

Inside, Cassandra swiped her arm over her mouth where the baronet's lips had touched hers. Rupert had caught her unprepared. She was unaccustomed to fighting at this close range. Viciously she trod on his toe, but her cloth slippers went unnoticed against his leather boots. When he bent his handsome head to nuzzle her neck, a paralyzing wave of disgust swept through her, but she had to keep her wits. The Marquess of Eddings kept very little in the way of servants, and those few were in all probability sleeping off drunken stupors in the distant basement. She was quite effectively alone in this little trap laid for her, and she had only herself to rely on.

As Rupert's hand crept across Cassandra's flesh to take more liberties with her person, the door crashed open. The furious struggle in the hall suddenly halted as the towering figure of the earl intruded.

Cassandra felt the full weight of Merrick's disgust as he discovered her wrapped tightly in Rupert's arms. She was nearly of a height with the baronet, and her hand in Rupert's hair must have the appearance of a lover's caress to the earl's untrained eyes. Trapped by a strong arm, Cassandra strained to escape, but the resulting position pulled her velvet gown taut over her breasts. Realizing how she must appear to Merrick, she struggled to right herself, but Rupert brazenly closed his fist over her breast.

As Thomas tumbled in behind him, Merrick pulled himself to his full height, and giving the passionate couple a look of disdain, growled, "Let us go, Thomas. I fear we are intruding." Cassandra's strangled cry brought him to a sudden halt.

"Damn you, Wyatt, help me!" Cassandra dug her nails deeper into Rupert's neck in an attempt to pry loose from his embrace.

Merrick's eyes narrowed as he turned to investigate the tableau more thoroughly. Only one candle burned in the sconce upon the wall, but Cassandra's struggle to escape had grown pronounced enough to discern. Whether this was an effect of his presence or not, he could not ascertain, but he could not ignore her plea. He stepped forward with the threat of his greater stature.

"I believe the lady protests your embrace, Rupert. I would recommend releasing her."

The smell of spirits was strong on the baronet's

breath as he threw the earl a sullen look and deliberately manipulated Cassandra's breast. "She's promised to me. She can protest all she wants, but I have
her brother's permission to make her mine. She just
needs a little taming, that's all."

Cassandra tugged harder on Rupert's hair, bringing
his head closer until she could twist and grab his nose
between her teeth. She bit hard until he screamed and
practically dropped her.

Merrick caught her before she fell, and she grasped
gratefully at his waistcoat and held on for dear life as
the baronet wailed and searched frantically for a handkerchief. One of them was trembling like a leaf, and
Wyatt wasn't at all certain that it wasn't himself, as
rage washed over him for the first time since childhood. He hadn't been this furious in years, but this
was none of his affair at all, and he had no real right
to interfere—as much as he desired to plant a facer in
the middle of the rake's already injured nose. Still, he
didn't release the slender form curled against his protection.

"Thomas, would you show the gentleman out?"
Merrick asked coldly, not daring to do more. The baronet could very well be in the right of it. Cassandra
needed a strong hand taken to her, but a fist wasn't
what he had in mind.

Rupert was in no state to offer a fight against the
brute strength of the younger Scheffing. He left reluctantly under escort. Throwing a glance over his shoulder, young Thomas followed him out and closed the
door after him.

Left alone in the darkened hall, Merrick instantly
set the lady in his arms at a proper distance. Cassandra
wiped at a suspicious glimmer in the corner of her eye
and offered a wavery smile.

"I apologize for cursing you, my lord. My brother's
practical jokes sometimes fail to strike me with their
humor."

She was lying, he was certain, but he pressed the

topic a little further. "Then you are not betrothed to him? I should think your brother would have to call him out for such behavior."

Cassandra took a deep breath to steady her nerves and give herself time to think herself out of this embarrassment. The smile on her face became a little brighter. "Oh, yes, well, I suppose I am promised to him for now, but in a week or so he will grow tired of my sharp tongue and Duncan will pay him back his markers and he will be gone like all the others. Sometimes it's an amusing game and most of the gentlemen play it properly. I fear Sir Rupert really believed it when Duncan said he would sell me to him. Would you like to buy me next, my lord? I'm certain after tonight he could use a little extra cash. Just don't expect to get it all back when I bite your nose."

She laughed, a brittle laugh that did not sound as if it belonged to one so young. Well acquainted with the drunken madness of the Howard family, Merrick couldn't separate truth from lie. Every word she said could very well be true, but whether it was a game, indeed, or a cruel farce instead, he couldn't say with any degree of certainty. Cassandra had proved herself every bit as much a liar as the rest of the family.

"You would have some difficulty reaching my nose to bite it, my lady," he responded gravely. "If you are alone here, perhaps I ought to take you to stay with young Thomas' parents. You are less likely to be the victim of practical jokes there."

Cassandra gathered up all her quivering nerves, and clasping her arms over her bosom, met the earl's haughty gaze with all the courage she could muster. She smiled. "How very thoughtful of you, but I assure you it is not necessary. My mother is asleep just up the stairs. I shall lock the door behind you and go smear jam on my brother's sheets. It was kind of you to see me home. I hope I was not too rude."

Merrick began to understand that the polite, formal statements she summoned from some long-ago train-

ing were the real lies, but he had lived too many years
by the rules of society, and those statements were a
formal dismissal. He made a brief bow.

"Very well, my lady. I must offer you my gratitude
for saving my young friend from his foolishness. If I
may, I will call on you and your mother on the morrow
to better express my appreciation and to be certain you
suffered no harm from this evening."

Cassandra's smile was beginning to grow a little
strained. "Of course, my lord. Good night."

She watched tautly as he closed the door behind him;
then she fell on it and bolted it thoroughly. Tremors
of disgust and tears and pure emotional hysteria swept
through her, but she would not give in to them. She
would not. She had to stand strong. Someone in the
family had to stand strong.

Raising her chin, she gazed up the stairs to where
her mother lay. She could do it. She could defeat Duncan. It was just a matter of planning.

Chapter 3

"I won't have it, Duncan, I won't, I won't!" Cassandra slammed the iron poker into the stand so hard the entire heavy ring of instruments threatened to tilt and fall. For a brief moment she contemplated taking one of the brutal pieces to her brother's thick skull.

The Marquess of Eddings sat with one thigh propped on the edge of his desk and his arms crossed over his chest. He was a powerfully built man with muscular legs that bulged at his tight buff pantaloons and shoulders that strained at the faultless tailoring of his navy broadcloth coat. A permanent sneer marked the elegant cut of his aristocratic features, and the puffiness about his eyes gave evidence of more than one night's dissipation.

"You have no choice in the matter, dear girl. I can no longer afford your elegant wardrobe with no return on my investment. Rupert is willing to overlook your lack of dowry and your nasty choice of family, not to mention your bad temper. How many of the *ton* are willing to do the same?"

Cassandra drew herself up and gave him a scathing glare. "It is not my lack of dowry that presents the problem. We have name and title enough for the worst of them. It is your rakish behavior that brings me to this. It is your pockets that Rupert will plump if you have your way. I am willing to help to gain the funds we need, but you aren't willing to listen."

Duncan gave a short laugh. 'Don't fool yourself, little sister. You are far too clever to believe that. You have the tongue of a shrew and the temper of a viper. Your behavior at the very few places we are invited has been inexcusable to an extreme. It won't take long for word to circulate of your presence in the city's most notorious gaming hells, should you try to attach anyone of respectability. How long do you think it will take for tolerance of our noble name and title to turn to cutting you dead for your wantonness?''

"I am not wanton! You are the libertine, throwing me into the arms of your disgusting friends. I will not go gambling with you anymore. You never pay attention to me anyway. Take me to respectable places and let me find someone decent, if I have become such a burden to your finances.''

Duncan stood up and started for the door. "You'll not find anyone with Rupert's wealth willing to take you. Sorry, old girl, but the deed is done. You'll find he's not so bad when he sets you up in that elegant house of his and dresses you in silks and furs. You can look for someone decent after you give him his heir.''

Cassandra slammed a book after his departing back, but it merely bounced off the door as it closed. She would not wed that lecherous fiend. She would not! What could he do if she refused to say the vows?

She didn't want to think about it. She knew her brother well enough to realize he would be prepared for that eventuality. Rape, drugs, and Gretna Green were not beyond him.

It wasn't that her brother didn't love her, she told herself as she started toward her mother's bedroom. It was that he didn't know what love was. Duncan had inherited his disgusting weaknesses from his father along with the title and the estate and the empty coffers. The Howards had been drunkards for generations. The only father-son relationship they knew was over a table and a bottle of wine. Drunkenness led to gambling and other vices, until there was nothing left for her brother to call his own.

Cassandra didn't fool herself into thinking she was

untainted. Had she been a male and introduced to her father's society, she would undoubtedly have turned out the same way. Her sex and her mother had been her saving graces. Ladies weren't supposed to drink, and her mother had warned her of the dangers of strong spirits. Too bad she had not been more of an influence on Duncan.

A servant in shabby livery hastened up the stairs before she had time to enter her mother's chamber. Cassandra raised her eyebrows at the man's appearance after an absence of several days, but his message prevented questioning.

"There's two gents below to see you, m'lady." He tugged his forelock respectfully, remembering the modicum of training he had received at an earlier time when there had been others to teach him.

"Gentlemen? To see me? Or Lord Eddings?" Any callers at all were highly unusual. Her mother had been an invalid for years and her brother's friends weren't of the type apt to make formal calls. Cassandra could safely say she had no friends. She had never been formally introduced to society, and her childhood playmates had been left behind in Kent.

"You, m'lady," the servant insisted.

Curious, Cassandra quickly followed the footman downstairs. Surely Rupert had not already recovered from his night's excesses and come with a friend to claim her. She didn't think the beast had any friends. Besides, the footman had said they were gentlemen. Even an untrained servant was discerning enough to recognize a gentleman.

When she entered the front salon she was conscious of the unaired mustiness of the room. The draperies had been drawn against the fading effects of occasional sunlight, and it was doubtful if they had been aired or cleaned in decades. She felt her breath catch in her chest in embarrassment as she recognized the two immaculately proper gentlemen standing in the center of the graying carpet.

"Lord Merrick, Mr. Scheffing, it is a pleasure." She made a careful curtsy, determined not to appear as shabby in manners as the room was in appearance. Duncan's scathing remarks on her behavior still rankled.

"Cass, you needn't stand on propriety with old friends," the elder Scheffing exclaimed, stepping forward to take her hand. "We've known you since you were in leading strings."

Cassandra threw a look over Bertie's shoulder to the stern, proud man behind him. That wasn't what Merrick had said. She gave his frown a slightly triumphant look and turned her smile to his friend. "But I am supposed to be a proper lady now, sir. Won't you have a seat? Let me open these draperies so we have some light."

She glided across the room to tug at the immense height of ancient brocade. The handful of fabric shattered in her hand and engulfed her in a cloud of dust.

A large, competent hand reached over her shoulder to lift the heavy material and drape it carefully over a mahogany serpentine bureau that had not been sold because of a sword gash in its side. Cassandra stepped warily aside as Merrick lifted another panel and draped it over the lion-clawed chair on the window's other side.

"Let there be light." With a flourish, he produced a gilt side chair built to accommodate hoops and panniers and gestured for Cassandra to sit in the gray light produced by the filthy window.

Thoroughly embarrassed but determined not to be, she settled her pale muslin skirt neatly about her as if it were silk and lifted her hand to indicate the nearby chairs for her guests. "I recommend these seats, gentlemen. The wood is sturdy and not so infested with dust as the upholstered ones."

The sarcasm did not sound right on the lips of so young and fair a maid, but both gentlemen agreeably pulled chairs forward to sit before her.

"I am not accustomed to gentlemen callers, my lord, sir. What does one talk about on such occasions?"

The brilliant smile was almost painful to see, Merrick decided as he admired the fire ignited in her hair by the few dismal rays of sun. The state of this room made the truth of her comment more than obvious. His reaction wasn't one of embarrassment for her but a decided urge to throttle her brother.

"You know full well why we came, Cass." Scheffing barged into the stray thoughts and odd emotions drifting between the other two. "I had to offer you my thanks for pulling Thomas out of the briars last night. He's new to town and not up to all the rigs. He learned a lesson he's not apt to forget anytime soon. He would be here himself to tell you but he's still suffering from a sore head and a stiff set-down from our parent."

Cassandra's smile faltered slightly, uncertain how to deal with gratitude. "I hope he will not hold me in dislike for the circumstances. Norton is an old friend of my father's. I fear I know his tricks too well."

Merrick had not been able to keep the circumstances of their encounter entirely from Bertie, and he hastened to soothe her fears. "We have said nothing of it to anyone else. We're all acquainted with the marquess's habits. Thomas is eager to further your acquaintance and will most likely do so once he is permitted out of the house again. We thought there might be some way of showing our appreciation."

Cassandra gave him a sharp look. She well knew the Earl of Merrick was a wealthy man who had little need to waste time on young misses not yet introduced to society. The way those dark eyes rested on her, she suspected he was remembering the encounter with Rupert last night. She gave him a smile of defiant hauteur.

"How enchanting!" She laughed brittlely. "Shall I demand that you accompany me for two turns around the park this afternoon? I daresay all heads will turn

at the sight of two such gallant gentlemen escorting a
mere girl about. 'Twould be most exciting indeed.''

"I'll gladly escort you to the park every afternoon,
Cass," Bertie offered exuberantly. "You'd make a
deuced fine sight on any gentleman's arm."

Merrick gave his thick-headed friend a frown. It was
patently obvious to him that Lady Cassandra had been
roasting them for their good intentions, but then, Bertie didn't know the full extent of her desperate straits
or deceptive tongue. He turned his frown back to the
undisciplined brat in the window.

"Since we understand your mother is quite ill and
unable to escort you to the proper functions, we
thought it might be appropriate if Bertie's sister takes
you under her wing. She has been wedded this year or
more and would make a suitable chaperone. And she
has already proclaimed herself thoroughly tired of her
family's all-male company. She would be delighted
with a little feminine companionship."

Merrick offered this with the air of one determined
to do a good deed whether his victim liked it or not.
Rebellion lay close to Cassandra's surface, too close
not to resent being manipulated in this way. He was
determined to teach her proper behavior, and she was
equally determined to show him she did not need his
help. Far too wise in the ways of the world to exhibit
open rebellion, she smiled complacently and crossed
her hands in her lap as a demure miss ought.

"How very considerate of you, my lord. You have
thought of everything. She's Lady Cunningham now,
is she not? I'm sure we'll get on swimmingly. I can
teach her to play cards and swear, and Bertie and all
his young brothers can escort me about town, and Lord
Cunningham can cut Duncan every time he comes
looking for me. Sounds great fun, does it not?''

The horror in Bertie's eyes made her giggle, and she
instinctively avoided Merrick's. "I'm sorry, Bertie."
She laughed as he tried to stutter some reply. "I should
not twit you that way. Your offer is very generous, but

I must stay with Mama. I really have done nothing to merit your generosity.''

Bertie tugged at his neckcloth and, red-faced, attempted to be polite. ''Dash it all, Cass, you and Christa would get along fine. You ought to be out and about more. You ain't still in mourning, are you?''

It was on the tip of her tongue to say she had never mourned her father, but she caught Merrick's eye and bit back the bitter reply. All this had been his idea, she knew. He wholeheartedly disapproved of her rackety family and upbringing. The Howard name and Eddings title dated back through centuries, but Wyatt's Puritan antecedents cared little for such things. Perhaps it was kindness that made him want to rescue her from herself, but she preferred to believe it was his smug moral righteousness. Experience had taught her kindness was not overabundant in this city.

With tired politeness Cassandra dismissed the subject. ''That's most thoughtful of you, Bertie, but really not necessary. Mama will be better soon, and I'll have a proper come-out then. I haven't seen Christa in this age or more. Perhaps someday you could take me to call. We haven't kept in touch with our neighbors from Kent very well. Would you care for some tea?''

She prayed they would not. In all likelihood she would have to go to the kitchen and prepare it herself, and even then it was doubtful that she could offer anything more. But it was the only polite phrase she had left in her repertoire to distract them.

Lord Merrick rose and made a polite bow. ''I fear we have other pressing engagements and must be leaving, Lady Cassandra. If it's convenient for you, one of us will be around tomorrow at this time to take you to Lady Cunningham's. I'm certain she will be delighted to have the visit.''

He was all that was proper, making her realize all that she was not. Resentfully she offered her hand and allowed him to bow over it. His grip was strong and firm and somehow disconcerting, but she knew how to disguise her feelings. "Thank you, my lord. It has been good seeing you again."

Less sensitive to the sparks and tension between the striking pair than his younger brother, Bertie waited impatiently for his friend to release his overlong grip on the lady's hand. "I say, Merrick, let's not do it too brown. Christa ain't exactly the Queen of Egypt."

Cassandra immediately transferred her hand to Bertie's and murmured polite farewells. She was quite uncomfortably aware of his lordship's thoughtful gaze upon her, but she had no wish to decipher what was behind those observant eyes. She would much rather not know Lord Merrick's opinion of her.

After they left, she sat staring at the lighter-colored square on the wallpaper where a portrait had once hung. Her argument with Duncan overshadowed the morning's events, and her fingers clenched and unclenched in her palm as she tried to sort out a strategy to be made of this visit. She shouldn't have been so hasty about declining Lady Cunningham's chaperonage. She might have met some decent gentlemen that way, but Duncan had been right. Her reputation and that of her family would eventually ruin any chance she had and potentially harm anyone who supported her. She had always considered it something of a lark to accompany her father to places other ladies would blanch to hear of. She wondered what they would think of her if they knew she was quite good friends with the Cyprian who had been her father's mistress these past years. Undoubtedly, she was corrupt beyond redemption, but she hadn't *wanted* to be that way.

All she had ever wanted was her parents' happiness and a decent home. That she had gone about it in all the wrong ways was a difficult lesson to learn—and not one understood when she was younger. Now that she was old enough to know better, there didn't seem to be any way out of the hole she had dug. She was tarred with the same brush as her brother and father.

Or would be soon enough. She stood up and began

to pace the room. Obviously her reputation hadn't preceded her yet. Perhaps she had behaved rather badly at the few social affairs Duncan had condescended to take her to, but that was because he had insisted on foisting her off on his miserable company of friends. She could do better. She knew how to behave. She only had to find a decent man to rescue her from this morass, and she would be the epitome of all that was proper. She could take her mother away from here and provide her with a decent home. If she worked fast enough.

She knew the very man to rescue her. It would take a man of immense respectability and wealth, one who was far above gossip. With a smile as much of spite as decision, she lifted her skirt and set off in search of the one remaining maid.

The illegitimate daughter of a long-departed parlormaid, Lotta had been with the Howards literally since her birth. There were some that said she was as much Howard as the legitimate son and daughter, but Cassandra and Lotta had long ago decided it was more likely that Lotta's father was one of the late marquess's rakehell friends. While admittedly Cassandra favored her mother and possessed little of her father's dark, aristocratic looks, Lotta bore no resemblance to anyone at all, not even her deceased mother. Her round cherub face and blond locks had more the appearance of a good yeoman than of any aristocrat either knew. But both girls were equally certain that Lotta's mother would never have given her virtue to a simple farmer. Somewhere out there a nobleman with a rotund face and a yeoman's build had a daughter he knew nothing about.

Cassandra rather favored Bertie's father as the culprit this day as she went from salon to kitchen in search of the maid. Wouldn't the new Lady Cunningham be surprised to discover she had a half-sister scrubbing ladies' linens in the Howard basement? She gave a sigh of exasperation as Lotta took the wash paddle to

the kitchen cat, spraying hot suds across the already
slippery floor.

"Lotta, how would you like to put on your best bonnet and go courting?"

That caught the older girl's attention. Lotta dropped
the paddle and hastily began to dry her hands on her
apron. "Courting? Who's to go courting, ye or me?"

"Both. First, you must find out where my beau will
be so I can make certain to be there too. That you can
do if you woo one of his lordship's men. Surely you
must know one or two on Merrick's staff?"

Lotta's eyes grew large at the prestigious name of
her employer's proposed suitor, but she had no reason
to question Cassandra's decision. She quite firmly believed that Cassandra could do anything she wanted.
One had only to look at her fiery gold hair and small
determined chin to know that. Cassandra was destined
or doomed to have her way. Lotta was only thankful
that she had chosen someone as eminently respectable
as Lord Merrick.

"If I don't know them, I soon will. Will you lend
me your old gloves, too, so I can look proper?"

Cassandra smiled in delight at this sign that her plan
was in motion. It would be only a matter of time now.

Lotta had long since returned with her devastating
news when Cassandra entered her mother's room with
the tea tray. She felt her stomach knot as she carefully
arranged the bed tray under Lady Edding's tender
glance. She couldn't let her mother see how many of
her hopes were pinned on the outcome of this conversation.

"There is entirely too much here for both of us to
eat, child. Are you expecting company?" Lady Eddings neatly arranged her napkin over her satin bed
gown and lifted large blue eyes to her daughter. It had
always amazed her that she had been able to produce
two strappingly healthy children. She herself had had
a heart murmur and other physical weaknesses since

childhood. It did not seem quite feasible that her children should be such tall, handsome creatures.

"Of course not, Mama. You must eat more if you are to get well. Will you have one sugar or two today?" Cassandra settled comfortably in the bedside chair and poured their tea. Her mother really ought to have full-time care, but good nursemaids did not stay long when their duties were not monetarily rewarded. The bell at her side had to suffice during those hours when she and Lotta could not be there.

"One, thank you. Lotta said you had gentlemen callers this morning. I trust they were respectful. It really is not proper to have callers with no other lady in attendance." She watched her daughter carefully, understanding the shadows behind her eyes better than any. As the daughter of a marquess, she was entitled to all that society had to offer. That Cassandra must settle for the crumbs that fell from the bounteous table was as much her own fault as the child's father. Had she possessed health, she would have managed a proper come-out, money or lack of it regardless. These things could be arranged. But her health had prevented her being there with her daughter, arranging the proper introductions.

"You need not worry about the conventions, Mama. Lord Merrick is everything that is proper. He meant to call on us both, but I had to explain that you weren't receiving. You remember Lord Merrick and Mr. Scheffing from home, don't you?"

Lady Eddings smiled faintly at the disguised eagerness in her daughter's voice. "Which Mr. Scheffing? It seems to me there are dozens of them. A quite respectable family, as I recall."

"Albert, of course, Mama. He is a little less than Lord Merrick's age, I believe."

The invalid nodded knowingly. "And never been married, now that I recall. A quite presentable young man. They're not wealthy, but I suppose young Albert would come into a competence one day. You could do worse, I daresay. Will he call again?''

Cassandra looked exasperated at this digression from her plans. "I don't know, Mama, he's just a friend. It's Lord Merrick I want to talk to you about. I wish to attach his interest, but he's to go away and stay at Hampton Court with some others for a week and I fear he will forget all about me while he's gone." Actually, she was quite certain he would forget. Her urgency was a result of her conversation with Lotta. The servants' gossip had the earl setting a date with Lady Catherine over this next week. It was quite expected there would be a wedding before the Season ended. She could overset a betrothal without a qualm, but a wedding would put finished to her plans.

Lady Eddings had the grace to hide her surprise. The Earl of Merrick was the last person she would expect her tempestuous daughter to fix her interest on. Or vice versa. She regarded Cassandra's innocent expression with some suspicion. "Wyatt Mannering is much too old and set in his ways for you. His first wife was a mouse who never spoke a word of her own. That harpy mother of his saw to that. Besides, haven't I heard you say that he has become betrothed to Lady Catherine? An unlikely couple, I admit, but their lands do march together.''

Cassandra had no recollection of Wyatt's mother or his first wife, but as a schoolroom miss she could scarcely be expected to come into their acquaintance. Her knowledge of Wyatt came more from his association with Duncan and the other young men of the area. She had always managed to find a way to seek them out. She was more comfortable in their company than that of the few young girls allowed to visit Eddings Hall. That had been before the fire, of course, but she remembered those times quite clearly.

"He won't be happy with Cathy. And our lands march alongside his as well. And we have a much higher rank than the Montcrieffs. I don't see why I shouldn't be the one he weds. Just think, Mama, we could go back to Kent. It would be just like old times.''

She said it with all the satisfaction and assurance of the young, Lady Eddings noted. It would not do at all, and she was quite certain the earl would know it. They were not at all suited. The child was merely dreaming of bringing back the past. Still, it didn't hurt to encourage her to dream a little. She had so little to dream about.

She gazed at her young daughter with a soft smile of affection. The child was so like her father, impetuous, rash to a fault. It nearly broke her heart every time she looked on her. But she wouldn't have done it over for all the coins in the realm.

Let the girl dream. Perhaps in striving to meet Merrick's rigid standards she would catch the eye of someone more suitable. Young Albert, for example. It would be good for her to get away from London and Duncan for a while. The more she thought about it, the better she liked the idea. It was time Cassandra found a husband to protect her.

''Very well, child, if your heart is set on it, I will write to your Aunt Matilda. She does not go out much anymore, but she is great friends of the dowager Lady Hampton. They will enjoy a visit, and I see no reason you shouldn't accompany her. Bring me my writing desk.''

Exhilaration swept through Cassandra. She had done it! Within a fortnight she would be in constant proximity to Wyatt. Surely she would find some way to attach him. It was just a matter of knowing her cards and playing them well.

The jackpot would be returning to the safety and respectability of Kent and providing the home that her mother deserved.

She would worry about the duties of married life later.

Chapter 4

The moment Cassandra walked through the portals of Hampton Court she had the premonition that she had made a dreadful mistake. The elderly butler greeted her great-aunt with respect and did not deign to so much as announce Cassandra's presence. An aging dowager in the sweeping silks and turban of another generation haughtily bore down on them, taking Aunt Matilda into her protection and leading her away, leaving Cassandra to trail behind.

Unhappily, she listened to the sounds of voices and gay laughter coming from various concealed chambers in this monstrous edifice, but none came to greet her, and Lady Hampton made no effort to introduce her to the other guests.

Well, she was quite accustomed to looking after herself. She would just have to learn to do the same in these strange surroundings. She was the daughter of a marquess. They could not keep her in hiding forever. Then she would show Merrick that she was all that she should be. Somehow, she would have to make him see that Catherine was not what he wanted.

The evening certainly began dismally enough. Duncan had refused to allow her any more gowns, so she had only the emerald and the primrose to choose from. Merrick had seen both, so she had to choose on the merits of the entrance she would make at dinner. Without a lady's maid to advise her, she settled on the primrose silk. It was more ball gown than dinner gown, but she was not unaware of how the pale yellow set off the golden highlights of her hair. Dressing her hair herself so that the disorderly strands fashioned into a neat coil on top of her head and only a few reckless wisps spilled about her face, Cassandra finally descended the stairs to meet her aunt.

The titters and shocked stares as she entered the salon warned all was not well, but Cassandra arrogantly held her chin high and surveyed the room in seeming search for her aunt. In reality, she wished for a corner in which to hide.

Her *faux pas* was immediately apparent. Most of the guests assembled were considerably older than herself, and one or two indiscreetly displayed as much of their bounteous charms as Cassandra, but it was obvious even to her that such a display in this proper household was the exception rather than the rule. In addition, the one or two young ladies of her own age wore modest muslins primarily of white with discreet dashes of color in their sashes or ribbons. None revealed more than a hint of the valley between their breasts, and even this much was concealed behind a properly draped shawl. Cassandra's vibrant silk with its daring décolletage was fit only for the wicked women of Duncan's world. Why had she never noticed that before?

Cassandra had no time in which to berate herself for her blindness. She could not run and hide. She was a Howard, and thereby of higher rank than almost everyone in this room. She had to smile bravely and wish she could sink through the floor by magic. And she had to keep going forward.

She had no awareness of Merrick's nearness until she heard the deep rumble of his voice behind her and felt his large hand upon her elbow. "The room is damp. Shall I send someone to fetch your shawl?" There was neither mockery nor warmth in the question.

Cassandra steeled herself from the condemnation in his eyes and looked up into his lean face. To her surprise, she found no emotion there, only a certain patience as he awaited her reply. She made a small nod of acknowledgment. "If you would, please. I was in such a hurry, I forgot it."

Doubting seriously that Cassandra would normally bother with the cumbersome nuisance of a shawl, hoping that she even possessed one, Merrick summoned a nearby footman and sent him on the errand. With any luck, the man would be enterprising enough to find something.

"I trust you are not within these illustrious halls without a chaperone, my lady. Perhaps you would introduce me to whomever you are searching for?"

Cassandra mistrusted the velvet softness of his voice, but she had vowed to be on her best behavior with the earl. She could see Catherine rapidly advancing upon them, and she daringly sent Wyatt a brilliant smile. "If you could find my Aunt Matilda in these cavernous spaces, I would be happy to introduce you. Perhaps she is by the fire. She has a fear of cold."

Subtly she edged Merrick away from the approaching Catherine and around the edge of the room, keeping their backs turned toward his angry fiancée. One of Catherine's shrewish set-downs would certainly make Merrick see her in a new light.

They did not advance far before Catherine came in front of them, her icy gray eyes sweeping over Cassandra's revealing costume with derision before turning to the towering earl. "You are making a spectacle of yourself, Wyatt." She turned her spiteful glare back to Cassandra. "You would do well to eat with your aunt in her room, Cassandra. The men here tonight are gentlemen. You'll not find them very entertaining."

Malicious mischief welled up behind Cassandra's eyes, and before she had time to think, she offered a venomous smile. "Cat, you have not changed. Do you still use handkerchiefs to fill your bodice?" Before any outraged reply could be uttered, she turned and made a proper curtsy to Merrick. Triumphantly she felt his gaze resting thoughtfully on her own obviously natural abundance, and she sent him a knowing gaze as she rose. "It's good seeing you again, my lord. I wouldn't wish to intrude upon a private conversation. Good evening."

Merrick had half a mind to catch the brat's arm and give her the proper verbal thrashing she deserved, but with a guilty start he realized it wasn't just a verbal thrashing he had in mind. Lady Cassandra Howard had grown into a proper armful, and he felt a long-denied surge of lust as he imagined any number of other chastisements he could offer her. It came to him suddenly that she hadn't minded the way he looked at her. Catherine would have very properly slapped his face for the thoughts he was thinking now, but he suspected Lady Cassandra would only laugh and encourage him. The idea of actually dipping his hands into her bodice so shocked the normally proper earl that he scarcely heard a word of Catherine's scold. It was time he married and found a release for his physical needs. And none too soon would it be, either. His gaze followed Cassandra around the room to where she took the shawl the footman offered.

That one small triumph scarcely weighed against all the minor disasters of the evening, Cassandra decided as she retired to her room later that night. To avoid being asked to play the piano, she had allowed a rather decent-looking gentleman to lead her out to the terrace. She had successfully fended off his amorous attentions with a slap, but not before Merrick had seen it. He had scolded and ordered her to her room, but she refused to go. It was the public humiliation of having her hostess suggest that she see to her aunt's comfort—at Merrick's behest, of course—that made Cassandra's blood boil with fury. She could hear them now, laughing and singing and chattering gaily in the salon behind her, and her ears burned at just the thought of it. She wasn't a baby. She was a woman grown. What would it take to make them realize it?

After seeing that her aunt was quite comfortably settled in bed and not inclined to accompany her downstairs, Cassandra made a grim face and, chin lifted in resolution, prepared to storm the citadel. She would not be sent to bed like a child.

The billiard room wasn't hard to discover. She had spent many lonely hours perfecting her game over her father's table. Who cared that ladies didn't indulge in such sport? That was their problem, not hers.

The two gentlemen lackadaisically knocking a ball around stood up in surprise when Cass helped herself to a cue and began to chalk it. It wasn't long before the game became so animated that the room filled with other eager males ready to take on the challenge of the Howard chit's prowess at the board. The fact that she discarded her shawl and seemed unaware of the bounteous show she provided only added to the excitement.

Heady with triumph, Cass scarcely noticed the sudden silence that descended upon the entrance of a familiar tall figure. The Earl of Merrick's disapproval visibly emanated through the room, and the callow youths crowding around the table shrank back from it, disappearing into the shadowy corners of the normally all-masculine room.

Cassandra did not look up until her shawl dropped upon the table, sending her balls cascading hither and yon. She leapt up with a start, and found herself caught upon Merrick's piercing frown.

"I believe your aunt is looking for you, my lady."

There was that about his voice not meant to be denied. Had it been Duncan or any of his friends, Cassandra would have flouted his authority and challenged him to a game. But this was Merrick, the proper, upstanding earl that she wished to marry, although at the moment she could not quite remember why. Still, she had set herself a goal and she was in danger of losing it. She couldn't afford to lose. She remembered that much as she met his glare.

Draping her shawl about her shoulders with studied grace, Cassandra made a demure curtsy and offered him a vapid smile. "Thank you, my lord. It is good of you to play the messenger boy. I bid you good night.'' This last encompassed the remainder of the company as she beat a hasty retreat.

The memory of Merrick's dark eyes upon her sent her scurrying even faster. He had been assessing her, she knew, and she feared she had come out lacking. Heavens above, how would she make him come up to scratch if he thoroughly disapproved of her? How was she to prove to him that she could be as she ought?

As the week drew on, it became quite plain that she could not, because she was not. Her lack of education did not merely encompass the inability to play a musical instrument. She had no notion of how to go about fluttering a fan and batting her eyes and speaking in musically modulated whispers. She did not know how to sit still and speak idly for hours on end in all-female company, waiting patiently for the men to join them. She much preferred to be in male company, riding, hunting, playing cards and billiards as she had done in the past. Every time she sought more interesting entertainment, Merrick was there to restrain her.

She cursed vividly and fluently to herself as she was ordered out of the card room again one miserably rainy day toward the week's end. The women were sipping tea and doing needlework and busily cutting into ribbons friends and neighbors unfortunate enough not to be present. Cassandra neither knew nor cared about the morals or finances of these subjects for gossip. She had come no closer to her goal than before, and things were looking decidedly grim. She was almost positive that the letter Aunt Matilda received today was a summons from Duncan to bring her home. She knew what that meant, and she dreaded it with every fiber of her being.

Passing by the library door, Cass heard her name mentioned and could not resist hesitating to see who was speaking. If she could only get Wyatt alone, perhaps she could make him understand the desperation of her plight. She was more than certain he had no love for Catherine, or she for him. More than once she had heard Cat speak of the changes she would make in Merrick when she was wedded. Cassandra was quite certain Wyatt would not approve of his betrothed's intentions. She listened as the first speaker laughed.

"She's a rare handful, I agree. I've heard it said she accompanies Eddings to the worst hells in town. Have you made a pitch for her bed yet?"

"Good Lord, no. Maggie would have my eyelashes out. The Howards never were ones for discretion, and word would be out faster than I could get between her legs. Besides, I hear she's promised to Rupert, and he would take the balls off any man daring to encroach on his territory."

"I heard him bragging about his latest conquest, but I hadn't put the two together. He's really getting leg-shackled, then? I shouldn't have thought it even of Rupert. She's a pretty piece, but she'll have horns on his head before the wedding bells quit chiming. Did you see that gown she had on the other night? It was all I could do to keep from dragging her into the bushes right there and then."

"She's a gauche little devil, admittedly, but what do you expect? I bet in bed . . ."

Cheeks flaming, tears burning at her eyes, Cassandra hurried on. Those who eavesdropped never heard good of themselves, she reminded herself, but the pain of those insults could not be dismissed as easily. Gauche! It was bad enough that they thought her free with her favors, but gauche!

She had done nothing right. It had been a mistake to come. She didn't belong here. They had made that plain enough all week. Why did she have to wait to hear it for herself? They were all laughing at her behind her back.

That thought made her angry. So Rupert had bragged of his conquests, had he? Did they all think the daughter of the Marquess of Eddings was so desperate as to settle for a dissipated baronet with the tongue of an adder? She would have his scalp first. She would thrust him through with his own sword. She would carve him into little pieces of bloodied meat not fitting for chicken feed.

She would marry Merrick. That thought came in a blinding flash that burned through every vein in Cassandra's body and brought a sheen of perspiration to her brow. Wyatt would never allow others to speak of her so. He would cut out their tongues first. They would have to respect her if she were the Earl of Merrick's wife.

Her feet fairly flew up the stairs. She had no time left. Desperate times called for desperate measures. It had become more than obvious that Wyatt would never do the dishonorable thing and jilt his fiancée for a wanton hoyden. It was just a manner of planning. She had been in worse predicaments before and managed to get out of them. She had no one else to rely on but herself. She could only blame herself if she failed. She wouldn't fail.

It took an hour's worth of pacing before she had the details complete. It would work if she could get the timing right. Wyatt would be furious, but she would deal with that later. He shouldn't have ignored her so boldly all week. He wouldn't even look at her, much less speak to her. Every time she approached, he deliberately turned his back to speak with Catherine. He deserved his fate.

Excitement began to replace the shame and anger of earlier. She had always wondered about the secrets of the marital bed. Perhaps she would find out soon enough. Surely Wyatt would find her as attractive as those two vipers in the study did. That was all that mattered in a marriage anyway. If Merrick could marry a plain-looking shrew like Catherine, he should be grateful for the opportunity of someone who would cater to his every whim. She fully intended to cater to Wyatt's every whim once they were married. The chance of having a real home and family was worth crawling on bended knees for, if necessary.

As she sat down at the narrow desk in the room she had been assigned and scribbled out the missives that would bring her plan to fruition, Cassandra allowed her mind to paint the pictures of her dreams. In a real home, there would be no drinking and gambling and whoring. There would be no screaming fights or slamming doors or violent curses. There would be no wondering where the coins would come from to buy the evening's dinner or worrying which bill collector should be paid first with the prior night's winnings.

In a real home, her mother wouldn't have to hide behind closed doors and doses of laudanum. She could come out and be her friend again, as they had been before they moved to London, before they had to live with her father and brother. They would have lady's maids again, and the men of the family would look upon them with respect. No one would curse them ever again, or strike them. She felt certain in Wyatt's home they would be safe.

It was worth whatever she had to do to accomplish it. Her reputation could scarcely suffer any more than it had. Wyatt would be angry with her, but he wouldn't beat her. He would do the honorable thing, and then she could explain why she had done it and offer her eternal gratitude. When he understood, he wouldn't mind so much. Surely he wouldn't.

Sealing the two notes, Cassandra summoned a maid. It would be better if she had Lotta with her. Lotta would understand and carry out her instructions to perfection. She would have to make do with this stranger and pray that things worked out as planned. It was the only chance she had. It had to work.

Once the maid left, Cassandra hovered with uncertainty in the room's center. It was already dark. Dinner was over and the company would be gathering in the salon. She doubted if anyone had even missed her. What should she do now? Wait and see if he came? What if he didn't? She couldn't think of that. She must think positively. She must think how to greet him when he came.

Wyatt had seen all the gowns she owned, but not her nightshift. Would the sight of her in dishabille shock him so thoroughly as to make the rest of her plan simple? Or would it warn him away? She would wear a robe. That was it. The robe might make him wary, but surely he would be just a little bit curious. Merrick was too honest to expect anyone else to be devious, particularly not the innocent he obviously thought her. Well, he was about to be disabused of that notion.

Hastily Cassandra unfastened her gown and let it drop to the floor. It seemed shameless to greet a gentleman with nothing covering her nakedness but the thin lawn of her nightshift, but she didn't think really wanton women wore chemises beneath them. She had to be really wanton to lure Merrick into this trap.

The chemise joined her gown on the floor. Opening a drawer, she quickly removed a freshly washed and ironed shift. The ribbon lacing seemed slightly girlish, but it was her best gown. It was a little tight across the bosom. Perhaps if she laced it loosely enough . . .

A knock came at the door, and in anguish Cassandra kicked the crumpled pile of clothing beneath the bed and grabbed for the satin robe in the wardrobe. In a few minutes she would be a fallen woman, and she hadn't even let her hair down.

Belting her robe beneath her breasts, Cass took a deep breath to steady her nerves. The knock came again, sending frantic jingling along her nerves once more. It had to be him. No one else would sound so authoritative but discreet. Without another thought, she opened the door and stood aside.

The room's darkness left Merrick momentarily nonplussed. Only a single candle burned on the far desk. The lamp in the hall behind him sent his shadow spilling across the uncarpeted floor, and he realized inconsequentially that Lady Cassandra had been assigned one of the lesser rooms despite her rank. He finally found her proud figure huddled uncertainly beside the door, and blinking his eyes against the gloom, Merrick made a tentative step toward her.

"Cassie? What happened to the lamps? What is this urgent matter you must speak of privately? Can you not come down to the study or somewhere proper so we might speak decently? Are you ill?"

Her muffled cry brought him further into the room. She had no one to turn to but him, the message had said, and Merrick realized the truth of that. Whatever gossip said, he knew her to be little more than a frightened, proud girl cast into a harsh world without her accord. Perhaps the gossip had reached her ears, and she did not dare face the guests below. He wasn't at all certain how to deal with that, if so.

He held out his hand, and the door closed behind him. Merrick turned to correct that impropriety, but Cassandra fell against him and he was forced to catch her up in his arms.

"Cassie? For pity's sake, Cassie, what is wrong? Where is your aunt? Let me fetch her."

She clung to him, and Merrick felt her slightness in his arms. She was more slender than any reed, and she smelled of some heavenly scent that filled his nostrils and clouded his thoughts. He was aware of her silken hair tickling his cheek, her breasts pressing against his waistcoat, and idly he tried to remember another woman feeling so comfortable in his arms. She was tall, taller than most, but there was nothing boyish about her figure. She had the slender curves of a woman full grown but not yet ripe. Wyatt had the sudden nonsensical desire to see her ripen and become the sensuous woman every man dreams of, but he hastily shoved aside such thoughts.

"Cassie, answer me. You are giving me the fright of my life. What is wrong?"

She pushed slightly back from his embrace then, her translucent face glowing up at him through the darkness. She had such lovely, liquid skin, he wished to stroke it, but he settled for catching her chin between his thumb and forefinger. "Speak, Cassandra, or I will choke it out of you."

She smiled then, an easy smile of friendship. "I am trusting you not to strangle me, my lord. You may wish to shortly, but I have put all my confidence in your integrity. Duncan will almost certainly beat me, but you will not, will you?"

Merrick was beginning to feel uneasy about the confidence now reflected in those glittering blue eyes. His desire to protect her had astonished him from the first, but now he had reason to remember the mischievousness he heard in her voice now. It would be better did he look to protect himself.

His hand moved to grasp her hair in a firm hold so he could keep her eyes on his. "What are you plotting, Medusa? I'll not hand you over to be beaten by your brother, but I am not averse to spanking some sense into you."

The smile disappeared and she made a wry grimace. "I had hoped you were one who would not lift a hand in anger, but I suppose that really was too much to ask. I deserve whatever you mete out, I daresay, and I will not complain of it, but you will find me much more compliant should you show me gentleness."

"What the deuce are you talking about?" Merrick practically yelled, although he had a sudden suspicion. Quickly dropping his hold on her, he reached for the door.

Cassandra moved swiftly to the opposite end of the room, to the window opened to a cool evening. As Wyatt discovered the locked portal, she dropped the key into the shrubbery below.

Chapter 5

Wyatt swung around in time to catch her treachery. With a hissing intake of breath, he strode across the room in a few steps, catching Cassandra firmly by the waist as he glanced out the window to discover the distance to the ground. They were on the third floor. There would be no escape that way.

He turned a furious gaze to the calmly conniving brat in his hands. Briefly, he contemplated shaking her until her teeth rattled, but that was obviously what she expected. Her air of patience and resignation as she waited for her punishment quelled his impulse instantly. She had to be desperate to do this.

Wyatt flung his hands from the temptation of Cassandra's soft curves and quickly removed himself from her proximity. He found a lamp and lit it with the candle, gathering his scattered wits as he performed the homely function. Unless he thought quickly they would be caught in a scandal of enormous magnitude, and he could be looking at his future wife.

That thought brought Wyatt's head up abruptly as he returned his gaze to the lovely girl waiting expectantly for his reaction. When it came, it surprised even himself.

"Why, Cass? Why me? I'm nearly old enough to be your father. I cut no dash about town. I harbor no misconceptions about my looks. Except for the title, I am little more than a staid old country squire. And I cannot think the daughter of a marquess is much impressed by titles."

Cassandra hovered uncertainly near the bed, clasping her robe at the throat. She had not anticipated this reaction from the man of her dreams. She had been prepared for anger. She had been prepared for rape. She had not expected this self-denigration. She stared at him with some surprise.

"I shall be nineteen in a month and you cannot have become thirty yet. You would have had to have been an extremely precocious child to be my father. I didn't mean it to be like this, Wyatt, but you are too proper to break your betrothal with Catherine, and I could not see any other way to it."

Wyatt contemplated lifting the little heathen to the bed and giving her the scare of her life, but his long-denied body warned that he was very capable of doing more than scaring her. He could not keep his gaze from straying to the creamy curves rising above the flimsy fabric of her robe. She had the body of a woman full grown, he had to admit. He seldom indulged himself in the pleasures of the flesh, and he could not remember ever indulging himself with anyone remotely attaining this girl's magical beauty. Just the thought of lifting her onto that bed incited war between his conscience and his physical desires. He wanted her. He very definitely wanted her. The question was, what could she see in him?

"This is ridiculous, Cassandra. There must be another key to that door. Why don't you fetch it, and we'll forget any of this ever happened. You have not thought this through very clearly. I am marrying Catherine because she will run my home with little interruption of my present life, because I need an heir and she will give me one, and because our estates are joined. I do not wish to break my betrothal. Before you create any further scandal for yourself, why don't you let me quietly leave?"

Cassandra shrugged her shoulders. Wishing only to bury her face in her hands and cry over his obvious rejection, she did the opposite. Boldly, she climbed

upon the step to perch on the edge of the high, cano-
pied bed. Releasing her death grip on her robe, she
met his gaze fully as the satin fell loose from her thin
shift.

"I am not the one who would wish to make changes
in your life, Wyatt. Catherine is. She is tired of Kent
and wishes to celebrate becoming a countess by entertaining all of London. I have no such desire. She is
practically on the shelf, my lord, and will soon be too
old to bear children safely, I heard Aunt Matilda say.
If that is so, you would have .much more chance of
success at heirs with me. And you know where my
lands lie."

Her brother's lands, not hers, but Wyatt did not
mention that small point. Despite the fact that she was
artfully leaning forward to reveal more of her lovely
curves and her glorious hair was slowly working its
way from its pins to wrap in tendrils about her throat,
she still appeared a confused child to him. He doubted
seriously if she even knew what she would be expected
to do to produce heirs.

He could be wrong. He had some experience in the
naivety of untried maidens and he was in no hurry to
repeat the experience. He stepped forward threaten-
ingly, letting his gaze travel knowingly to the bare flesh
revealed by her open robe. "Is that so, my lady? And
what are you willing to do to give me those heirs,
Cassandra?"

Putting on a bold front, she leaned beckoningly toward him. "Kiss me, Wyatt, and I will show you."

Amused as she closed her eyes and pressed her lips
primly together for his kiss, Wyatt halted in front of
her. "What else, Cass? Show me how you will give
me heirs."

Cassandra reluctantly opened her eyes and gazed at
him in puzzlement. In truth, she had no idea where
heirs came from, had scarcely given it any thought.
Duncan was her father's heir, so obviously sons were
the secret, but she had never had much contact with

children. She didn't know where they came from and didn't want to know. She just assumed Merrick knew these things and would teach her when they married. What on earth was he asking her to do now?

"You're the one who wants them, my lord. I should think the matter was up to you." Cassandra arranged herself cross-legged in the bed's center and gazed up at the tall man standing with hands in pockets gazing down at her. She suspected he was laughing at her, but his gaze seemed more reflective than amused. "In any case, it does not matter. They will come looking for us soon enough, and you will have no choice but to do the honorable thing. Will you be dreadfully unhappy to lose Catherine?"

Merrick wondered what would happen if he answered in the affirmative. Would she set him free from this trap out of guilt? He rather suspected not. She had done this for a purpose, and he doubted that the purpose would change because of a small matter of unhappiness. And he really didn't think he would suffer any great pains of anguish from replacing plain-spoken Catherine with this treacherous but lovely little witch. His mother would undoubtedly have the vapors. The servants would probably all quit after a day of her improper escapades. His reputation would be ruined. But he didn't think any of that would disturb him greatly. He had learned to overcome a great deal in his thirty years. A child-wife wouldn't be a major challenge. But there was one thing he would insist on, and he doubted that Cassandra had given it any consideration.

"You are asking to be tied to a man who prefers the solitude of the country and the fidelity of a proper wife, Lady Cassandra. I don't drink, I don't gamble, I don't entertain lavishly, and I don't exchange my wife for the beds of others. You would find it an exceedingly tedious life compared to the fast one you are accustomed to. Why don't you just unlock the door and end this charade, Cassie? If you have a problem, I'm certain we can come to some more satisfactory conclusion than this.'' A horrifying thought suddenly entered his head, and he blurted out, ''You are not pregnant, are you?''

''Of course not!'' She wouldn't know if she was since she had very little concept of what the word meant, but he sounded so horrified at the possibility, Cassandra answered instinctively. When he looked relieved, she lifted a hand wistfully toward him. ''I do not mind being bored, Wyatt, really I don't. I'd much rather live in the country. You would let me have a dog and a horse, wouldn't you? I shall never stand in your way. And I can learn to be very proper.''

His lips set in an angry line at her continued refusal to be reasonable, and she watched warily as he leaned forward beneath the canopy, bringing his face closer to hers.

''We are talking marriage, Cassandra, not a romp in the country. We are talking of spending the rest of our lives in each other's pockets, sharing meals and beds. Have you given any thought at all about what it would be like to wake up to my face every morning?''

Cassandra gave him a smile of relief and reached to caress his sturdy jaw. ''Much better yours than Rupert's. Marriage is a gamble anyway you look at it, isn't it? But I think I prefer the cards you hold to Rupert's. I'm just sorry you think Catherine's is the better hand. I'm willing to wager my life that you're wrong.''

Wyatt closed his eyes in exasperation and against the temptations of her inviting loveliness. The sunset glow of her hair burned against his lids, and the enticingly fresh scent that was all Cassandra's own lured him even without vision. He felt himself leaning closer, wanting to know the taste of full strawberry-tinted lips, wanting the sweet brush of her breath against his mouth. Any more of this, and he would wonder why he was fighting her.

As if sensing his capitulation, Cassandra swayed closer. Wyatt could feel the warmth of her breath against his cheek. He turned his head slightly and her lips seared across his.

There was nothing for it but to pull her closer before he lost his balance. He couldn't release the ripeness of those innocent lips. He gathered her closer, pulling her to her knees, and she came without hesitation, her fingers curling in trembling balls against his chest as he pressed for more, demanding a parting of the soft temptation of her lips to gain the entrance of her heated mouth.

In one moment, she didn't seem to know what he wanted. In the next, she was opening fully to him, moaning slightly in surrender as her hands flattened and slid up his chest and clung to his shoulders while his tongue plundered and plunged and stole all the innocent passion of her mouth.

Only whores had ever kissed him like that, and not with this amount of pleasure. Wyatt felt his body hardening in response, and caution fled with the winds. He gripped her arms tighter, pulling her closer, twisting his mouth against hers until he received the maximum pleasure of their proximity. As her breasts crushed against him, her tongue tentatively came out to meet his, and an undulation of intense desire swept though him, dashing all reason. Wyatt groaned as her tongue twined with his and his senses filled with her heady scent and warmth.

His hands moved to her back, stroking, caressing, learning the fine-boned curves of her fragile figure. The satin of her robe slid gently through his fingers, falling loose. He wanted to pull her hips against his, feel her response to his arousal, but he wasn't ready to frighten her yet. She was so incredibly responsive. He hadn't expected this, had never dreamed such passion was available for just a touch and a kiss. In the back of his mind, he knew what he was doing and condemned himself for it, but such pleasure did not often come his way. He couldn't release her just yet.

Cassandra made a soft sound in her throat as Merrick's hand found the curve of her breast and explored there. The thin cotton of her shift offered no protection from his heated fingers, and when he found the hard nipple pressing eagerly for release, she could not control the shudder of pure need sweeping through her. She had never understood a kiss could be like this. A burning sensation started somewhere in the center of her being, driving her wildly into Merrick's arms, clinging to his shoulders as his hand continued its ardent exploration, and his kiss seared her soul.

They scarcely heard the timid knock when it came. The pins were rapidly coming loose from her hair as Merrick's hand traveled over her body and his kisses bent her backward. The knock jarred Cassandra's senses as an unwelcome intrusion, but she couldn't release him, couldn't fight his heated hold. Feeling triumphant, she clung to Wyatt, ignoring the outer world.

A louder knock rapidly brought Merrick back to his senses. His mind woke instantly to his plight, but still he felt reluctance in releasing her. His first wife had never allowed such liberties, and his experience with whores had left a bad taste in his mouth afterward. Strangely enough, he felt quite exuberant as he heard the knock again and recognized the voices outside the door.

With a wry, mocking look, Wyatt sat Cassandra back against her heels and smiled down into her stunned loveliness. "I think you are about to be granted your wish, my lady. I hope you know what you're doing."

Cassandra clung to his arm a moment longer, not trusting her ability to sit alone. She squeezed her eyes shut in hopes of gaining composure, but her head swirled with the still racing sensations he had aroused in her. "Answer it, my lord, for I fear I cannot."

Sympathetically, Wyatt caressed her heated cheek, then hardening his resolve, he released her. "The door's locked," he yelled curtly over his shoulder to the anxious rapping at the door. "You'll have to find a key."

To the shrill exclamations of surprised and concern from the other side of the door, Wyatt turned a deaf ear. His body had not been so totally out of control since he was a boy with no experience and no outlet for his sexual tension. Should anyone walk in here now, he could not disguise his state of arousal. For a man proud of his control and behavior, that was the ultimate humiliation. He turned away from the trembling temptation on the bed and schooled his rampaging emotions to coldness.

"My Lord Merrick, is Cassandra in there? What has happened? Why can't you open the door?" The high, quavering voice of Cassandra's elderly and respectable great-aunt pierced the heavy paneled door with anxiety. Merrick grimaced.

"There has been a misunderstanding, Lady Matilda. Cassandra is fine. The key seems to be down in the bushes somewhere. I trust the butler keeps an extra set." Merrick turned his glare on Cassandra, who responded woodenly to his unspoken demand.

"I am fine, Aunt Matilda. The wind blew the door shut, that is all. Merrick has been everything that is proper."

That was a bouncer that wouldn't pass the first inspection, but for quick thinking, it would have to do. Merrick took a deep breath and walked to the open window. His loins still ached with the fullness of unquenched desire, but he tried not to think about it. He tried not to think about anything. He had been successfully using that ploy since he was a youth and the victim of his mother's scathing tongue. It was remarkable how many situations one could get through without thinking. The outcome of this one was a foregone conclusion. It certainly didn't need any of his thought in it.

"You had better do something with your hair," he warned without turning to look at the forlorn creature

in the center of the bed. The image of red-gold hair
falling in wanton tendrils about translucent skin burned
indelibly across his mind's eye. He didn't need to see
her to visualize the abandoned disarray that would
meet the gaze of the curiosity-seekers outside the door.

Cassandra obediently began stabbing pins through
thick curls. She had little patience with her hair. A
maid had arranged it earlier this day, but she had no
knack for recovering that lost sophistication. But she
had promised herself to be obedient to Merrick's every
whim. Now that fate and her own deviousness had
closed the door on them, she would have to start living
up to her vows. She felt the coldness emanating from
Merrick's corner of the room and shivered.

When the scrape of the key came in the lock, she
froze. Merrick reluctantly turned to face the condemnation of his peers. Too late, he discovered Cassandra's mermaid stance in the middle of the bed, her
arms raised to her wanton tresses, her satin robe sliding loose to reveal the tight bodice of her thin gown.
He groaned inwardly and felt the sudden surge of heat
in his loins as the door flew open.

Tiny, stooped, gray-haired Aunt Matilda stepped
through first. Behind her thick spectacles no emotion
could be discerned, but Merrick rather expected they
concealed resignation. Cassandra was, after all, a
Howard, and Lady Matilda had no very high opinion
of her niece's family. Her gaze swerved sharply to him,
and Wyatt bore her regard impassively. Behind her
surged all the guests that he had once considered
friends.

"Wyatt!" Catherine's shriek cut the silence, followed by a low moan as she discovered Cassandra's
scandalous position. Despite the fact that Cassandra
had recovered her senses and lowered her arms, Catherine's moan resulted in the inevitable faint. Wyatt
watched callously as one of the other male guests
caught her up in his arms and carried her off with a
curt nod. Randolph had need of a rich heiress. They

would suit each other fine. Merrick managed this cynical thought easily enough.

Their host pushed his way through the crowd, gave the earl a shocked look, then, murmuring something about "simple explanations," ushered the sightseers from the room, leaving Lady Matilda to hear their story alone.

Wyatt stepped forward and made a polite bow. "My apologies, my lady. This was all a simple misunderstanding, but of course I am sensible of the damage done to your great-niece's reputation. I will repair at once to London to seek her hand from Lord Eddings. I trust you will find it in your heart to forgive what must appear to be an unseemly situation."

Matilda sniffed, lifting her haughty nose in the air to shift her spectacles backward as she regarded the formally correct earl. His cravat was mussed and there was a decidedly rakish dishevelment to his normally smooth chestnut hair. She gave him a knowing look. "Balderdash, Merrick. I know an unseemly situation when I see one, and this one is beyond unseemly. As much as I hate to admit it, I must assume you are the injured party, however." She threw a look to Cassandra, who—now that the guests had departed—had finally managed to return her feet to the floor and stand upright. Matilda gave another sniff at the sight of Cassandra's still-stunned expression, then returned her gaze to the more sensible earl. "However, you are old enough to know better, Merrick. I suggest you leave tonight, before that shrewish fiancée of yours decides hysterics are in order."

"That would be cowardly, my lady," Wyatt murmured, although he heartily wished he could take the coward's way out. He knew Catherine of old. One of her temper tantrums was not a pretty sight to see. "Hysterical" would only be a mild term for it. "I must apologize and make my explanations to the lady. I think it would be best if I escorted you and Lady Cassandra back to London in the morning."

Matilda gave an inelegant snort. "Let Cassandra pay the price of this escapade. She has been given entirely too much freedom in the past. It is time she faces the consequences of her rash actions. She will apologize to Catherine. You write her a brief note of explanation and tell her you will understand if she calls the engagement off. You will be in a ticklish situation until she does, but it's no matter. She'll come around. Just don't let that young Howard wastrel rob you of more than is proper. He will only gamble it away."

Merrick was unable to find a respectful manner in which to argue with the elderly lady. In truth, he had no desire to do so. He lifted his gaze to Cassandra's bewildered beauty, and felt a sharp pain strike his midsection at the thought of possessing this fiery creature. He ought to be ashamed of himself, but he felt only a certain amount of triumph, as if his life of respectability had finally been rewarded.

He hid his thoughts well as he had learned to do long ago. Approaching Cassandra, Wyatt took her cold hand and bowed formally over it before looking down into the depths of her iridescent eyes. He had thought them blue, but now he saw they contained all the aquas and greens and midnight colors of the ocean. He could no more see what lay behind those long lashes than she could see into his.

"I will come to call as soon as you return to town, my lady. There are a number of things we will need to discuss."

"I'm sorry, Merrick," she whispered brokenly, meeting his polite gaze.

"I'm not," he heard himself saying, to his own horror. She was a lying, conniving, scheming little witch who would make his life hell. And the thought of her in his bed made his blood race. He had married for all the right reasons the first time and found no happiness. Why not marry for all the wrong reasons and at least obtain some small measure of pleasure?

Cassandra offered him a startled look before hastily

lowering her lashes. Grimly Merrick imagined he'd given her something to think about in the days to come. He had no idea of whether she was a virgin or not, and to his own surprise he really did not care.

Feeling much as if he had just gained wings and been caught in a hurricane wind, Merrick made a formal bow and left the ladies alone. He needed time to learn the vagaries of this wind that carried him along. He greatly suspected Cassandra needed time to acquaint herself with the ball and chain she had just acquired. He envisioned troubled days ahead, but the nights . . .

Remembering those impassioned kisses, Merrick warmly admitted the nights would be worth every bit of trouble she caused him. If he could keep her to himself.

Chapter 6

Duncan Howard looked liked death warmed over, Merrick observed as he entered the study of the marquess's home the next afternoon. Duncan was a year or two younger than himself. They had more or less grown up together until Merrick had inherited the estate at the age of twelve and their lives had taken different roads. Duncan had gone the idle way of his titled peers who had naught to do but wait for their fathers to pass on. Merrick had taken up the reins of an estate so large he had not known the boundaries or extent of it until he was nearly twenty. Not that the difference in their paths hadn't been a foregone conclusion from the first, Merrick wryly admitted to himself. His rigid, religious antecedents were exact opposites of the wayward Howard ancestors, as if living next to each other through the centuries had driven neighbors to opposite extremes.

Duncan scowled and offered no hand in greeting as Merrick approached. "What is your complaint today that you must hunt me down in town to make it? Has another damned tree fallen on your turnip crop? Surely I have no tenants left to poach your land?"

That was scarcely an auspicious beginning for a marriage proposal, but Wyatt rather calculated Eddings' humor would change once he learned he would be rid of a costly liability in the form of his sister.

"I am not here to discuss our estates, Eddings, not in the matter of land, leastways. Am I allowed to sit or must I stand on formality?"

Not looking completely mollified, Duncan took a seat behind his desk and indicated a chair to his neighbor. Merrick noted the new marquess did not look entirely comfortable in this position of authority, as if he had tried on his father's shoes and found they did not quite fit. He had the puffy eyes of a confirmed roué and the sulky mouth of a spoiled child. Beyond that, he was as handsome as his sister was lovely. Merrick prayed the family excesses had not yet affected Cassandra.

Wyatt took a seat and looked for a place to begin. "I have come about Lady Cassandra." That sounded formal and innocuous enough.

Duncan grunted and relaxed. Reaching for the decanter of brandy, he admitted, "She's a rare handful. I expected her to be sent packing well before this. Well, you need not worry. I've ordered her home. She should be out of your hair shortly."

"That's not precisely what I had in mind." At the moment, Merrick wished it was. He disliked being put in the position of admitting a moral failing to the rakehell Marquess of Eddings. He resented Cassandra for placing him in that position. But he knew his duty and would not shirk it. "I have come to ask you for Lady Cassandra's hand in marriage."

Duncan choked and spewed the mouthful of brandy he had just taken across the desk. He gasped and gaped at the earl as if he had just taken leave of his senses. "Cass? You want to marry Cass? Why? Is she blackmailing you into this?"

Duncan knew his sister well. Merrick grimaced and crossed his arms over his chest. "There was a minor incident at the country party. I feel obligated to make reparations. I'll take care of her, you can be sure of that. She'll not lack for anything in my hands. I'm prepared to make a handsome settlement on her behalf. I think it best if we wed quickly and remove to the country. I don't believe city life suits her."

Duncan began to grin. "You sound as if you're about

to buy a pound of conscience. She ain't even come out yet, Merrick. What would you want with the little hellion? She ain't your sort by far.''

Wyatt stiffened. "She's young and impressionable. We'll grow to suit after a while. The main thing is to avoid the scandal.''

The marquess leaned back in his chair and suffered the earl's discomfort with gladness. "The main thing, Merrick, is her settlement. The chit has cost me an unholy fortune, and I'm not ashamed to admit that I am in need of funds. She's a lively little thing, and quite a few are taken with her. The scandal won't scare them away unless you've got her with child, and somehow, I rather doubt that.''

Merrick felt his temper rise to an uncomfortable degree. Although he did not come to town often, he was well aware of the gossip that circulated behind his back. The sobriquet "St. Wyatt" was as nothing to the rumors of why his first wife had never produced children after years of marriage. To have Eddings throw that up in his face at a time like this added fuel to the fire already simmering. He did not have to endure this. Only the memory of Cassandra's stunned expression after he kissed her kept him firmly in his seat.

"You are speaking of your sister, not a prize horse,'' he informed Eddings coldly. "I have reason to believe she is not averse to my attentions. While I am not prepared to ransom her for an unreasonable sum, I am prepared to accept full financial responsibility for her from this day forward. I will provide her with an annual income, and settle a fair sum on you and her mother. And I will provide her with the home and security a lady should be able to expect. You will not need to worry about her ever again.''

"I never worried about her before, why should I start now? Cass can take care of herself. Why the deuce she would choose you above the others, I cannot fathom, but she's free to make that choice, provided that you can make the same settlement as her other suitors.'' Duncan sat back in his chair, smiled comfortably, and named a sum that would have bought and sold his entire holdings twice over.

Merrick made a cold smile. ''I may be wealthy, Eddings, but I am no love-bitten fool. Anyone willing to offer that sum is buying your silence.'' He leaned over and scribbled an amount on a piece of paper on the desk. ''I'll not bargain for her. You're the one who must live with your conscience. You know she will be safe in my hands.''

Duncan glanced at the number and shrugged. ''As I've told you, Cass can take care of herself. You may be well off, Merrick, but Rupert can dress her in diamonds if she wishes, and offer her a trifle more pleasure than a country parson. My conscience doesn't nag me in the least by accepting his offer. She's whetted his appetite and he's chewing at the bit. I daresay he's more her type than you. So I suppose we have nothing further to discuss.''

He rose from his chair and Merrick rose with him, his ire seething uncontrollably, although he revealed only an outer coldness. ''Rupert is an unscrupulous rake with the morals of a degenerate rabbit. If you can accept his suit over mine, the matter is on your conscience. I wash my hands of it. Should you change your mind, you know where to find me.''

Duncan whistled softly to himself as the earl stalked out. He had rather thought Merrick gullible enough to be incensed by his talk of Rupert marrying Cassandra and to offer the inflated sum. Well, he had lost that gamble, but Rupert's offer was still higher. On a gamble like this, he could not lose. And Rupert could be relied on to come through with extra cash when funds grew tight, whereas Merrick was a tightfisted bastard. No, it was much better this way. Cass would have been back on his doorstep within a fortnight of marriage to the earl. Rupert would keep her in hand. These things always worked out for the best.

* * *

The scene with Catherine left a bitter aftertaste in Cassandra's mouth, and she rode in silence beside her aunt as the carriage carried them back to London. Catherine had every right to be outraged, but she had said unforgivable things about Merrick as well as herself. Cassandra was willing to admit that she was a wanton hoyden. She didn't think she was a whore, but she was willing to let the epithet slide by. But to call Merrick a debauched old goat seeking filthy pleasures with children was an unfeeling and irrational thing to say. Unfortunately, Cassandra realized that Catherine might not be the only one saying these things.

Wyatt was such a proud and proper man, she hated to be the one to blacken his name. He would never forgive her for that. Why hadn't she thought more about his feelings before she got them into this situation?

Because she had no choice. Lifting her chin, she stared proudly out the carriage window. Aunt Matilda had scarcely said two words to her since they left. She would not be sympathetic to Cassandra's plight. No one would. How could she explain that Rupert made her skin crawl? It was her place to accept her brother's choice for her, they would say. Well, she wouldn't. She had made her choice and acted upon it. She would rather live with her own wrong decisions than someone else's.

By the time they arrived in London, Cassandra was prepared to defy the world in defense of her decision to marry Wyatt. He must have spoken to Duncan by now. He would come to see her in the morning. The earl would be angry and coldly formal, but she would win him. She knew she could. His heated kisses had caught her by surprise, but she was willing to learn where they led. More than willing, if the truth be known. She had never felt anything like them, wasn't entirely certain if it was proper to feel like that, but Wyatt's kiss had been the most exciting thing that had ever happened to her. She hoped he wouldn't be horrified if he knew. Perhaps ladies weren't supposed to feel that way. She was quite certain they weren't. She couldn't imagine her mother feeling like that. Or Aunt Matilda. Since they were the only proper ladies she knew to emulate, Cassandra stifled a giggle at her thoughts. She might be wanton, but for a little while, Merrick had been too.

Holding that thought as she marched into her mother's bedroom under Matilda's command, Cassandra smiled blithely and rushed to her mother's bedside. Lady Howard appeared paler than usual, and Cassandra brushed a light strand of golden hair back from her mother's face as she perched at the edge of the bed.

"Do not look so gloomy, Mama. I am quite fine. The cloud of disgrace will soon pass over after I am wedded."

Faded eyes that once were blue settled searchingly on her daughter's face. "You are happy with the idea, then? You are so very young, but I thought you wiser than I. Do you know something that I don't?"

That was an odd tack to take over a daughter's impending marriage. Duncan must have been saying reprehensible things behind her back. Cassandra tried to smile her mother's doubts away. "Don't you think he'll make a good husband, Mama? I thought you would be pleased. He has asked, hasn't he? He said he would." She tried to hide the note of anxiety in her voice. Surely a man like Wyatt wouldn't have second thoughts and turn tail.

"But I thought . . . He is so much older than you, more worldly." Lady Howard lifted her gaze to her aunt's disapproving expression. "Did the visit not turn out well? Why are you back so soon? I had hoped . . . Cassandra was so set on . . ."

Cassandra was accustomed to her mother's unfinished sentences, but she did not like the sound of these. Perhaps Merrick had not mentioned the reason for his sudden proposal. That was extremely generous of him, but something still did not seem quite right. She hated to be the one to reveal the scandal, but how could she get a complete thought from her mother at this rate?

Aunt Matilda was not so silent. She gave Cassandra a scornful glance. "Your daughter behaved as any Howard would and got herself sent home in disgrace. I trust the young man has offered for her as he said? Otherwise, we must find somewhere to send her. She cannot show her face in London again."

Cassandra bit back her irritation. Her mother was nearly white. Had Aunt Matilda no sense at all? "It's quite all right, Mama. Merrick will give me his name and there will be no scandal. We really did nothing wrong. It was an accident. But you know he is the perfect gentleman. He will be a fine husband and I shall be a proper countess."

Lady Howard appeared even more faint. "Merrick? Merrick has offered for you? But you are to marry Rupert anyway?"

"Of course not. Why would I marry Rupert? He has clammy hands." Anxiety took a deeper hold, and Cassandra hurriedly asked, "Wyatt has offered, hasn't he? He said he would. He's a gentleman. He must."

"It is your marriage to Rupert that Duncan has just shown me in the papers, Cassie. Surely you knew? Even Duncan would not marry you off without telling you the bridegroom's name."

Her mother seemed to be seeking some reassurance Cassandra could not give her. She stared at her mother with incomprehension, her own face becoming as pale as the invalid's. Duncan would not. He could not. Surely Merrick. . . ?

Without another word, Cassandra rose from the bed and woodenly stalked toward the door. She would find him, and she would kill him. She would take a red-hot poker to Duncan's head. She would find a butcher knife and run it through his invisible heart. She would murder him, she knew she would.

She caught him on the way out for the evening. The marquess's valet glanced up in surprise and stepped away from the final straightening of Duncan's immaculate cravat. At the certain signs of fire in the lady's eye, the valet discreetly retired from the battleground.

Duncan gathered up his gold-knobbed walking stick and beaver hat and gave his sister's wild-eyed look a cursory glance. "Threw you out, did they?" He began to button his last glove.

"Did Merrick offer for me? Did he, Duncan? Don't lie. I know he did. He's a gentleman, a fact you'll never understand. I know he offered."

Duncan lifted one dark eyebrow. "Haven't you outgrown these childish tantrums yet? Yes, he offered, but he didn't offer enough. Rupert is agreeable despite the scandal. He was on his way to obtain a special license the last I saw of him. He thought an extensive wedding trip might be called for to let the scandal die down. Very considerate of him, I thought."

Cassandra picked up the elaborate snuffbox on the table and launched it at her brother's dispassionately handsome face. "No! A thousand times no! Did you hear me, Duncan? No! I'll not marry that smug bastard! I'll run away with Merrick before I'll let that toad near me. You can't make me, Duncan!"

A hairbrush and a deck of cards followed the snuffbox. The brush sent Duncan's hat flying, and the cards slithered and slid about his feet as he stalked her. She heaved a century-old carved night table in his path and grabbed wildly for a weapon, any weapon at all.

Her hands burned at the touch of a lighted oil lamp behind her, but she lifted its crystal shade and flung it wildly. It smashed into shards on the floor after bouncing harmlessly off Duncan's broad chest. The crash had to have been heard by the entire household, but no one entered to intervene. No one ever had.

"You're wasting your energy and mine, Cass. You know very well I can make you. Now, stop shattering the furniture before you give Mother a spasm."

Cassandra went deadly still. Her mother was all she had left in the world. She lived in dread of the terrible attacks that left the invalid blue and gasping for air. She had promised time and again to curb her temper, but she was justified in her fury this time. She gave Duncan a scathing glare.

"Touch one hair on my head, Duncan, and I will scream the house down. Aunt Matilda is still here. You'll never inherit a cent from her if she knows you beat me."

"I'm not likely to inherit more than loathing from the stiff-necked old biddy in any case. I haven't time to beat you, Cass. I'm meeting Rupert so I can begin collecting your settlement. I'll leave you to him. I daresay he'll know how to settle your childish tantrums." He caught Cassandra's wrist firmly in his gloved grip as she reached for his box of pistols. "Merrick isn't man enough to beat you and bed you until you're biddable. Rupert is. I'd suggest you learn to curb your temper in this next week, Cass. I'll not come to your rescue if your new husband feels called upon to make you mind. My sympathies are entirely with him."

Duncan made no attempt to hide the threat in his voice. He never had. Her father had beat her on more than one occasion, but he would never allow Duncan to touch her. He had encouraged the competition between brother and sister instead, until they were not to be outdone in their fight to obtain their father's favors. But once the marquess was dead, Duncan had it all. He had beat her only once after that, but Cassandra had learned to avoid him deftly ever since.

"I won't, Duncan," she whispered as the pain of his grip twisted her arm backward. "You can't make me marry him. Let me marry Merrick. Then you will be rid of me."

"I would have, if he'd offered enough. It would have served you right to marry such a milk-livered man. But he's too clutch-fisted to waste his coins on the likes of you, Cassie. Go order up your bride clothes, little sister. Saturday is your wedding day.''

Cassandra blanched. Less than a week. She had to find Merrick and make him elope with her. Surely he'd understand. He'd offered. He would make his offer good.

As if reading her thoughts, Duncan smiled and released her hand. "Don't even think it, Cass. I need only tell Merrick who your real father is, and he'll cut you cold. You wouldn't want our dirty linen aired in public, would you, now? Or should I say, our mother's dirty linen?''

He donned his hat, leaving Cassandra staring white-faced and cold at the portrait of the late marquess over Duncan's mantel: the devilish black-haired marquess who had fathered a changeling child like Cassandra.

She shivered and slid into a hunched ball at the bottom of the closed door. No one could save her but herself.

Chapter 7

Merrick lifted the beautiful hand-blown crystal goblet to the fire's light and admired the flash of gold and diamonds created by the contents. The heady liquor left burning trails along his palate, and he savored the fire of it thoughtfully. He had almost possessed just such a fire of his own. He could still taste the passionate liquor of her mouth, still feel the fire of red-gold silk against his palms. One brief moment to last a lifetime. Life was full of brief moments. He had never expected more.

Sighing, he took another deep draft of the expensive brandy. He was well on his way to being solidly in his cups, but a man had a right to an occasional lapse from sobriety. The wedding night of his intended bride was one of them.

"Never saw a lovelier bride. Never did, old boy. Wasn't she splendid? All that shimmery gauze, and hair like fire. Never saw the like. Never will. How did we let her go, Wyatt? Rupert don't deserve her. Not our Cass. She was a wild one, but young. She'd come around. What happened, Wyatt? How did she get away?"

Wyatt wished Bertie to hell, but then he would be drinking alone, and he'd sworn he would never drink alone. He lifted the glass for another sip, but it was empty. Staring at the goblet blankly for a moment, Wyatt shook his head to clear the fog.

"She wasn't ours, Bertie. Never was. She's a Howard. Was a Howard. Not country folk like us. They're off to Paris on their wedding trip, I hear. Would you have thought to take her to Paris? I never would. They were just fighting battles over there a few months ago. We're getting old and dull, my friend. We need to settle down and set up nurseries, not chase the wind. She was a vision, you say?''

''Aye, a vision. Floated down the aisle. Funny thing, that,'' Bertie mused, as if just discovering it. ''She didn't take Eddings' arm, just walked at his side, proud as any princess. Rupert caught a rare one there. Scarcely fair, practically stealing her from the nursery. What was that talk about you and her at Hampton Court?'

Merrick ignored these wanderings, chasing after thoughts of his own. ''You think you know women, and then you find you don't know them at all. Take Catherine, f'rinstance. Known her all our lives. Like a sister. Not hard to look at, just a country girl more our style, practically on the shelf, if the truth be told.'' Merrick poured a hasty drink as he repeated Cassandra's outrageous remark. ''Think she'd be happy to be wedded, set up a nursery, have an establishment of her own. But more I think of it, Cass was right. She was like a cat ready to pounce. Once she had me in the bag, whoosh, off she'd go, haring into town.''

Bertie gave an inelegant belch and reached for the decanter. ''Mixing the old metaphors, old boy. Cat can't hare.''

''Cat can't wed,'' Merrick answered inanely.

''Yes, she can, too. She'd have you back in a trice if you'd like. Go ask her, see if she won't.'' Bertie sipped contentedly at the shockingly expensive French liquor. Merrick seldom brought out the really good stuff except on special occasions.

''And Cass, there's another one.'' Merrick went on with his train of thought as if his friend hadn't spoken. ''To see her in that gambling hell, you'd think her up to all the rigs. Then you look at her trailing around the company like a stray cat, and you know she just ain't been brought up right, damn her unholy father to hell.''

"*I* don't know nothing of the sort. *You're* the one that said that,'' Bertie reminded him callously.

"And then it turns out she's just looking for a meal ticket, and the richer man won. I just can't fathom that.'' Merrick shook his head again in confusion, but the fog was getting thicker. He took another drink before continuing. "I thought to myself, now here's a maiden in distress. Why else would she take to the likes of me? And then I see that announcement and think, old Duncan's up to his tricks again, but I'll rescue the lady. But she doesn't want to be rescued. Can you figure that? She sits there, just as cool and calm as you please, smiling like she's just discovered the sun, and saying it was all a misunderstanding, thank you very much. Misunderstanding, by Jove! She locks herself in the room with me, causes the scandal of the decade, and it's all a misunderstanding! Now, I ask you, Bertie, is that anything your sister would have done at ten-and-eight? It don't make good sense.''

"Better off without her, old boy. She'd run you in circles. Rupert's the right one for the likes of that. Shame, though. Sure was a fetching little thing.''

"Mother was right about one thing,'' Merrick said gloomily, stretching his long legs out toward the fire. "Never marry a pretty woman. They have no heart or soul and think only of themselves.''

"Cat ain't pretty and she's got the heart of a shrew. What say we round up a few others and make a night of it? Wine, women, and song, that's what we need.''

Wine, women, and song. Merrick stared at the fire while the words danced in his head. For one instant he had possessed all three in one lovely package. He'd never known such things were possible. Where could he find the like again?

With a sudden twist of his wrist, he flung the lovely shimmering goblet and its fiery contents into the flames.

* * *

In a far different corner of the city, a cadaverously tall man looked gloomily around the rag-patched walls of the room housing a frail woman of nearly half his size and a small boy who hid behind his mother's skirts and stared at the newcomer with fear and curiosity. Into this tiny space between four walls was squeezed a pallet for sleeping, a broken-legged table, and a single chair of dubious integrity. The man remained standing rather than take a seat as urged.

"You can't let him do it!" Despite her frail stature, the woman's plea was vehement. "It's unholy, that's what it is! You've got to stop him."

The man shrugged with an even more gloomy expression. "Not likely. Too late for that. It's not our worry. She's bound to be just another of them what deserves a comeuppance. It's not her we're to worry about. It's a nasty cough you have, Lucinda. It's you we've got to take care of. Use those coins I brought to get you and the boy out of here, somewhere in the country where it's healthy. I'll take care of him when the time comes. We'll just have to be patient, that's all."

"You didn't used to be like this," the woman cried. "You've grown hard, Jake. What if it were me he wedded today? Would you do nothing?"

Despair briefly filled the tall man's eyes as he gazed upon the once lovely woman in rags staring beseechingly at him now. But condemnation quickly took the place of despair. "I'd kill him, but it's not worth my neck to do the same for his noble bride. I'll take care of you, Lucy. Just be patient."

"I heard a story today I didn't like at all." Drunkenly the elegantly clad Marquess of Eddings pinned his new brother-in-law between wall and mantel as the noisy reception swirled around them. Being the larger of the two, Duncan had no difficulty in keeping his audience captive.

Casually straightening his rumpled lace and examining his cuff as if Duncan's proximity were a mere nuisance, Rupert inquired, ''Oh? Then I trust you won't repeat it.''

''No, but before you go up to my sister, you'd damned well better deny it.''

Duncan's tone was menacing, and Rupert hid a sudden frisson of alarm. While Duncan repeated the sordid tale he'd heard, Rupert's eyes darted nervously to their surroundings to be certain no one else listened. Who had repeated this story to the marquess, and why? No one else could possibly have known. There wasn't a soul in this room who knew the truth. Somewhere, there was a traitor.

When the sodden marquess hiccuped to an end, Rupert summoned a chilling smile and signaled to a servant for another glass of champagne. ''Don't be ridiculous, Eddings. Would I have settled that kind of sum on you if that were the truth? Have a drink and wish me happy. Your sister will not regret your choice of husbands, you'll see.''

When the marquess wandered off with his drink, Rupert clenched his fist until the stem of his goblet cracked. Flinging the shattered crystal at the wall in much the same manner as another man in another house not so far away, he signaled a servant discreetly waiting near at hand.

In furious whispers he sent the man scampering into the night.

Caught up in her own problems, Cassandra scarcely took consideration of any other's. The drunken revelry from below had begun its last, dying chatter. She recognized the signs from experience. The male laughter coming from her father's all-night card parties and, later, Duncan's, had always ended just so: riotous laughter, breaking glass, a few loud arguments, and then the drunken farewells. Rupert would be up soon. Her husband.

Nervously she turned and contemplated the full-length mirror filling nearly all one wall between the dresser and the wardrobe. The gilded frame glittered garishly in the light of the crystal chandelier. She had never seen a chandelier in a bedroom before. She didn't know if she ought to call a footman to douse the candles or leave it as it was. She preferred the light.

The mirror revealed a pale ghost with haunted eyes, and she turned away from the image. She had to hang on to her courage, and she couldn't if she looked at that formless waif in the mirror. The rest of her life depended on her performance tonight. She must think of herself as invincible.

She tugged the spun gold of her wedding dress upward, but the bodice wasn't cut to completely cover her breasts. Damn Duncan and his disreputable modistes. Cassandra opened the wardrobe and found her shawl upon a shelf. The servants had already unpacked all of her meager belongings, but that didn't make this strange room any more hers than before. The room was as cold and unpleasant as her husband. She would cast them both off shortly. She just wished the servants hadn't unpacked her things and taken away her trunk. That would make things awkward.

It didn't matter. Tonight she would cast herself upon the world. No longer would she rely on anyone but herself. If her own brother could sell her into a life of bondage, then there wasn't a man alive who could be trusted. For the first time she was beginning to understand what men saw when they looked at her, and she didn't like it a bit. Even Merrick had treated her as if all she were was a body to ease his desires on.

Cassandra ground her teeth together and tried not to think about her mother's warnings of the physical side of marriage. She still didn't know where kisses led, but her mother had made it clear it wasn't necessarily pleasant and had to be endured, that a husband would expect it. That was what Merrick had been trying to

tell her. She would have to give him credit for being
honest, but if she did so, then she would have to acknowledge that Rupert had done the same, only in a
less polite manner. Rupert's bruising kisses held none
of the gentleness of Merrick's. Perhaps that was all the
difference she could expect by a choice of husband.
One would be cruel, the other tender. But both would
want the same thing, some unspeakable violation of
her body.

Cassandra glanced surreptitiously down at the pale
curve of her breasts above the gold fabric. She knew
men liked to look at her there, and Rupert had made
it clear that he intended to do more than look, had
already done so. His hands on her had been humili-
ating, but that act couldn't be the one that made her
mother speak in horrified whispers. She didn't intend
to stay long enough to find out the source of her fears.
Once she was free, she would buy a burlap gown that
swathed her to the ears. Then she needn't worry about
men again.

Her thoughts had distracted her sufficiently so she
didn't hear her husband's footsteps until they were almost to the door. Cassandra swung around, her heart
pounding wildly as the door opened.

Rupert stepped into the room. He was not a tall
man, but he possessed a certain wiry grace that revealed an athletic physique. Garbed elegantly in
starched cravat, black tailed coat, and silk knee
breeches, he was the epitome of a fashionable gentleman. Had he the character to match his wealth and
looks, he could have had any woman he wished. One
look in his heavy-lidded gray eyes gave fair warning
of the truth behind the facade, however.

Cassandra forced herself not to step backward as
Rupert's gaze found her. He did not appear to be
pleased to see her still fully clothed and standing in
the circle of chandelier light. She could tell that by the
flick of his gaze to the covers Lotta had turned down

earlier. Still, he did nothing more than loosen his cravat as he approached.

"I did not take you for the missish type, my lady. My apologies for lingering overlong with our guests. Shall I send for a maid to help you undress, or will you allow me that pleasure?"

Unctuous. That was the only word she could think of to describe his voice. Cassandra distrusted the sound of it wholeheartedly. Trying to hide the quaver in her voice, she moved toward the dresser and away from her husband.

"There is something you must know, Rupert," she answered, keeping her chin high and allowing defiance to creep into her voice. She did not meet his gaze, but reached for her brush instead.

Amused, Rupert cast his cravat aside and began unfastening his coat. "Pray, inform me, wife."

"I do not intend to be your wife."

The words came out so coldly and curtly, he looked up in startlement. She was still the tender young child he had seen as he entered the room, but he mistrusted the stiff set of her shoulders. He shrugged out of his coat and kept his voice casual. "You should have thought of that before you said the vows in church. It's too late to change your mind."

Cassandra heard the coldness in his reply and tried not to shiver. "I didn't change my mind. I never wanted to marry you, but Duncan forced me to. I daresay he lied to you about my willingness. He never let me near enough to you to explain my feelings." When Rupert made no immediate reply, Cassandra swung around to finally face him.

She was appalled to discover he had continued undressing as she spoke. The sight of his bare, lightly furred chest beneath his unfastened shirt struck her like a blow to the stomach, and she steadied herself against the dresser behind her. "I never meant to cause anyone any trouble, but you really should have asked me first, Rupert. Then we wouldn't have to have this discussion.''

Rupert eyed her dispassionately and began unfastening his cuffs. "What discussion? We are married. You are nervous. I didn't expect it of you, admittedly. I thought you a trifle more experienced, but I find I prefer it this way. Before the night is over, you will be my wife. In the morning, we shall be on our way to the pleasures of Paris. I will see you gowned in the latest fashions. We will frequent the halls of the highest society. With your name and rank and my wealth, we should even be welcome in the Bourbon palaces. What is there to discuss?''

Cassandra took a deep breath to steady her nerves. He was entirely too close for her comfort, but at least he was being reasonable. That was more than she could say of Duncan. She sought for the words that would make him understand her plight.

"I am sorry, Rupert. I'm certain there are more willing women who would gladly accompany you to Paris. I don't want the latest fashions, and I'm not entirely certain I even know what a Bourbon palace is. All I want is to go home to Kent and make a home for my mother. I don't want a husband. So I thought . . . I mean, I talked to someone who knows, and they said . . .''

Cassandra stumbled over the words as Rupert lifted the shawl from her shoulders and dropped it to the floor. She was grateful for the length of silk covering her as his hand closed about her upper arm, but it wasn't sufficient to protect her from the coldness of his grip.

"Stop prattling, Cassie. We're married and there's an end to it. Now, kiss me as a wife ought.''

She swerved her head to avoid the heated liquor of his breath, but Rupert caught her jaw with his other hand and pulled her around. She gagged as the fumes of his breath filled her senses, but his grip forced her lips to part. His tongue was a punishment, not a sweet excitement, and she felt a sweeping dread through her middle as he crushed her back against the dresser and plundered her mouth. This wasn't how it was supposed to be.

As his hand released her jaw, Cassandra jerked her head away and pushed at his chest. "Stop it! Can't you see I don't want to be your wife? Let me go now, Rupert, before Duncan steals any more of your money in exchange for favors I don't intend to give you. I'm trying to help you get the best of the bargain. Why won't you listen?"

"Because I have what I want, Cassie. Now, be a good girl and get in bed and I'll show you that you have nothing to fear from me. I'm said to be an accomplished lover. You needn't worry about any old wives' tales of our marriage bed. You'll be begging for more before the night is done."

Rupert's hands moved to her breasts, kneading them urgently as his mouth sought to cover hers again, and Cassandra knew an instant's panic as she realized he was thoroughly inebriated. She had meant to argue this out with a rational man, but she knew from experience that a drunken man was beyond reason. His fingers bit cruelly through the thin fabric, and his kiss brought a sudden burning nausea.

She reacted insensibly then. She had meant to be sensible. She had meant to be calm and sympathetic and agreeable and show Rupert how he was being cheated. But fear and loathing and panic replaced all thought as his hands began to jerk her bodice down. With all the strength she could muster, she brought her knee up in a trick her father's mistress had once taught her. Her aim was poor, but her intent was obvious. Rupert yelped and jumped back, covering his bruised parts as Cassandra shoved from his grasp.

Not injured severely enough to remain still, Rupert leapt after her, grabbing Cassandra's arm and flinging her toward the bed with a strength she would not have thought of him. She stumbled on the length of her gown and heard it rip as she fell. Before she could right herself, he was upon her.

She screamed as she was crushed against the bed by his heavy weight. Cassandra's fingers recoiled from the cold flesh of his chest as she attempted to shove him away. Rupert caught her wrist in his hands and pressed her back, smothering her breath with his punishing mouth. He was stretched full length against her, and she felt the hardness of him rubbing at her hips. When Rupert bit her lip and began to shove his hips in some manic fashion against her, all trace of rationality fled Cassandra's mind. She fought one hand free and grabbed Rupert's hair and yanked until he yowled with pain.

"Bitch! I'll teach you . . ." Rupert grabbed her wrist and with his free hand smacked her violently across the cheek.

The world whirled and went black for a minute, but the scrape of Rupert's hand across her breast as he ripped at her clothes gave Cassandra strength to fight back the dizzying nausea. Again she brought her knee up. This time, her aim was better.

He screamed in pain, and she shoved him backward, hearing his thud with satisfaction as he toppled against the washstand. Grasping at her torn gown, she dragged herself from the entrapment of the feather mattress and groaned as she tried to straighten and stand.

She could hear him trying to get to his feet. It was too late to salvage the evening. Far from being rational, her husband was more animal than Duncan, and with a greater power to harm her than her brother had ever possessed. It was late to learn that now, but with the feral caution of a cornered creature, Cassandra ran.

There were servants clearing up the wreckage of the public rooms downstairs, but none stood in her way as the new bride fled down the stairs in her tattered wedding remnants. Tongues might clack on the morrow, but none owed the master the kind of loyalty that demanded they stop her. Without orders to the contrary, they merely looked up and gaped as Cassandra struggled with the huge front door, wrenched it open, and fled into the night.

The cold night air struck her with the same force as Rupert's blow, tearing her breath away. She had no wrap, no shawl to protect her bruised flesh, but already she heard Rupert's furious shouts in the house behind her. She could not stop to contemplate a need for warmth. With frantic speed, she raced down the lonely street.

She had no idea where she would go. Her only goal was to lose Rupert somewhere in the streets of London. Unfortunately, these were the broad gaslit streets of Mayfair and not the narrow alleys of the East End. Anyone could spot her fleeing figure with a modicum of effort.

Rupert's shout sounded as if it were right behind her. It echoed eerily between the tall brick edifices, as out of place in these elegant environs as a jaguar's cry. She shook with cold, but shivers of fear increased her discomfort. He was drunk enough to beat her right here on the street, and not a single window would open to investigate her cries for help.

Her breath hurt in her chest as she raced faster. The pain in her jaw ached, but not so much as the rasping gasps for air and the sharp pangs in her side as she fought to outrun her pursuer.

It didn't take far for Cassandra to realize she would never make it. Her narrow skirts hindered her pace despite the tear that had ripped one seam and left the hem flapping behind her. Her thin slippers were already destroyed by the rough stones underfoot. And her lungs gasped for chilling air that somehow did not quite relieve her distress.

When she stumbled, she could hear Rupert's leather shoes pound on the walk behind her. If only there were a hackney, some innocent passerby, some witness to protect her from his fury. She took a breath, righted herself, and ran on.

And collided with a solid masculine chest that teetered, then caught her firmly as he fell back against the gate from whence he had just come.

"Dashitall!" The words came out in a whoosh as they struggled in a dance for balance.

The voice sounded hazily familiar, and Cassandra darted a hasty look upward. In the darkness, she could see little more than a blond halo and broad shoulders, but that was sufficient to jog her memory.

"Thomas! Thank God, Thomas! Help me. Hide me. Please." The grating gasp of her own voice terrified her, and Cassandra clung unsteadily to the youngest Scheffing's coat front.

"Lady Cass?" Thomas barely had time to identify her before the sound of pounding footsteps approached.

Cassandra squealed and tried to break away from the young man's steadying embrace, but it was too late. Rupert's ragged breathing cut menacingly through the air as he tried to control his breath long enough to demand the return of his wife. Faint with fear and physical illness, Cassandra still attempted to push away and seek the gate that Thomas had come through.

"Let her go." Rupert's voice almost managed the tone of cold authority that normally served him.

Cassandra felt more than observed Thomas' puzzled glance downward, but the state of her gown told the tale that she could not. His large hands placed her firmly behind him.

"You've insulted a lady."

Cassandra shuddered at this dangerous approach. Thomas had no responsibility for defending insults to her name. All she needed was the bulk of his physical protection for now. But he was young and hotheaded and not very sensible. She would have to be sensible for him.

Before she could disentangle herself and assert her

rights, she heard Rupert chuckle drunkenly, and she cringed at the sound even before she heard his words.

"Damned young puppy, that is my wife you're holding. I ought to call you out for this."

"You ought to be shot for what you've done to her!" Thomas replied belligerently, even as Cassandra reached to cover his mouth with her hand.

Realizing that his wife was acquainted with the young knight-errant, Rupert smiled smugly. "I've pistols back at the house. Shall we try them out?"

"Thomas, no!" Cassandra screamed, breaking from his grip. "He's drunk! He'll kill you. This isn't your argument."

"Ahhh, my lovely wife, you've gained your voice. Come along now and you can watch the fun. I rather fancy I'll have to defend your honor more than once in the months to come. You might as well become accustomed to the sight."

Rupert caught Cassandra's arm and tried to drag her along with him, but she swung wildly with her fist, connecting with his shoulder. He raised his hand to slap her again, but Thomas lunged at him.

"Run, Cass! Get out of here!"

She did as told. Perhaps without her there, Thomas could knock Rupert out and escape. It seemed the only sensible thing to do. Even she knew of her husband's deadly reputation as a duelist. She had thought the worst of the talk to be rumors, but tonight had proved her wrong. Rupert enjoyed violence.

Suddenly she found a goal for her fleeing feet. Wyatt had protected young Thomas in the gaming hell. He would certainly protect him from this worse danger. If she could only just remember which of these elegant streets contained the imposing London town house of the Earl of Merrick.

Sheer luck steered her down a vaguely familiar crossroad. Gas lamps paved the way, but the tall houses on either side towered dark and unfriendly behind their facades of stone and closed, draped windows. No light beckoned from any of them but one. That was the one she remembered.

Gasping with relief, Cassandra staggered down the street, drawn by the single light in a lower window. Wyatt had to be there. Surely the proper Earl of Merrick could not be out carousing at this hour. He had to be there. The light in the window was not to guide his wandering feet and welcome him home as it had been for her father and Duncan. It just meant he was still up. Please.

Feeling the last of her strength drain out of her, Cassandra dragged her quaking legs up the steps between the stone lions and dropped the knocker. Once. Twice.

It took an interminable time for anyone to answer. Perhaps Merrick had sent all his servants to bed. She didn't know the hour, but it must be late. Leaning against the wooden panel, she pounded the knocker again and again.

Finally she heard the echo of boots against the parquet floor inside. She remembered seeing that floor once when she was a little girl. She didn't remember the occasion. She just remembered how it shone like polished glass. None of the floors in her home looked like that.

She almost fell as the door jerked open. A startled masculine gasp and a hard arm greeted her, and she was lifted bodily into the entry. The door slammed swiftly behind her.

Chapter 8

"Cassandra!"

Merrick felt his stomach lurch sickeningly at the bedraggled waif collapsing in his arms. The shimmering silken sunset curls he remembered had become damp tendrils hanging in limp tangles about a fragile face misshapen by an ugly, swollen bruise. A silent scream of rage welled up in him as dull blue eyes lifted briefly, then closed. He caught her up in his arms and carried her toward the warmth of the fire in the study. Suddenly sobered by the sight of shadowed bruises marring the pale breast spilling from her torn gown, Wyatt reined in his rage with an icy calm.

Scheffing staggered to his feet at the unexpected sight of the earl appearing with the lost bride who had set off their drinking spree. Remembering how he had tried to persuade Merrick out for a night of wine, women, and song, he sighed with relief that his friend had been wise enough to stay home. Had he known she would come here?

Bertie's thoughts on that subject quickly fled as Cassandra's eyes opened and found him. Aqua pools widened in silent horror as Wyatt set her down in a chair near the fire, and she instantly swayed upward, shoving Merrick's arms aside as she stepped toward Scheffing with an imploring hand.

"Thomas! He will kill Thomas! Help him, please."

Her words blasted the lingering fumes of brandy from their brains. Merrick reached out and caught

Cassandra's arm, steadying her, while Scheffing hurried forward with a small tumbler of drink.

"Here, take this. Catch your breath, then talk."

The smell of alcohol reached her nose and Cassandra wearily attempted to push it away, but Scheffing forced the glass to her lips while Merrick held her still. She choked on the burning liquid, but it swept fire through her veins. She took the second sip more readily.

"Gently, now. It won't help to get her drunk. Cassandra, what happened? Where is Thomas?"

Merrick felt her terror rip through him as her dangerous eyes turned upward to seek his. He could feel her fear radiating through his body. The fiery woman who had swept through a hall of gamblers with a radiant smile shouldn't know such fear. There was an awareness in her eyes now that hadn't been there before, and Merrick flinched guiltily from it as if she had accused him. This was her wedding night, or rather, the morning after. The tattered state of her dress left only one inevitable conclusion. He had not thought even Rupert so low as to stoop to rape, but the evidence was damning. The only question remaining was how Thomas had become involved in this.

Gathering his strength, Wyatt held her tight. "You don't have to explain, Cass. Just tell us where Thomas is. We'll find him."

Cassandra went limp with relief. Finally, someone who would act in her behalf. His arms around her were far from frightening. They comforted and offered a security she had never known. Merrick had tried to teach her a lesson once, but it was Rupert who had made it clear. Merrick's touch could never frighten her.

"Down the street. Rupert challenged him. Hurry, please, Wyatt. Don't let him hurt Thomas."

The sudden intake of breath behind her told her Scheffing didn't find this an easy task to undertake. He was right. Only Duncan had the right to interfere with

Rupert. Or herself. Straightening her sagging shoulders, Cassandra pushed from the earl's comforting arms.

"I'll go with you. Let us hurry."

Merrick caught her and held her back, studying the black smudges beneath her eyes and the painful swelling of her jaw. "Let me call a maid to take care of you. We'll find Thomas."

"No, it won't do. You can't stop Rupert. It's me he wants. Give me your coat." The weariness of how it must be wrote its lines across Cassandra's face as she held out her hand. She didn't know why she had thought running away would save her. She didn't know why she had thought marrying Rupert would solve her problems. She kept reacting instead of acting. She would never get anywhere that way.

When Merrick still hesitated, she pinned her gown with her fingers as best as she could and started for the doorway. "I can't stay here. You will have to come with me."

That made about as much sense as anything else that had happened this night, Merrick decided drunkenly. Peeling off his coat, he wrapped it over Cassandra's slender shoulders as they started down the hall. He ought to be calling for maids and a physician, but he sensed Thomas' danger was immediate. There wouldn't be time for argument.

There wasn't time to order a horse saddled or a carriage brought around either. They walked out into the frosty night and let the cold air sweep away the last of the brandy fumes. Between them, Scheffing and Merrick half-carried Cassandra down the street in the direction she had traversed so frantically earlier.

By the time they reached the tall wall where she remembered leaving Thomas and her husband, there was no one in sight. Cassandra gave a moan of frustration and wilted against the earl's arm. She didn't have much strength left. The pain in her jaw throbbed, and the blisters on her feet made each step one of torture.

Merrick held her up and thought as quickly as his drink-befuddled mind would allow. "We'll have to send for a carriage, Bertie. We'll need to go to Rupert's and your family, see if they're there. And Lady Cassandra needs to be taken home."

The thought of facing Duncan made Cassandra shiver, but she didn't object. Duels required seconds. Rupert would go to her brother for support in this. She nodded agreement.

But when the curricle was harnessed and they finally arrived at the Howard town house and discovered Lord Eddings had just been called out on an urgent matter, they both knew his destination, and Cassandra refused to be left behind.

"We've got to stop them, Wyatt. It's all my fault. You can't leave me here. Perhaps we can stop Rupert before he leaves." She clutched his coat around her shoulders and met his worried dark eyes without hesitation. Wyatt had thrown a cloak around him earlier, but she could see the gleam of his shirt sleeves and waistcoat beneath the dark material. That seemed to make him look even broader and taller than before. She remembered him as a gangly young man, but his poise now was stately.

"I cannot drag you back out again. You need medical attention. Stay here, and we will come back to you as soon as we have word."

"No!" Frantically Cassandra grabbed his sleeve. She was beyond reasoning. She only knew she could not be parted from Merrick. He was the only one who could save her. "You can't leave me here. Duncan will just send me back to Rupert and all will be for naught. I must go with you. I've got to make them understand."

She was practically hysterical, and it was obvious even to Merrick that the only servant here was the smirking valet. Resignedly he followed her out to the carriage. Scheffing had taken one of Merrick's horses and ridden home to try to stop his brother there. The earl privately offered a prayer that he was successful.

Steering the curricle back into the street, Merrick debated the wisdom of returning to Rupert's house. Instinct told him to take the girl to Scheffing's parents and pray that Thomas was safely under their roof. Logic told him that too much time had been lost already and that the answers lay on Rupert's doorstep. Whether wisely or not, he raised his whip and raced across the park toward Lady Cassandra's new home. She had married the madman, after all. She had to face up to her choice sometime.

As the curricle pulled up to the doorstep and came to a rapid halt, the town-house door swung open and a young maid raced down the step to meet them.

"My lady! He's gone. He's furious, Jacob says. I thought he'd gone for you. Oh, thank goodness you're safe."

The maid would have swept into the curricle after Merrick stepped down, but Cassandra lifted the reins and whip and froze both Wyatt and her maid with her look. "Where did they go, Lotta? They cannot be far ahead of us."

The maid glanced nervously at the impassive earl, who reached in and snatched away his whip, but she answered eagerly. "To St. James. Not far. Sir Rupert said he hadn't time for leaving town to do it proper. Jacob says there's a corner there that's kind of protected—"

"I know it." Wyatt swung back into his seat and calmly removed the reins from Cassandra's hands. He didn't have time either. The stubborn chit would have to go with him.

Cassandra clung to the sides of the carriage as it flew through darkened streets. The night sky was beginning to brighten in the distance, signaling the onset of dawn, but it was still the blackest night of her life. Never had she imagined this would come to pass of

her decision to lead her own life. She still didn't know
how it had come to this. Perhaps it was a nightmare
from which she would soon wake. She scarcely knew
Thomas. Surely he would come to his senses before
going to meet Rupert. Or his family would stop him.

She gave a cry of fright as the curricle tilted on the
turn, but Wyatt righted it with an expertise she had
not expected of the quiet earl. She grabbed the side of
the carriage and held on as he guided it recklessly
through the gray dawn and empty streets. An occasional early riser jerked his head in surprise as the
curricle and horse stampeded down the normally staid
streets, but the drunken revels of wealthy young men
were well known and none gave their passing more
than a second thought.

The early-morning twitter of birds in the park
quickly silenced at the intrusion of the horse and carriage. Cassandra paled as the gray light revealed another reckless rider careening down a crossroad, but
in a moment she recognized Bertie's stolid figure.

Merrick recognized him too, and cursed vividly at
realizing he rode alone. Either young Thomas had not
returned home or no one had been able to stop him.
As the first rays of dawn began to lighten the eastern
sky, he applied the whip for a final burst of speed.

Reaching a small copse of trees in an out-of-the-way
corner of the park, Merrick steadied his horse to a
halt, and throwing the reins to Cassandra, jumped to
the ground before the wheels stopped rolling. Without
stopping, Bertie galloped his horse in the same direction.

Cassandra threw down the reins and on shaking legs
climbed from the seat and set out after them. She
would plead with Rupert if she had to. Her pride wasn't
worth another man's life. Perhaps the drink had worn
off by now. She would agree to be his wife if he insisted. Anything. Please, just let poor, harmless
Thomas be all right. She could deal with the shame of
being Rupert's wife, but she could never live with the

burden of a man's death. Merrick and Scheffing would hate her then, and rightly so. This was all her fault. She had been foolish to think she could pit Rupert against Duncan and come out unscathed.

She could see Bertie leaping from his horse at the edge of the copse and Merrick disappearing into the dark shadows of the trees. The shot sounded before she could reach the path they took.

No second shot followed. Gasping with horror, Cassandra raced on slippered feet through the forest terrain until she stumbled upon the glade at the center.

Rupert stood at the far side of the clearing, a pistol smoking in his hand as Bertie cried out and knelt beside the fallen figure of his youngest brother. Merrick approached Rupert and Duncan with fists balled in anger, but Cassandra did not linger to see the outcome. Rupert still lived and Thomas was dead. There was naught for her to do now. She fled back in the direction of the curricle.

As Merrick neared the notorious duelist with murder in mind, Duncan grabbed his brother-in-law's arm and began to whisper hastily in his ear. Rupert nodded once, twice, then spun on his heels and strode off through the trees before the earl could reach him.

Ice in his eyes, Merrick regarded Duncan with venom. "I never believed a gentleman could lower himself to the height of a worm, but you have succeeded this night, Eddings. Did you send him safely home to rape your sister again?"

Duncan paled slightly but held his ground. "Rupert has no need to rape anyone, and Cass takes care of herself. They will be in Calais by evening and on their way to Paris before the next dawn. This unfortunate incident will prevent him from returning to England anytime soon. I tried to stop him, but the young man was rather belligerent. I had not realized Cass had acquired so many followers."

"If he dies, I'll personally see that you do not walk among polite society again, Howard." Merrick did not reveal the fact that Cassandra was safely in his curricle only a few hundred yards away. Let Rupert fly to Paris alone. He'd not make a victim of another helpless female this time. Swinging on his heel, he retreated to where Bertie lifted his young brother in his arms. He ought to kill Rupert for this, but now was not the time to do it. He had to get Thomas to a physician and Cassandra to safety before contemplating the pleasure of removing the vermin of society.

What he would do with the hauntingly lovely, no longer innocent Lady Cassandra never once crossed his mind.

The lovely Lady Cassandra was far from waiting patiently for the warrior heroes to come home. Tears streaming down her cheeks but no longer hysterical, she calmly rent the skirt of her wedding gown and mounted Bertie's horse. They would need Merrick's curricle to transport Thomas.

It was her fault that all this had come about. She had rushed headlong into this without giving a thought to the consequences. And because of her, Thomas lay dead or dying on the cold ground back there. Had she not meant to have her revenge on Duncan, had she not used Rupert as an instrument of that revenge, had she not been so damned stupid and arrogant . . .

She was too tired to continue the litany of self-flagellation. Rupert would be coming after her shortly. She had to get away. It was obvious he would never agree to an annulment or go along with her plan to beggar Duncan in retaliation for foisting off an unwilling wife on him. How very naive she was to believe Rupert might care whether she was willing or not. Naive! The notion was so ridiculous as to be laughable. She had seen things no lady should see, been places no gentleman would acknowledge, and still she had no understanding of the people around her.

She slid off Bertie's horse in the mews behind Rupert's town house. No sign of another recently used horse gave any evidence of Rupert's arrival. With luck, she would get away before he came back. Without luck, she would kill him. Or he would kill her. It scarcely mattered anymore.

Lotta gave a scream of fright as Cassandra entered the bedchamber like a vengeful ghost. A taller, lankier figure rose from the same couch, and Cassandra gave Lotta and her cadaverous lover a cynical look. These two did not waste much time mourning her imminent demise.

"Pack whatever you can, quickly. We're leaving." She had neither the patience nor the strength to reprimand her maid's scandalous behavior. At least they were still fully clothed. That saved a little time. She strode wearily to the wardrobe to find a gown suitable for traveling.

"Where are we going?" Lotta anxiously ran to the dresser to begin removing the few intimate garments stored there. Rupert's valet loped off in search of a bag.

"Away." Cassandra struggled out of the remains of her gown and grabbed her old riding habit. It was too tight in the bosom but it was warm. They might end up walking to Kent. She had best be prepared.

By the time she had the skirt and shirt in place, the valet was discreetly scratching at the door. Lotta let him in and sent her employer an anxious look.

"How will we go?" Cassandra was nothing if not inventive, but even Cassandra couldn't manufacture gold or horses with which to travel far. Lotta had no idea what had transpired this evening, but the ugly bruise all along her employer's fragile face spoke volumes. She would follow Cass to hell, but she would rather know the route in advance.

As if Lotta's words jarred her memory, Cassandra began tugging at the various drawers in the room. It was obvious to her that this was Rupert's room, that he had not stirred himself to provide a chamber of her own. He had to keep his spending money somewhere.

The lanky valet watched impassively as she dumped out drawer after drawer. Well over six feet, stoop-shouldered, with a face as lean and haggard as the rest of him, he appeared ancient beyond his years. Yet he surmised the lady's problem swiftly enough.

"There's a door at the rear of the desk, my lady. You'll find a coin box in there."

Without so much as a grateful look to the laconic servant, Cassandra ran her fingers over the polished wood at the side of the desk until she found a latch similar to the one in her father's. The door sprang open and she grasped inside until she found the money box. Opening it, she discovered Rupert very conveniently kept his coins in the pouch from the bank. Without counting the contents, she swept the bag from its hiding place, shoved the box back, and slammed the door.

"Let's go." Gripping the pouch, trailing the skirt of her habit, ignoring the long tendrils of hair streaming from her once neatly arranged coiffure, Cassandra strode across the garish bedchamber to the door.

Sending the valet an anxious look, Lotta started after her. "How will we go, my lady? You cannot travel unprotected. Is someone waiting for us?"

Cassandra swung around and gave her plump maid a look of disgust. "Rupert will be if we do not leave at once. Are you coming?"

The lanky manservant stepped forward with an impassive bow. "If I may suggest, my lady, there are pistols in the wardrobe."

Cassandra's stiff, haughty features suddenly crumpled. "Not anymore, they're not." Without another look back, she proceeded into the hallway.

With a shrug at Lotta's pleading look, the valet donned his best dignity and followed after them.

Chapter 9

"Wyatt! You're not listening to me!" The Countess Merrick drew her wattled chin to an indignant height and glared at her only son, or what she could see of his dark head from behind the newspaper.

"No, Mama," the earl replied absently, innocent of the irony of his answer.

"Wyatt, put that paper down this instant and listen to me! You have been gone far too long. Now that you're home, you must right the situation. It's wicked, what she's doing, and you must put a stop to it! You are the magistrate, it is your responsibility!"

"Yes, Mama." Not having heard a word that was said, Merrick continued scanning the contents of the paper while sipping at his morning coffee. The scandal of Sir Rupert's and Lady Cassandra's disappearance after an illegal duel in the park had finally died down to an infrequent rumor in the gossip columns. It had been impossible to keep the episode quiet. Thomas' large and noisy family had rampaged through Bow Street and Parliament seeking justice; Rupert's disloyal servants had told stories to every reporter willing to wave a shilling: and Duncan's arrogant denial of any knowledge of the event had infuriated the nobility as well as the general populace. Merrick gave a grateful sigh as he finally set aside the printed pages. He prayed Cassandra had not been caught in Rupert's clutches: Duncan had sworn the baronet had sailed alone. Cassandra's brother had looked gray and harried enough to almost make his promises believable.

Merrick removed his spectacles and toyed with his empty cup. It was no concern of his where Lady Cassandra might have gone, but he couldn't help an uneasy feeling in the pit of his stomach. He had been with Duncan when they returned to Rupert's house to see if she had returned there. The knowledge that Cassandra's maid and Rupert's manservant had also disappeared did not reassure. He had insisted on hiring investigators to be certain the lady hadn't been abducted.

The investigators had brought a mountain of confusing information these past weeks, but all Merrick had learned was that Cassandra wasn't in Paris with her husband and that France was an extremely expensive place to send hired investigators. Shrugging mentally, he started to rise before his mother's constant carping finally penetrated his thoughts.

"Are you going over there today? She needs to be sent back to her brother, or to that scandalous monster she married. It's not right that she remain here causing talk. I don't know why the Scheffings haven't had her arrested."

Thoughtful brown eyes finally focused on his mother's powdered, wrinkled face. "Who arrested, Mother?"

The countess favored him with an irate glare. "The wanton Howard chit, of course. Honestly, Wyatt, sometimes I believe you don't listen to a word I say. I have been waiting for you to come home to straighten out the matter. What are you going to do about it?"

Merrick felt the pain in his stomach grow a little tighter as he finally listened to his mother's railing. Had he spent all these weeks scouring London when the little witch was actually right here at his doorstep? Impossible! Cat would never take her in, and the Scheffings would have notified him. Surely she wouldn't be staying in the village. His mother's mind must be weakening.

"What am I going to do about what, Mother?" he asked wearily. The countess was quite capable of ordering him to purchase the papers publicizing the scandal, but since Cassandra Howard's marriage could have no effect on the Merrick fortunes or family name, he rather doubted that was what his mother had in mind. Except that it seemed to concern Cassandra, Merrick rather doubted he wanted to hear any of it. And why he should care what his mother had to say about Cassandra, he didn't wish to push his tired brain to think. Married less than twenty-four hours and a duel fought over her already. He was well out of that trap.

The countess rose to her full, somewhat shaky height and glared at her obtuse son. Although Wyatt was tall by any standards, his mother nearly reached his chin, almost exactly the same height as Cassandra, Wyatt remembered for some odd reason. Few women could match his height so closely. Perhaps that was why he felt more comfortable in Cassandra's presence: he felt less awkward. It made slight difference now.

"What are you going to do about Cassandra Howard living in that tumbledown wreck of a house and enticing our tenants away with promises she can't keep?" The countess enunciated each word firmly, as if speaking to a child.

"Don't be ridiculous, Mother. Even Gypsies avoid that place. Someone's been telling you Banbury tales." Merrick folded his newspaper and strode across the room. Cass couldn't be living in that pile of burned-out timber and rock, but she might be living in the area somewhere. It wouldn't hurt to look around now that he was home.

Wyatt heard his mother's cry of frustration behind him as he left the room, but he paid her cries little heed. When he was young, he had allowed her to guide his hand in the managing of his life as well as his estates. She seemed to have some difficulty in recognizing that he no longer needed her advice. He had finally heeded it in the matter of his proposed marriage to Catherine Montcrieff, but only because it agreed with his own thoughts. He had recently come to doubt his ability to

choose a proper wife, but he had not yet informed the
dowager countess of that. She had been pushing Catherine at him for years. He wasn't in any humor to have
another frigid shrew pressed upon him.

Mounting the horse he had ordered saddled and held
for him, Wyatt set out to see how his lands had fared
during his absence. He was unaccustomed to being
gone during the spring planting, although his steward
was quite capable and well able to carry out his duties
without constant supervision. Merrick found it difficult to believe the estate had now reached a running
order that seldom required his attention. To do so
would be to admit to his own uselessness.

Near the edge of the field where the men were planting the early corn, he espied the robust figure of his
steward, John MacGregor. The older man seemed to
be in conversation with a woman who matched him
eye-to-eye, although her willowy figure was half the
breadth of the older man's. She wore her hair hidden
beneath a cotton kerchief, but something in the graceful movement of her hands as she used them to emphasize her words stirred Merrick's recognition—that,
and the fact that MacGregor spoke to her at all. The
steward was a notorious woman hater.

Feeling an odd catch in his throat, as if his breathing
had suddenly become labored, Wyatt kicked his horse
in their direction. Lady Cassandra Howard—Percival,
he added belatedly—did not belong in cotton kerchiefs
and broadcloth gowns. She might be a glittering star
in the firmament, but he could not see her grubbing
in the dirt. This must be a newcomer to the area, and
he was eager to greet her.

Too eager. Wyatt felt his pulse begin to race even as
he reached the pair on the field's edge. Just the possibility that it might be Cassandra had the strangest
effect on him, one he hadn't felt since adolescence,
one he had no desire to succumb to now. Scowling,
Wyatt swung down from his horse.

The blue gaze smiling up at him matched the color

of the spring skies this morning, and Wyatt's knees nearly fell out from under him. She was only eighteen and another man's wife, his conscience told him, but his senses swayed under the brute force of her sensual perfume, the generous curve of her full lips, and the lithe figure that seemed a perfect fit for his aching arms.

Knowing he was surely losing his mind, Merrick continued to stare down into her cream-and-rose features, caressing the fading bruise on her jaw with his gaze while clenching his fingers into a fist to keep from touching her. Cassandra's smile faltered slightly at his continued silence, but he had never been one for small talk and he didn't dare speak what was on his mind now.

"Lord Merrick?" Her soft voice whispered like the wind through the leaves, and Wyatt finally jarred himself back to his senses.

"Lady Cassandra." He made a perfunctory bow for the benefit of their audience. "I did not know you had returned." He did not mention that he and her brother had spent the better part of three weeks looking for her.

A small dimple appeared beside her lips at his curt tones. "I did not know I was supposed to inform you." Wanting to say more but encumbered by the presence of the steward, Cassandra flicked her eyes in Mac-Gregor's direction to indicate she was hampered by a third party.

Merrick ignored the hint as well as the light jest. Turning to his steward, he gave a nod of greeting. "John, I take it you have met Lady Cassandra?"

The cold tones were not natural to the earl's usual easy conversation, but the steward gave a nod. "It's been a few years since she trampled my wheat making hiding places for her dolls, but aye, I remember her well. We were discussing which of her fields requires the least work to put it into production. I'd guess that back lot the tenants been using to run their cows."

Merrick raised incredulous eyebrows as he returned his gaze to Cass. "Is your brother planning to restore the estate?'' He fought back another scowl as her eyes danced with amusement.

"*I* intend to restore the estate, my lord. My estimable brother has nothing to do with it. What do you think my chances are of earning enough to buy it from him?''

Both the earl and his steward stared at her as if she were mad, Cassandra noted. Perhaps she was. The last three weeks of her life had been the most miserable and the happiest she had ever known. She was still not able to fully accept that she was responsible for a young man's death. She woke up in the night screaming with the memories of that smoking pistol and Thomas' crumpled body spilling blood at her feet. She would never lose that memory, never put another man in that same position again. She hadn't yet figured out how she could ever show her sorrow to Thomas' family or make it up to them, but she would.

That was why she was happy. She had found her home and knew this was where she was meant to be. She could make something good here so Thomas would not have died in vain. It would take time, but she knew she could make a better life for many people if she worked hard at it. And then she would go to Bertie and his family and say, "Because of your son, I could do this," and offer her sorrow and gratitude.

It would have to work that way. She could not live with herself otherwise. Looking up in Merrick's cold face, she felt a momentary trepidation for the scorn she felt lay behind that icy gaze, but she would overcome even that. The proud and righteous Earl of Merrick would someday look at her with respect. She would see that he did.

But for now she amused herself with teasing the scowl from his face. Wyatt had grown too stuffy with age and responsibility. Perhaps he disapproved of her now, but she could still make him smile, she wagered to herself. It would do him good to smile more often.

He looked at her now as if she were half-crazed, but she would show him differently. Smiling brightly and nodding a polite dismissal to the steward, Cassandra slid her hand around Merrick's arm and steered him toward the hedgerow that marked the division of their properties.

"You do not think a woman can manage these fields?" she taunted him.

"I do not think anyone can manage these properties without a large influx of wealth and labor. Has your husband signed over his fortune for such use?" Merrick knew the idle baronet too well to expect any such thing, but he had to say something to keep his tongue from sticking to the roof of his mouth. The memory of a certain heated kiss returned to haunt him, and he felt none of the chill of this cool spring day as his blood warmed with sight and sound and touch of the woman who had generated that kiss.

A frown briefly crossed Cassandra's delicate features, and then she waved her hand regally as if to dismiss her husband in the same manner as she had the steward. "Rupert knows nothing of this. Do not mention his name or that of my brother again in my presence. They are not topics I wish to dwell on. I will work these lands on my own, without anyone's help."

Despite his physical attraction to her, Wyatt maintained his practical nature, and he shook his head. "Lady Cassandra, you have no idea of the size of the undertaking. The lands and tenants have been neglected for years. You have no cottages left. You do not even have a house in which to live. Where are you staying, by the way? Your brother has been looking for you."

Cassandra snatched her hand away and finally returned his scowl of earlier. "I daresay he is, and he'll find out soon enough, but certainly not by my words. If all you will do is offer discouragements, my lord, I will bid you good day."

Wyatt knew he ought to let her go. There was nothing he could say to her that she wished to hear. But in the brief space of a few weeks she had given him more vivid memories than he held of a lifetime. He could still see her now in the daring primrose gown, dashing into his arms, and later, with her glittering wedding dress torn and hanging from her shoulder and her jaw swollen and bruised as she begged him to save a young man's life. She had shed no tears, offered no hysterics. He had to admire her for her courage, if nothing else.

He caught her elbow and prevented escape. "Let me escort you, my lady. You should not be walking these fields alone."

Cassandra shivered with relief as his hand clasped protectively around her arm. She had not wanted to lose this man as friend. Even now, he offered a shield of security and she felt coddled and protected as he helped her across the stile. No one else made her feel that way, and sometimes it grew terribly lonely to always have to look after herself.

"I did not mean to be sharp with you, my lord," she answered quietly. "It is only that I am tired of being told what I cannot do."

"You used to call me Wyatt. Can we not be friends and return to the informalities?"

Eyes of liquid blue turned up to scan his face, and a smile crept about the corners of her mouth. "Are you sure you would cry friends with such as I, my lord? Or do you just wish to preach me sermons?"

The faint mockery in her voice raised a similar mood of his own. Merrick quirked an eyebrow at her. "I believe I wish to show you that you chose the wrong man, but that wouldn't be very gentlemanly of me, would it?"

Shock hit her that she could very well have hurt this proud man who had offered her his name. She had thought he had done it out of obligation, but could there have been more to his offer? No, that was an impossible thought. The kiss that had overpowered her with the possibilities of what the future might bring could have only been a dalliance for the Earl of Merrick. His mockery now was just that, a gallant ploy to raise her spirits. Hiding the pain, Cassandra lifted a smile to him.

"Oh, no, I did not. Husbands are easily come by, but not friends. I would hate to lose your friendship by becoming your wife."

There was truth in what she said, Wyatt knew from experience, but how had an eighteen-year-old child come to possess such wisdom? Holding his smile so as not to disturb her, he shook his head in disbelief.

"I'll not debate platitudes with you. Tell me where you are staying so I might reproach your hostess for allowing you to run wild and unprotected. Or is it the countryside that must be protected from you?"

Cassandra sent him a sidelong look, but he seemed merely to be jesting with her. Still, she replied with a newly won caution. "I am a married woman now, my lord, you must remember. I am entitled to a household of my own."

"You have found a bower of honeysuckle and roses over which to preside?" Merrick asked in amusement as they trampled across a neglected field in the direction of her former home.

"Something like that," Cassandra replied absently. Was it a mistake to allow Wyatt to see her home? Would he write to Duncan immediately? Of course he would. She had known the truth couldn't be hidden forever. She just hated for her idyll to be disturbed now that she had found a modicum of peace.

She stopped as they crossed into the weed-strewn remains of the old carriage yard. A few blackened stable timbers stood in stark relief against the cloudless sky. Ivy had covered much of the fallen debris, and a wild morning glory bloomed rampantly over a fallen beam. The once magnificent stable had returned to nature, but she did not regret its passing. Her only strong memory of the building was its emptiness after the horses were sold, and her father's furious spanking when she had thrown a tantrum at discovering her pony was gone.

She held out her hand to the puzzled earl. "Thank

you for accompanying me, my lord. I do hope you will not mind if I take occasional liberties with Mr. MacGregor's knowledge. I promise not to interfere with his work.''

Wyatt looked from the vine-covered stable across to the empty stone walls of the once enormous mansion. Some former Marquess of Eddings had shipped expensive limestone from north of London to the Kentish countryside to build this palace of his imagination. That had most likely been the beginnings of the end of the Howard fortune. The impressive edifice had outshone the countryside, but the surrounding lands could not support the army of liveried servants required for upkeep. "Pride cometh before a fall" was as apt a quotation for the Howards as any.

"I mean to see you safely home, my lady. These ruins are no safe place to be. The roof on that section there is likely to crumble at a moment's notice, and any loud noise or vibration could send some of those stones cascading to the ground. I know you must feel sentimental about your home, but it needs to be razed to the ground. I have told Duncan so on several occasions. The local children are fascinated with it, and they can only come to harm if allowed to play here.''

Cassandra made a wry moue. "I am aware of that. I have had to persuade several of the more intrepid youngsters that it is not polite to play in other people's houses uninvited. I think they are beginning to get the message.''

Wyatt felt as if the message were escaping him. Cassandra made no move to return to wherever she was staying, but remained standing on the broken cobblestones of the carriage drive, the ghostly gray walls rising up behind her. She had removed her cotton kerchief in the warmth of the sun, and her red-gold hair shone gloriously against the backdrop of evergreen vines and blackened stone. Daringly he looked into the vivid aqua of her eyes and read the truth there.

"You are not staying here?" he managed to whisper hoarsely.

"I will agree with you if that makes you happy." Cassandra shrugged blithely. "Just take my farewells and leave me here. Perhaps it is better if you remain uncertain. I have no wish to have Duncan or my husband informed of my whereabouts at any foreseeable time in the future."

Unreasoning anger swept through Wyatt at this callous dismissal of his fears and worries of these last weeks. He had spent weeks chastising himself for having left her alone in the carriage, for not having forced Duncan to give her up in marriage, for not having done any of countless things to prevent the tragedy of that night. He had berated himself and piled guilt upon sin at the thought of her innocence violated at the hands of a brute like Rupert. He had greatly feared she had done away with herself, and only when no trace of her body was found had he allowed himself to believe she might still live. She had turned his life into a raging chaos never before endured and which had only now begun to return to its peaceful origins, and she dared dismiss his concerns with a shrug and a lie!

Grabbing her arm and ignoring the startled look she threw him, Wyatt dragged Cassandra toward the crumbling pile of stones that had once housed the family of the Marquess of Eddings. "Show me where you live. Convince me you are safe and protected here."

Cassandra jerked her arm from his grip. "It is no business of yours whether I am safe or not. It has not mattered to anyone but myself and my mother for these past nineteen years. Do not extend your concern at this late date, my lord."

Nineteen. It was mid-May now. Wyatt vaguely recollected gala birthday parties thrown in the child's honor when she had lived here long ago, right about this time of year. She had turned nineteen alone in this crumbling pile of stone. Merrick strode quickly after

Cassandra as she slipped from his grasp and disappeared around the corner of the house.

He followed the drive around the blank, staring walls
of the kitchens, the private side entrance now buried
under an avalanche of scorched rock, and to the once
impressive grand facade of the front. The fire had
burned hottest at the rear, leaving the porticoed front
steps relatively unscathed, but even a casual observer
could see the sky through shattered casements. The
tiled roof had fallen through to the attics, and years of
rain and neglect had gradually rotted any unburned
portions of the interior into collapsing. She couldn't
possibly live in here. Yet he could see no sign of Cassandra's unmistakable coloring anywhere.

A torn vine waved in the breeze over the gaping hole
of the front entrance. Merrick angled his long legs in
their high riding boots over a fallen lintel and ducked
beneath the canopy of greenery to enter the towering
foyer. One glance upward revealed glimpses of sky
through moldering wood and crumbling dusts of plaster. Little of the magnificence that had once belonged
to this lordly edifice remained. Scavengers had carried
off polished wood that the fire had missed. What stones
could be lifted had been trundled off in wheelbarrows
and added to barn foundations and pigsties over half
the county. The tiled floor had deep cracks through
which weeds and shrub trees pressed, or had the last
time he had been here. Merrick noted their lack now
with suspicion.

Voices further into the interior of the house provided
the final piece of evidence for his suspicions. Carefully walking over tumbled laths and eyeing the tim-
bered remains of the walls with caution, Merrick
traversed the center hall in search of the occupants.

The laughter spilling through the abandoned rooms
could have only one source. Merrick stopped and hesitated beneath the railless circular stairway. She had
not invited him in here. He was trespassing in every
sense of the word. He had no right to intrude. Every

moral precept that he had ever learned insisted that he leave at once.

Instead, he strode ahead to throw open the charred door to the flagstoned terrace room and conservatory.

Cassandra halted with a bright-colored tulip in her hand, caught in the act of arranging a bouquet of flowers obviously picked by the young maid laughing with her. Blue eyes lifted to regard him—not with surprise—but with curiosity.

"My lord." She made no curtsy, but the tone in her voice bespoke the same formality.

Lotta gave their neighbor's forbidding look a swift glance and hastily departed. Merrick scarcely saw her leave. His gaze swept the newly cleaned floor, lifted to the charred but still solid stone and tile walls, and glanced cautiously upward to the cracked cherubs on the ceiling. The wall of shattered windows facing the south slope of the park had been recently boarded over, and Merrick could see that the airy ironwork and glass in the conservatory beyond had received the same treatment, blocking out light as well as the elements. Lanterns placed around the room provided the only illumination other than the vision in red and gold at the room's center.

"I apologize for intruding, my lady," Merrick replied stiffly to the question in her eyes. "I could not in all conscience allow you to come to harm because of my failure to warn you of the dangers of these walls."

"They are my walls." Cassandra calmly set her tulip in its place in a cracked but still usable delft vase. "You really need not concern yourself over my safety, my lord. As I told you, it is none of your concern."

Merrick felt what remained of his patience running out. "Cassandra, you are behaving like a petulant child. You are endangering yourself and your servant by remaining here when there is no need. I will be only too happy to provide you with shelter of whatever sort you choose. Come back to the house with me, where we can discuss these things reasonably."

Incredulous blue eyes lifted to bowl him backward with their volatile fire. "Your home? To that termagant mother of yours? She has all but turned the dogs loose on me. No, thank you, my lord. I am quite comfortable here."

Merrick sensed her impatience for him to leave. She had put him in an insupportable position. He could not leave her here in this crumbling ruin. Equally, he could not carry her off screaming to his own home. Only a Howard would be mad enough to dream up this bedevilment.

An emaciated scarecrow of a man entered silently to interrupt Wyatt's quandary. The anxious maid crept in behind him.

"Could I be of assistance in seeing you out, my lord?" The man bowed courteously from the waist, but the insolence in his tone was thinly disguised. He straightened and regarded the earl with jaundiced eye. "The path can be somewhat treacherous to the uninitiated. Let me lead the way."

She was having him thrown out! Merrick turned to the marquess's lovely daughter for confirmation and caught the faint nod of her head. The smile had gone from her lips and a shadow of sorrow darkened her eyes as they met his, but she had no words to stop this charade.

Irate, Merrick whirled on his heel and stalked out ahead of the cadaverous butler. Butler! He shook his head in bemusement at the thought.

The brilliantly lovely daughter of the late Marquess of Eddings, the wife of the fabulously wealthy Sir Rupert Percival, an Incomparable yet to grace the halls of London society—living like a hermit in an abandoned ruin with a butler and a lady's maid to attend her.

Only a Howard could do it.

Shaking his head, Merrick marched out into the spring sunlight and wondered where the clouds had come from.

Chapter 10

Cassandra closed her eyes against the crack of sunlight coming through the chink in the ceiling. Once there had been two floors and a roof above this room to keep out the elements. She didn't even want to know what remained between her and the world outside right now.

She snuggled deeper into the goosedown pallet on which she slept. Lotta and Jacob were amazingly resourceful. She wondered what farmer's wife had been persuaded to part with this lovely bedding, but she didn't dare question the pair too closely. Lotta's lack of the basic scruples of honesty she had lived with long enough to know. That the correct and proper Jacob could be partner to her crimes was impossible to conceive. She was just grateful for whatever small comforts they could provide.

Musing over the oddity of the disparate coupling of the voluptuous young maid and the lanky, formal gentlemen's gentleman, Cassandra was slow to notice the pounding and sawing some distance away. As the noise gradually intruded on her consciousness, a scraping sounded at the doorway.

"My lady, Cass, are you awake?"

They had been friends too long for Lotta to maintain the proper decorum between them. Cassandra stretched and wrapped her woolen blanket around her shoulders. The spring nights were still chilly and they had yet to discover any safe way of providing heat. What parts of the chimneys still remained standing had become a harbor for sparrows and swifts, and there wasn't a chimney sweep in the world who would risk climbing out on these roofs to clear them out. By winter some solution would have to be found to the problem.

"What is it, Lotta? And what's that noise? Surely Jacob isn't trying to put up more boards?" She remembered with a shudder the day the valet-turned-jack-of-all-trades had attempted to cover one of the broken windows. It had become quickly apparent that hired handymen would have to be found to prevent the loss of their only male protection.

The door jerked and creaked as Lotta lifted it on its rusty hinges so that she could slip through the narrow opening. The shaft of sunlight from the ceiling provided the room's only light.

"That's what I come about. There's a swarm of men up there on the roof hammering and banging away. Do you reckon Duncan sent them?"

Cassandra looked mildly alarmed before she stopped to think and shake her head at the impossibility of such a notion. She didn't know how much money Duncan had connived out of Rupert before the wedding, but it was a certainty that he had received none since. He would not spare his few coins on her.

"Send Jacob out to find who sent them. I'll get dressed and join you in a minute. I suspect I know who's behind this." Cassandra reached for the simple gown she had worn the day before. Her muslins and silks weren't made for weeding floors and sweeping plaster, and her limited funds could more easily afford the rough cotton. The fact that she looked like a scullery maid didn't deter her in the least. She wanted to look like a scullery maid. She had no desire to ever see another smoking pistol used in her name again.

When she had dressed and tied her hair back in a ribbon, Cassandra let herself out through the newly built wooden door at the rear of the conservatory. The tile and stone that had once kept plants cool and moist in the summer had withstood the fire much better than the elegant paneling and woods in the rest of the house.

She patted the limestone walls cheerfully as she stepped into the sunlight.

A bevy of workmen crawled and pounded and worked at the low roof over the garden wing that housed their small living space. They had already leveled off a portion of the upper walls to provide a surface for new beams that men on the ground were hastily sawing to size.

Cassandra could think of only one man who could single-handedly summon so much efficiency on such short notice. When Jacob loped unhurriedly across the lawn to greet her, she was not surprised to hear Lord Merrick's name on his lips.

"They say they're here on his lordship's orders, my lady," Jacob explained at her question. "They won't leave without his lordship's orders."

Cassandra bit back a vivid curse just as she knew Jacob had omitted the rest of his explanation. Work was hard enough to come by in these parts. These men wouldn't be deprived of a day's wages without a fight. She had found them all too eager to come at her beck and call for nigh on to nothing whenever she needed work done.

Well, Merrick could just put them to work on his estate. She couldn't afford them and she wasn't accepting his charity. She needed farmers, not carpenters, not yet.

Lifting her hand to shade her eyes, she glared up at the men clambering about on her roof. "All right, Jacob, I'll see to this. Tell Lotta to see if that lazy hen has laid any eggs this morning. I'll be needing a decent meal by the time I get finished traipsing across these fields."

From beneath hooded lids Jacob gave his new employer a speculative look. "Perhaps his lordship is apologizing for his unwarranted intrusion yesterday. Would it not be proper to be gracious and accept his unorthodox manner of apologizing?"

Cassandra sent him a sharp look. "I realize a sound roof will be more comfortable when it rains, but I am not about to compromise his reputation or mine any more than they have been. If I have learned nothing else, I have learned gentlemen expect a return for their favors. No, thank you, Jacob. I am not my brother or Rupert. I will get by without *anyone's* charity. I will be sure to save sufficient cash to see you and Lotta paid at the end of the quarter as usual. You know I will provide adequate references should you wish to seek employment elsewhere.''

The butler/valet straightened stiffly. ''I did not doubt your word, my lady. I merely sought your comfort. You are in the right, of course. Forgive me.''

He managed to sound insulted and aggrieved at the same time, but Cassandra ignored his demonstration of loyalty. She had seen more servants come and go in her short lifetime than most people would did they live to be a hundred. She knew theatrics when she saw them. She used them herself upon occasion. Jacob did it very well. She gave him a polite smile and stalked off across the field to Merrick House. Wouldn't the Countess Merrick be surprised to see the bane of her life at the breakfast table?

The Countess Merrick couldn't believe her ears when Lady Cassandra Howard Percival was announced. She couldn't believe her eyes when she raged into the drawing room when the unwanted visitor refused to leave. The wanton hoyden who had spread scandal across London so thickly she had even managed to tarnish Wyatt's good name appeared no more than a slip of a village maid amidst the grandeur of the silk-lined walls of the salon.

''Good morning, my lady.'' Cassandra smiled brightly and turned innocent eyes of blue to the heavily fleshed woman in brocade entering the room. ''Please pardon my not calling upon you sooner. The exigencies of moving from city to country are probably not known to someone who has led such a staid and respectable life in the same place for so long. I do hope you never have to undergo them.''

The countess heard a threat in the sweet tinkle of

that voice, and she straightened herself to her full magnificent height. "I am certain that I never shall move about in such a harum-scarum manner. Did my servant not tell you we are not receiving today?"

"But this is a business and not a social call, my lady." Not having been offered a seat, Cassandra sat anyway. She threw an admiring glance around the room, noting the age of the draperies, the dust motes under the hundred-year-old furniture, and the signs of wear in the carpet. Wyatt would not note such humdrum details but his mother ought certainly to have seen such things if she were to play lady of the manor. She had heard much of this dragon Wyatt called mother. It would be interesting to try pulling a few of her teeth. "I have come to see Lord Merrick. I will be quite content to sit here until he has time to see me."

The dowager's jaw dropped and her bulging eyes appeared to protrude a little more as she regarded this wanton display of bad manners. "You most certainly will not! I will tell Wyatt you wish to speak with him, and he will call upon you when and if it is convenient for him. He is a very busy man and hasn't time to be bothered with trivialities."

Cassandra smoothed the rough weave of her blue broadcloth skirt as if it were silk, then lifted her lashes and smiled graciously at her hostess. "And to think you were almost my mama-in-law. Do you think we should suit?"

The high-pitched wail emitted by the dowager's pinched lips brought instant reaction. A liveried footman raced to catch the countess's suddenly wilting figure, and a vibrantly masculine voice echoed with irritation from down the hall.

"What the hell is wrong now? Hanley, go see what is happening. James, see if my curricle is ready yet. Why the deuce a man can't have a moment's peace . . ."

His words stopped abruptly as Wyatt stepped into the salon. Caught in the act of drawing on his gloves, he froze as he encountered the sight of his mother being lowered to a couch while a certain pert and prim strawberry-blond sat mischievously watching him. His blood ran cold at the thought of what had transpired between these two to cause such a scene.

"Lady Cassandra." He recovered himself sufficiently to acknowledge her presence.

"Lord Merrick," she mimicked perfectly, with a smile of startling sweetness. She said nothing further, leaving him to wallow in the mire and find his way out of this social nightmare.

Lady Merrick resolved the dilemma. "Send her home, Wyatt! Do not let her corrupt you with her scheming wiles! Send her back to her husband."

Scheming wiles? Merrick lifted a puzzled brow at his prostrate parent, then turned a quizzical gaze to Cassandra's deceptively guileless expression. "My lady, perhaps a breath of fresh air would do us good?"

"Very neatly done, my lord," Cassandra said approvingly, rising from the elegant Queen Anne chair with the same stately grace as the queen herself. Taking Wyatt's arm, she stopped before the haughty dowager taking smelling salts from a terrified maid. "I'd recommend fresh air and exercise, Lady Merrick. My mother prospers greatly if lavished with those rare commodities when given the opportunity. Thank you for your hospitality. I will be pleased to call upon you on a better occasion."

Smiling lightly to herself, she swept out of the room on the earl's arm, well aware of the eyes of all the servants upon her. The contrast between her simple cotton dress and Merrick's tailored coat and immaculate breeches must be striking, but she felt more comfortable this way than in the scandalous evening gowns Duncan had provided her with. At least, swathed from head to toe in crude cotton, she could know men weren't staring at her breasts or imagining her unclothed.

Had Cassandra had any idea of her effect on the Earl of Merrick, she would not have been so confident of that belief. He did not need the temptation of low-cut bodices or clinging gowns to taunt his imagination. He could feel the slightness of her long, graceful fingers along his arm, sense the movement of her breasts and hips as they brushed close to him when they walked, smell the heady scent of lilacs wafting up to him. He did not even need to look at her to desire her.

Curtly dismissing this treacherous trend his thoughts had taken, Merrick halted at the foot of the wide stairway where his curricle awaited and turned to watch her. "To what do I owe the honor of this visit?"

The smile disappeared from Cassandra's face as she met his dry gaze. "You know very well to what you owe this visit, Wyatt. I did not expect it of you, indeed, I did not. I will not apologize for upsetting your mother. You deserved it. I cannot believe you were so very wicked. I want you to call those men away right now, and I want you to give them their day's wages even if they don't finish the job. Find them employment elsewhere, I don't care, but do not seek to varnish your reputation at the ruin of mine."

Wyatt gaped in astonishment at this tirade from one so young and seemingly helpless, but then he remembered to whom he spoke and gathered his wits about him again. Cassandra's looks were her greatest asset, and not in the usual way that was meant. Her beauty was quite stunning, but Wyatt had seen beautiful women before and not been swayed. It was her childlike innocence that kept deceiving him. He had to remember this vision of sunshine and roses could swindle a man to his last penny and drive a grown man to desperation. The last was the only possible reason he could conceive of for the catastrophe of her wedding night.

"I had no intention of doing more than offering a neighborly hand, my lady," Merrick responded coldly. "As you say, the men needed work and I offered them some. I would have done the same for anyone."

"Then send them to mend Mrs. Smith's chicken-house so the fox won't eat her hens again. Get them off my property now, Merrick!"

She stamped her foot and put her hands on her hips and scowled at him with a ferocity that would have put her brother to shame. Merrick grinned.

"Since you put it so politely, of course, my lady. If you will join me, we can drive over there now." He offered his arm to assist her into the waiting carriage.

"I will walk." Cassandra resisted the ever-present temptation of Merrick's strength. She had given in to the need for his friendship yesterday, and he had taken advantage. She would not repeat the same mistake.

"I will not come." Clever brown eyes beamed with amusement when she turned and gave him an irate glare. "You have had things your own way too long, Cass. I'll not be browbeaten by a pretty face and a sharp tongue. You wish me to accompany you back to your house, then it shall be at my convenience, not yours."

Her hands flew to her hips again. "I thought you were a gentleman, Wyatt Mannering! You are the one who turned my house all into an uproar, now you must undo it. I don't know why I must suffer your company for you to do so."

Wyatt didn't know either, but he was adamant. "I don't know why you should object to a simple carriage ride. I have no intention of abducting you."

The argument was petty and ridiculous and Cassandra felt it, but she hated being bested by anyone. She was almost tempted to tell him to forget it and leave the workmen alone. Almost. When she realized he would win of a certainty that way, she surrendered. Better a pawn than a knight.

Huffily she refused his arm and climbed into the light curricle on her own. The open vehicle tilted slightly under Wyatt's weight as he joined her, but she stared straight ahead, refusing to acknowledge his presence. The Earl of Merrick knew too much about her affairs for her to be entirely comfortable in his presence. She didn't know how it had come about, but she couldn't even mention her grief for young Thomas in his presence. They had nothing in common. She didn't now why she had once thought he would be the ideal husband.

"Sulking is scarcely ladylike, Cass. I still cannot fathom why you will not accept my offer of help. If we are neighbors, we need to be friends."

Cassandra put a lid on her simmering anger, but her sarcasm escaped without effort. "Had I been Duncan, would you have sent workmen to repair his roof without permission?"

Merrick whistled softly to himself and whipped the reins of his horse as they turned onto the rutted roadway that ran along the front boundaries of their estates. "I had not thought of it that way. Of course I wouldn't have. But then, I wouldn't care if raindrops fell on Duncan's head for the rest of his life, either. He got himself where he is today, let him reap the results."

"And you think I am so helpless that I had no responsibility for getting myself where I am today?" Cassandra inquired scathingly. "Little do you know the power of a woman, my lord. I got myself here, and I will get myself out. Without your help."

There was little he could say in reply. She was in all probability quite right. He had offered her an alternative to Rupert, and she had refused him. Wyatt couldn't quite find his way around that. He did not have Rupert's handsomeness or social grace, and he certainly did not possess Rupert's wealth. And Rupert was a few years younger than himself. From the viewpoint of a young girl, he could see why Cassandra had made her decision. Yet he could not quite get over his disbelief. She had kissed him with a passion he had never before experienced in his life, yet that kiss had obviously meant nothing to her. He was leading much too restricted a life. It was finally time to consider taking a mistress if he let one kiss from a girl fresh out of the schoolroom go straight to his head.

Deliberately reviewing the potential candidates for the position of mistress, Merrick drove the curricle the remainder of the way to Eddings Hall in silence.

Chapter 11

"I'm that sorry, m'lord, but I won't be helping with the planting this year. You see, well, me and Meg been talking of marrying, and what with what I figure to make working for Lady Cass, we'll be able to set up housekeeping come fall. I'll understand if you'll need the cottage to let to someone else. I know her ladyship ain't got nothing to let me, but I'm figuring I'll get by till the weather turns. And her ladyship says I can have a choice of places to build when I'm ready. You see how it is, your lordship. A man has to take care of his own the best he sees how."

Beating his riding crop thoughtfully against the top of his leather boot, Merrick regarded the young farmer with a slight frown. Wigginton was one of his best workers, ambitious, hardworking, self-driven. He hated to lose him. What could Cass possibly have offered that he could not?

"I understand, Wigginton. A man must look out for his own. Can I not match what Lady Cassandra has offered?"

The tow-haired young man scuffed his old shoe in the dirt without looking up to the tall gentleman who had been his employer and his landlord for as long as he could remember. "She promised me half of everything made from the crop I raise. I know that land, your lordship. It's been fallow a long time. This first year won't be the best, but I can make it grow. It's the best chance I got."

He was beginning to sound defensive, and Merrick

understood his position. Merrick could provide a cottage and equipment and seeds, but the cost of that cut into his profits to such a degree that he could never match Cass's offer. Cass, on the other hand, had nothing to lose by her generous proposition. She was just teaching the young man to gamble.

"What will you use to plow the fields?" Wyatt inquired mildly.

Wigginton straightened his shoulders and dared a quick look at the earl. "My grandpap built a plow of his own. It's not like one of yours, of course, your lordship, but it's sturdy and I'm strong. Maybe by next fall, there'll be money to buy a better."

"Well, Wigginton, I hate to lose you, you know that. And if things don't work out as you plan, you're always welcome back. I can't afford to lose too many workers like you. Are there others considering taking up Lady Cassandra's offer?"

The young man glanced down at the ground again. "One or two, m'lord. Them without families, leastways. It's an opportunity that don't often come our way, and it's better than the mines."

"Yes, I can understand that. I wish you the best of luck, Wigginton. I'll not need the cottage immediately. You can stay on awhile longer, if you like. There will be a reckoning to pay come harvest, of course, but I'll make it fair."

Wigginton tugged his forelock gratefully. "Thank you, m'lord."

Wyatt whistled softly to himself as he strode back to his horse. He began to understand his mother's tantrums over Cass's arrival. Lady Merrick had never been one overconcerned with the scandalous lives of her neighbors so long as they did not affect the Merrick estate or family. Cass could have held midnight orgies and practiced witchcraft and the dowager would have frowned and pointedly looked the other way. It wasn't Cass's reputation that was driving his mother wild. It was her interference with their tenants, and thus the estates, that set off the uproar. Wyatt found himself greatly aggravated at her ploy.

She was clever, he would grant her that. What cottages remained on the Howard estate had gone to rack and ruin. The equipment and animals had been sold off long ago. The fields were a mire of bramble and weed, but the land beneath was good soil that Wyatt would have given a fair sum to own. It was all Cassandra had to tempt a farmer. It was all she needed. As Wigginton had said, no one would get rich that first year, but with a little luck and a lot of work, they would prosper in years to come. And Lady Cass with them.

Not enough to make her wealthy by any means, Wyatt amended as he rode toward the village. There had never been enough land there to support an extravagant style of living. It wouldn't even be a comfortable life for a long while, and one bad year could potentially wipe her out, but Cass had been raised to be a gambler. She might not have all the cards, but she knew a good hand when she saw one.

He would have persuaded Duncan long ago to sell that land had he known it was available. He had always presumed it entailed since Duncan neither sold it to pay his debts nor gambled it away. Cassandra could be risking everything if her brother discovered her intentions and jerked the lands away from her. Wyatt scowled at the thought.

It was his responsibility to write to Duncan and inform him of his sister's whereabouts. The marquess had seemed truly anxious over his sister's disappearance, although he had hidden it well by scoffing and repeating his usual phrases about Cass taking care of herself. Whatever the situation between Eddings and his sister, Wyatt had a moral responsibility to report her whereabouts.

That he had not yet done so ate at his conscience. He told himself he no longer had a right to interfere in her life. Duncan had assured that when he refused Wyatt her hand. But Cass was living in unsafe conditions, with a disreputable pair of servants as her only companions. For her own protection, her brother must be notified.

Turning Cassandra over to her brother would solve all his problems, but Wyatt still had not resolved to do it by the time he rode into the village to discover the object of this thoughts sweeping through town in her colorful skirt with a market basket on her arm.

Cassandra could not miss the sight of the massive stallion or the elegantly erect rider on its back riding through the narrow street of low stone cottages. Although Merrick had not bothered with hat or intricate cravat for a ride to town, he still managed to maintain the polished aura of an aristocrat in his tailored riding coat and tight trousers. The immaculately polished riding boots alone distinguished him as a man with the resources to employ a skilled valet. Cassandra felt her lack of even a decent means of bathing, and abruptly she turned her back on him and started toward the bakery.

A familiar shout behind her caused her to swing around with a mixture of hope and despair. Merrick would never be so rude as to shout, but Bertie had never been bothered by such niceties. His sturdy figure hurried after her now, even as Merrick swung down from his stallion to follow. She was fairly caught, and she tried not to look too closely at the scowl marring the earl's noble forehead.

As long as she was caught, she ought to make the best of it. Quickly she walked toward Bertie before Merrick could reach them. Holding out her hands, she forced Bertie to take them in his own. With a catch in her voice she managed to gasp a small whisper. "I'm so sorry, Bertie, I have never been able to tell you . . ."

Cassandra's voice broke and she hastily dropped Bertie's hands and turned partially away to hide her tears as Merrick came up beside them.

"It ain't nothing to weep over, Cass," Bertie was hastily assuring her. "Tom was half-bosky or he'd never been fool enough to go out. He's learned his lesson the hard way."

That seemed a callous way to regard a brother's death, and Cassandra wiped her eyes and turned to stare at him through incredulous blue eyes. "Hard lesson? Bertie, he was the bravest, sweetest . . ."

"Most foolish idiot that ever walked the earth," Wyatt finished for her. He gave Bertie a warning look. "Lady Cassandra has been somewhat out of touch with the city these last few weeks."

Cass shot him a furious glare. "You will not talk about Thomas that way in front of me. I owe him my life, and I intend to make it up to his family one way or another. It might take me years . . ."

Bertie grinned cheerfully. "Just come over and hold his hand for a while and you'll have made it up to the pestilence. Worst patient my mother's had in years. She'd be grateful for a little reprieve, and Tom would be over the hoop with joy at having you for nurse."

Cassandra caught her breath in astonishment and growing hope as she stared at Bertie with this announcement. Merrick gave her a wry gaze.

"You've stopped her tongue, Albert. Mark how you did that. I'm certain we'll have cause to recall it in the future. I believe the lady was under the mistaken impression the lad was a martyr to her cause."

That was the outside of enough. She had never given Merrick reason to insult her like that, or make little of her feelings. Perhaps she had tricked and humiliated him when she was desperate, but she had tried to make up for that by giving him his freedom. He had more than got even with her by not telling her Thomas lived. She gave him a scathing look and took Bertie's arm.

"You are as thoroughly unpleasant as my brother warned you were, my lord," she informed him coldly before turning back to Bertie. "Tell me about Thomas. Please come in and have tea with me at Mrs. Singer's and tell me how he fares. You cannot imagine . . ."

Panicking at the thought of entertaining the marquess's lovely daughter all on his own, Bertie turned hastily to his friend. "I say, Merrick, you better come with us. You do a better job at explaining these things."

Wyatt hadn't taken his gaze from Cass's indignant face. He couldn't tell if she were really as shallow as she sounded, or so distraught that she said anything that came to mind. Whichever it was, she had nearly cost a young man his life. Someone needed to teach her the results of rashness.

"I need explain nothing, Scheffing. The less said, the better, in Lady Cassandra's case. I have told you from the first that it is not wise to talk about what happened, or the results. The gossip has been scandalous enough, and Thomas is lucky the authorities have not set about arresting him. I don't believe the lady would want it to get about that there's some chance the lad might live. Rupert might take it into his head to return from exile if he thought he was safe from the law."

Cassandra blanched at that possibility, but she held her head high and continued to clutch Bertie's arm. "I certainly have no intention of informing the odious monster of anything, and I can see no harm in my lending a hand to nurse Thomas. I owe him much more than that."

Merrick gave his friend a scowl. "That was an idiot notion to give her, Bertie. She is neither sister, nor mother, nor wife, and has no right to be tending an unmarried gentleman."

Cassandra and Bertie both began to reply at once, but Cassandra rode roughshod over Bertie's much less emphatic replies. "I shall do as I see fit without your instruction, my lord. I am a married woman now, and not your wife. I shall go right now to extend my gratitude." Dropping Bertie's arm, she lifted up her stiff cotton skirt and petticoat and started down the street.

"Disturb the Scheffings anymore, and I will tell your brother where to find you," Merrick warned as she turned her back on him and began to stride away.

Her step faltered, but she did not stop.

Merrick gave a growl of irritation deep in his throat. Looking from friend to irate young lady, Bertie hesitated.

"I can't let her walk all that way alone," he finally decided when Wyatt made no further attempt to stop her.

"Cassandra would walk all the way to London alone did it serve her purpose. I wish you the best of her."

Irritated at his own inability to control the situation, even more irritated that it bothered him, Merrick strode off down the street in pursuit of the errand that had brought him to town. Lady Cassandra Howard Percival was none of his business. He was well rid of a high-handed, temperamental female like that one. Somebody should have beat a little sense into her long ago. Thank heaven it wasn't his duty to do so.

Cassandra sat beside the wounded man's bedside, tears streaming down her cheeks as she watched his labored breathing in sleep. Someone had discreetly pulled his covers up, but the bare muscularity of Thomas' shoulders and upper arms could not be disguised. Cassandra scarcely took note of that as she watched the youthfulness of his features in sleep. Except for her father and brother, she knew little of men, but the golden fuzz along his cheeks did not compare to the harsh dark shadows of Duncan's or Wyatt's jaw late in the evening. Men in general were a crude, rough lot, but not Thomas.

Bertie and the maid stirred restlessly behind her as she clasped the patient's lifeless hand. She wanted to send them both away, but Wyatt's admonitions had taken hold, and Bertie had taken back his suggestion of playing nurse to his brother. His mother had not approved of the visit either, Cassandra knew, but out of politeness she had not refused. They all wanted her gone. If only Thomas would open his eyes . . .

As if in response to her thoughts, Thomas' eyelids

flickered and his hand twitched between her fingers. Then he was staring up at her, and Cassandra beamed with delight. Impulsively she leaned over to kiss his cheek.

"My hero," she whispered wickedly against his ear.

Thomas grinned a slow, sleepy grin. "Lady Cass. Have I died and gone to heaven?"

"You'll not find me there," she admonished, sitting up again. "If you want to see me, it will have to be in this world and not the next one."

His gaze did not leave her face. "This world's fine. Will you stay?"

Bertie hurried forward to put a halt to his brother's meanderings. "Lady Cass just came by to see how you fared. Now that she knows mere bullets don't stop us Scheffings, she'll have to be on her way."

The boy's warm expression suddenly grew remote, and restlessly he removed his hand from Cassandra's. "Of course. You will be joining your husband. Thank you for your concern. I apologize for any trouble I have caused you."

Cassandra threw Bertie an impatient look and reclaimed the hand picking at the covers. "I have no intention of ever seeing Rupert again. I owe you my life, Thomas. I would repay you in any way I can."

The grin returned to his lips as he opened his eyes to look at her again. "Marry me, and we'll call it even."

Cassandra laughed, squeezed his hand, and kissed his cheek in farewell. "Of course. How can I do any less? I must leave now before Bertie worries himself into a fit. You must get better so you can come and court me properly."

Bertie watched his brother's face glow with more color and animation than he had shown since his injury, and he had to give the girl credit. If he'd had all that sunset-blond beauty bent over him, kissing his cheek, he'd glow like a lantern too. For a chit scarcely out of the schoolroom, Lady Cass certainly had a way of turning men's heads without even trying. Why, then, was Merrick so grumpy with her?

It didn't matter to Bertie. Were she not already wedded, he'd court her himself. Of course, he was supposed to make a wealthy match, but Cass wouldn't mind if they weren't rich. Driving her home after the visit, he threw her pale face a speculative look. A wife without a husband, and not even had a Season yet. But that was a Howard for you. Did everything backward.

Cassandra met Bertie's bewildered gaze when she asked him to let her off at the drive to the Eddings' estate. 'I'm meeting friends, Bertie. You needn't worry about me. Do you think I might visit with Thomas again?''

Easily distracted, the squire's son nodded eagerly. ''You'll do him good. He's been moping around, calling himself a gudgeon, and not much interested in getting well. Shall I call for you sometime? Where are you staying?''

Deftly avoiding that troublesome subject, Cassandra held out her hand in farewell. ''I'll send a note around, shall I? Thank you for being so forgiving, Bertie. I think I would have hated me in your place.''

Red-faced, Bertie shrugged. ''It ain't your fault, Cass. Duncan never should have let you marry a rum one like Rupert. Sure you don't need an escort? It ain't right wandering these fields alone.''

''Oh, but I'm a married woman now, and this is my home, after all. I'll come to no harm. Good day, Bertie, and thank you.''

She set off down the overgrown drive, leaving Bertie no opportunity to protest further. The rhododendrons had gone wild and now towered well over her head. She was quickly out of sight of the road. When she was certain she was no longer observed, Cassandra allowed her shoulders to slump slightly. It had been an emotionally draining day.

She hadn't wanted Merrick to despise her. And she certainly didn't deserve Thomas' adulation. All she wanted was a few good friends she could talk to, someone to understand her predicament, someone to fill her loneliness. Would she never be allowed that small luxury?

Not as things stood now. Breaking off a dead twig from an overhanging bush, Cassandra tried to gather the strength to face the ruin that was now her home. She could never bring her mother out here, nor could she ever go home again. She couldn't live under the same roof with Duncan. He had sold her to a madman, and now she was caught betwixt and between, neither wife nor maiden.

Well, still maiden. She crumbled the twig between her fingers and dragged her hand along the scraggly plants as she slowly approached the house. Peggy, her father's former mistress, had explained about annulments, sort of. She had said a man and woman could marry and not go to bed together and the church would say they were never married if they wrote a petition for annulment. That was what she had wanted Rupert to do. She had hoped Rupert would settle a small sum on her to be rid of her when she refused to be his wife. Peggy hadn't mentioned that the man could take what he wanted without the wife's consent. Surely those few minutes in Rupert's bed didn't make her a wife. How did one go about petitioning for an annulment?

A solicitor would have to be hired, obviously, and she had no money for such. Besides, what did it matter if she were married or not? No man would have a penniless female with a reputation as blackened as hers. Just as long as Rupert stayed in Paris, there was no problem. She had more freedom as a married woman. And Duncan couldn't try to trade her off to someone else.

It was better to be lonely than miserable. Picking up her feet, she hurried toward the ruins she called home. Lotta would scold if she kept their meager supper waiting. Another day was gone, and she had survived. One day at a time was all anyone could ask.

Chapter 12

"We can't keep going to the butcher's or these coins won't last till harvest. Can't you hunt something?" Lotta dawdled over her second cup of tea while regarding the blackened fireplace with distaste.

Across from her, Jacob lifted his cup with the same elegance as his betters. "Even if I could nab a squirrel or hare, would you know what to do with it?"

Ignoring the implied scorn in his words, Lotta turned a grin to her lover. "Not a bit. A pampered life, I lead. When are you going to keep me in the style to which I'm accustomed?"

The lean face broke into a flashing smile as Jacob recognized the look in her eyes. "There's many a way to do it. We could do it honestly and seek employment elsewhere."

"And leave my lady here alone? Never. We look after each other, we do. Besides, no one else would look kindly on our pairing off, would they now? Soon's I had a bun in the oven, off I'd be in the streets. No thankee, sir. I'll stay here."

Jacob glared at her. "You told me you knew how to prevent that sort of thing. Don't neither of us need that kind of trouble right now."

Lotta bent forward to reveal a tantalizing glimpse of her plump breasts beneath her loose blouse. "Ain't any of us perfect. We all get caught sometime. Now, what are your other suggestions for making a few coins?"

Eyeing the view, Jacob gave the matter some

thought. "Selling information always works well, but the only one with any coins to buy is our high-and-mighty earl. He'd not take kindly to paying for information. The marquess hasn't got a ha'pence to spare. There's always Rupert. He might be willing to spare some of the ready to know where his wife is, but that rather defeats the purpose, doesn't it?"

Lotta sat up and adjusted her bodice with a glare. "You bloody well better believe it. That bedlamite would have our arses for helping my lady to escape. And she wouldn't be left in any condition to protect us. Come up with a better one than that, my genius."

Jacob shrugged. "Your lady gambles well, didn't you tell me?"

A noise in the hall outside caught Lotta's ears and she hurriedly signaled for silence as she began to speak quite loudly. "You'll have to steal a hen, Jacob. We can't spend any more at the butcher's. His prices are too dear."

Cassandra drifted through the doorway to take in this domestic scene. Lotta should have been baking bread, and Jacob had promised to look for the leak in her bedroom roof. But their conversation set her thoughts on a different path.

"You can't be stealing our neighbor's hens. We'll raise our own if need be. Surely it can't be too difficult a matter."

Lotta stood up and carried her dishes to the washbasin. "That won't help us none tonight. What are you planning on living on until then?"

Cassandra's face lit with a blaze of remembrance. "Fish! We can have fish. There's a pond the next field over stocked full of them."

Jacob removed his lanky frame from the chair with a glum expression. "I expect you will be wanting me to catch them?"

Cassandra continued to beam with delight. "Not at all. I am very proficient at it. You can clean them."

Ignoring the butler's crestfallen expression, Cassandra slipped out the makeshift door in search of a suitable stick for use as a pole. The look on Lotta's face had been sufficient reminder that the pond in question belonged to Merrick, but the small matter of property lines had never inhibited her. A pond was made for fishing, just as apples were meant for eating. The property beneath them made little difference.

Feeling as if she were finally being of some use to their small household, Cassandra quickly gathered her rudimentary fishing gear and set off across the fields. The sun had risen warm and high, and the heavy cotton of her coarse gown weighed down on her. By the time she reached the pond, she had loosened the tucker to let her skin breathe.

She found a grassy overhang beneath a towering beech and settled herself comfortably on a tussock. Removing her shoes and stockings, she discovered she could just touch her toes in the water, and she wriggled them joyfully in the wet coolness. Rolling her skirts up to her knees, she reveled in the breeze off the water. This was much better than trudging out to the fields to see if her new workers were making any progress in the weed-grown pasture. The slowness of their pace was depressing.

The fish bit willingly this day, and soon she had a small string of them floundering in the water. Unwilling to return so quickly, she sent her line out one more time, wondering if the huge trout that used to hide on the bottom had ever been caught. Feeling quite at peace with the day, Cassandra began to sing softly to herself.

Rather enjoying the joyful noise she made, she tried out a more boisterous tune. The water seemed to carry the sound back to her better than the choir loft of a church, not that she had tried that holy place on many occasions. Still, the round tones made pleasant music, and dabbling her bare toes in the water in accompaniment, Cassandra filled her lungs and began a haunting lover's lament in full soprano.

By the chorus, a rich male baritone had joined her, and Cassandra hid a grin as she added dramatic emphasis to the pathos of "his lovely lids closed over his sad, dark beautiful eyes." The ringing high notes blended smoothly with the deep counterpart, and she launched into a livelier tune as Merrick crouched down beside her.

His brown eyes were crinkled with amusement, but he met her note for note with a voice smooth enough to raise the hairs on Cassandra's arms. Garbed in a rough pair of broadcloth breeches and an open-necked white shirt, he did not wear the cold formality of the earl. Cassandra started on a rolling "fol-de-rol-ra-ra" that caught the best of tongues, when a sudden sharp tug on her line jerked her attention from Merrick's rather pleasing smile.

Nearly tumbling forward, Cassandra caught herself in time and hauled backward in an attempt to draw in the line.

"Hang on, I'll get it. Old Bess must have liked our singing." Crouching behind her, Merrick added his strength by wrapping his arms around her and grabbing the pole. "Steady now, or she'll break loose. What the deuce did you use for bait?"

"Worms. What else is there?" Cassandra gasped as the fish struggled harder. Raising the pole in tandem with Wyatt's efforts, she tried to pull her catch toward shore. In the next instant, the pole snapped, she tumbled backward, and Wyatt collapsed with a soft "Oomph" as he hit the ground with Cassandra on top of him.

Giggling, Cassandra tried to extricate herself from the entanglement of line, pole, skirts, and Wyatt's long legs. "Such a good pillow you make, my lord," she murmured happily. Fairly caught, she gripped Wyatt's thigh to balance herself. The muscular hardness beneath her fingers caught her by surprise, and liking the way this touch made her feel, she made little haste to

escape the encounter as she turned to smile pertly at
the trapped earl.

Whatever words Cassandra meant to say disappeared swiftly, seared away by the look in Merrick's
eyes. Lying flat on his back, his arm clamped around
her waist, he was prepared to remove her from this
awkward encounter, but the heated warmth of his gaze
gave Cassandra other ideas. The soft curve of Wyatt's
lips and the desire igniting in his eyes as his arm lingered at her waist sent more than shivers through her.
Knowing what she did was brazen beyond all the
bounds of propriety, Cassandra turned more fully in
Wyatt's grasp. Still lying between his thighs, she rested
her hands against the rough weave of his shirt and bent
forward to place a kiss upon his lips.

The grip at her waist tightened forcefully, hauling
her upward so she no longer possessed all the advantage. Cassandra found herself sprawled full length
along a man's hard body, her breasts pressed against
an unyielding surface, her legs entwined about limbs
stronger than a young tree's. She scarcely had time to
register these facts when Wyatt's lips began to move
against hers, drawing her concentration back to the
wondrous blending of their mouths and breaths and
tongues.

Sighing with pleasure, Cassandra gave herself up to
the kiss she had feared would live only in her imagination. It burned like fire but sent shafts of pleasure
through her center, causing her to seek more while her
body reeled with the heady sensations his kiss and
touch engendered.

Wyatt groaned softly as Cassandra parted her lips at
just a touch of his tongue. His growing possession
brought further awareness, and Cassandra relaxed and
melted against him, wanting to know more of the hard
male body beneath her. She sensed his tension, but
the sweetness of his kiss and the tenderness of his hold
were too new an experience to let go lightly.

As the kiss deepened, Merrick's hands began to

roam, and Cassandra felt a shiver of some instinctive knowing that made her wrap her fingers in the thick hair at the nape of his neck and hang on. When one large hand encircled and cupped her lightly covered breast, she moaned against his mouth but made no effort to escape. The shivers had become something else, a need, a yearning for more, and she eagerly awaited the next step along this path he took her on.

A gasp escaped Cassandra at the hot, tingling sensation of hard brown fingers caressing her bare flesh, but she scarcely had time to explore this new avenue of pleasure. A loud male voice yelling ''Merrick!'' somewhere just beyond the bushes brought their idyll to an abrupt end.

Cursing, Wyatt swiftly rolled Cassandra to the ground and sprang to his feet. Grateful he was wearing loose breeches, he adjusted himself and strode to the pond's edge, avoiding the tumbled beauty lying in the grass. One sight of her might destroy all the good intentions in the world. Just that brief glimpse of fair, full breasts had nearly crippled him. Fully aware of Cassandra's hasty attempts to right her appearance, he called out to the intruder.

''Bertie, you damned fool, don't you know better than to yell around fishermen?'' He stooped to retrieve the broken pole.

Wyatt couldn't turn around until his ardor cooled somewhat, and he listened with disgruntlement as Cassandra greeted their neighbor with pleasantries. He heaved the snapped pole into the water after the treacherous trout and greeted their jests with grunts.

''He got away, Bertie, the biggest fish you ever did see! Snapped my pole right in two! You should have seen it. I'll have to come back tomorrow with a stronger pole.'' Throwing a careful glance at the angry straight back of the man at the water's edge, Cassandra chattered senselessly. She didn't know the source of Wyatt's anger, but she had no wish to have it turned on her. What they had just shared was too precious to end in anger, even if her cheeks flamed in embarrassment at her forwardness.

"I'll bring one of my lines down for you to try if Merrick's are so flimsy as to break at a mere tug." Bertie threw his friend's back an inquiring look. "He hasn't got time to idle away. They're raising a hue and cry for him back at the house. I just came to ask if our lofty earl will honor our poor house with his presence on Friday eve. And now that I've found you"— Bertie glanced down at the girl sitting cross-legged with some maid's discarded skirts billowing around her—"I would ask Lady Cassandra the same. It will just be an informal dinner and musicale. Do say you will come, Cass."

Merrick turned then, his dark eyes regarding her with some fathomless expression as he awaited her reply. Feeling as if she dangled on the edge of a precipice, Cassandra averted her gaze and began gathering up the remains of her equipment.

"It is very kind of you to ask me, Bertie, but it would probably not be appropriate for me to attend a respectable neighborhood gathering. I would like very much to see your brother again, if I might."

Merrick hauled in her catch line. "She'll be there, Scheffing. I'll bring her with me. If Thomas is up to it, I'll bring her over for a few minutes this afternoon."

"Merrick, of all the high-handed—"

Bertie grinned and cut her off as he helped her to her feet. "His lordship speaks. We must obey. We keep country hours. You needn't worry."

Cassandra angrily shook out her skirts and glared at both men. "It is all very well and fine for you to say, gentlemen. You do not have to show up in cotton skirts and be the butt of gossip. I will accept your offer to see Thomas, Merrick, but I cannot attend a social occasion."

Bertie looked dismayed, but Wyatt merely handed her the line of fish. "You will have to face them sometime. It might as well be among friends. You can wear what you have on for all I care. I'll be by this afternoon to take you to Thomas. First, I better see to the uproar at the house.''

He turned and strode off without leaving a chance for reply. Bertie gaped after him, but left with the choice of following at the earl's heels or staying with the disheveled beauty, he chose the latter.

He reached for her line of fish. "I don't know what's got into Wyatt these days. He didn't used to be so toplofty. Let me see you home.''

Cassandra felt a tug of sadness as Merrick deliberately increased the distance between them, but she put on a light smile and disengaged herself from Bertie. "My maid would be all up in the boughs did she know anyone saw me like this. I thank you for your offer, but I had best see myself home.''

She gave a quick curtsy and hurried away before Bertie could object.

Merrick climbed over the stile and into the carefully manicured park of his estate. Ancient evergreens with their lower limbs long since turned to dust beckoned him with their shade, but he trudged determinedly toward the sunny cascade of the flower gardens in the side yard.

He didn't know why he had even gone to the pond this morning. He had just felt misplaced and out of sorts and wanted some time alone. The quiet reflections and musical bird calls of the pond had always been one of his favorite escapes. Too favorite, obviously, he grunted to himself. Elsewise, Bertie would never have found him.

Imagining what might have happened had Bertie not arrived, Merrick bit back a deep groan and covered his eyes briefly. Neither action appeased the surge of lust in his loins. Never in his life had a woman driven him to this sort of behavior. He had considered himself a dispassionate man. He enjoyed the brief plea-

sures of a woman's body, but not to a degree to distract
him from the goals he had set for himself. Even his
first wife had been chosen to accomplish those goals.
The fact that he had already succeeded at everything
he had set out to do—except for producing an heir—
should have no bearing on his behavior. He had a score
and ten years to his name. It was no time to behave as
an untried schoolboy.

Awakening to the fact that he was in danger of tram-
pling his mother's prized flowerbeds, Wyatt halted to
watch a butterfly flit from tulip to spirea. Cassandra
was like that butterfly: beautiful, flighty, and purpose-
less, to be admired and left behind.

Shaking his head at this incongruous thought, Wyatt
turned his gaze on the unopened new buds of the rose-
bush. That was a more apt comparison. Cassandra had
her roots in the mire of Howard ancestry, but she still
produced the heady, sensuous beauty of a perfect rose.
No man in his right mind clasped a rose to his bosom.
Particularly when that rose belonged to another man.

Wyatt glanced up to see his mother bearing down
on him, followed by a harassed and angry MacGregor.
It would not do to make MacGregor angry. The man
was worth his weight in gold. But then, Lady Merrick
on her high ropes was not a pretty sight to see either,
nor an adversary to be discounted. Cursing his un-
lucky stars, Wyatt stretched his long legs in the direction of the coming battle.

His mother gave his rough garb a hasty glare.
"Where have you been, traipsing around like some
Gypsy? You even have grass in your hair!"

With a tired sigh Wyatt ran his fingers through his
thick hair to remove the offending article. "Bertie says
there is some problem, Mother. I assume my offensive
appearance is not what he had in mind."

"Most certainly not! You have no cause to be rude,
Wyatt. The men are planting turnips in the south field.
We always plant oats in that field. Your father swore
the soil was best for them there. You must order them

to stop at once. MacGregor won't do it. He is above all insolent.''

The earl sent his steward a sympathetic look and gave him a slight nod of encouragement. "Quite right, Mother. The soil in the south field has been diminished by too much planting of oats and no replenishment of nutrients. I told MacGregor to have turnips planted there." As his mother choked on her outrage, Wyatt dismissed the steward before he could be subjected to another scathing attack of the countess's particular brand of vitriol and watched the man stride away, wishing he could do the same.

"You never told me, Wyatt! I should have been told. You cannot go making decisions behind my back and leaving me ignorant in front of the servants."

Wyatt offered her his arm as he steered her toward the house. "If you did not interfere in what is not your concern, Mother, there would be no reason to show your ignorance. Why can you not visit the other ladies and hold teas and parties and play cards and leave me to running the estate?"

Lady Merrick sniffed arrogantly. "I always helped your father run the estate, and I am sure he did not object. But if it is parties you want, you will be pleased to know we are entertaining this evening. I have invited Catherine and her family. It is time you mend this foolish breach. You must have heirs, and even you have admitted that Catherine is the ideal candidate for your wife."

As he helped his mother up the terrace step, Merrick caught sight of an early yellow rose nodding in the sunlight in a protected corner of the wall. At its base an encroaching dandelion had not yet been discovered by the gardeners. Wyatt had the sudden urge to get down on hands and knees and root out the interloper. Instead, he nodded politely to his mother's chatter and concentrated on the day's chores ahead.

The fact that the day's chores included driving Cassandra to visit Thomas presented both irksome and

pleasing aspects to the afternoon, Merrick decided
later that day as he guided the curricle down the rutted
drive of the Eddings estate. He had changed into suitable attire for an afternoon visit, and glancing down
at his companion, he could see that Cassandra had
done the same. Rupert could not have left her entirely
impoverished. The high-necked sprigged muslin gown
she wore was of the highest quality, he ventured to
surmise.

Clearing his throat, he began the speech he had
practiced these last hours. "I wish very much to apologize for this morning, my lady."

Blue eyes the color of gentians flashed up at him.
"I should certainly think so. You cannot imagine how
awkward a situation you place me in. I am quite certain Mrs. Scheffing had no intention of inviting me and
polluting the polite air of her company. Even if she
did mean well, I could not possibly go. I left those
hideous evening gowns Duncan bought for me behind,
and I could not possibly attend in one of the two morning gowns I came away with. I had quite enough of
that embarrassment at Hampton Court. It is bad
enough that people gossip behind my back, but to walk
into a room and hear whispers follow me all about is
the outside of enough. I am happy to hear that you
finally see reason."

Merrick didn't know whether to laugh or weep that
his hours of agonizing over the insult he had offered
her had completely gone by Cassandra's pretty head.
His lips tilted in a wry quirk as he bent a quick look
to her pert features. "That is not precisely the incident
to which I referred, Cass."

That brought a sudden flush of color to her cheeks,
a rarity if he ever recognized one.

"Oh, that, well, you were hardly to blame, were
you? Does a lady apologize for forwardness?"

"A lady is not forward, so she has no reason to
apologize. But you did not know what you were doing,

and I did. Therefore, I must extend my most abject apologies and promise it will never happen again.''

Cassandra thought about that for a minute. The curricle in which they rode was quite small, and she had a new awareness of the hard male thigh not inches from hers. The tight pantaloons encasing his muscular leg heightened her fascination. Broad shoulders moved with expert grace as he guided the horses, and she knew their strength now. There was a subtle difference in the way he treated her, as if he had suddenly become aware that she was a woman. She didn't want their relationship to go back to the way it had been before. She wanted Merrick to think of her as a woman.

''Why do you think I did not know what I was doing?''

Merrick turned to give Cassandra a startled glance, then flicked the whip and continued to watch the road. ''You are not old enough to know what you were doing.'' Rupert could have taught her, his mind said, but his heart refused to believe.

Cassandra flounced on her seat and gave him an angry glare. ''I am old enough to be married. I should certainly think a married woman ought to know what she was doing.''

''This is a ridiculous argument. I will rescind my apology, if you prefer, but you will still go to the musicale Friday. You cannot hide forever. The frock you have on will be far grander than anything the other ladies will have.''

Cassandra sat stiffly beside him pondering this. Wyatt was no arbiter of ladies' fashions, obviously. She knew perfectly well that what she wore now was suitable for morning company at home, not even appropriate for this afternoon call, and certainly not suitable for evening attire. But the question was more of her courage than her attire. Did she dare face a house full of condemning, critical people, even with Merrick at her side? Why should she?

"It is easier to slay dragons while wearing armor. I'll not go. You may make my apologies to Bertie."

"You had best be dressed and ready when I come for you, or I shall take you wearing whatever you have on."

Cassandra sent his determined jaw an uncertain look. Wyatt's unprepossessing demeanor did not speak of a man capable of physical violence. A shock of chestnut hair fell down over his forehead even now, and whereas his high brow and square chin might have classical proportions, his nose had a sharp look to it that diminished the image. He did not possess the deep romantic eyes of a Byron or the sardonic piratical features of a Raleigh. He was just Wyatt, the toplofty Earl of Merrick. He wouldn't carry out his threats.

Cassandra crossed her arms and repeated, "I won't come."

Wyatt shrugged. "We'll see about that."

Wyatt had forgotten that conversation by the time he staggered out of the stable later that night and turned his weary legs toward the house.

It had been a monstrously long day, starting with that tussle with Cassandra and ending with the foaling of his favorite mare. The birth had threatened to be a breech, but the blood and filth halfway up his arms testified of the struggle to prevent it. All Wyatt wanted now was a long, hot bath and some of his best brandy.

As soon as he walked through the door he realized his mistake. Voices and light drifted from the first drawing room, which was never used except for entertaining. His mother's words of earlier that day vaguely came back to haunt him, and he groaned inwardly. Catherine was here.

Any attempt he might have made to escape was quickly thwarted by his mother and Catherine. They must have been lying in wait for him, or else he had a traitorous footman on the staff. Glaring at the closest servant, Wyatt waited as the two women came forward to greet him.

His mother gave a screech of dismay at his appearance, and Catherine's venomous glance spoke volumes before she even opened her mouth. Merrick bowed mockingly.

"Forgive me, ladies. I had not meant to offend your delicate sensibilities with my appearance. I was inexcusably delayed by Mother Nature. Perhaps you could go in to dinner without me?"

By this time Catherine's parents had joined them in the foyer, and Merrick gave Baron Montcrieff a brief bow. The jovial older man gave him an understanding grin, but the thin set line of his wife's lips kept him silent.

"I have had quite enough of your insults, Wyatt." Catherine spoke before anyone else could offer a placating word. "You had time enough to escort that little trollop through the countryside, but you do not have the decency to let your grooms handle their own jobs while I sit waiting for you to put in an appearance. I'll not be treated as an old shoe by anyone. I demand an immediate apology."

Wyatt gazed down into her small, tight features as she spoke, wondering at the hostility in her voice. She was twenty-five, well able to attend a small family dinner without her parents in attendance, but she continued the act of demure young maiden except at times like these. When loosened, Catherine's tongue could be as strident as any jackdaw's. He heard the fear and despair behind her anger, but he didn't care.

He couldn't help wondering what Cassandra would have done in this situation. Knowing the little wanton, he rather imagined she would do something completely perverse like calling for his bath and insisting on bathing him.

Merrick started with the shock of that thought. Where had it come from? Why would he even imagine such a lascivious thing about a gently bred young girl? He must be more tired than he thought.

The sight of his mother's face at learning he had spent the afternoon in the ''little trollop's'' company frayed what remained of his patience. Cassandra's grateful visit to Thomas had brought sunshine to the sickroom and laughter to a household that had lived on the edge of hell these last weeks. Whatever Cassandra might be, her heart was in the right place. The Earl of Merrick frowned his displeasure at Catherine's self-serving speech.

''We have already had this argument, Catherine. We have agreed we do not suit. Now, if you will excuse me . . .'' He gave a curt nod and strode off, leaving his mother to deal with the consequences of his rudeness and her own overbearing interference.

What he needed was a bath, a bed, and a willing woman. Catherine offered none of these.

Chapter 13

The package arrived late Friday afternoon. The grubby little boy who delivered it insisted that he had already been paid and rode off in a splatter of mud on an equally bedraggled pony. When Lotta carried it to her mistress, Cassandra stared at the package as if it were a can of worms.

"I ordered nothing else from the dressmaker's, just this gown I have on and the other. It cannot be for me."

The maid gave her employer an impatient look. "Why question it? If a mistake has been made, someone else must pay, not us. Or perhaps your brother has condescended to spend some of your husband's money on you. Enough money exchanged hands to pay for a thousand gowns."

Not wishing to hear more along these lines, Cassandra tentatively peered at the papers wrapping the package. Ordinary dressmaker's wrapping, it explained nothing. Only the word "Armor" blackened in one corner gave any clue to the sender. Cassandra gulped and hid her dismay.

Lotta removed the paper and eagerly withdrew a lovely blue-green- and white-striped silk with a simple bodice draped in lace and a skirt ending in a flounce and a slight train. Both women stared at the confection in awe and admiration.

"Look at the wider skirt," Cassandra whispered in delight. "It is the very latest thing. And the trim . . . It is so much lovelier than those plain straight things I have been wearing for years. How could he . . . ?"

She bit her tongue. Under no circumstances could she reveal her knowledge of the giver, but she knew of a certainty who it was.

Even she knew it was highly improper for a gentleman to give a lady a personal or valuable article unless they were betrothed. What had possessed the proper Earl of Merrick to do such a scandalous thing? Her eyes widened as she thought of the expensive gifts her father and brother sent to their Fashionable Impures. This was the kind of gift a man gave his mistress.

Not totally displeased with this idea, Cassandra began to shed the hideous cotton gown she had been disguising herself in. It was all very well and good to swear never to be looked at by another man, but her heart longed for the feminine niceties she had forsworn by coming here. She could resist silks and satins when Rupert was attached to them, but Merrick was another story entirely. Only a married woman was supposed to wear silk, so he was acknowledging her status by the choice of fabric. Yet the gown was entirely appropriate for a girl of her age. The only inappropriate thing was the status of the giver.

It didn't matter. She wanted to try it on. She didn't know how the dressmaker in the village had come by such a fashionable pattern, but she ought to have her measurements correct. With Lotta's help, Cassandra slipped the silk over her worn chemise.

It fitted beautifully, the draping of lace adding a becoming modesty to her generous figure, the silk clinging enticingly to her small waist. Beneath the silk lay matching ribbons, and Cassandra gazed at them longingly before glaring at her rebellious tresses.

"How I long to cut all that off! Wouldn't it look nice with just a fringe of curls and those ribbons? I hate Duncan for not allowing me to see a hairdresser."

Since of all the things Duncan had done, that was the least, Lotta ignored this childish tantrum and reached for the brush. "Sit down. You just don't know how to work with hair."

With a few deft twists and turns and a number of precious pins, Lotta succeeded in taming Cassandra's unruly hair into a neat roll at the back of her head, with only a few wispy curls dangling in a tantalizing cloud about her face and throat. The ribbons wound through the strawberry tresses added the finishing touches.

Cassandra gazed at her reflection in delight. ''You're an artist! I almost look like everyone else now.''

Lotta snorted. ''You'll never look like all those other insipid misses. You can just pretend to for the ladies' sake. The men will see the difference soon enough.''

Cassandra's shoulders slumped slightly as she stood to seek out her cotton gown. ''I don't want men to see the difference. I've caused enough trouble as it is.''

A knock at the side entrance put an end to this argument. The two women exchanged glances as Jacob's august footsteps walked steadily across the flagstone floor to the conservatory entrance. The room Cassandra had chosen for her own had been little more than a potting shed off the conservatory, just steps away from the entrance. But the door on that side was swollen shut and impossible to open. Their gazes drifted toward the partially open door on the other wall. It didn't close properly, and there was no way of barring it. One could only hope the intruder was still another delivery boy.

A man's deep baritone quickly dispelled that hope. Cassandra glanced nervously toward their entrance hall. Merrick! He had come for her just as he said. Glancing down at her gown, she knew his timing to be impeccable. He had probably watched the box delivered and waited just long enough to be certain she had time to try on the gown. Despicable cad! How had he known that she would try it on and not send it back, as would have been proper?

Foolish question. Cassandra listened as Jacob insisted the lady was not at home, as she had told him to do. Merrick's deep voice did not seem angry in reply, but it did not go away either.

At the door, the earl was pinning the lanky butler

with his noble stare. "The lady has a previous engagement with me. Move aside and let me in and I will wait for her."

"There is no salon, my lord, I cannot do that. Lady Cassandra would be most upset should her friends see the inadequacy of her establishment. You will have to come back later."

"Over your dead body, my good man. You will step aside or I shall remove some of those rotten boards in the window and enter that way. Cass will be upset no matter what either of us does. You might as well accept that fact right now."

The earl certainly had the right of it, Jacob thought gloomily as he stepped aside. Lady Cass's temper was notorious. Neither of them would win this battle.

Merrick walked into the dark interior Cass called home. While it was still daylight outside, in here all was black as night except for the occasional sunbeam through a chink in the walls or ceiling. Setting his jaw at this abomination of a house, Merrick stalked unerringly across the flagstone floor. He shoved at the nearest door, finding it thoroughly embedded. He had seen a light shining through the boarded window beside the door, so he knew someone was on the other side of this wall. They wouldn't waste candles on unoccupied rooms.

Reaching the roofless corridor outside the conservatory, Merrick turned to his right and discovered the light streaming through a partially open door. This, then, was her hiding place.

He shoved the door open and stared at the vision glowing in candlelight. The soft blue-green made her hair more gold than red, and he wasn't at all certain that he approved the change. Yet she looked as demure as any mother could desire. Her armor was quite complete. She had been right. The proper attire would sway the old biddies before ever a word could be said.

He made a stiff bow before the startled silence of

the two women. "I see you are ready. Excellent. My carriage is waiting."

"I'll not go, Merrick," Cassandra responded nervously. "I don't wish to cause more trouble. I just want to be left alone."

That was entirely unlike the Cass he knew, and Merrick sent her a puzzled frown. "You'll cause no trouble. Mrs. Scheffing knows you are coming and is agreeable. You are gowned appropriately. You have Bertie and me to stand at your side. What trouble can you possibly cause?"

Lotta gave him a look of scorn as she marched past him to stalk out of the room. "You can look at her and ask that? I did not take you for a blind man."

Merrick looked back to the strawberry-golden tresses dancing tauntingly about long eyes that slanted upward and fanned outward in a magnificent fringe of lashes. Full pink lips formed a natural pout to beckon a man's kiss, and skin fair and rich as any bowl of cream enticed the touch. All that, without even looking lower. Merrick kept his groan to himself.

"You're beautiful. I'm not blind. But beautiful women walk this earth all the time. They don't hide their looks in dismal caverns. Now, come, they're waiting for us."

"Look what I've done to Thomas," Cassandra whispered entreatingly. "And Rupert. That was my fault. All my fault. I'll not have it happen again. Leave me be, Merrick. Stay away from me."

It was much too late for that, Merrick could have told her, but she was frightened enough as it was. Like this, he could see a girl-child in a woman's body. She had learned grown-up games much too young to know how to deal with the results.

Patiently he walked to her side, took her hand, and placed it on his arm. "Cass, you're braver than that. I've seen you walk through a gambling hell that would have made an Amazon faint. You can face a room of old biddies and a few young striplings. What happened between Thomas and your husband was one of those things that life hands out upon occasion. There was nothing you could have done to prevent it.''

Oh, yes, there was. She could have agreed to be Rupert's wife as promised, and none of this would have happened, but Cassandra didn't say that out loud. That was her shame. She would bear it in silence.

Reluctantly she took Merrick's arm and walked out, ignoring the incredulous look on Jacob's face. She couldn't yell at her servant for allowing the earl in when she had given in to him herself. It was amazing how Wyatt was able to do that. With a minimum of noise and bother, he managed to twist everything his way. Duncan would do well to study his technique.

Dinner was an agony of form and address, but Merrick somehow maneuvered a place at her side and kept a running commentary that allowed Cassandra to relax to a degree and follow his example. When some particularly catty remark reached her ears, or when someone asked a pointedly personal question, Merrick stepped in before Cassandra's temper could ignite. To be defended was such a novel experience that she managed to complete the meal in a silence of amazement.

Due to the entertainment, the gentlemen weren't left to linger over brandy and cigars while the women withdrew. Cassandra was grateful for this small favor, although she was becoming increasingly aware that she was now a target of disapproval for monopolizing the earl's time.

Drawing a breath as they entered the music room, Cassandra bravely disengaged her hand from Merrick's arm. ''The ladies will expect you to circulate, my lord. You need not stay by my side all night.''

Merrick glanced down into her pale face and wished he could do just that. He had no burning desire to talk with anyone else in this room. He found it much more flattering to listen to Cass's laughter at his jests, bask in the admiration of her eyes, and wait for the occasional pearls that fell from her lips when she thought no one but himself listening. He was in a fair way of becoming obsessed with his role of protector, he decided guiltily. That was a rather foolish notion with a woman who could walk with ease through the most notorious alleys of town, the same woman who had driven men to duels and set up housekeeping in a moldering castle. Cass was not likely to need his protection now or ever, and he was certainly in no position to offer it. He would do better to place some distance between them.

Cassandra felt more than saw his departure. A gaping emptiness opened beside her where Wyatt had stood, and even though others came to fill it, she felt curiously alone without Wyatt's company. She didn't know why that should be. She had spent nineteen years on her own. Aside from Lotta, she had never had a close friend or someone to confide in. It was oddly reassuring to be able to speak her thoughts to someone, but she couldn't fathom why it was Merrick who invited these confidences.

Bertie sat by her side through the recital, and she lost herself easily in the music, supremely unaware of his presence. It would be marvelous to play like that, but she had never been able to beat out more than the most perfunctory of tunes.

When the recital ended, the audience demanded selections from its members. Proud mothers paraded their daughters' talents gladly, and Cassandra felt the fear building inside. Surely they would not call on her. She did not need the humiliation of displaying the meagerness of her abilities.

As if sensing her weakness, Mrs. Scheffing smiled benevolently at her son's companion. "And you, Lady Cassandra, will you not play? I can remember your parents had a grand music room. Surely you have absorbed some of their love for music?"

Cassandra bit back a sharp retort. The only music the late marquess enjoyed was the sound of his own voice brutalizing a tavern ditty. If her mother loved music, she had not stirred from her bed in years to acknowledge it.

"Thank you, Mrs. Scheffing, but I really cannot spoil the lovely sounds I have heard here tonight. Perhaps another time."

A polite murmur of insistence arose around her, and Cassandra nearly panicked until a familiar male voice intruded.

"Lady Cassandra has an excellent voice, Mrs. Scheffing. I could be persuaded to play for her if she would sing."

Cassandra met Merrick's dark eyes with a slight flush of embarrassment, but the happy applause sounding around them prevented refusal. Obviously Merrick's talents were known. Reluctantly she rose to join him by the pianoforte.

"What if we know none of the same tunes?" she whispered in anguish as he seated his tall frame on the bench.

There was laughter in his look as he glanced up at her frightened features. "I can assure you, I know every tune that you know, and I know which ones not to play before polite company. Shall we try 'Greensleeves'?"

A brilliant smile of relief swept over her face, instantly quieting their audience and nearly startling Merrick into forgetting where he was. Deciding if Wellington had only had Cassandra at Waterloo she could have stopped Napoleon's army with that smile, the earl returned his attention to the instrument. The music should be sufficient distraction from the slender figure standing beside him.

The first haunting notes of the old melody rang out from the pianoforte with startling clarity. Cassandra's voice joined in so smoothly that it was a second or two before anyone knew she had begun to sing. The music rose and swelled with the refrain, and she followed it without hesitation, filling the room with a haunting tale of lost love. By the song's end, many were surreptitiously drying their eyes.

Shaken by the intensity of the musical joining they

had created, Merrick hastily stood and made a quick bow as applause thundered around them. He felt as if they had just bared their souls for all to see. Never had he shared the intensity of his fascination with music with anyone, but in Cassandra he sensed he had found a soul mate. Judging from Cassandra's dazed expression, she felt the same, and he pressed her fingers protectively against his arm as she dipped a polite curtsy. They shook as they gratefully clasped his sleeve, and he refused any encore.

When no one was able to match such a resounding favorite, the evening trickled to an end. With the music still ringing in her ears, Cassandra made no pretense of letting Merrick leave her side again. Her heart ached with the joy of the sounds he had created out of that impossible instrument, and she wasn't at all certain that she wouldn't float away if she released his arm.

The carriage was finally brought around, the last farewells were said, and they stepped out into the cool evening starlight without exchanging a word. Merrick assisted her into the closed carriage and silently followed. The music continued to swirl around them, and Cassandra reached for his hand as he settled beside her.

"How do you play like that?" she whispered in wonderment, her eyes wide in the lantern light as she gazed up at him.

Merrick raised a dark eyebrow. "Shall I ask how you learned to sing like that? Even a nightingale couldn't hit some of those notes you reached tonight."

How had she thought his face not handsome? In this light Wyatt's eyes had a romantic darkness that even Byron couldn't hope to duplicate, and the gentleness of his smile made Cassandra's heart swoon with something she very much suspected to be desire—a desire to see that smile again and again. Her gloved fingers wrapped trustingly around his.

"I have tried to play 'Greensleeves' on every instrument imaginable. It is one of the few tunes for which I know the notes. I cannot make it sound the way I

want it to except when I sing. You played it better than
I heard it in my head.''

Merrick remained silent. His mother deplored his
useless habit of wasting hours at the pianoforte. He
could not explain to her that he was happiest during
those hours. The music challenged him, absorbed him,
and carried him to other worlds. The child beside him
tonight was telling him she felt the same, or perhaps
he was only imagining that in her simple words. He
was afraid to find out.

"You are welcome to try out our instrument anytime
you like, my lady," he answered formally.

Cassandra shook her head vigorously, loosening a
shower of curls. "I could never make it sound like you
did." Hesitantly she watched his profile from the corner of her eyes. "Would you, sometime, play more for
me? I'm certain the musician tonight was very talented, but I was not familiar with the music. Perhaps
you could teach me more?''

He was asking for trouble to even consider it. Cassandra was an untamed spirit, a willful sprite who en-
chanted and tormented with just her presence. To
unleash that spirit in his quiet household would be akin
to opening the gates to heaven and hell. Merrick smiled
and squeezed her hand.

"You are welcome any evening. We will polish our
duet, shall we?''

Her joy rippled through him, and he knew he was
committing the unpardonable, but Merrick never felt
more satisfied than when she reached to kiss his cheek.

Insane to think a kiss on the cheek was worth more
than a pleasant tumble in bed, but he resisted the lust
rising in him and merely pressed a kiss to her brow as
they said their good-nights.

Strange, but it wasn't the scent of roses that lingered
in the carriage after she was gone; it was the fresh
spring scent of dew-moistened lilacs.

Chapter 14

"I will not take up gambling, I will not!" Cassandra stomped her foot, threw her head haughtily, and glared at her servants. The effect was slightly spoiled by the fact that her gown was less elegant than their attire and that she stood in the remains of a burned-out kitchen holding an iron skillet over the fire.

"Not gambling, just a few friendly social games now that you are appearing in society again. A few coins won here and there will tide us over to the harvest."

Since the work progressing in the fields was so slow as to make the possibility of a harvest almost laughable, Jacob might as well have said "until our ship comes in," but Cassandra shook her head vigorously.

"Absolutely, uncategorically, no! We will starve before I cheat friends."

"We will starve undoubtedly," Jacob intoned gloomily. "It is just a matter of how soon. You have spent the bulk of your money on repairs to this monstrosity and to the fences and hedgerows. How were you planning to eat this summer?"

"We have a garden," Cassandra pointed out. "It will grow in due time, provided you and Lotta spend more time weeding it than complaining about it."

"My lady, we aren't farmers." Lotta interrupted their argument with her protest. "Can you not write to Duncan or Rupert's solicitor and demand they provide you with funds for support? Surely there must be some law that says they must provide for you."

Cassandra's expression grew even more mutinous. "Certainly, they will provide me with one-way tickets to France. I'll return to gambling before I return to them." At the relieved look on her servants' faces, she hastily added, "And I never intend to return to gambling."

As she set out later to meet Merrick for their evening music lesson, Cassandra pondered this conversation. She could not ask Jacob and Lotta to starve with her, and their funds were running desperately low. She had not meant to mend that hedgerow just yet, but when the deer had cropped nearly their entire planting, she knew she had to do something. She had not realized how expensive farming could be. She had thought it just a matter of clearing some land and dropping some seed and watching it grow. Deer and too much rain followed by too much sun had never occurred to her. And now that they finally had a crop growing, the men were beginning to murmur things about wagons to haul the grain to market and tools with which to thresh it and any number of other impossibilities. If she did not have the funds now, she was less likely to have them at the end of the summer.

Merrick met her at the stile, as had become his custom. She had insisted he was not to waste his valuable time coming to fetch her every evening, but he was unwilling to allow her to wander through the forested park unaccompanied. So they had silently compromised on this arrangement.

Cassandra was still amazed that they managed to get along so well. Merrick was everything that she was not. She was ever conscious of their differences. He dressed in sartorial splendor, never raised his voice, gave orders with a quiet authority that sent people scurrying. She couldn't manage the two miserable servants she possessed without screaming arguments. He was half a score years senior to her with a world of experience and sophistication she could never attain.

Yet they came together over their music in complete accord.

Tonight, however, there seemed to be a change in plans. Beside Merrick waited two beautifully groomed thoroughbreds patiently champing at the grass along the fence. Cassandra cast the earl's impassive features a glance askance. "Do you have company?"

"Not with me." Merrick watched Cass's solemn upturned face. These last weeks had drained some of the sunshine from her smile. The radiance was still there when they worked with the music, but whenever he encountered her elsewhere, he couldn't help but remark the change. His field hands had reported the various disasters that had struck her crops. He could afford to replant when the rain rotted his fields or the sun scorched them, but neither she nor her tenants could have continuing funds for such uncertainties. He often wondered if that were the only source of her unsmiling expression, but he couldn't inquire into her personal life. She was reticent on the subject, and he was too polite to pry.

"My mother has some cronies of hers up at the house playing whist. It was such a nice evening, I thought you might enjoy a ride rather than their exalted company."

Cassandra gave a wry grin as she stroked the nose of the little bay mare. "She has finally found a way to drive us out of the house. Your mother is a clever woman."

"She is also manipulative, overbearing, and bored, but we will not go into that. We can go up to the music room if you prefer, but I remember you once mentioning you wished to have a horse. I thought a little exercise might be beneficial. You have looked a trifle peaked lately."

"Thank you, my lord, just the words a lady likes to hear." Cassandra caught his pained expression and hastily added, "But you are right, of course. I have been out of sorts and a ride is just what I would like."

It was curious how easily she could hurt him. Merrick never had been known as a ladies' man, and over these last weeks she had come to understand why. Despite his wealth and title, he possessed little assurance when it came to women. She had watched Mrs. Scheffing and her friends run rings around him, and they were probably the kindest women in his set. He managed well by holding his tongue and bowing politely and obliging their requests, but Cassandra sensed his unease. He never offered a comment of his own, never began a conversation with them, never offered a flattery, or suggested any continuance of the dalliances the single ladies pressed upon him.

She had finally concluded that he was actually shy around women, but not with her. That puzzled her for a while until she remembered her own extreme forwardness. She had never given the poor man a chance to be shy, and he had responded by treating her as a friend. Their shared interest in music had helped, and the difference in their ages and marital status had perhaps eased some of his concerns. She was not a woman he needed to impress, but the neighbor's wayward child and a married woman beyond his reach. If it suited him to think of her as such, she would not complain. She needed his company too much to ever object to the circumstances of it.

The sun was well above the horizon when they set out. Thunder rumbled in the distance as it had this past week, but no rain ever came of it. Cassandra glanced anxiously to the sky, hoping this time to find a cloud to water her wilting crops, but only a purple haze in the distance gave any promise.

Merrick noted the sudden slump of her shoulders and, surmising the reason, offered consolingly, "It will rain before week's end. MacGregor's aching bones never lie. One of these days you will have to consider irrigating that field. You have quite an adequate stream nearby."

Cassandra nodded silently and adjusted the skirt of

her gown more comfortably over the sidesaddle. Had she known they would be riding, she could have worn her habit, but the heat would be excruciating in that wool. It was just as well that she hadn't known about it.

"You are terribly silent tonight, Cass. Have I offended you? Or would you have preferred to go to the music room?"

Cassandra summoned a bright smile and urged her mare to a canter. "This is what I want to do. Race you to the crossroad?"

Before Merrick could agree or disagree, she dug her heels in and her mount sprinted off.

They raced through the gathering gloom of the trees and into the sunset light of the road. A wind dancing through the treetops dipped to tear at their hair, and Cassandra's wild mass of curls began to tumble down her back. Merrick kept one pace behind her just to admire the fire of the sun's dying gleam in that red-gold brilliance.

The crossroad loomed ahead and he kicked his mount to greater speed, crossing the finish line a nose ahead and cantering toward the beckoning banks of a stream below. He heard Cassandra's laughter and the hoofbeats of the other horse following as he led the way through the shrubbery to the streambed below. He hadn't heard her laughter in days, and it warmed him to know he had produced it.

He dismounted and turned to help Cassandra down. Merrick knew his error as soon as his hands touched her waist, but it was much too late by then. His fingers were already sliding her from the saddle, her breasts were brushing against his chest, and her face had turned expectantly toward him, her lips parted with promise and her eyes bright with joy.

Cassandra slid into his embrace so gladly that Merrick wondered how he had kept away this long. Or why. Her mouth was warm and eager and as willing as he remembered in all his joyous dreams. It was like being touched by magic when she was in his arms. All the old uncertainties disappeared, and there was only the music of her mouth against his.

Wyatt pulled her closer, fitting her willowy slenderness against him. The wind caught at Cassandra's skirts, whipping them around her legs, but he could feel the straight firmness of her thighs pressed against his, her hips rubbing where he needed her most. It seemed incredible that she did not pull away in terror. Instead she wrapped her arms around his shoulders and parted her lips and bent fully into his embrace.

Their breaths mingled with sweet heat while Cassandra's hair tugged from its pins and swept around them. Merrick gathered the silken curls in both fists and drank deeply of the heady wine she offered. He couldn't get enough, and he lifted her from the ground to have her closer.

Cassandra dreamed she had died and gone to heaven. Nothing could equal the rapture of Wyatt's kiss. She felt his need, knew his desire, and they matched the churning excitement of her own. Maybe this time he would teach her where these kisses led. She felt as if she would die if he did not. There was more, she knew it with age-old instincts, and she cried out her joy as his kisses strayed to her ear and throat. Her breasts pressed eagerly against her bodice, awaiting his touch.

When it came, Cassandra sighed happily and felt the molten heat rise through her middle to greet Wyatt's hand. She wanted to shed all her clothing and give him free rein to touch where he willed. Surely then she would know the relief her body sought in his embrace.

Merrick returned his kiss to her swollen lips as his hand fumbled with the various fastenings of her bodice. He could feel the heat of her beneath his fingers as he finally gained the entrance he sought, and then he was lost to thought as he encountered no further barriers to the firm white flesh he had imagined in his dreams.

Somewhere in a disconnected portion of his mind, Wyatt knew what he was doing. He felt Cassandra moan against his mouth, knew the shiver of passion sweeping through her as his fingers located the sensitive peak of her breast and began a fusillade of sensation there. But his mind had no control over his body. He could not force his hand away, any more than he could release her from his hold.

His long, sensitive fingers were warm against the coolness of her flesh as the wind crept beneath her clothing and curled around her. Cassandra wished he would hurry as Wyatt found the rest of the fastenings and peeled her bodice downward, freeing both her breasts to his explorations. His hands splayed across the swelling ache he had created, and still it was not enough. Cassandra clung to his mouth when he would pull away, and her fingers wrapped in his hair to prevent any parting.

Reassuringly Wyatt's lips brushed against hers, burning tiny trails to the corners, then heartbreakingly moving onward. Only when she realized his destination did Cassandra emit a sound of joy deep in her throat as she threw her head backward and allowed him to lift her to his kiss.

Fire, swift and searing, swept through her from where Wyatt's mouth closed over her breast. The tingling in her lower parts became something stronger, headier, more demanding as she cried aloud and moved against him. She could feel herself swelling to fill Wyatt's passionate claim, and she wanted nothing more than to give him all he asked.

It no longer mattered that he was the Earl of Merrick, a man of stature and importance in the community and society. It no longer mattered that she was married to a brutal rake who had nearly killed a friend of the earl's. All that mattered was that they were together, at last.

A crack of thunder broke overhead, startling their horses into anxious whinnies. A fat raindrop splattered across Cassandra's breast, running downward until Wyatt caught it with his tongue. She shivered in his embrace, and he could feel the hot, hard points of her breasts pressing hungrily against his palm. He knew what she offered, but the thunder had reconnected his brain. Gradually Wyatt returned his kisses to her lips and banked the fires with tender strokes as he pulled her bodice together again.

"That is not why I brought you out here," he murmured regretfully against her lips.

"It doesn't matter, Wyatt," Cassandra whispered urgently, catching his hand and holding it against her breast. "Don't stop now."

"Not here, my love. Not ever, perhaps. Come, let's get you dressed and back to the house before you are drowned."

His will was strong, but his flesh was weak. It took a long time to find all the hooks and ties and fasten them properly between each kiss to the loveliness about to be covered. They were both weak with desire before she was respectable again.

Azure eyes gazed uncertainly, expectantly up to him as Wyatt straightened but continued to hold her against the telltale signs of his arousal. He didn't know what to say or do. Had she been unmarried, he would be obliged to offer for her, and would have done so gladly, even if it would be the single most insane thing he had ever done. He had no illusions about what life would be like with a tempest like Cassandra. She had already made life at home a living hell simply by existing against his mother's wishes. But she was married, and he was not a man who dallied with other men's wives.

"I don't know what to say, Cassandra. There is no excuse for my behavior, nor any remedy. Will you forgive me anyway?"

She felt an emptiness clawing at her insides as Wyatt retreated behind his polite facade. She would not let him escape like that. She could not. They had both been so close to finding what they needed—how could he back away? She wrapped her fingers in his stiff shirt and turned to him beseechingly.

"Don't set me aside, Wyatt. I know I've not always treated you kindly. I should never have embarrassed you like that at Hampton Court, but I tried to relieve you of that obligation by marrying Rupert. And I know they're whispering all over the neighborhood about our being so much in each other's pockets, but I promise never to be seen in public with you again if that will help. Just do not abandon me entirely, Wyatt. Tell me you will still see me."

Merrick wasn't quite certain he believed what she was saying. Cassandra could be a melodramatic little flirt if she put her mind to it. But he couldn't believe she would lie to him, nor did he think she was normally given to begging. No woman had ever begged for his company before, and that only served to raise his incredulity.

"You married Rupert to relieve me of my obligation? Forgive me if I appear a little caper-witted, but wasn't that a rather drastic means of settling the matter?"

Now she had done it. He was angry with her, and she would never be able to explain. Cassandra pulled from his grasp and turned to tend to her nervous mount. The sky was getting darker, but no rain had come of it yet. She wished for a quick drenching downpour to soothe her fevered skin.

"I had very little choice in the matter, Wyatt. Let us not argue now." She kept her chin steadily up as she waited for him to assist her into the saddle.

He did not immediately oblige. Standing behind her, willing his hands to his side, Wyatt continued his interrogation. "Perhaps my memory is ailing. Did I not come to see you after the announcement was put in the paper? Did I not offer for you again, even though I was no longer under an obligation to do so?"

"Yes, you did," she whispered at the saddle.

''But you still felt you had no choice but to marry Rupert? That is not how I see it.''

She didn't want to know how he saw it. She didn't want to explain why she had to marry Rupert. She didn't want anyone to know how great a fool she was. She led her horse to a fallen log and prepared to climb into the saddle without his assistance.

Her cold silence left little choice. Furious, but not at all certain with whom, Merrick strode across the distance between them and threw her up in the seat. Unable to think of a word to say in the face of her silence, he held his tongue.

The silence stretched out between them as they rode back the way they had come. It grew like a tangible thing, a briar patch of thorns between them that could not easily be discarded or traversed, and neither made any attempt to do so.

There were too many things between them, too many things left unsaid, too many impossibilities to confront. Merrick stopped when they reached what served as Cassandra's front door. He jumped down and reached to help her. Remembering the disaster of that last attempt, he hastily offered his hand instead of taking her waist.

Silently Cassandra accepted his offer and climbed down without further assistance. She gazed briefly into his set face, then turned away and went inside, gently shutting him out.

Chapter 15

The thunder continued to roll as Cassandra lay sleepless in her lonely bed, waiting for the patter of rain to begin. Her body ached with a fierceness hitherto unknown as the past hours came back in fleeting, startlingly clear images.

Closing her eyes, she could feel Wyatt's hands still on her, smell the masculine scent of his skin as his beard-roughened kiss chafed her cheek, see the smoky desire of his eyes as his arms closed around her. If she had anything at all to give, she would give it now to have Merrick by her side again. She just wanted him to hold her, to lie here beside her so she wouldn't be so alone.

She had once asked Peggy, her father's mistress, what happened between husbands and wives in bed. Peggy had always been honest with her, and she had replied that husbands and wives held and loved each other in bed. That was what Cassandra wanted: to be held and loved.

A tear slid down her cheek and she hastily rubbed it away. When she was twelve years old she had resolved never to cry again. Crying accomplished nothing. When she felt like crying, she hit something instead. After Duncan hit her back, she had refrained from hitting anything but inanimate objects, and that helped for a while. But as she got older, the pain of rejection grew progressively worse, and it was harder to find satisfaction in bruised knuckles.

She loved her parents. They were all she had. And

sometimes, she knew, they loved her back. Even though she wasn't his true daughter, the marquess had paraded her before his friends and called her his little princess. When he was in funds, he would buy her pretty trinkets and ribbons and carry her beside him on his horse or carriage. She had never even known he wasn't her father until Duncan had told her when she was twelve.

That was the last time she had really cried. The marquess hadn't answered her hysterical demands for denial, and when she heard Duncan being thrashed soundly later that night, she had cried until there weren't any tears left to cry. Then she had punched Duncan in the stomach the next morning and walked away, head held high.

But it had never been the same again. The marquess never called her bastard, but when he was drunk, he cursed and thrashed her just as frequently as Duncan. The older she grew, the less able he was to face the facts, the more he drank. The more he drank, the more he abused them. Cassandra couldn't hit him back, so she learned to smile in retaliation. The marquess cringed and wept like a baby whenever she did that, and it made her feel stronger. But it didn't take away the pain.

Tears crept faster down her cheeks now, and Cassandra choked on them, tossing on her pillow as she tried to drive away the need building in her. She had only wanted their love. She had felt like she had it when she helped her father win at cards, but then he would come home and she would hear the violent arguments in her mother's chamber, and the feeling would go away again. She knew they argued over her. It was all her fault that her father drank and her mother couldn't get out of bed. It was all her fault, and there was nothing she could do about it.

The helplessness overwhelmed her. Maybe if she behaved better they would love her and everything would be all right. But everything she did was wrong.

If she went out with her father, her mother cried. If she tried to stay home with her mother, her father raged and cursed, and her mother cried. She couldn't win their love no matter what she did, but she stopped crying about it.

Until now. The tears swelled and choked and came without ending. Was it so wrong to want to be loved just a little? Whom would it hurt? Merrick needed her as much as she needed him. She knew that. He wouldn't have done what he did otherwise. She had to believe that. But now she had made him angry, and he would never love her. It was happening all over again. Why couldn't she ever do anything right?

Cassandra was only a pale shadow of herself when she approached the stile the next night. Dark circles beneath her eyes bespoke the sleepless night she had spent; colorless unsmiling lips gave evidence of her inner struggle. She had forced herself to the meeting place with arguments too obscure to ever repeat to herself. She just knew she had to see Merrick again.

When he didn't come, she let anger build over the pain that would have swallowed her. She refused to think that what they had done was wrong. It had felt right. She knew it was right. She wouldn't let him make her think otherwise. Anger carried her over the stile. Anger stalked her feet toward the mansion in the park's center.

There were no lights in the front drawing room, so they weren't entertaining. Maybe Merrick wasn't there at all. Maybe he was out courting Catherine, as his mother had made plain that he must do. Let him marry Catherine. All she wanted was a little of his love. Catherine would never have that.

The knocker sounded hollow against the great front door. A servant answered with smooth efficiency and stared at her as if she were some waif washed upon the step by a wayward tide. Cassandra met his blank stare with livid fury.

"Let me in, James. I wish to see Lord Merrick."

"His lordship is not at home, my lady." Caught in a quandary, knowing full well the earl welcomed this oddly dressed female and the countess did not, the servant equivocated.

"I daresay he will be soon enough. I will wait in the music room until he comes." Anger made her brave. She held on to it with every ounce of strength she possessed.

The servant tentatively opened the door a little further, but their confrontation had taken enough time to give Lady Merrick a chance to hear them. She sailed down the hall now, bearing down upon them, her silks flying in the breeze.

"You are letting in a draft, James. Close that door at once." As if just noticing the drably dressed female on the doorstep, she made a startled gesture. "Lady Cassandra, what brings you here tonight? Wyatt has gone out and I don't expect him to return soon. I am so sorry you have made the journey for nothing."

The malicious gleam in the widow's eyes was fuel enough to keep Cassandra's ire kindled. With equal maliciousness she replied, "I am so sorry to have missed him, my lady, but it is you I have come to visit. I have been meaning to this age, but you have been busy and I had no wish to intrude. Since Wyatt isn't here, we should enjoy a good long *tête-à-tête.*" She deliberately used the earl's given name to watch his mother blanch.

Shocked to the toes by this blatant untruth garbed in social flattery, Lady Merrick hesitated. Cassandra took advantage of her hesitation by stepping into the foyer, her chin held high and a brilliantly false smile upon her lips. Her gaze quickly took in the cold formality of the interior, the lack of any welcoming vases of flowers, the polished tiles without so much as a tiny rug to warm them, the towering walls with only a stern-faced ancestor to beautify them, and her determination intensified.

"It is so good of you to see me, Lady Merrick."
She mouthed the words she had heard uttered in some
earlier time and place while she sought a welcoming
light to guide her. She longed to head for the music
room, but no melodic tones drifted from that direction. Now that she was here, she meant to stay until
she and Merrick had this straightened out.

"I really cannot. There is so much for me to do . . ."
The countess's words drifted to an end as her high-handed
visitor proceeded down the hall without her.

"Merrick tells me you are bored, my lady." Cassandra espied a light and a fire in the room on her left
and turned unerringly toward it. "That seems hard to
believe when there is so much to be done with this
house." She hid her triumph as she spotted the countess's tea tray with a steaming pot still waiting.

Fascinated despite herself, Lady Merrick watched
as the brazen child sat down in the love seat beside the
tray and arranged her dowdy skirts across the satin.
There was no doubting the challenge in her eyes, and
accepting it, the countess sat regally in the chair beside her.

"I cannot imagine how you received that impression, child. There is scarce time to be bored on an
estate the size of Merrick. I am constantly busy.
Sometimes I must take time to breathe. That is what I
was doing before you arrived. I insisted that I have
one night a week to myself, and Wyatt graciously
agreed."

When the countess made no effort to offer tea to her
guest, Cassandra signaled the footman to fetch her a
cup. She had not grown up in the house of a marquess
and learned nothing. Perhaps a properly coached
young lady did not order other people's servants about,
but she had no timidity in doing so. Half the battle in
winning Merrick's affections lay here, and she was
about to dig in her heels and fight.

"I am certain Wyatt is a most considerate son. He

has been very kind in offering me the use of his music room. He is very fond of music, is he not?''

The servant arrived with the cup, and the countess ungraciously poured a splash and handed the china to her uninvited guest. "He is very good at whatever he does. However, he is much too busy to continue entertaining you as he has been doing. He has been neglecting his other estates by lingering here overlong this spring. It would not surprise me if he left shortly to tour his other holdings.''

"I do believe he has a steward and a man of business who are quite capable of managing much of those lands without his constant attention,'' Cassandra replied demurely over her teacup. "Perhaps he should turn his attention to renovating the interiors here. If I am not mistaken, there is a serious water stain on the brocade of that drapery.'' She indicated a window to their right.

The countess drew herself up in a flurry of ruffled feathers. "Wyatt has better things to do than consider the furnishings, and so have I. When we have the time to turn our attention to it, we will hire an architect to make the necessary changes.''

"You would do better to hire a housekeeper,'' Cassandra said wryly. "What this house needs is someone to love it. I don't think anyone has looked at it for years.''

"How dare you!'' Finally outraged, the countess set her cup down with a bang that should have cracked the flowered china beneath.

Before she could speak further, a masculine voice in the hall warned that the master had returned.

Cassandra kept her expression carefully neutral as Merrick entered the room. He had obviously just come from outdoors. His hair was still wind-tousled, and the fresh scent of the coming storm carried with him. He was so strikingly handsome in his informal tweed habit with only a twisted length of linen at his throat that Cassandra almost had to look away to fight down the pain. That same man had held her in improper embrace just the night before. She had difficulty in juxtaposing the formal earl on the improper lover.

The flicker of surprise left his eyes as quickly as it came. Merrick bowed briefly to the ladies, sent a questioning glance to Cassandra, and formally addressed his mother. ''I see you are entertaining. Am I intruding?''

''No, you are not. Lady Cassandra was just about to leave. You may summon James to see her out. I have some things to discuss with you.''

Cassandra remained smilingly where she was. ''I am in no hurry, my lord. Perhaps you would permit me some time with your pianoforte while you and your charming mother have your discussion.''

The polite words hid a powder keg about to explode, and Merrick hastily moved to stomp out the burning fuse. ''Of course, my lady, I will be with you directly.'' He signaled the servant hovering in the doorway. ''James, see Lady Cassandra to the music room.''

Merrick watched in admiration as Cassandra rose, gave a proud nod to his irate parent, and swept off in a trail of lilac scent. She seemed paler somehow, but the fire in her eyes was unmistakable. He was about to receive a bear-garden jaw from one woman and a sharp set-down from another. He found himself quite eager for the second.

''I will not have that wanton female in my house, do you understand me?'' The countess's tirade began as soon as the door closed behind their guest.

''It's my house, Mother. I will entertain whom I wish.'' Merrick waited wearily for the next wave of venom. They had had this argument in varying forms over the past few weeks. He had always tried to treat his parents with respect, but he found himself increasingly impatient with the prospect of listening to this for the rest of his days.

''She has insulted me! You cannot allow that to go unavenged.''

Amusement quirked a corner of his mouth. "I shall challenge her to a duel. What weapons do you suppose she will choose?"

"Wyatt, do not treat this lightly! She has scandalized all society, exiled her husband, nearly destroyed that poor Scheffing boy, and now she is after you. Do not let her do this to us! Put her out at once and forbid her the door."

"Actually, Mother, Cass quite had me once and set me free. Had she not married Rupert, she would be Lady Merrick now. I do think you owe her an apology. Now, if you'll forgive me, I must see what she needs. Cassandra seldom goes visiting without reason." His dry tone left no room for argument, and Wyatt walked out without further intervention. His mother's shrieks for a maid and smelling salts left him untouched.

He could hear the hesitant tinkle of the pianoforte as Cassandra sought the notes to "Greensleeves." Even her inexpert fingering had the power to return the night of the musicale to him. In some odd way, they were closer to each other in this room than they were in each other's arms. That realization made his palms sweat and his heart catch in his throat as he opened the door. He didn't know what was happening to him, but he was certain it was some form of madness. Perhaps the Howard insanity was contagious.

A strand of red-gold hair curled about the nape of Cassandra's slender neck as she bent over the keys. The branch of candles above her sent shimmering light across the knot of hair pinned at the top of her head. She appeared so fragile sitting there, yet Merrick knew her to be stronger than any other female he knew. In some ways. Perhaps not all.

She looked up as he approached, and moved over to give him room on the bench. The poignant scent of lilacs wafted around him, wrapping him in memories, but he resisted the call. His fingers automatically found the chords she had been attempting, and the music came without thought.

She didn't sing, only watched avidly as his hands moved easily across the keyboard. He switched to a more complicated piece that he had been trying to teach her to appreciate, but recognized his error at once. He needed her to sing. He wanted to hear her voice opened in pleasure. He didn't want what he had done to spoil what they had in here.

"Sing, just for a little while," he murmured as he switched to a simple lullaby.

He chose the right piece this time. A love song would have made her cry, but a lullaby was a child's song, simple and without the complicated emotions of some others. Cassandra sang it obediently, with practiced ease, but it wasn't the same.

With crashing chords Wyatt switched to a boisterous tune requiring both their voices. Cassandra's sweet melody sought that plateau of mutual understanding they had found before, almost reaching it, but not quite.

He knew what was missing but he wouldn't give in to it. He found a faster song, one that required all their attention and usually ended in laughter when one or the other tripped over a note and lost pace. They sang it with perfection this night, and it wasn't the same.

Slamming the cover down, Merrick rose and peremptorily held out his hand. "I had best get you home before the storm breaks."

It hadn't broken last night and might never break, but Cassandra rose and willingly took his hand. She understood that whatever they had to say to each other would not be said in here. This room was to remain their haven, unmarred by the distress of the outer world. Perhaps Wyatt would return here alone and never share it with her again, but the memory of this pleasantness would not be shattered.

Wyatt ordered two horses saddled, and they waited restlessly in the protection of the shrubbery along the drive. The wind tossed and rattled the upper branches, and clouds scuttled rapidly across the setting sun, but a beam of light still brightened the horizon. Cassandra stared at that gleaming ray against the black clouds and held tightly to Wyatt's ungloved hands. Neither of them had donned gloves when they came outside. She liked the intimacy of his bare fingers wrapped around hers.

The horses were brought and Wyatt allowed one of the grooms to throw Cassandra up in the saddle. If she noticed, she said nothing as they moved out onto the drive. The wind wasn't conducive to talk, but the words had to be said.

"I can't bring myself to apologize for what happened last night. I did not think you would wish to see me again." Merrick started stiffly, not daring to look in her direction.

"Then I will not apologize either. And I don't think I could bear it if I never saw you again."

Her voice was low and quiet and Merrick wasn't certain he had heard her aright, but the lurch in his stomach told him he had. "You don't know what you're saying," he answered quietly.

"Probably not, but I don't care. You're my only friend, Wyatt. I couldn't bear it if I lost you." The pain was creeping into her voice. She hadn't meant to let it, but last night had brought all the anguish to the surface and there had not been time to bury it again.

Merrick sat in stunned contemplation of this fact. She needed a friend, not a lover, but he didn't think there could be any separating the two. He had paced the floor last night in an agony of unquenched desire. He didn't know how it had come to this or why, but the one woman in the world who drove him to unbridled lust was the one woman he could not have.

"Cassandra, there are some basic truths you must understand. Friendship between a man and a woman is looked upon with skepticism by our society. People are not going to believe we are merely friends. And they would be right. You don't understand yet what is between us, and as the older, more responsible party,

I cannot let you learn more. That is why women take husbands. I hate to say this, but you chose Rupert. It is his place to teach you the relationship between a man and a woman.''

"You cannot forgive me that, can you?'' Cassandra asked bitterly. "I have a hard time forgiving myself, so that is understandable. It is too late now for regrets. It could not have been done any other way. I just don't know why I have to suffer for it for the rest of my life.''

"I wish I knew how to help you, Cass, but I don't. You must have had reasons for choosing Rupert. I do not know what happened that night, but is it something that might be corrected with time and patience? Perhaps you just didn't understand . . .'' Merrick found that a difficult topic to express, and he changed his direction. "Rupert was quite drunk. Perhaps he didn't mean to be cruel. You can try a man's patience at times, Cass.''

Cassandra threw him a spirited look. "And men can try mine equally. Rupert is a drunken bully and I'll never go back to him. You're right. I didn't understand what was expected of me, and it doesn't make matters any better now that I do. I loathe him. I've always loathed him. But now that I'm married, Duncan can't sell me again. I've accomplished that much. I just don't understand why it should mean an end to our friendship.''

Wyatt wanted to ask her just exactly how much Rupert had taught her. After all, they'd had a day and a night of marriage. Almost a night. It was quite possible that Rupert had practiced his skills on her before their marriage and only revealed his beastlier side after he had her firmly bound. Wyatt didn't want to think about what a man of Rupert's nature might have done to a lady as lovely and innocent as Cassandra. As much as it was the proper thing to do, he could not bring himself to persuade her to return to her husband.

"It doesn't mean an end to our friendship, Cass.

I'll always be here if you need me. I just don't think it would be very good for either of us to continue seeing each other as we have.''

The clouds overhead were thicker now, blotting out what remained of the sunlight. As they entered the forest, the trees danced wildly in the wind, and a sudden bolt of lightning in the distance made the horses jerk nervously. This was no time or place for argument, but these words had to be said. Merrick tried to increase their pace, but Cassandra hung back, oblivious of the fury of the storm growing around her as she was overcome by the storm within.

"Not see each other? What kind of friendship is that? You sound like a bored lover trying to rid himself of an unwanted mistress. How many times have I heard my father use that line? Not see each other! Pardon me for being so offensive to your delicate tastes, Merrick. I did not mean to fling myself upon you. You may stop seeing me now if it pleases you. I will have Jacob return your horse in the morning.''

So saying she kicked her mount into a canter down the narrow trail. A streak of lightning followed by a paralyzing crack of thunder directly overhead spooked the horse into a gallop, and Merrick screamed a warning even as the rain began to beat down upon his shoulders.

The path she took was not a riding trail. The branches were not kept trimmed to a horse's height. Panic drying his mouth, Wyatt lowered his head and sent his horse into a gallop after her.

Chapter 16

The sky exploded in flash after flash of light. Wyatt could see only the silhouette of horse and rider ahead of him. The horse was clearly in control now, the drenching rain and thunderous cracks overhead driving the spirited mare into panic. Cassandra was either too angry or too frightened to care. She clung to the reins and let the horse have its head.

The next flash set the silhouette into a slow motion that drove Merrick's breath back into his lungs. A low-lying limb loomed ahead. He could see Cassandra duck to dodge it, but not soon enough. He could almost hear the crack as her uncovered head connected with the branch. Then she was tumbling, and he was racing forward, and there was nothing he could do to stop any of it.

Mud splashed around his boots as Merrick leapt from his horse. The crumpled figure on the ground lay very still, and he couldn't bring himself to breathe as he knelt beside her. Bright hair lay soaked in filthy water, and rain poured in muddy rivulets down Cassandra's pale face as he lifted her from the path. His own heart thudded too loudly to be certain he felt hers. Her eyes remained closed, and he groaned in despair at what his careless words had wrought.

She had come to him, lowered her pride, and let him see her vulnerability, and he had returned her favor by setting her aside. He had listened to his head and not his heart. He had always thought that the wisest way to live, but sometimes wisdom wasn't enough. The lifeless girl in his arms might not be wise, but she had a heart that might have welcomed him if he had let her. He might never know now. Moisture not entirely from the rain slid down Wyatt's cheeks, and his insides clenched into painful knots as he raised her in his arms.

He had to get her out of the rain. Their clothes were drenched and clinging, and the air was rapidly turning colder. Even if she still breathed, she would have pneumonia from this weather. Holding on to his horse's reins, Merrick carried his still burden down a shorter path. The playhouse should still be there. MacGregor kept an eye on all the outbuildings. He would have reported it if one were damaged.

The small square cottage appeared in the next flash of lightning. There was little protection for his horse here. Wyatt debated the merits of riding the miles back to the house or sending the horse home. If nothing else, the arrival of two riderless horses would signal something was wrong. The lifelessness of the woman in his arms made the decision for him. She would be safer here, out of the cold, than riding miles in a drenching rain.

Wyatt's mind grasped one logical step at a time. He dared not think further. Smacking his mount on the rump, he prayed the horse would have sense enough to find the stable on a night like this. Grooms would come looking for them soon enough.

He carried Cassandra inside and cursed the darkness. It had been a long time since he had set foot in this child's territory. A flash of lightning revealed the cot still in the corner, and he moved toward that.

There would be no tinder or flints for fire here. His mother's admonitions about playing with fire came back as clear as if they had been yesterday. At least it was dry and out of the wind. Merrick laid his burden down upon the bed and discovered the woolen blanket still folded at the bottom.

There would undoubtedly be moth holes and mildew in it, but it was better than nothing. His own teeth chattering against the chill of sodden clothes, Wyatt quietly set himself to his next task. Cassandra had to be made warm, and that was impossible in that soaking gown. Although it made finding the fastenings nigh on to impossible, this time he gave thanks for the darkness. Just touching the tender skin beneath the sodden clothing aroused him. Were he able to see what he touched, he wouldn't be responsible for his actions.

Cassandra groaned and stirred slightly as he drew her arms from the bodice. Wyatt caught his breath in hope, but there was no further sign of life. Determinedly he lifted her limp shoulders and pushed the bodice of gown and chemise down to her waist. The full curves of her breasts pressed against him as he balanced her against his chest in order to free his hands to strip her. It was better not to think of her passion the night before when he had touched her there. It was too easy to imagine it happening again.

With some degree of difficulty he managed to slide the sodden garments over her hips. For a moment Wyatt hesitated, wondering if this was the wisest thing to do, but once he'd set on a course, he refused to turn back. He must get her dry. He would have to stop thinking of the soft nest of curls his fingers encountered and the fact that he hadn't been with a woman in months, maybe longer.

Wyatt dried her with a soft cloth from the cabinet, then wrapped her in the blanket. Still, she didn't wake. How long would it be before anyone came for them? In this rain, probably hours.

He began to discard his own soaked clothing and wished again for a fire. The wetness chilled to the bone, but he could find no suitable garments or blankets in any of the tiny cabinets. This was a child's playhouse. It did not come adequately supplied with adult conveniences.

Stripped to his wet breeches, Wyatt stooped beside the bed to test Cassandra's brow for fever. He had little experience in nursing anyone or anything, but he remembered this gesture from childhood. She didn't feel warm. In fact, she felt icy.

He knew only one other way to make her warm, but the implications of such an action were resounding to an extreme. The proper thing to do would be to just sit and wait for rescue. It could be dawn before that happened.

To hell with proper. Standing, Wyatt peeled the rest of his wet clothing off. Cassandra would have hysterics if she woke and saw him like this, but he would prefer hysterics to this present state of lifelessness. Drying himself off with the damp cloth, Merrick crawled beneath the blanket with her.

He tried to concentrate on generating warmth. There was scarcely room for the two of them, and he turned Cassandra on her side, wrapping his arm around her waist to hold her close. She stirred slightly and snuggled closer into the curve of his body, leaving Merrick to wonder if she had not planned this all along. She fitted perfectly. He could move his arm neither up nor down without encountering female places meant for exploring.

If she were warming up as quickly as he, they could dry their clothes over the bed with the conflagration they made. The rain continued to pour on the tile roof, and Wyatt made himself more comfortable on the old pallet. It would be hours yet before anyone would come. He could feel Cassandra's breathing. Surely nothing could be seriously wrong if she breathed.

He drifted into a light sleep. The wet smell of moss and old leaves mingled with the faint fragrance of lilacs to soothe his slumbers.

Cassandra woke to the pounding of a drum, and she clenched her eyes closed against the pain until she could determine its source. Disoriented, she wondered if the leak on the roof of her bedroom had grown larger. The rain sounded so much closer and the air was damp and sticky. The feather mattress felt hard, and she stirred restlessly.

The pounding stopped with her breathing. Holding her breath, she tentatively tried moving again. She seemed to be quite naked. Worse, there seemed to be someone equally naked lying behind her.

Her first thought was: Rupert! But there was something too comforting and safe about the warm arm wrapped around her for it to belong to Rupert. She felt cozy and protected, and even though her head hurt dreadfully, she smiled and imagined Wyatt beside her. She didn't wish to wake from this dream just yet, and listening to the patter of the rain overhead, she slept again.

Somewhere in the dark before dawn, Cassandra woke again, and she knew something had changed. The pounding in her head had subsided to a dull roar, and she sought the difference with her senses. She must have turned over in her sleep. She could feel her companion's breath upon her face.

The arm around her waist tightened, and she knew the difference at once. He was awake. Raising her hand tentatively to the broad, lightly furred chest not inches from her nose, she whispered anxiously, "Wyatt?"

"Thank God," came the reply.

Then he stiffened and started to move away, but Cassandra couldn't bear to lose this dream so quickly. She ran her fingers exploringly through the soft curls of his chest, testing the unyielding surface beneath. "Don't go. It's cold."

She didn't know what she was doing, but he was virtually helpless to leave her side. Soon she would discover the extent of his arousal and run screaming in fear from the bed. He would deserve whatever happened then, but Wyatt could no more move from this exciting luxury than he could stop the rain. It was much simpler to lie here and feel the soft heat of Cassandra's body close to his and imagine what it would be like to be joined together.

Unaware of where these dangerous games led, Cas-

sandra moved closer. The brush of something hard
and heated against her thighs startled her, but she was
intent on seeking Wyatt's kisses. She would win him
somehow. Kissing was the only way she knew to start.

The sweetness of her lips eased some of the ache in
his loins, and Wyatt succumbed to them without a
fight. In his mind, he knew what he was doing was
wrong, but he had given up using anything so useless
as his mind last night. When it came to Cassandra,
logic no longer prevailed. He eased his tongue between her lips and felt the heady sway of desire begin
to throb through his blood.

It was much better this way, without the layers of
cloth to prevent touching. Excitement ran through her
fingertips as Cassandra responded to Wyatt's kiss and
ran her hands over his broad shoulders. She could feel
the ripple of muscle in his back as he shifted position,
and she felt no surprise at all when she lay half under
him, her lips parted to encourage his plundering.

Excitement ran all along her skin where he gently
touched her. She could never have dreamed such sensations, and she responded eagerly as his hands began
to wander. His kisses burned and tingled all at once,
and she felt a liquid fire slide through her center to the
very core of her being as his sensitive fingers stroked
the crest of one breast.

She was breathless when he lifted his head to stare
down at her, but in the darkness she could see nothing
of his expression. She heard the whisper of her name
mixed with anguish and what she very much hoped to
be desire, and she lifted her hand to pull him down to
her lips again.

It was like nothing she had ever known, and more
than she had ever hoped it would be. Wyatt's strength
cradled her against his shoulder, and his touch was
gentle and heated all at once. When he bent to suckle
at her breast, Cassandra felt herself moving a little
closer to ecstasy.

She wanted to give him the same, but she didn't

know how. She wrapped her hands in his hair and cried out her joy at his touch and tried to lift herself closer to the heavy weight lingering just out of reach. She felt the brush of his hardness once again, but it matched a growing emptiness inside her and felt right.

Cassandra's hands slid downward, exploring the firm muscles of Wyatt's shoulders and arms, traveling to his broad chest as his kisses moved to trail living fires across her breasts. He gently set her exploring fingers aside so he could trace his own across her body, and Cassandra eagerly submitted to this exploration. When he brushed lightly at the heat between her thighs, she instinctively closed her legs tighter, but his gentle insistence brought a new urgency to the liquid fire consuming her insides, and she parted her legs slightly to allow his hand entrance.

What followed then was the beginning of the end, although Cassandra had no way of knowing that. She knew she was somehow going too far, that they teetered on the edge of some beginning, but she could not stop him. His exploring fingers stirred a wild urgency in her, and she rose against him, again and again and again until she could no longer help herself. Wyatt murmured reassurances against her ear, but she was beyond hearing them. When he removed his hand, she cried in protest, but he was quick to find her breast and distract her as he shifted position again, nudging her legs a little wider.

She knew what he was doing the instant he entered her, but she was too far gone now to offer even the slightest denial. She drowned in the wine of his kiss and lifted her legs under his gentle touch and felt the piercing pressure that filled her. It happened too swiftly, and his sudden intake of breath as the pain shot through her had no more reality than the urgency in her blood demanding that she rise to meet him.

Once thoroughly sheathed in the tight heat between her thighs, Wyatt could no more stop his movement than he could have removed the earth from its axis. He

had had a virgin once before and knew full well what
he had done as the membrane sundered beneath his
thrust, but it was too late now. He could only hope that
he did not hurt her as he had his first wife. Cassandra
was too fresh and eager to destroy with his clumsiness.

Cassandra closed her eyes and gave herself up to the
sensations exploding through her. She felt Wyatt's
weight concentrated at the place where they were
joined, knew his body to be a part of hers, and gave
herself up to the rhythm of his thrusts. Over and over
again he filled her until she no longer knew whether
she floated or swam and her body was a mere extension of his.

And then his thrusts became fiercer, more intense,
and the liquid fire ignited and raged through her womb
and exploded in rapid bursts that ripped a cry of wonder
from her throat and a rumble of some deep pleasure
from Wyatt. She felt him bury himself deeper with a
groan, and then she was flooded with the wet warmth
of his seed, and he collapsed heavily against her.

Drained, they lay quietly together a few moments
longer, absorbing the newness of this joining. Cassandra felt a throbbing between her legs where he lay, but
she had no desire for it to go away. The wonder of
what they had done was too new, and she wanted to
know more.

Their mouths met in a long, sweet kiss, and Cassandra felt the stirring between her legs where he
rested. Restless excitement urged her to touch Wyatt's
body again, to stroke the strong build of his chest and
shoulders. His kiss became fiercer, and sweet triumph
filled her as she realized her ability to stir him. He did
need her. That thought opened her heart without reservation. Without giving any thoughts to the propri-
eties, Cassandra opened herself entirely to Wyatt's
needs, and accepted whatever came of it.

He took her more slowly this time, bringing her to
the edge of passion and delaying it and letting the desire build inside until she cried his name and rose

greedily to receive him. The ecstasy they achieved was more binding still. Unable to speak of it, they drifted slowly back to sleep afterward.

Wyatt was first to wake with the morning. The rain had stopped, but the overcast skies prevented the dawn from bringing more than a gray haze to the room. Cassandra lay curled in his arms, her brilliant hair providing the only curtain for her silken skin.

Deep inside Merrick, a knife twisted in his gut, but the inevitability of what he had done could not touch him while he held her trusting body close to his. This was the way it should have been with his first wife, this gentle giving and receiving, the passion, the closeness that should have led to happiness and, eventually, children. That was what he had wanted, longed for, and been denied.

He wasn't a cruel man, just a lonely one. He had thought a wife would end that loneliness, would give him the pleasant companionship he so desired. He hadn't expected and didn't need one of the Season's Incomparables. Their flirtatious conversation and coy attractions made him uneasy. He had thought he had chosen well when he had taken Alice to wife. She was young, but so was he. She had been small and quiet and pretty in a subdued way that did not draw a bevy of suitors. There had been little difficulty in wooing her. She had seemed pleased with his courtship, agreed with his conversation, and had accepted his proposal with shy smiles. He had been quite pleased at how easily the dreaded task of finding a wife had been accomplished.

And then they had married. That was when disaster had struck. He'd never had time to develop a sexual relationship with any woman, isolated as he had been in the country much of the time. There had been the occasional willing whore when he visited London. They had never commented on his prowess or lack of it. It had never occurred to him that there would be any complaint from a wife.

But Alice had not stopped complaining from the first night he had taken her to his bed. She had screamed and cried when he had taken her virginity, until he was forced to halt and wait for another night. She had lain like a statue the next time he went to her, visibly holding back her revulsion while he came into her. After he had spilled his seed, she had rolled away and cried into her pillow.

Determination to beget an heir, and a belief that she would soon feel more at ease with her wifely duties, had kept Wyatt returning to her bed for the first months of their marriage. Instead of becoming more relaxed and comfortable with each other, their infrequent encounters outside the bedroom became strained and tense. Inside the bedroom, the tension made it almost impossible to perform.

Eventually Alice had become pregnant, and he had retired with relief to his own chambers. When the miscarriage occurred not long after, he hadn't the heart to return to her bed to start all over. He kept telling himself he would wait until she was fully recovered and willing. That time never came.

Wyatt adjusted Cassandra's sleeping softness a little closer in his arms. Here was the comfort and the passion he had envisioned, all wrapped up in a tempestuous package of trouble he should be fleeing from in horror. She sighed softly and rubbed closer to his warmth when he cuddled her breast in his palm. Although his mind shrieked hysterical warnings, he couldn't let her go.

By the time Cassandra woke, Wyatt had smothered even the cries of warning in his head. He had dishonored her. He must face the consequences. Not that the consequences were unpleasant to face when they opened sleepy blue eyes and looked up at him with a slow smile that would cause a clock to stop.

"How do you feel?" he whispered with a little more uncertainty than he desired.

Dreamily Cassandra touched her finger to Wyatt's

beard-stubbled jaw, caressing the hard plane of his cheek down to the corners of his mouth, watching his lips quirk slightly upward with pleasure at her touch. "Magical," she whispered.

He wanted her again, but it was broad daylight and there was no excuse for lingering. He had to be the one to be strong until they could untangle this infernal mess. He could see right now that it would never occur to Cassandra that what they were doing was highly improper.

"You are undoubtedly a sorceress," he murmured against her ear, returning her caress with the gentlest of touches, just enough to be certain she was real. "But unless you can make the world go away, we will have to get dressed before we're found."

Cassandra made a moue of distaste. She had no desire to leave just yet. She wanted to know more of what they had done, and it would be easier in daylight. She could see the broad width of Wyatt's shoulders now, the shadow of hair splaying across his chest and narrowing as it trailed downward. He kept the blanket pulled around them so she couldn't see more, but she felt him. The tingling began again where he pressed against her. It didn't seem fair to have to stop just yet. Daringly she began to move her hand downward.

"Our clothes are still wet." Cassandra lifted her gaze to watch his expression as her fingers traced and explored the tight points of his nipples and continued downward. The curve of Wyatt's mouth softened, and desire burned more brightly behind his half-closed eyes. Just that look drove the tingling sensation into something much stronger, much deeper, a little more terrifying. Even though they were only touching, she could feel him deep inside her. Such possession made her uneasy, but she wasn't ready to call surrender.

"Good," he murmured, "I'll need the damp to cool me off, and so will you, it seems." Wyatt caught Cassandra's hand in a firm grip and raised it between them.

His eyes searched her face. "You are certain you are well? How is your head?"

"It aches. Can we not stay here until the ache goes away?"

Wyatt smiled at the ingenuous innocence of her wide-eyed gaze. "The ache won't go away this way, wanton. Close your eyes and I will get up first."

Her rebellious look warned she had no intention of obeying, but he knew it was only a matter of minutes before they were found. Heedless of her stare, Wyatt turned and swung from the bed. The chill air of morning struck his skin, but he needed the cold to dampen his ardor. He could still feel her against him as he picked up their damp clothing. He doubted that he could ever go without wanting her again.

Cassandra blatantly stared as Wyatt rose from their bed. The gray light concealed much, but her heart slammed against her ribs as she absorbed this first full look of male nudity. She had never thought about the differences between a man's and a woman's body, but she could see now that Wyatt was admirably suited to complement her. There was no softness in the hard lines of his muscled back and narrow buttocks, but she could give him softness. She could catch only a glimpse of the part of him that made him male, but she knew there, too, they were suited. She sensed her own emptiness when they had joined last night. They would fit together well.

She stretched tentatively, testing aching muscles and chafed skin. Desire still burned with a center between her legs, but she ached there too. When Wyatt turned to bring her her clothes, she caught another glimpse of his maleness, and wondered that she had been able to accommodate him at all. It did not seem quite possible, but she was willing to try again. She did not rise to take the clothes, but threw back the covers in a welcoming gesture.

Wyatt could not keep his gaze upon her face. He didn't know if she was conscious of what she was doing to him, but he indulged himself in a brief inspection of what she offered. He had known her breasts were full and high, but he had not known how perfectly they curved down to her slender ribs. The narrow valley of her waist beckoned a man's grasp, and the wide flare of her hips with the downy nest between made his throat dry with need. Long, slender legs stretched out to perfectly shaped toes, and he wondered at once what it would be like to have those slim thighs wrapped around him as he thrust into her. Just the thought made him harder and brought a burning ache to his loins.

"Get dressed," he muttered thickly, dropping the clammy gown over the slight concavity of her stomach.

Cassandra jerked at the sudden coldness against her skin. She had grown warm under his thorough observation, but the cold cloth he forced on her was an insult to her well-being. She leapt from the bed to confront him, and came up against the full extent of their differences. Wyatt towered a head taller and considerably wider, and there was that strong lance of maleness between them. Thrown off guard by her own brashness, she didn't know how to react, but there was no retreat. The bed pressed against the back of her knees.

Wyatt's hand came out to steady her, and the contact of heated flesh against flesh melded them with a sudden shock of electricity. Cassandra found herself balancing against him by wrapping her arms around his shoulders, and when he lifted her for a kiss, she could feel him sliding between her thighs. She parted her lips to receive his tongue just as she parted her legs to receive the rest of him. It seemed a perfectly natural extension of the longing she harbored deep inside. Only Wyatt had come this close to touching her. Only Wyatt would possess her.

He caught her hips firmly in his hands and guided her to him. Cassandra flinched slightly as she felt him pressing at the vulnerable entrance to her body, and realized more fully than last night what this meant.

But when he pushed a little harder, she opened to him, sliding her legs upward until he held her fully in control and could plunge as deeply as he desired.

Wyatt stared down at Cassandra's abandoned beauty with amazement. A flush of desire tinged her breasts and accented the rosy hues of the hardened tips. Her face was blurred with passion, and her lips curved in a sultry smile of pure delight as he moved inside her. No man could resist such wild innocence, least of all him. He had never known a woman's desire, never imagined desire could be like this. She had abandoned herself entirely to his care. He would oblige her gratefully.

He wished desperately for the high bed of his home so he could keep her like this, pressed against the side of the mattress while he buried himself over and over again into this welcoming haven. But the child's bed they had shared was too low to maintain this position, and he would not take her against the hardness of the table. Gently he lowered her back against the mattress and knelt over her.

If nothing else, she had learned the advantage of lifting her legs around him. Cassandra gave a deep primeval cry as Wyatt sank hard and strong into her and repeated the thrust until she felt him deep against her womb. The sensation made her wild with need, and she lifted her hips to meet him again and again, until all thought of tenderness and care disappeared under an onslaught of hungry desperation.

In minutes, they must part. The real world would intrude. But for now they were together. When Cassandra could no longer fight her release, she surrendered to him in wanton abandonment, feeling his seed hot and deep inside as he came into her.

It would never be like this again, she knew, but just once, she wanted to know perfection.

She sighed in pleasure and despair when the knock came at the door.

Chapter 17

Cursing softly, Wyatt kissed Cassandra's cheek and climbed from the bed. He pulled the cover snugly around her, not giving himself time to admire the soft flush of pink of her silken skin. Drawing on his disgustingly clammy breeches, he strode to the door.

To his surprise, Cassandra's cadaverous butler waited outside, his expression one of stoic virtue as he met the earl's eyes. There was a dark knowing behind his gaze before it dropped to a respectful position somewhere about Wyatt's naked chest, but his tone remained neutral as he spoke.

"My lady did not return home last night. Has there been some accident?"

"Yes, but she is quite well. I think it would be best if you have her maid pack her clothes and send them over to the house."

Cassandra sat up with a start at these words, but having nothing other than a blanket to cover her, she could not raise a violent protest. The sounds of dogs in the distance brought a sudden realization of their predicament, and she leapt for her clothes as soon as Wyatt closed the door.

"You do not lie fast enough, my lord," she scolded as she struggled into her damp chemise. "Now Jacob knows we spent the night together. He will keep quiet, I believe, except for telling Lotta, but you had best let me talk to the next one who appears. Go back to the house, indeed. I can just imagine what your mother would have to say about that."

Wyatt reluctantly held himself aloof as she jerked on her cotton gown. He hated to see the coarse material touch her lovely skin, but he, too, heard the dogs and knew they would soon be discovered. There wasn't time to send for decent clothes. There wasn't time for explanations either, but he knew damned well he had no intention of letting her go back to that hovel again.

"My mother has no say in the matter. The house is mine and will soon be yours. She will have to make her own choices whether to stay or not." He reached for his shirt and carefully began to tug the clinging material over his arms.

At his words, Cassandra stopped to stare. Wyatt seemed perfectly sane standing there with his shirt half on and half off, his dark hair falling in careless locks across his forehead as he struggled with the unmanageable material. He was magnificently made, and she had to stop and gather her wandering thoughts by transferring her gaze back to her own clothing.

"I cannot believe this is St. Wyatt speaking. You cannot set me up as your mistress under your mother's nose. If you have no respect for her, have some for me."

Wyatt grimaced at the hated appellation but he held firmly to his resolve. "If you require a chaperone, I will send for your mother. It may take time to locate Rupert and obtain an annulment, and I have no intention of letting my future wife live in a derelict castle."

Cassandra's head jerked upward at his calm reproof. "Wife? Have you taken leave of your senses? It is impossible. Rupert will never agree. We will never suit. You are all about in your head to even consider it."

Wyatt forced the last of his buttons closed and began tucking his shirttails into his breeches while he held her gaze. "Rupert will have to agree. Last night I took your virginity. The evidence is right there on that bed. Your marriage was never consummated, therefore it is not valid. There is only one honorable course for us. We will be married as soon as it is legally feasible."

Panic held her in thrall. Cassandra stared at the man she had given herself to and watched the authority of the honorable earl emerge. She could never marry the Earl of Merrick. He would find out she wasn't the daughter of a marquess but the bastard of some commoner. Duncan would blackmail him dry. The dowager would have apoplexy. All of society would be scandalized and he would be cast out by his peers. And she could never act the part of proper countess no matter how hard she tried. He was mad even to consider it. Or as desperate as she had been when she had tried to trick him into it. That thought firmed her resolve.

"Don't be ridiculous. I'll not marry you, Wyatt. I'll be your mistress if you like, but I'll not spoil both our reputations by doing it so blatantly as to move in with you. Now, if you will step aside, I shall go home before your men discover us."

The dogs were getting closer. He had to leave and head them off. Wyatt stared at Cassandra's rebellious expression and felt anger begin to build. "You will wait here until I can send my men away. I don't care if the whole damned world knows we spent the night together, but I'll not have them looking at you with scorn. When I come back, we can discuss the best manner of breaking the news to everyone." Reading Cassandra's expression quite clearly, he added softly but warningly, "We will be married, Cass. There is no longer any question about it. Wait here."

Wyatt strode out with a pervasive sense of foreboding. He knew better than to leave her alone. He ought to carry her wet and half-naked through the park and fling her on his bed and proclaim loudly to the world that she was his. But a lifetime of propriety was hard to break. He had to protect her from as much scandal as possible. If she ran, he would run after her. In time, she would learn.

Cassandra darted out the door as soon as Wyatt disappeared into the trees. The thin edge of panic urged her on. It wasn't in her nature to consider consequences, but she would never have imagined this even if she had stopped to think. Why couldn't Wyatt be like her father and brother and take his women as he found them? Did he propose to every woman he bedded?

He hadn't even proposed. He had ordered. That would never do. She couldn't spend a lifetime with a man who ordered her about. She had just discovered freedom. She wasn't prepared to give it up just for the pleasure he gave her in bed.

She wouldn't think of that pleasure. To do so weakened her will to mindless jelly. She had to remain strong and reason this out. In time, Wyatt would begin to see reason. It was just his damnable sense of honor standing in the way. Perhaps when he realized she was not the same honorable person as he, he would see the sense of settling for a mistress. She was not prepared to let him go entirely. The thought did not even bear considering.

Merrick felt little surprise when he returned to the cottage to find her gone. She had already rejected his offer once. He had hoped these last days had brought them closer and that last night had sealed the bonds, but he should have known better.

Gathering up the soiled sheet with the evidence of their coupling, Wyatt felt the strength of his resolve. In that way, at least, she did not find him objectionable. She had been too innocent to feign passion. There were worse things on which to build a marriage. He was a living example of that.

Returning home only to change clothes and saddle a horse, Wyatt evaded his mother's hysterical questions and set out for the Eddings estate. There had to be some way to make Cassandra see reason.

He was met at the door by the lanky butler. The man gave no indication of their earlier meeting but merely informed him that Lady Cassandra was not at home. Wyatt clenched his teeth and refused to budge.

"I must speak with her. Jacob, isn't it? If she's not at home, then I must speak with you and the lady's maid. The business of living in this dangerous pile of rocks has to come to an end."

That received a flicker of attention from the man's impassive expression.

"The only chairs are in the kitchen, m'lord. It does not seem proper. I will tell her ladyship that you have been here."

"I've sat in kitchens before. This concerns you as well as Lady Cassandra. Let me in, Jacob, I'm not leaving until I know I have your cooperation."

Jacob hesitated; then, throwing a glance over his shoulder to Lotta waiting in the shadows, he stepped aside to allow the earl to enter.

Merrick glanced around in hopes of finding some sign of Cass, but he could sense the room's emptiness. She wasn't here. She had known this would be the first place he would look. Disappointed, he followed the servant into the burnt-out remains of the kitchen.

His glance took in everything, from the cracked bowls piled beside the caldron of water to the tense expressions on the servants' faces. The maid was a bounteous lass with a golden face and a defiant expression. Wyatt couldn't blame the butler for hovering protectively near her. Both must harbor some loyalty to Cass or they wouldn't be here. He came immediately to the point.

"One way or another, I intend to marry Lady Cassandra. Until I can, I want to know that she is safe. That means getting her out of this piece of hell. I am willing to set her up anywhere that she might be comfortable, so long as it is safe. I am asking your cooperation in helping with this, assuming you have her ladyship's best interests in mind as well as your own. I am willing to take you into my employ starting today if you are in agreement with me."

Neither servant hesitated. Smiles replaced reservation as they gave their agreement to the tall earl trans-

forming the kitchen with his authoritative grace. A
trace of relief tinged their voices with their solemn
vows. Merrick kept his smile to himself as he turned
to walk out. Stronger men than Cass had been brought
to their knees by nagging servants. Her loyal army had
just decamped to the other side.

"Don't be ridiculous, Lotta. The room is no more
damp than it has been, and I shall not die of con-
sumption for it. Leave off your complaining. You and
Jacob have been the souls of misery for days now.
What has got into you?" Cassandra jerked on her best
morning gown and began to fasten the bodice without
her maid's help.

"You've been looking sickly lately, and we worry.
You shouldn't have spent the night in the rain. You
ought to see a doctor. You could be ailing for something."

She felt worse than sickly. She felt humiliated,
frightened, anxious, and worse: she wanted Wyatt
again. She had avoided him at every turn while wishing desperately to fall into his arms again. If only she
knew how to make him see reason, but the one thing
that would certainly convince him of the wrongness of
marriage was not her secret to give. She couldn't hu-
miliate her mother by revealing to Wyatt the indiscre-
tion that had led to her birth.

"There's nothing wrong with me, Lotta. I don't
need a physician. This room is fine. I don't intend to
look for another house. We haven't the money. Now,
I want to hear no more about it. If you wish to leave,
I will be happy to provide you with references."

Cassandra dreaded the day when Lotta and Jacob
would take her up on that offer. She didn't know if she
could stand the loneliness of this life with no one to
talk to but herself. Lotta and Jacob weren't just servants, they were the only friends she had. But she
couldn't let them see that. She had chosen this life,

not they. The time would have to come when they
would want to leave.

"You can't go on living like this, no more than we
can," Lotta protested. "It just ain't right. You'll have
to take up gambling soon just to keep this place in
rags and boards to keep out the wind. You'd best be
thinking about it."

Cassandra got the same sermon from Jacob when
she went in to breakfast. He came at it from the per-
spective of Lotta, who had been feeling poorly lately.
And his own joints were feeling the damp. They would
need fires to ward off illness, and where would the
money come from for coal or kindling?

Cassandra was tempted to reply that they could chop
down Merrick's prized forest, but they were quite apt
to do that without her encouragement. And the first
blaze they set in the ruined fireplaces would burn down
what remained of the house. Just the small fire they
kept in the kitchen filled the house with smoke. It did
look hopeless, but she wouldn't give in.

Now that she was feeling a little stronger should she
come face-to-face with Merrick, she felt safe in visiting the village again. The hens they had bought were
producing a few extra eggs that might be traded for a
small pat of butter. Perhaps she would see Bertie and
he could take her to visit Thomas. He should be sitting
up in a chair by now, and she had promised to teach
him a few card tricks.

Her patience was to be rewarded this day. She found
Bertie so easily it was almost as if he had been waiting
for her. Expressing delight, he agreed to accompany
her on her errands if she would accompany him on
his. In the meantime, he would send a boy with a
message to warn Thomas of their arrival.

Cassandra realized later that she should have been
suspicious, but it was the first sunny day in forever,
and she was feeling better, more confident. It didn't
matter what the world threw in her way, she could
overcome it. She smiled graciously into Bertie's eager

round face and took his arm. She might be a fallen
woman, but the world didn't know it yet. The fact that
she could still feel Merrick's possession, knew now
what a man could do to a woman's body, did not seem
to be revealed on her face for all to see. She would
survive.

Bertie dawdled over his decision at the leather shop,
and then he expressed a deep desire for tea before setting out of town. Cassandra blindly accompanied him
to the tea shop and thoroughly enjoyed the fresh scones
and jam. She had never thought much about the food
put upon the table as long as it settled the pangs of
hunger, but a steady diet of Lotta's meager cooking
had left a definite desire for something more. The
scones left her well satisfied.

When they stepped out into the street again, it was
to meet Wyatt just climbing down from his curricle in
front of the shop. Bertie had seated her so she could
not see out the window, and she threw his happy face
a suspicious look as he greeted his friend, but she
could not pin the blame entirely on him. He could not
possibly know how much she wished to avoid the earl.

Merrick greeted Cassandra with a deep bow, then
caught her hand and held it firmly against his arm as
he turned to Bertie. "Well met, old boy. I was just on
the way to fetch Lady Cass. On her brother's instructions, I have been scouting the perfect residence for
her, and I have finally found one I think will suit. I
am most eager to show off my discovery. Shall you
accompany us?"

That malicious lie was quite the outside of enough,
but when Cassandra opened her mouth to object, Bertie interrupted.

"I've told the family I'll be directly home. Bring
Cass by when you're done inspecting the property and
we'll have a rousing time discussing whether or not
she should settle for your choice." He bowed politely
to Cassandra. "It will be good to know you'll be a
permanent neighbor."

What could she say? That Merrick meant to make her his mistress and she needed rescuing? That idea was absurd. She wanted to be Merrick's mistress. Sort of. She just didn't want to be ordered around. And she didn't want to put Merrick in the position of protecting her. The thought sent chills up her spine, but involving Bertie would only compound the problem.

Silently she nodded agreement, waved farewell, and allowed Merrick to assist her into the curricle. She held her tongue until they were on the road out of town.

"That was not very noble of you, my lord." Cassandra crossed her arms and glared at the dancing larkspur along the roadway.

"It's the perfect solution. Wait until you see it," Wyatt answered calmly, trying not to look too closely at the delicately pert features set stubbornly on the woman beside him. Wisps of red-gold hair escaped her bonnet and sparkled in the sun like gleaming copper. He wanted to catch them in his hand, but he concentrated on the argument to come.

"I will not allow you to set me up like some light-skirt, Wyatt. I have my own home, and I'm doing quite nicely without your help."

"You are living in a leaky cave and courting pneumonia. I expect nothing of you. You know better than that. All I want to do is keep you safe until I can make arrangements with Rupert."

Cassandra's jaw set even harder. "You must stop talking like that at once or put me out right here. I'll not trade one husband for another as a man does horses. What is between Rupert and myself is none of your affair."

"I'll not argue that now. First, we must get you into a decent house. I don't think you'll disagree with my choice." Wyatt steered the curricle down an overgrown lane. "There hasn't been much time to make improvements. I'll have men to clear this lot now that the rain has broken."

Cassandra couldn't hide her curiosity as she gazed up at the overhanging elms and around to the riot of rhododendrons lining the drive. The direction seemed vaguely familiar, but it had been a long time since she lived here, and she had not yet reacquainted herself with all the area. They seemed to be fairly close to her home, but they had come at it from a different direction.

The trees opened onto a small clearing. A climbing rose sent sparkles of red up the side of the stone cottage set in the center of the clearing. The thatched roof had been newly mended, and Cassandra drank deeply of the scent of fresh-cut grass. The diamond-paned windows gleamed with recent scrubbing, and she knew Wyatt was responsible. She had no doubt that the inside would be as fresh and scrubbed as the outside, and her fingernails clenched into her palms as she tried to keep herself from feeling the longing for just such a home.

It was little use. She scrambled down from the curricle with Wyatt's assistance and practically ran beside his eager stride as he led her toward the door.

"Your land runs just the other side of the hedgerows. I'll have a stile built so you can supervise your planting. The cottage isn't large, but it's snugly built. The bailiff before MacGregor had a family and used to live here. It's been empty for some time and suffers from neglect. You will be doing me a favor to look after it."

"Wyatt, I can't," she protested as he threw open the door, but she stepped inside anyway. Her heart raced as she felt his hand grasping her elbow as they crossed the threshold together. This was the way a husband should introduce his bride to his home, with pride and excitement. But this wasn't Wyatt's home. It was one of his many properties. She had to remember that.

She couldn't seem to cling to that harsh thought. The wide whitewashed hall looked onto two sun-filled

front rooms with low beamed ceilings. Wyatt proudly
pointed out the hand-carved built-in cupboards, and
Cassandra ran to inspect them. The rooms were so
clean and dry and full of light, she couldn't suppress
her delight. A home like this was all she asked. She
didn't need mansions. She just wanted to be warm and
dry and left at peace.

She raced on light feet to the kitchen and servants'
rooms in the rear, then danced up the narrow center
stair to the low-ceilinged rooms above. Again, latticed
windows thrown open to the air filled the rooms with
light, and Cassandra crowed with delight at the view
over her bramble-strewn pastures.

Merrick watched her with patience and growing excitement as she flitted from window to window. For
one brief moment he saw her as a caged bird, but he
shook the image away. This was only temporary. Soon
she would have full rein over his entire holdings. She
was much better off here than in that hovel down the
road.

He saved the largest upstairs room for last. Cassandra had thrown off her bonnet, and her hair glinted in
the sunlight as she stepped into the spacious room
equipped with fireplace and a crochet-draped tester
bed. No curtains yet hung on the windows; there hadn't
been time for that. But this was the room he meant to
be hers.

Her light muslin gown clung to her slender figure as
she swung around to face him with a smile of happiness upon her lips. "It's truly lovely, Wyatt. Do you
really think you might persuade Duncan to pay the rent
on it? Just for the summer. After harvest, I should be
able to pay it myself."

Merrick knew full well that Duncan would part with
none of his coins for a sister who had thrown away
their chance for riches. He was not accustomed to lying, but the truth would only send her flying back to
her ramshackle cavern. The truth was, he had never
even notified Duncan of her whereabouts and had no

intention of doing so until their marriage was a fact. He stepped closer to brush a wisp of hair from her cheek.

"Of course. The rent is very reasonable since you will be looking after the property for me. You will stay, then?"

Wyatt's gentle caress meant more than his words. Cassandra saw the emotion in his eyes, and felt the warmth welling up in her heart as his hand lightly rested on her shoulder. She ought to be angry with him, but she could not remember why. Instead, she lifted her hands to his shoulders and rose on her toes to kiss his lips.

She was unprepared for the blaze of hunger leaping between them. This sudden fire in her belly always caught her by surprise, but now she knew where it led and what to expect. Instead of resisting, she leaned more fully into Wyatt's embrace. This was what she wanted: a lover, a home, and freedom. She had not known it before, but it seemed so natural now.

Wyatt crushed her against him, and Cassandra parted her lips in complete surrender to his demands. She could feel the tension in him, the resistance to the desire flaring between them, and she kneaded her hands over the taut muscles of his neck. The tension slowly drained out of him, and his kiss became ravenous, demanding more as he succumbed to the pleasures she offered.

It was as if they had been apart years and not days. Cassandra wasn't certain how they came to be upon the bed, but she arched eagerly to Wyatt's caress as his hand cupped and lifted her breast and his mouth continued to plunder hers. It was a reckless madness that he had taught her, but it was a madness that gave her more pleasure than she had ever known in her life. She could not stop even if she wanted to.

The breeze from the window blew across her skin as Wyatt undressed her, but it didn't cool the heat that made every inch of her sensitive to his touch. Cassandra gazed up into his dark eyes and felt something in her middle clench and grow tighter as his gaze bored into hers. She knew what he was going to do to her now; she was no longer innocent of a man's touch, and the knowledge became a powerful aphrodisiac.

Wyatt's shirt fell open beneath her nimble fingers, and she explored the rough texture of his hair there, comparing it to the glossy thickness about his head and neck. He breathed her name as he divested her of gown and chemise, and little flames ignited along her skin where his breath touched.

It was a magical fantasy world where he took her, one where the toplofty Earl of Merrick and the Countess of Eddings' bastard daughter didn't exist. They were just man and woman, Adam and Eve, discovering the delights of forbidden fruit. Cassandra cried a little and shivered as Wyatt's hand explored and possessed the aching junction between her legs.

When he finally eased into her, she gave a cry of relief and pulled him down to take her kiss. Their tongues met in the same union as their bodies, and she shuddered as she felt Wyatt's quickening heat. It was happening again, but she was no more prepared for it now than she had been the first time.

The bed creaked as they gave of themselves, tasting, touching, abandoning their restraints to find a plane where they could both exist in joyous union. For a few short moments they found it, claiming and being claimed, acknowledging the power and possession, before slowly slipping back to the more natural boundaries of existence.

A bird chirped and sang outside the window, and Cassandra slowly turned her head to watch the branches of the tree for the singer. Wyatt's kiss whispered along her cheek and throat, and she closed her eyes to better absorb the sensation of his heavy weight pressing her down into the mattress. She wasn't quite so sore this time, but she was still sensitive to that part of him inside her. It didn't seem quite possible yet.

Wyatt, Earl of Merrick, her staid and proper lover. She smiled softly to herself.

Wyatt watched the slow curve of her lips jealously, wishing he had the right to know her thoughts. He kissed her cheek where the thick fringe of lashes lay, and idly brought his hand between them to play at the still-swollen tip of her breast. "Tell me what you're dreaming," he whispered against her ear.

"Of this. Of holding you. Of having you near and hearing you speak. Will you come to me often if I agree to stay here?" The words came out in a hushed rush. She always spoke too hastily, without thought, but she needed to know. She wanted him here every night, and in wanting, knew it was impossible.

Wyatt kissed her cheek and rolled on his side, pulling her with him. The breeze from the window felt good against his heated flesh, but he could see little bumps rising on hers. He rubbed her arms thoughtfully as he stared into her flushed face.

"I would be with you every night and every day if I could, Cass, you know that. It will take time, but that day will come. I promise."

Bitterness welled up inside her and Cassandra turned from his honest gaze. "It can never come. You will never understand, so please just accept it. I will be happy just to know you are close by. Perhaps I could still come once in a while to sing with you."

Wyatt caught her chin and forced her to face him. "I won't be happy knowing you are here alone and I can't come to you. Be reasonable, Cass. We must marry. Let me deal with Rupert."

The anguish marring her perfect features was so deep and so unalterable that Wyatt felt his heart shrivel and die even before she spoke.

"I'll not agree to an annulment, Wyatt. If that is the cost of staying here, I will not come. If you go against my wishes, I shall leave here and never come back."

She meant it. He knew better than to underestimate

the power of Cassandra's will. Her words hurt like all the brands of hell, but he refused to let her see the damage.

"You are willing to settle for being my mistress?" he demanded harshly, still holding her face between his fingers.

"For me, it is not settling," she whispered, tears in her eyes. "It is a great leap upward to my heart's desire. Please, Wyatt. I need you to be my friend and to hold me. Just that. Can that not be enough for you?"

His whole body grew taut with the need to reject that proposition. He didn't need a friend. He needed a wife. And despite all the differences between them, all the reasons that made them unsuitable for each other, he needed this woman to be his wife.

But if he couldn't have what he wanted, he would take what he could get. He didn't think he could drive the need for Cassandra out of his soul anytime soon, if ever.

Knowing that she asked the impossible, knowing the world would come crumbling down upon their heads soon enough, Wyatt bent to take her kiss. "Friend and lover," he corrected her.

Chapter 18

Wyatt paced the library floor like a caged animal, stopping to stare at the shelves in search of a book that didn't exist, roaming between the tables and leather wing chairs as if they were trees in a jungle where he didn't belong. He halted at the far end of the room overlooking the park, pulling back the heavy draperies to stare into a darkness that gave him no glimpse of the lights he sought.

He dropped the draperies and cursed and forced himself to face a shelf of philosophy. He needed a good sound philosophy right now to persuade him what he was doing was right. He knew by society's code he was doing the honorable thing, but that wasn't enough to keep him from feeling enormously wretched. He didn't think Socrates had anything that would apply to his situation, but if he were lucky, the Greek would put him to sleep. He felt as if he hadn't slept in years.

It had been only a week. One week. Wyatt stared at the shelf, his search for the Greek philosopher forgotten. Except for the briefest and politest of social calls in the company of others, he had not seen Cassandra since she had moved into the cottage. She had seemed so happy and content feathering the nest he had provided for her that he couldn't think of sullying her happiness by forcing her into a relationship that could only be disastrous for both of them.

That wasn't quite right. He could think of it. He thought of it all the time, night and day without cease. But he couldn't bring himself to do it. It was wrong.

All his moral precepts told him it was wrong. She was young, innocent, and had no understanding of the complexities of the relationship they had been contemplating. In the end, she would hate him for it. He couldn't allow that to happen. Cass needed all the friends she could get.

But he couldn't stop thinking of her as she lay naked beneath him on that sun-blessed bed, her hair spilling in wild abandon across the sheets, her skin flushed with ecstasy, her eyes speaking her desire and happiness. Had she despised him, he could stay away. Had she been cold and unfeeling, or even experienced and cynical, he could have stayed away without this battle. But she wanted him as much as he did her, she needed him, and that drew him more powerfully than any magic potion mankind could distill. It was an aphrodisiac and a love spell all stirred into one tempestuous package, and Wyatt had no defense against it.

So instead of himself, he had sent presents. Any little thing that caught his eye that he knew would please her, he had sent by way of messenger to her door. He tried to imagine her reaction when she opened the box with the crystal vase that captured the sunlight and filled the air with color. He liked to think of her sipping from the china teacups he had found stored in some ancient cabinet of the kitchen. They were fine Chinese porcelain, but the set wasn't complete and was never used anymore. He had known Cassandra would love them as they ought to be. He wanted to send her music, but even if he could smuggle a pianoforte into the cottage, she wouldn't be able to play it. So he had searched the attics until he had found a wooden music box he remembered from his childhood. He hoped she would understand when these tokens reached her door without a message.

But the gifts didn't appease Wyatt's restlessness. He needed to talk with her, to hear her voice, watch her smile, touch her hand. She soothed something inside of him that he hadn't realized existed until she came

along. Her laughter had awakened him and her song
had stirred his soul just as her caresses had eased his
longing. She was the part that had been missing from
his life all these years, and he never would have known
it had she not dashed into his arms that fateful night.
It was cruel to find what he sought after all these years,
only to be separated by fate.

Wyatt stiffened at the sound of footsteps in the hall
outside the door. He schooled his expression to boredom as he pulled down a volume and opened it to a
page he didn't see when the door opened. The anguish
in his soul was his own private torment, not there for
anyone else to peruse. To his household, he was the
quiet, authoritative earl, unchanged by the events of
these last weeks.

The butler came in with a card on a salver, hesitating to disturb the man so absorbed in his reading that
he did not look up at his entrance. Lord Merrick was
a busy man, seldom taking time for his own pleasures.
The butler wasn't at all certain whether this intrusion
was a welcome one or not, but the earl had seemed so
preoccupied of late that the servant thought he might
appreciate this particular visitor. He stood silently until the distinguished gentleman turned to acknowledge
him with a stiff nod, then presented the card.

A muscle twitched in the earl's cheek as he read
the small white piece of pasteboard. Without a word to
the butler, Wyatt turned on his heel and strode out. The
servant stared after him with curiosity. Had there been
a slight straightening of the earl's tall frame as he
reached the hall? Had that been just a hint of eagerness
in his stride? And surely he hadn't seen his lordship
lift a hand to his neatly cropped hair to brush it into
place?

Ignoring the man's curiosity, Wyatt took the stairs
at a pace greater than was customary. He was making
a fool of himself, but he didn't care. At the bottom of
the eternal length of mahogany stairway stood a tall,
slender figure garbed in a gold pelisse of silk that he

remembered ordering just last week. She wore no hat, and the light caught in strands of red and gold more brilliant than the expensive fabric. Her eyes turned up to him as he approached, and seemed to shimmer briefly as their gazes met.

And then he was beside her, taking her hand, guiding her toward the one room that they could regard as theirs alone, and his soul soared. He read the questions in her eyes, but he couldn't answer them here, not with words. He helped her discard the pelisse, seated her at the piano bench, and took his place beside her. The music could speak his thoughts more clearly than he could, and he let his fingers roam over the keys until they found the right notes.

Cassandra watched, her slender frame seemingly unbreathing as the music poured around them. The scent of lilacs lingered on the evening breeze from the open windows, where no lilacs bloomed. Her shoulder brushed his as she reached for the sheets of music that bore no resemblance to the song he was playing. Her hands trembled on the paper, and when he switched the song to one she knew, her voice quivered slightly as she sang the words.

She had come to him. There would be no holding him back now.

Wyatt waited outside the cottage in the darkness beyond the square gleam of golden light from the window overhead. Cass had not yet installed draperies, and he could see her slender shadow moving across the room. She had dismissed her maid and was undressing herself, softly singing a tune they had shared earlier.

He had done his best to stay away. He knew his mother was suspicious of his decision to rent the cottage to Cassandra. The neighbors running in and out all week helping her set up housekeeping had eased those suspicions to a degree. His presence would have

been conspicuous. He had given Cass a chance to feel
as if she had some choice in the matter.

But when she had turned up on his doorstep this
evening, he had known he could not stay away. There
had been no accusation in her eyes, only questions.
He hadn't needed any more invitation than that.

So he stood here now like some lovesick fool, staring up at her window, wondering how he could enter
his own house and take her to his bed without com-
promising both of them. Her two servants weren't
fools. They knew what he wanted. Why should he care
what they thought of him?

The back door opened and slammed behind two incongruous shadows, one tall and lanky, the other short
and plump. Wyatt could hear soft giggles as they
strolled arm in arm through the moonlight. There was
no mistaking the pair, and Wyatt smiled grimly to
himself. He didn't know whether to reward them or
sack them for their desertion, but he wasn't going to
waste the opportunity.

As soon as the disparate pair disappeared into the
shrubbery, Wyatt strode for the door.

Cassandra looked up in surprise when the bedroom
door opened, but her lips curved into a joyous smile
at sight of the tall man outlined in the doorway. Garbed
only in a thin nightrail that revealed every curve of her
body in the lamplight, she lifted her arms in welcome.

Merrick hesitated, aware, as she was not, that they
set a pattern for the nights to come in what they did
now. She came to him as a wife would, or should, he
amended to himself, without guilt or self-consciousness,
with only joy at his presence. He would not allow her
to feel ashamed for what they felt.

In a few strides he was across the room and taking
her in his arms. Never would he let her feel anything
but joy for what they did now. This, he vowed, even
as he carried her to the bed that would make them
adulterers before all the world.

* * *

Cassandra awakened to the sun streaming through the open casement. Summer was finally in the air, and the gentle breeze made her warm and languorous as she stretched joyfully, reveling in her nakedness against the sheets.

Her foot brushed the long, muscular limb of the man beside her, and she turned to smile at the sleep-tousled face on the next pillow. Wyatt's usually neatly arranged hair lay all rumpled in barbarous imitation of London's dandies. She ran her fingers through the thick chestnut locks and watched his eyes open suspiciously.

"I'm glad you stayed," she whispered as she bent to press a kiss along his beard-stubbled cheek.

A hard arm circled her waist and pulled her closer. He hadn't meant to stay. There would be no disguising their relationship for very long if he never slept in his own bed, but the world could be damned for all he cared this morning. Wyatt covered her mouth with his kiss and soothed her halfhearted struggles with his hand.

A half-hour later they were both more tousled than before, but any tension between them had disappeared. Cassandra lay against Wyatt's shoulder, her eyes closed dreamily as his long fingers idly caressed her breasts.

The knock on the bedroom door startled them back to the moment. Cassandra threw him a panicky look, but Wyatt merely pulled the sheet up over her nakedness and ordered the maid to enter.

Lotta failed to conceal her smirk as she came in with a tray of tea and toast and silently laid it on the bedside table.

"Have you any coffee, Lotta? I prefer coffee in the mornings." Wyatt calmly sat back against the pillows and awaited her reply.

"I'll buy some in the village this morning, my lord." Lotta bobbed a beaming curtsy and departed, softly closing the door behind her.

Cassandra turned her flaming cheeks in Wyatt's direction. She was thoroughly embarrassed, but his high-handed manner of ordering her servants around gave other outlets for her emotion. "That was uncalled for, my lord," she remonstrated. "Lotta has no idea how to brew coffee, we have no pot to brew it in, and we cannot afford the extravagance. And if you offer to pay for it, I shall kick you from this bed."

Wyatt watched her with amusement, waited until she was done, then pressed a kiss to the swell of her breast above the sheet before swinging his legs out from beneath the covers and reaching for his discarded shirt.

"You may as well grow accustomed to it, my love. If we are going to shed all propriety and meet the world as lovers, then we may as well take advantage of the comforts of such a situation. I will provide the funds for what I need to be made to feel at home. I do not expect you to shoulder the burden."

Cassandra heard his calm words with suspicion, but she was distracted by the sight of his bold masculine nakedness in her heretofore feminine room. Even in undress, he was very much the earl when he spoke like that. Her mind tried to grasp the consequences of his words, but her eyes traced the dark band of hair disappearing beneath his shirt as he tied it.

"You are going to tell the world that we are lovers?" she asked a trifle breathlessly.

"I don't need to." Wyatt reached for his discarded trousers. "My servants will have already discovered that I did not sleep in my bed. They will begin whispering among themselves. Someone will mention that your servants were seen buying coffee in the village. The dressmaker will remember the gown I ordered for you. The whispers will get a little noisier. It will not take long before the whole town knows of it, no matter how discreet we may try to be."

As usual, Cassandra hadn't thought of that. She was so used to keeping her own company that she had managed to shut out the gossip around her. She knew it was there. She was too often the target to be unaware of malicious tongues, but she had never considered the source. Her eyes widened with dismay as he turned to gaze on her with curiosity when she said nothing.

Wyatt wanted to take the wounded look from her eyes, but he had to be ruthless for her own good. She had to be made to see the consequences of what they did. It was the only way to persuade her to do what was right.

"I will take you to London, if you prefer, Cass. These things are more acceptable there. A vast amount of society will still receive you. You are a married woman, after all. It is done all the time."

Cassandra shook her head slowly. "No, I don't want to live in London. I want to live here. This is my home. I'll not be driven away from it again."

She was ignoring the consequences again. Merrick sat on the bed beside her and tilted her chin upward. "Do you wish me to stay away? You have only to say the word."

Her eyes began to gleam the aquamarine color he was beginning to recognize as confused emotions. She shook her head.

"I don't need anyone else, just you. Will it be very hard for you? I don't wish to make you an outcast."

That wasn't quite the reply he wanted, but Wyatt could see it would take time before she realized their position. In the meantime, he would have his solicitors locate Rupert and begin drawing up the papers necessary for an annulment. He would have them ready for signatures when the reality finally reached her.

"I will not be outcast by any but my mother. There are different rules for men. I might lose my halo"— he smiled bleakly at this reference to his reputation— "but I will not be blamed for taking a mistress. You, I fear, are the one who will suffer. I would keep you from that if I could."

Cassandra straightened and pulled away from his protective hold. "I cannot possibly suffer any more than I have. My reputation will not keep workers from my field if they think they can earn good coin from it. That is my only concern.''

Wyatt did not want to contemplate what kind of life she must have lived to make such a statement. His anger at her family began to build, but he did not let it show. He kissed her brow and stood up. ''I will do what I can to keep the gossip at a minimum for as long as possible. Thomas would be disappointed if you no longer came to visit.''

That sank in. He could see the horror slowly write itself across her face. Wyatt felt a twinge of jealousy, but he stubbornly repressed it. Thomas was too young to think of marrying. Cassandra needed someone who could protect her. He had given little thought to the benefits of his wealth and title, but he knew they would stand her in good stead now. As his wife, she would be welcome everywhere. He would see to that.

''Shall I send Bertie by this afternoon to take you visiting? It would be better if we were not seen so much together in public.''

Cassandra nodded helplessly. She didn't want to spend the afternoon with Bertie. She wanted to be beside Merrick, laughing at his jests, holding his hand, sharing his life, but she was the one who had denied them that fate. She could only agree to his common-sensical suggestions now.

After Wyatt left, she threw herself into her work with determination. She had everything she wanted, more than she asked for. She would not feel sorry for herself. When Lotta returned from the village with much more than the coffee and pot, she did not ask where the money had come from. Pride no longer had a place in her life.

Thomas was dressed and sitting in the salon when Cassandra arrived that afternoon. She gave a cry of delight and ran to kiss his freshly shaved cheek. She felt his wince of pain when he lifted his arm to her, but the schoolboy grin on his open face was all she could ask. He would be better soon and wouldn't need her. It wouldn't matter when she was soon barred from polite society.

As had become their custom, the three of them and whichever of the large Scheffing family happened to wander in took out the cards and indulged in a madcap game that involved more cheating than rules. In some way, Cassandra hoped she was teaching Thomas not to be quite so gullible when it came to gambling. She had very little knowledge to offer others, but this was one field where she specialized.

She drew a card from the bottom of the deck, added it to her hand, and proudly spread it on the table. "I win. You now owe me half a million pounds, two estates, and three horses. Shall we wager for a fourth horse and a carriage?"

"Use some of the half-million pounds to buy them, my lady." The amused male voice in the doorway caused Cassandra's heart to leap even before she looked up to meet his gaze.

He was so incredibly proper and elegant—in his dove-gray swallowtail and wine-colored vest with just the simple fold of white cloth at his throat—that she could scarcely believe he was the same man whose tousled head had rested on her pillow that morning. Her breath caught in her lungs, and the way he stared at her, she knew that he felt her constraint. Wyatt's gaze quickly took in the green morning gown that she wore interchangeably with the sprigged muslin whenever she went visiting, but she felt no condemnation at her lack of wardrobe. In fact, she very much feared he had just made a mental note to buy her more gowns.

"I need the half-million pounds for principal so I might live off the interest, my lord," she replied with as much insouciance as she could muster. She felt as if everyone in the room were staring at them, but she knew they were not. Bertie was ringing for refreshments and Thomas was happily shuffling the cards in preparation for another game.

"Do you have any idea how much interest that would

be?'' Openly laughing now, Wyatt entered the room,
shook Bertie's hand, and cuffed Thomas' when offered
the deck of cards.

"Just sufficient to keep me in gowns, I'm certain. I
daresay I'll need another half-million to provide car-
riages and servants and suchlike. Have you come to
gamble away your wealth, my lord?''

"I have come to save the Scheffings from bankruptcy and to deliver a surprise." Merrick gave
Thomas a wink as the sound of female voices carried
up the stairwell. "Your sister could no longer bear to
remain in hiding and not read you a proper lecture.
Prepare yourself.''

Before Cassandra could piece this together, Mrs.
Scheffing and a lovely but heavily pregnant woman
joined them. The blond curls and wide cheekbones
bespoke still another family member, and she realized
this was the Christa she had not seen since childhood.
Cassandra stared with fascination as the newcomer
awkwardly advanced across the room, her light muslin
skirts emphasizing rather than concealing her condition.

"Cards! I cannot believe it of you, Thomas! Gambling, and you just out of sickbed. And corrupting
gentle females at the same time. For shame." She bent
and placed an affectionate peck on her brother's brow.
"Please, do not attempt to rise because of me. I cannot sit and you cannot stand. A sad pair we make.''

She turned a questioning gaze to Cassandra, but before Thomas could make the introductions, her face
lit with recognition. "Lady Cass! My goodness, you
have grown up. I can remember you only as a little
girl in braids.''

The conversation became general then, and feeling
as if she were an outsider, Cassandra glanced to Merrick for rescue.

Wyatt had watched Cassandra's wide-eyed curiosity
at Christa's appearance, but he had thought it only her
astonishment that a lady would appear in public when

so heavily with child. He began to doubt his notions later when they were in the curricle and a puzzled frown appeared upon Cassandra's brow.

"Christa seems excessively polite, does she not? It is odd that she is so very much larger than her mother. I do not remember her as being that way."

The questioning way she said it and the knowledge that Cass was not given to rude remarks about other people's appearances kept Wyatt from mistaking her words. That led to another interpretation, and Wyatt shot his companion an incredulous look.

Sometimes it was very easy to forget how young Cassandra actually was. Married at eighteen, never out in society, and her only company being her father's drunken cronies, she had no access to the polite world of gentlewomen. Wyatt knew very little of her mother, but he suspected Lady Eddings had communicated little more than complaints to her daughter. It was very possible that Cassandra had never seen more than a glimpse of a pregnant woman in her life. She was intelligent enough to figure it out eventually, but Wyatt felt a sudden shudder deep down in his soul as he contemplated the entire depth of her ignorance. Could she possibly not know . . . ?

Gathering his wits about him, Wyatt tried to offer her some explanation. Never in his imagination had he thought it would be necessary to explain the facts of life to a young girl. He wasn't at all certain where to begin, particularly in light of their current situation.

Hesitantly he said, "After the baby is born, she will be her normal size again. I belive it is expected any day now."

Cassandra absorbed that information quietly. She had a dozen more questions to ask on the subject, but she disliked showing Wyatt her ignorance. She could feel his reluctance to speak, and not wanting to embarrass him more, she smiled brightly. "Of course, how foolish of me. See how lovely the bluebells are today. It's a pity they do not make good bouquets. Wouldn't they look lovely on the kitchen table?''

He was making a great mistake in ignoring the subject, but Wyatt nodded with relief and allowed her to carry off the conversation. Cass was bright enough to figure it out sooner or later. This was the country, after all.

He didn't let himself consider the fact that she owned no animals and no farmer in his right mind would allow a Lady Cassandra into his barn or stable. Someone would explain it to her soon enough.

Chapter 19

Cassandra sang to herself as she arranged the bouquet of roses in the lovely porcelain vase Merrick had brought for her last evening. She really ought to refuse his gifts, but when he insisted he was accustomed to flowers on his breakfast table, she hadn't been able to refuse him.

Not any more than she had been able to refuse the lovely peach satin robe or the walking dress or the riding habit or any of the other extravagant gifts that arrived in so many unexpected ways these past weeks. Coaches from London pulled up at her door to spill trunks of clothing with no name attached. Barefoot boys pulling wooden carts unloaded crates of delicate china. Merrick always evinced surprise at their arrival, then agreed she really ought to keep them since she didn't know whom to return them to, and he did prefer seeing her in satin and silk and was accustomed to eating from china.

He was becoming a worse liar than she, but since they both knew he was lying, it didn't seem so much of a sin. Nothing he did seemed a sin. Remembering what the proper earl had done to her in bed just the night before, Cassandra felt her cheeks blaze with color, but she welcomed the heat rising within her at the memory. Only Wyatt had the power to do this to her. She couldn't be a wanton if only one man made her life complete.

The sound of a horse trotting up the drive brought a flush of expectancy. Wyatt never visited during the day.

He played the part of gentleman to perfection in public. It would not be seemly for him to visit unaccompanied, since she had no companion or chaperone. The sound of a horse meant another package was arriving. She really ought to refuse this one. She had never needed all these beautiful things before. She had no right to them now. But how could she go about refusing a package from an anonymous deliveryman who would only be disgruntled at having to cart it away again?

The knock sounded at the door, and she hesitated. Jacob had gone into the village and Lotta had taken lunch to the workers in the field. It wasn't much of a lunch, admittedly, but they always seemed grateful for whatever was given. It looked as if they might have a crop, after all. Wiping her hands on a towel, Cassandra hurried to answer the door herself.

She stared in astonishment at the tall, immaculately garbed horseman on the doorstep. For a brief moment she considered slamming the door in his face. As if anticipating her thought, Duncan caught the door and strode across the threshold.

"You are looking well, Cass." He gave her a curt nod before gazing around at the orderly cottage. A polished walnut table gleamed on one side of the hall, and he could see a satin settee and a lamp hung with crystal on the other side. His gaze returned to his sister's expensive French muslin, and he hid his frown with a smile.

"I see you are doing well for yourself, little sis. Rupert has been a generous husband. Are you not going to invite me in?"

"You are already in," she answered bluntly. Then, unbending slightly, she led the way to the front parlor. Merrick had insisted the pieces of furniture he had sent down from the house had been collecting dust in the attics, and they were, indeed, not of the most recent fashion, but they were of too expensive a quality to be condemned to attics. Perhaps earls lived differently. She was in no position to know. She gestured at the French side chair beside the window. "Have a seat and I will fetch some lemonade. I fear we do not stock brandy," she said mendaciously.

Duncan made a face at this choice of refreshment but offered no objection as she hurried off to the kitchen. He paced the room slowly, mentally calculating the cost of the antique settee and chair, the rather valuable Chinese vase filled with common wildflowers, and the aging Persian carpet beneath his feet. The house could have come provided with these things, but the house itself led to rampant speculation. He gazed up at rafters darkened with age.

By the time Cassandra returned, Duncan was sitting amiably in the chair, swinging his crossed leg, and smiling to himself.

Not fooled by his pleasant expression, Cassandra set the tray down beside him and without further ado spread her skirt across the settee and came to the point. "Why are you here, Duncan? Has London become too hot for you?"

He continued to smile. "I'm tolerably well, thank you. Do you not wish to ask after our esteemed parent?"

No, she didn't. Guilt seeped through the back of her mind. She had wanted to bring her mother to the country where she might grow healthy again, but she could not let her mother know that she had become Merrick's mistress. It was a topic she tried not to think about. Curtly she gave the reply that Duncan expected. "How is Mother? I trust she is well?"

"Tolerable, as usual. She would do well here, I venture to say. Shall I bring her for a visit the next time I come?"

A visit would be perfect. Cassandra's eyes lit for a brief moment; then suspicion replaced joy. "Why would you do that? Why are you here at all, Duncan? I thought you detested the countryside."

"So I do." He sipped at the sweetened drink and winced at the taste. "I just wished to check and see how my little sister fared. I've heard rumors for weeks now, but I knew you were one to land on your feet. And so you have, it seems.''

"No thanks to you," Cassandra responded sweetly. Under the pretense of lounging idly on the settee and sipping on her drink, she glanced out the window, praying for some glimpse of Lotta or Jacob. She disliked being along with Duncan. His temper was uncertain at best. The window revealed only the now neatly trimmed drive. She turned back to observe her half-brother.

He looked thinner, somehow, and not nearly so terrifying as she had once thought him. He was still quite large, shorter than Merrick perhaps, but broader through the shoulders. Of course, the only work Duncan's shoulders had ever known was an occasional idle bout at Gentleman Jackson's, but she did not underestimate his strength. She just didn't fear him as she once had. He had done his worst. There was little more that he could do to harm her.

"Have you come to stay awhile?" she asked casually.

"No longer than it takes to see that you are comfortable. I had not expected Rupert to provide for you so well, under the circumstances. How did you do it?"

They trod dangerous ground here, and Cassandra smiled to hide her uneasiness. Merrick had said Duncan was paying the rent. She had assumed that was how her brother had found her. But Merrick had developed the bad habit of lying to get his way, and she had developed the equally reprehensible habit of letting him get away with it. She very much suspected she was about to get caught in the web of deceit.

She shrugged blithely. "Rupert had nothing to do with it. The cottage was in a sad state of neglect and I offered to take care of it. The neighbors have been all that is kind in helping me."

"You always were a shameless baggage, Cass. Don't bother giving me your Spanish coin, for you know I don't buy it." Duncan set his glass aside and rose to pace the room. "There's money here, and don't make

me think our righteous country-bumpkin neighbors
have given it. Even Merrick wouldn't lower himself to
helping a wanton wife who deserts her husband and
instigates duels. You have somehow found your way
into Rupert's pockets. Tell me how, Cass.''

Cassandra felt the danger in him but didn't know its
direction. Thankfully, he did not even consider Merrick. She didn't want Wyatt caught up in this battle.
This was a family matter, and Wyatt wasn't family.
She lifted her chin and met Duncan's gaze squarely. ''Believe what you wish, brother. I cannot tell you more
than I know.''

A dangerous gleam leapt to Duncan's eyes. He knew
that look of Cassandra's. She was hiding something.
Cass could fool others with her bright smiles and defiant tempers, but he knew all the fears and insecuri-
ties hidden behind that brave facade. He was getting
close to something.

''Fine, keep your little secrets, Cass. I have other
plans. Actually, you have done us both a favor by running off. Rupert would have made me beg for every
penny, but you will not, will you, Cass? Once we have
his wealth, we can be a happy family again, maybe
even rebuild the old mausoleum so you and Mother
can live happily content in the country as you prefer.
Wouldn't you like that?''

She had a suspicion she wouldn't like anything that
made Duncan happy, but she did not trouble him with
her opinion. ''What are you talking about, Duncan? I
have no wealth, and I see no chance of Rupert sharing
his. What maggot do you have in your head now?''

Duncan shrugged and shoved his hands in his pockets as he turned to observe his beautiful half-sister
lounging in the sunlight. He should never have worried
about her. In retrospect, it was quite foolish of him.
Still, there was no need to put any of them through this
again.

''Rupert is something of a monster, I have found
out. He enjoys killing. He enjoys women too, so I

never thought he would harm you, but I can see that he might be a danger to you. You have not exactly got an obedient spirit, Cass.''

"I never pretended to have, dear brother," she responded sardonically. "So what is this leading up to?"

"Tell me where he is, and I will rid you of him." Duncan was tense and expectant as he watched the emotions scuttling across her face.

"You are quite mad," she finally announced with a measure of calm. "It is much too late to defend me. In all cases, even if you managed to win, you would be tried for murder or exiled, as he is. Put the matter out of your mind. Why don't you help me put the farm back to work? There is money to be made here. We will not be wealthy, but we will not starve." Excitement crept into her voice as she allowed her secret hopes to creep out. If only he would accept this plan, they would be a real family, like the Scheffings. The excitement withered quickly enough beneath Duncan's scorn.

"I'd rather starve." He dismissed the offer out of hand. "You are married to a wealthy man. Someone is bound to take exception to his villainy sooner or later, and you will be a wealthy widow. Tell me where Rupert is, and I shall see that it is much sooner than later."

Cassandra stared at him in horror.

Lotta noticed the horse first. Coming from the field, she had dawdled in the lane waiting for Jacob, and they had taken their time returning to the house and their chores. It took a moment before she reacted to the sight of a horse in front of the cottage, and she tugged at Jacob's hand to halt him.

"Who around here rides a nag like that?" she asked in low tones at his surprise.

Jacob bent a skeptical look to the object in question. "None that would admit to it. A sorry hack, if you ask me."

Lotta gave him a disdainful look. "And what would

you know of horses? You'll be telling me next that you were a groom before you were a valet.''

"Actually, I was in the army before I was a valet. Not cavalry, mind you, but I've been around enough horses to recognize a sorry specimen when I see one.''

Lotta lifted her brows at that, but she didn't let go of the subject. "Who would ride a hired hack out here?''

Jacob gave her an impatient look. "Wouldn't it be easier to go inside and see?''

She turned on him as if he had lost all his wits. "Not if we need to get away again, it won't. Come, let's go around the back and see if we can hear their voices.''

Not in the least disturbed by this odd manner of approaching a visitor, Jacob led the way around the house to the kitchen door. Even from here the angry voices in the front room could be heard. The pair exchanged looks and crept through the kitchen to hear better.

"Duncan!'' Lotta whispered, clutching Jacob's arm and pulling him back. "I knew the devil would demand his due.''

Jacob closed the kitchen door. "You'd best warn his lordship. It won't do to have him come up unexpected.''

"Aye, I'll warn his lordship to bring his pistols,'' Lotta replied grimly. "You go in there and see that my lady is protected. He's a brute when he's angry like that.''

Jacob's stoic expression changed a hair, but his voice reflected only a solemn calm. "I'll do as I can. Be quick, then.''

Cassandra looked up with relief when Jacob appeared bearing a tray and a decanter. She had rather he kept the brandy out of Duncan's hands, but now that she was not alone, she felt safer. She gave Jacob a nod of acknowledgment when he entered.

"Thank you, Jacob. That was most thoughtful of

you. My brother is undoubtedly weary from his ride. Would you see that a room is prepared for him?''

Duncan waited until the servant was gone before pouring the brandy and facing his sister. ''That was Rupert's valet. Are you still going to insist you know nothing of your husband's whereabouts?''

Wearily Cassandra rose from the settee. ''He came with me when I left London. Think what you wish. I must go see about dinner. Jacob will show you to your room.''

Duncan held his temper. It did not pay to raise Cassandra's fury too far. It would be simpler if she just told him how to find Rupert, but there were other ways. And when she became a wealthy widow, it would only be natural if he, as her only male relative, became guardian of her estate. They rubbed along well enough when they weren't at cross purposes. Cassandra would be too caught up in the society and gowns that wealth brings to care who administered the funds. It would work out to his advantage soon enough. He didn't know why he hadn't thought of it earlier.

By the time Lotta's message reached Merrick, it was almost dark. Setting his jaw grimly, Wyatt approached the dowager countess in her salon.

''We need to make an evening call, Mother. It seems Lord Eddings is in residence, and I have several things I need to discuss with him. You can see that it would be more appropriate if you accompanied me to visit with his sister while we talk business.''

Lady Merrick gave her son a stiff look and sniffed superciliously. ''I can see nothing of the sort. I daresay she entertains single gentlemen every night of the week. I have nothing to say to her.''

''I had not realized you had grown so bored with the country, Mother,'' Wyatt replied without a trace of hostility. ''It is past time that I set you up with a house in town. You should have mentioned it much sooner. Perhaps Lady Cassandra could make recommendations as to the most fashionable streets. I have not kept up with them myself.''

The implied threat brought her nose up a little higher, but the countess knew when her bluff was called. She gave a gracious nod. "Very well, have the carriage brought around. I will not travel in that flimsy rig you gad about in.''

Cassandra gasped in surprise when Wyatt appeared at her door with Lady Merrick on his arm, but she held her curiosity and graciously beckoned the countess to the cushion beside her on the settee. Since Duncan had appropriated the only other chair in the room, she had an anxious moment in placing Wyatt, but he solved the dilemma with ease.

"So sorry to intrude at this hour, my lady. I did not realize you had company, but this is a fortuitous occurrence. While my mother speaks to you of her reason for visiting, perhaps I can persuade your brother to speak privately with me for a moment on a matter of business?''

Panic raced through Cassandra's veins as she contemplated all the things that might be said between brother and lover. It wouldn't do at all. How would she ever stop him? Duncan was looking bored and irritable and ready to entertain the notion of baiting Merrick. She cringed at the thought of where such a conversation would lead.

Taking the reins into her hands, she gestured to the servant waiting in the doorway while speaking quickly. "You cannot think of deserting us for business at this hour of the evening, my lord. Jacob, bring a chair for his lordship, please.''

Wyatt appeared ready to object, but Cassandra turned gaily to the disapproving countess. "Men are such a trial, always business, I vow. We must take a stern stand on these matters, mustn't we? Shall you have some tea? I understand you play whist very well. I have so longed for a good game. Perhaps we could persuade our men to a challenge?''

Duncan began to smirk at how easily his sister commandeered the haughty Merricks. Their rigid manners would not allow them to insult her by refusing her requests, and he could sense the earl's frozen anger. He didn't know what game she was up to, but this was as amusing as any for the moment. He wondered what stakes he could persuade out of the dowager.

Merrick alone sensed Cassandra's nervousness. Giving her brother a speculative look, he nodded vaguely in agreement and let her run with the show. There wasn't a thing he could say to Duncan that hadn't already been said. He had only meant to impress the fact on him that Cass was protected. It didn't appear as if they had come to blows. Perhaps he was hasty in his assumption that she needed protection.

The evening proceeded on a stiff but amicable basis. Merrick concealed his amusement at his mother's obvious approval of Cassandra's handling of the cards. The women stayed several points ahead of the men, but he couldn't catch Cassandra flagrantly cheating. For that matter, he couldn't see Duncan using any sleight of hand either. For a brief few hours it almost felt as if they were meeting as families should meet.

He threw Cassandra a quick look at that thought. They would be a family if only she would agree. Admittedly, he could not imagine a more preposterous combination of relations, but if it could work for one evening, it could work for many. What were the possibilities of persuading her to it?

Just as Wyatt began to grow complacent with the thought, Duncan smacked his hand loudly against the table. The marquess had been imbibing steadily all evening, but his lack of control had not surfaced until now.

"Cass, that deuce went out at the beginning! You swore you'd use none of your tricks with me. It's an easy few shillings. What's a few shillings to you and your toplofty friends?"

As his tirade threatened to continue, Cassandra smiled brightly, made a discreet signal to the servant hovering in the background, and spread her cards on the table, all with a smoothness that would have gone unnoted by a casual observer. Without any seeming relation at all, Jacob's hand slipped on the decanter and the brandy he was pouring spilled in a golden waterfall over the marquess's lap. At the same time, Cassandra calmly stood and held out her hand to the countess.

"I believe we have trounced them enough for one evening, my lady." Ignoring Duncan's screams and curses as he danced back from the table and flailed drunkenly at the servant, she turned to Merrick, who had risen when she did. "I thank you for your company, my lord. It has been a pleasant evening. I do hope you will bring Lady Merrick again sometime. We will give you an opportunity to beat us. Perhaps we could set a handicap?"

The dowager stared in astonishment as the servant made every appearance of removing Duncan's saturated trousers right there and then. She gulped, stepped back, stared with horror at Cassandra's outstretched hand and bright smile, then out of pure inbred courtesy accepted the offered hand and smiled perfunctorily.

"Of course, my dear, anytime. It has been a delightful evening. Come, Wyatt, we must go."

Cassandra followed them to the door, stiffly ignoring the brawling argument escalating behind her. As he left, Merrick bent over her hand and in a whisper murmured, "Shall I come back?"

For a moment Cassandra clung to his hand. More than anything, she wanted Wyatt's strength by her side while she endured Duncan's company. She didn't want to be alone tonight, but she had done this to herself. Summoning her courage, she met his gaze squarely.

"It won't do," she answered quietly, then turned away before he could see the tears in her eyes.

Chapter 20

"Who is that man out in the bushes?" Lotta whispered as she hurried in the back door with her basket of eggs.

Jacob glanced uneasily out the window. "I don't know. He's been there most of the night. Ugly big brute, ain't he?"

"Should we tell Cass? She has so much on her mind . . ."

Jacob shook his head. "We'll keep an eye on him. The marquess won't be lingering, I'll be bound. We'll see if this brute goes with him."

An angry remark carried down from the upper story, and Lotta grabbed a tray and a teapot. "They're at it already. I didn't think his royal-pain-in-the-arse would be up so early after last night."

"He'll be wanting to get away, I suspect." Jacob shot Lotta's full figure a quick look. "You stay away from him."

Lotta flashed a smile. "After all these years, don't you think I've learned a trick or two?" In flagrant imitation of her mistress, she tossed her head and flounced out, the smile plastered happily on her face. A little jealousy was good for the soul. She must tell Cass that sometime.

"You touch one single thing in this house and I'll break it over your head before I let you have it! They're not mine to give away. Now, leave off, Duncan." Cassandra smacked her brother's hand away from the lovely watercolor of a child at a spinet that Merrick had given her. He had said it was just a silly memento he had picked up on his Grand Tour, but she could tell from the way Duncan was eyeing it now that it had much more worth than that.

"I never begrudged you the coin to live, Cass. Now that I'm a little short of the ready, it wouldn't hurt to part with a bauble or two. Did you come away with no jewelry at all? That was very shortsighted of you."

Cassandra stamped her foot and flung a pillow at him. "Nothing, nothing at all! Shall I give you my gowns to sell? Would that make you happy, Duncan? I came here in rags. Shall you reduce me to rags again?"

The pillow missed Duncan and hit the door just as Lotta entered with the tea tray. She gave a scream and bobbled the tray and almost had it under control when Duncan turned abruptly to brush by her.

"Out of my way, slut." He shoved savagely past, careless of the teetering tray.

Raising her eyebrows and emitting a feigned squeal, Lotta let the tray tilt. The teapot and its steaming contents tumbled in a scalding cascade down the marquess's newly pressed trousers while she cried and carried on and filled the air with her protestations of apology.

Jacob was up the stairs in an instant, his lanky frame seeming to stretch and tower like a malevolent giant as he burst in upon the scene. Already near tears, Cassandra could scarcely hold back her laughter as Duncan yelped and cursed, Lotta continued shrieking, and Jacob added his highly vivid invectives to the melee.

His legs burning with the scalding pain, Duncan cursed and danced and tried to remove his trousers while Jacob rescued the remains of the tray and tried to quiet Lotta's malicious cries. Clasping her robe closed, Cassandra tried to gasp out words of calm, but she was shaking too hard with laughter. She would have to reward them somehow. Duncan would think twice before intruding on her peace again.

To the conspirators' surprise, a crash sounded below and heavy footsteps bounded up the stairs. Duncan had his shirttails down to his knees and his trousers down about his ankles when the intruder burst through the door, nearly knocking Jacob into his lordship's shoulders.

This time Cassandra screamed in truth as she spotted the great pistol in the stranger's hand. Lotta's cries instantly halted as she tried to judge the direction of her employer's distress. Upon discovering the source, the maid raised her tray and slammed it down against the stranger's gun hand.

The gun exploded into the floor, the air filled with sulfur and smoke, and the angry giant let out a howl of pain and rage as he grabbed his bruised knuckles.

With the echoes of gunfire ringing in their ears, no one even noticed the pounding of boots upon the stairs. Merrick and Bertie burst through the open doorway, whips and riding crops brandished in their hands, and halted to survey the chaos in Cassandra's bedchamber.

Cassandra, hair a riot about her shoulders, tears streaming down her cheeks, one hand frantically clutching her robe while she pulled a terrified Lotta away from the hulking farmer's angry howls, commanded their attention first. Their gazes then traveled to Duncan's half-clad form as he and Jacob fought to overwhelm the intruder.

Raising one eyebrow at this bedlam, Merrick hid a smile as he turned to an astonished Bertie. "I do believe we have just witnessed a circus rehearsal, old boy. Do you wish to tame the lions while I congratulate the lovely rope-walkers?"

"Wyatt!" Cassandra cried before he finished speaking. "Do make them go away. They've put a hole in my lovely carpet. Just look at it! And the tea will stain if it's not removed at once."

Mirth twitching at the corners of his mouth, Merrick

made haste to do as told. Only Cassandra could entertain a scene like this and worry about the carpet. He
would have to analyze that reaction sometime, but now
wasn't the time. With a firm hand he separated from
the marquess and the butler the berated bodyguard he
had ordered to watch the house, and shoved him into
Bertie's protective custody. His appraising glance
quickly brought the other two combatants back into
line.

"Make a habit of undressing before ladies, Eddings?" he asked coolly.

"Deuce take it, Merrick, what are you doing here?"
Duncan grabbed for his trousers. "You're showing
quite an interest in my little sister, ain't you?"

Cassandra gasped as Duncan's irate accusation hit
too close, but he didn't seem to be cognizant of his
accuracy. He gathered up his clothing and glanced at
Merrick, who blocked his escape.

"Sound tends to carry in the country, Eddings.
You'd best remember that before you send the ladies
into hysterics again." He bowed politely and stepped
aside so Duncan could pass.

"I'll wager no lady's cries are heard from your
chambers, St. Wyatt. Do you fear the sounds carrying
or do you not know how to produce them?"

Bertie stepped hastily forward to prevent Merrick
from striking him, but to his surprise, the earl was
smiling pleasantly.

"I trust you have a pleasant journey homeward, Eddings. Shall I have Jenkins here escort you?"

Duncan brushed past him with fury, shouting at Jacob to follow and repair his ruined clothing. Jacob
glanced from Wyatt to Cassandra, and at the earl's
faint nod, hurried after the marquess.

Wyatt made a polite bow. "Excuse us for intruding,
my lady. Shall we wait below until order is restored,
or would you prefer that we leave?"

He was laughing, she could tell, but he had been
concerned enough to leave one of his men to watch

over her. Cassandra shook Lotta into quieting and replied unsteadily, "If you would care to wait, perhaps we could provide you with some breakfast. Have you eaten?"

Calm restored some while later, Cassandra clung to Wyatt's arm as she waved farewell to her disgruntled brother. Bertie's presence inhibited her, but not enough to keep a formal distance between herself and Merrick. She felt Bertie's curious glance when she continued to hold the earl's arm even after they stepped outside when the men returned to their horses. She shouldn't be so obvious, but she didn't want Wyatt to go. She desperately needed to talk to him.

Merrick covered her hand with his and cast her a worried look. As Bertie mounted, he murmured under the guise of saying farewell, "I'll be back. Practice our song and pick me some roses and I'll be here before you're done."

Cassandra took a deep breath of relief and released him. "It was so good of you to stop by, my lord, And, Bertie, you will remember me to Thomas, will you not? I expect to see him up and about when next I come."

Bertie grinned and raised his hand in salute, but when he and Merrick were down the road, he turned an angry glare at his old friend. "What the deuce plays here, Wyatt? I'm not some blind schoolboy. She holds a *tendre* for you, and if I'm not mistaken, you are encouraging her. That's not at all like, you know."

Wyatt stared stiffly ahead. "Sometimes I try to imagine what it must be like to have grown up knowing nothing but a drunken, abusive father and life on the thin edge of poverty. A person would have to learn to be very strong to survive such surroundings."

Bertie stared at him thoughtfully, then applied his own knowledge of life to the situation. "A person with a family like that would know nothing of love. She would be very weak when confronted with it."

"Just so, Bertie, just so." Merrick rode on ahead and said nothing further.

Wyatt found Cassandra wandering in the remains of the cottage rose garden when he returned. In these last six weeks or so that they had been together he had come to learn her many moods, but "pensive" had never been among them. He felt a momentary tug of fear as he watched her expression now. The visit from Duncan had obviously set off some unpleasant train of thought. He wasn't at all certain that he wanted to hear it.

With a growing sense of foreboding, Wyatt walked quietly through the overgrown garden. The fact that she was too absorbed in thought to notice his presence seemed even more ominous. He snapped a yellow rosebud from its scraggly branch and laid it on top of the blossoms in her basket.

Cassandra looked up then. Her fleeting smile of relief quickly disappeared behind a cloud of apprehension, and she looked away from Wyatt's questioning gaze. Gathering up her basket and scissors, she started slowly down the garden path, away from the cottage.

"I need your help, Wyatt." She spoke softly, almost to herself.

"You know you have it without asking, Cass. Just tell me what I can do."

Instead of sending him her usual flirtatious look of gratitude, she continued looking straight ahead. "Can you have your man of business find Rupert for me?"

Wyatt's heart plunged to his feet. He caught her shoulder and swung her around. "Why, Cass? Tell me why."

She couldn't look at him. She held her gaze somewhere near his shoulder and tried to be strong. She was too confused and emotionally battered to think straight. She didn't want to hurt Wyatt. The last thing in the world that she wanted to do was hurt this kind, gentle man who had taught her what life could be like if she were not cursed with the name of Howard. But she could not live with the knowledge of a man's death on her conscience. She had suffered that agony once, and when given a reprieve, had vowed never to do so again. Merrick's love versus the life of a man she despised was an unfair choice, but she had to make it.

"Does it really matter, Wyatt? You need a wife and we can never marry. It's been unfair of me to even pretend otherwise. If you cannot help me with this, I will understand." She turned away and began moving back toward the house.

Fighting a growing desperation, Wyatt caught her again. This time he held her close, forcing her to feel the power of the emotions that brought them together. He felt her shiver, then melt against him, and he enclosed her tightly in his embrace when she rested her head against his shoulder.

"We are in this together, Cass. I will find Rupert for you, but in return, you must promise never to leave me without telling me to my face. No more disappearing acts, no notes on my pillow. I want you to come to me and tell me why you're leaving so I have some chance of presenting my side."

He knew her too well already. Cassandra rested in his embrace and wondered how she could ever explain that she could never marry him because her brother would in all likelihood attempt to have him killed in order to obtain his estate. Failing that, he would drain Wyatt dry. Even Wyatt wouldn't believe that.

It didn't matter. Just living as they had been, they would be found out sooner or later. Duncan would blackmail him blind. Wyatt's gifts would begin to disappear to feed her brother's rapacious greed, and she would be left to explain their disappearances. Sooner or later Wyatt would be forced to call Duncan out, and it would start all over again. She didn't know how she had allowed herself to be fooled into complacency for this long. Happiness wasn't meant for the likes of her.

"You won't be able to argue me out of it, my love.

Our time is limited, we both know that. I had so hoped . . .'' Cassandra shook her head, unable to voice her dreams. This was a good-bye of sorts. There might be a few days or weeks left to them, but the dreams were gone. Duncan had done that to her again.

Wyatt heard the choked-back tears in Cassandra's voice and lifted his face to the sun in an effort to scald away the threat of moisture in his own eyes. He wouldn't let her go. He refused to believe that what they shared was just some fleeting episode of lust. It would be easier if he could believe that, if he were more like his peers who could take up mistresses and discard them as they would a rumpled cravat. But he couldn't, and he wasn't even going to pretend to try. He had known from the first that Cass had the power to make his life hell. He'd rather live in hell than without her.

''I won't give up, Cass. I'll find Rupert for you, but I won't let you go back to him. You deserve better than that. There may come a time when you realize there is more to life than a dull farmer such as myself, but I would see you happy before I let you go.''

She nodded against his coat sleeve. He had just provided her with the means to make her escape. For his own good, she would use every power within her grasp to sever this connection between them. Someday, she hoped he would understand.

''You may rest easy on that account, my lord. I will never return to Rupert. I only wish to speak with him.''

Merrick wasn't fooled, but he sent a messenger to his solicitor later that day anyway. It had been over a month since he had requested that Rupert be found. Surely they must have word by now.

Chapter 21

"I am going with you."

Cassandra turned up her lashes and stared at her quiet earl with disbelief. He had donned only his tight pantaloons and stood there in the sunshine from the window in all his masculine glory. The light accented and shadowed the play of muscles under his skin as he reached for his shirt, and she felt an overpowering surge of pride that a man like this would seek her out. She felt sorry for those who saw only the surface man, the staid and formal earl in his conservative frock coat and top hat. She had been blessed with the sight of the real Wyatt Mannering, and her smile was one of joy as she approached him.

"You are being ridiculous, but I thank you for the offer." Cassandra ran her fingers over the hardened muscles of his chest to the wide breadth of his shoulders. She heard his sharp intake of breath when she pressed a kiss to the hollow of his throat. When Wyatt's arms closed instinctively around her, she came happily against him. "Is it so very late yet?" she whispered against his skin.

It was late. MacGregor would be waiting for him. His mother would soon be retiring with the vapors when he did not appear at the breakfast table. The post would be arriving soon, and he expected some important letters. None of that mattered while he held this enchanting fairy child in his arms. Woman, he amended. She was all woman now, and he had done this to her.

Wyatt pressed a kiss against her glorious hair and rubbed his hands up and down her arms. She wore only her chemise, one of the silken things with the low-cut bodice he had ordered for her. The full curve of her breasts pushed temptingly against the frail lace of the edging, and he bent to place a kiss on the narrow valley between those lovely curves.

Cassandra's gasp encouraged him to seek further, finding the taut rosy peaks beneath the lace with his lips. She writhed in his arms, fighting him only slightly, then wantonly offering herself for more. That was what excited him, her readiness wherever and whenever he demanded.

Wyatt lifted her onto the rumpled bed and teased the chemise down until he had the full glory of her high, firm breasts revealed. To hell with breakfast and taciturn stewards. The surge of heat in his loins increased the pressure against his confining clothing, and he needed the release she offered. Afterward he would remind her of their argument.

Cassandra felt the press of his flesh between her thighs as Wyatt released his pantaloons. She wanted the possession that would drive the world away a little while longer. This might be the last time they would be together like this. She couldn't let it end so easily.

Before he could take her, she pushed against his shoulders, pressing him away from her. Wyatt looked down at her questioningly, but pulled back slightly. Cassandra pushed harder and swung her hips to the side, unbalancing him enough that he got the message and rolled back to the bed and off her, tugging her with him.

That was what she wanted. With a grin of triumph Cassandra climbed astride. Now she was the one in power, and she bent to take full advantage, tormenting him with her kisses, keeping him from the goal he sought.

"Minx!" Wyatt muttered with tortured breath as her fingers found the hard crests of his chest at the same time her lips seared flaming trails down his throat. He could feel the moist heat of her against his throbbing manhood, and the proximity drove him to a frenzy of lust. Never had she been so bold. He sensed the farewell hovering behind her frantic overtures, but he had no intention of letting her go. With firm hands Wyatt grasped her hips and lifted her on him.

Cassandra gave a wild cry of joy and surprise at this mixture of impalement and freedom. She was free to do as she desired, to seek her pleasure by being still or quick, to take him as he had taken her to the heights of ecstasy, but it was only this man that could take her there, his body inside hers that produced the pleasures of this joining. She could not escape the firm tether on which he held her—not without destroying the joy for which she lived.

The pleasure was bittersweet with that knowledge. Wyatt's thrusts carried her away to a realm where the world couldn't reach, but it was a fantasy kingdom from which escape meant a kind of death. Cassandra wept as his body consumed hers and they found that world together.

Wyatt erased her tears with his fingers as he pulled her back into his arms. "Don't cry, Cass. I won't let it end like this. You haven't learned yet that I'm not your brother or your father. Your happiness is mine. We'll seek it together."

That seemed an incredible fallacy to her. She knew she gave Wyatt pleasure, but any woman could do that, he was just too shy and proper to seek another. Perhaps she needed to find him another woman before she left. The idea of some full-blown painted female in Wyatt's arms made her stomach knot painfully, and she buried her face against his shoulder.

"You had better go. It is getting late."

She said this while she lay on top of him, pinning him down, and Wyatt chuckled. "Shall I go like this, sweet? That should declare my intentions to all the world. Unfortunately, they may lock us both in Bedlam.''

Cassandra pounded his shoulder with her fist and rolled off him to the floor. Her hair fell in glorious tangles about her shoulders as she tried to pull her chemise back in place. "We belong in Bedlam. It is past time that we regained our sanity.''

Wyatt lay awhile longer, watching her. She had matured in many ways these past weeks. The careless girl who had so easily fallen into his bed had suddenly grown into a woman who realized the consequences of their actions. He wished he had the power to relieve her pain, but that power lay in her hands alone. Only she knew what was between herself and Rupert and Duncan. He could only stand by to catch her if she fell, or try to keep her from danger until she was strong enough to wield her power.

He rose and reached for his trousers for the second time that morning. "I have made arrangements to take a packet from Dover. We are to have their two best chambers. Lotta isn't much of a chaperone, but as a married woman you can probably be excused for traveling with just a maid. I'll arrange for separate rooms in the hotel too. We shall be all that is proper.''

Cassandra stopped to stare at him. Wyatt calmly continued dressing as if he hadn't just tipped the boat and turned her out. She shook her head and came up for air with a gasp. "Don't be absurd! We cannot possibly travel together. Your mother would disown you. The neighbors will be scandalized.'' And Duncan would know of a certainty what was between them, but she didn't mention that.

Merrick pulled on his shirt and pinned her with his glare. "Try to go without me, Cass. France is not all that stable even now. Wellington may have put an end to Napoleon's reign of terror, but there are still bitter factions and rivalries that make travel a danger, particularly for the English. Can you even speak a word of French, Cass?''

She shook her head. Her ignorance was abysmal, and she felt ashamed to let him see it. Wyatt was so intelligent and well-educated, she found it amazing that she had held his interest this long. Would he develop a scorn of her if he knew the full extent of her stupidity?

"Wyatt, I cannot let you do this. I'll travel simply with Jacob and Lotta. No one will be interested in a poor gentlewoman traveling in reduced circumstances."

Merrick held his exasperation. Catching her shoulders, he turned to make her face the mirror. The reflection revealed a wanton sun goddess newly risen from her fiery bed. Flame-gold hair curled in wild abundance about creamy breasts tinged with the rosy heat of their lovemaking. Brilliant sea-green eyes framed in long lashes stared in innocent confusion from a pale face constructed of porcelain delicacy mixed with aristocratic lineage. No man in his right mind would mistake her for any other than what she was: a woman of proud heritage and passionate beauty.

Cassandra glanced uncertainly from her own familiar reflection in the mirror to that of the man behind her. He towered over her by a head, though she knew herself awkwardly tall. He held her with firmness and care, though his hands dwarfed her small shoulders. Those deep brown eyes that had held her from the start now met her gaze with a look that spoke of unfamiliar and rather frightening emotions. There was no evidence of that tiny dent beside his mouth now, and his lips held a determination that she dared not brook. It wasn't just earl or lover looking at her now, but a man with his own will and thoughts who was not about to be cast aside until he was ready to go.

She gave a sigh of mixed relief and surrender. He would follow her should she even slip away at night. "I cannot like it, Wyatt. We must pretend to travel separately. It would not do at all for Rupert to discover you are with me."

That thought did not bother Wyatt in the least. With his first opportunity he intended to confront the cad, but Cassandra didn't need to know that yet. He brushed a kiss along her cheek.

"I shall be discreet. I shall be a gentleman on holiday. I will give you time to make your peace with Rupert and decide what you wish to do. Just remember your promise, Cass. Do not leave without telling me."

That was tantamount to asking her to hold a gun to her head. She would do it because she had no choice. It little mattered whether it were here or there.

She nodded and he released her. The matter was settled with little argument and no harsh words, but the tension remained in painful degrees. Both knew the time was drawing near when some decision must be made, and Merrick could read the choice in her eyes. He refused to admit defeat, however. Whatever hurdle she had erected between them, he would tear down eventually.

That night, as he approached the cottage door, Wyatt crunched the damnable letter in his pocket with nervous fingers. The past week had worn his patience and his nerves to ragged ends. He didn't know why Cassandra had resolved to see her husband again, but he knew Duncan had to be the source of her decision. That did not make this waiting period any easier, or ease the pain of Cassandra's gradual withdrawal from him and from the small society to which he had introduced her. He could strangle Duncan, but he doubted if that would resolve their problems.

Standing before the wooden door that separated him from the welcoming home of his dreams, Wyatt forced himself to raise the knocker. His dreams were built on ashes. He knew that, and Cassandra knew that. While they stayed behind these four walls, they could pretend all was well. They could pretend he was the husband come home to his wife after a hard day's work, but the pretense was wearing thin. He was tired of the lies and the excuses and the pretense when he wanted to give her a gift, dress her in the clothes she deserved, take her about to dinners and routs, or even share their musical evenings together. She belonged in his home, in his bed, his wife for all the world to see.

The world could scorn him as it would for his choice in brides, he didn't care. She was young in years, but old in the ways of the world, perhaps older than he in that respect. It scarcely mattered. She was beautiful and he was plain. She was dashing and he was dull. She was an untamed spirit and he had succumbed to the rigid routine of the staid life long ago. But all that disappeared the instant they were together. The air trembled and the earth moved and all their differences came together to make one whole. He had no desire to live without her ever again.

So why did he carry this letter in his pocket that would tear their world asunder? He was tired of pretense, true, but wasn't pretense better than nothing at all? And he greatly feared he would be left with nothing at all once he imparted this information to Cassandra. She had made some decision in that willful mind of hers, and nothing he could do or say would persuade her otherwise.

But he didn't want to keep her by trickery and lies. He had made this argument with himself a dozen times and lost every one. That was the reason he was standing here with his solicitor's letter in his pocket. No matter how he felt, Cassandra was Rupert's wife and a person with her own needs and desires. If she chose to return to Rupert, Wyatt could not stop her, no matter how he longed to do so. She had spent all her life under the pressure of some man's thumb, and the result had been disastrous. He had to hope that her feelings for him were strong enough to lead her to the right decision. He had to give her the freedom to make that decision.

As the door opened and a burst of red-gold exploded into his arms, Wyatt knew the anguish of loss even in this moment of happiness. His arms wrapped around her, but it was like holding the wind. What insanity had led him to believe she could ever be his?

Wyatt gave her the letter with Rupert's address that night, before they went to bed. Cassandra went white. Not opening the letter, she laid it carefully on the mantel. With her back to Wyatt, she repeated the phrases she had rehearsed all week.

"You made me promise to warn you when I decided to leave. I'm leaving you now, Wyatt. It would be better for both of us if you would let me go alone."

Wyatt felt his soul ripping from his body as he stared at her slender back, and her words pierced him like bullets. He had known the words were coming, knew the justice of them, but he refused to let her go without a fight.

"We've had this discussion before. Will you give me an explanation for your change of mind, Cass? Do I not deserve that much?" he asked quietly.

She couldn't face him, couldn't risk the torment of his face releasing the pent-up anguish in her soul. He was merely losing a mistress. She was giving up her life. She had never lied to herself before and there was no use starting now. She would leave Wyatt because it was best for him, and what was best for him was best for her. But she had no illusion of being happier for having done it. She would be miserable beyond belief, but it was better she suffer the misery alone.

"How can I say what you must already know?" She stared blindly at the blur of light that was the candle beside her. "You are better off without me. You need a proper wife and I cannot be it. I think it would be better if you left now."

That was utter nonsense and they both knew it. Wyatt came up behind her, wanting to put his hands on her shoulders and turn her around and kiss her until she regained her senses. But that wasn't the way to logic. He hated emotional scenes, and she would hate him for causing one. If she were determined to be cold about this, so would he.

"I'll leave if that is what you want, Cass, but don't expect me to believe a word you say. You've taught me too much to believe you're indifferent to my caresses or unhappy with my company. I'll go, but I'll be back."

With luck, he wouldn't be back in time, Cassandra vowed. She didn't turn and watch as he walked away. Every footstep tore another hole in her heart. The gentle closing of the door decimated what remained. Tears rolled down her cheeks, and she clung tightly to the mantel while shudders shook her body.

She had never done anything so hard in her life. Why did doing the right thing have to feel so bad?

Chapter 22

By morning Cassandra had a single bag packed and her small store of coins tucked safely in several different places. The letter with Rupert's address was tucked in Jacob's coat. She had sworn and cursed and tried to persuade the two servants that they must stay behind, but both refused to obey. Resignedly she watched as Jacob tugged two more satchels to their growing stack of luggage.

"I trust there will be room for all this in the mail coach," she grumbled as Lotta entered with still another small case.

Jacob ignored the complaint and swung open the front door. "This is the most shatter-brained scheme you've dreamt up yet. Rupert ain't worth the time nor the money, and I can't see why you're in such a hurry to find that out."

Cassandra had heard this all before. Picking up her bag, she swung out the door without his help. After Wyatt had left last night and she had explained her intentions, Jacob had been particularly mutinous. At one point she had thought him about to read her a lecture, but she had hastily explained about Duncan and why she couldn't ever marry Wyatt, and he had grown quiet, if somewhat sulky. She didn't need a repeat of last night's arguments. She wasn't at all certain she could remember them in the light of day. She didn't want to contemplate what she was leaving behind. She had cried all the tears she intended to cry last night.

As she stepped outside into the muted light of a gray

day, she gave a cry of frustration. Up the lane cantered Wyatt, followed directly behind by a coach and four.

He didn't look the least friendly as he doffed his beaver hat and made a stiff bow. With a few curt orders he had their bags stored in the boot of the carriage. He didn't even bother to dismount as the footman assisted her in. Whatever his coach driver and footman might think of this improper journey, they couldn't say it was in the least romantic. They barely exchanged two words before Wyatt made the signal for the coach to move out.

It began to rain before the morning was over. The light mist didn't slow their rapid pace, and Cassandra's stomach began to churn long before they reached a place to halt for luncheon. Wyatt hired a private room for them to dine in, but she refused to join him. She had burned her bridges last night. She wasn't about to try to build them again.

She knew he was furious when he strode out a while later and snapped at the grooms to hurry as they changed the horses. Cassandra clasped her hands in her lap and stared at the velvet squabs of the opposite seat. Anger was better than sorrow. Let him be angry. He would be rid of her sooner.

She half-expected Wyatt to join her inside the carriage as the rain grew steadier, but he merely forced the driver to a fiercer pace. The carriage lurched and rocked as it hit the ruts and rocks of the rough road, and Cassandra held desperately to the meager contents of her stomach.

They did not stop for an inn as the day darkened, but traveled on after another change of horses. Cassandra began to wonder if Merrick were driven by the devil, but, pale and proud, she refused to complain. Thick bread and a little roasted chicken had settled her stomach momentarily, and she continued to stare stonily at the drizzling rain as the scent of the sea grew stronger.

As the lights of Dover grew closer, she set her chin

with firm resolve. She had told Wyatt she was leaving him. She couldn't take the blame if he refused to believe her. If he thought she would continue to share his bed and company, he was sadly mistaken. She had meant to do this herself, and she would.

When the coach stopped, Cassandra sent Jacob off to the nearest inn for accommodations. When Wyatt came to hand her down from the carriage, she refused. He glared at her in disbelief as the water dripped from his hat to roll down his neck and saturate his already sodden cravat.

"You intend to sleep in the carriage?"

"I intend to sleep at the inn, by myself. I did not ask for your company."

"We discussed this before, Cassandra. I see no reason to change our plans. There are two perfectly respectable cabins on board that packet. I am going to claim one of them. You may stay here all night if you like, but when the boat sails in the morning, I will go without you. Your husband and I will find much to talk about while you catch up with me."

He swung on his heel and strode off to the dock. It had been a long time since he had spoken to her like that, and Cassandra bit back the tears as she watched him walk away. She hadn't wanted it to be like this. She had wanted only to have pleasant memories. Why must men be so damned difficult?

When Jacob returned to inform her the inns were full, she cursed as vividly as Duncan had ever done. Swinging down from the carriage before anyone could assist her, she stalked down the dock to the waiting boat. She'd be damned if she let Merrick get to Paris before her.

Before she could walk up the plank waiting for her, two bedraggled horsemen galloped to the end of the street, hailing the boat loudly. Cassandra hesitated at the familiar note in their voices. Jacob caught her arm and tried to lead her aboard and Lotta turned anxiously to see what kept them as Cassandra resisted being led. The horsemen had dismounted and were racing toward the dock.

A tall figure emerged out of the shadows of the boat as the shouts grew clearer. Ever aware of Wyatt's presence, Cassandra shivered and instinctively drifted closer in his direction. The shouts grew wilder, and she heard Wyatt curse. Wyatt never cursed. Startled, she looked toward him, only to see him hurriedly descend, scarcely giving her a second glance.

"Get Cassandra inside, Jacob, quickly," he ordered as he passed, but Cassandra refused to be so summarily dismissed. She jerked her arm free and turned to see where Wyatt was going.

"This is an outrage, Merrick! You can't do it!" The shorter, broader horseman stopped with hands on hips and legs akimbo before the tall earl.

Bertie! Even as she made this discovery, the taller horseman leapt forward and swung wildly at Merrick's middle.

"You bastard!" The cry was more tearful than angry, and Cassandra's heart jerked in pain. Lifting her skirts, she hurried toward the confrontation.

"Thomas! Thomas, stop that right now!" she cried as she ran. The blow had struck Wyatt squarely in the abdomen but he hadn't flinched or made any effort to halt his assailant. The irate youth swung again, but Cassandra's cries distracted him and he missed. Only Wyatt's long arm kept him from falling to the wet planks beneath their feet. Still enormously weak and drained by the mad ride, Thomas grasped his opponent's arm for support.

"I won't allow it! He can't do this," Thomas protested as Cassandra reached them. He shook off Wyatt's protective hold and stumbled toward her.

Bertie caught his brother and stepped between Wyatt and Cassandra. "Cass, you needn't do this. You can come home with us and no one will ever say a word. My mother has always mourned the fact she had only one daughter. She'll gladly welcome another."

Thomas threw off Bertie's restraining hand. "I'll marry you, Lady Cass. I'll find Rupert and kill him. You don't need be any man's mistress while I'm around, Cass. You know that."

Cassandra heard Merrick's angry intake of breath, but the tears choking her throat prevented any easy reply. She rested an imploring hand on Thomas' saturated coat and shook her head. What had she ever done to inspire such loyalty? He must be mad, but she couldn't help being touched by his brave defense. When Thomas grabbed this moment to wrap her in his suffocating embrace, Cassandra merely rested against his wide chest and hid her tears.

Wyatt's warning tone broke the spell. "Unhand her, you young lout. Bertie, take the sapskull to an inn and dry him out before I heave him into the harbor."

Thomas' grip tightened around her shoulders, but already Cassandra was backing away. She was doing it again, destroying all that was good and right and making it something evil. Maybe she belonged with Rupert and not the likes of these good people.

"Merrick, I ain't never been ashamed of you before, but I never thought you a rutting bounder before. She ain't naught but a girl. Find a loose bit of muslin to take advantage of and leave Cass alone. Ain't she had it hard enough without you to lead her astray?"

Bertie's challenging tone raised Cassandra's protective instincts and she stepped away from Thomas' possessive hold. "Albert Scheffing, you apologize at once! Do you think me some bacon-witted wigeon with no thought in my head of my own?"

"Cass, go aboard before you are soaked, and let me deal with this." Merrick's voice was low and meant to be steadying, but Cassandra ignored it.

She swung around and glared at him. "I told you to stay home. I told you I had to do this myself. But you wouldn't listen. Men! Just look at the three of you, fighting over nothing after being best of friends all your lives. I suppose you want to take pistols now and settle this like gentlemen. Fie on the lot of you! I wash my hands of you.'' Catching her cloak and skirts, she marched proudly back to the boat and her waiting servants.

Thomas stood stunned, watching her go, but Bertie turned a knowing glare on Merrick. ''I think explanations are due, old boy.''

Wyatt shook his head slowly and watched Cass safely hurried away by Lotta and Jacob. ''No, they're not, Scheffing. They're not any of your damned business at all.''

''Well, then, let's get on with this.'' Without any warning, Bertie swung his massive fist at Wyatt's jaw, sending him sprawling backward along the planks.

It was much later when Cassandra heard the stumbling footsteps and hushed whispers and muted curses as someone settled into the cabin next to hers. She pulled the covers more tightly around her and tried to force herself to sleep. Last night had been the first night in almost two months that she had slept without Wyatt's arms around her. She had to get used to the loneliness.

She scowled at Lotta's light snores in the hammock above her. Lotta had grumbled and complained when it became obvious that Merrick intended for her to stay with Cassandra and Jacob to stay with him. The only other alternative would have been for them to seek shelter in the common room with the other passengers. Lotta had grumblingly assented to this arrangement and fallen quickly to sleep. Cassandra had lain waiting for Wyatt's return.

She wondered at the extraordinary amount of noise he managed to make by himself. He was usually quite graceful despite his awkward size. Yet he seemed to be stumbling over everything in the room. He must be drunk, she decided, and her eyes opened wide at the thought. She had never seen Merrick drunk.

She didn't like the idea at all, and she cringed beneath the blankets, wondering what beastly incident would rise out of this new development. Her father and brother had never been satisfied in getting quietly drunk. They had grown more boisterous and belligerent with each drink. From the sounds next door, Wyatt was not much different.

Yet the sounds gradually quieted without any further disturbance. She lay there listening, remembering what it had felt like to have Wyatt lying beside her, his lean length keeping her warm, his strong arms holding her close. There was no room for him in this tiny bunk, but she could wish him there anyway. She was mad to cast him out.

Remembering Duncan and his threats, Cassandra closed her eyes and prayed for strength. With the increasing pounding of the rain outside, she finally slept.

The boat lifted and dipped and tilted to one side and Cassandra's stomach did the same. Groaning, she felt last night's bread and chicken reach her throat, and she grabbed for the bowl on the washstand. It was securely sunk in the hole cut out to keep it in place for just such weather, and she couldn't manage to stand to release it. The contents of her stomach spilled across the tilting floor.

The morning could only grow worse from there. Cassandra buried her misery beneath the covers as Lotta clucked with concern, strange people appeared to clean up the mess, and Jacob was consulted. Foggily she recognized Wyatt's voice, but when she tried to open her eyes to look at him, she saw a bruised and unshaven stranger in his place. She groaned and wished the apparition away and turned her back to the room.

She tried to eat a small luncheon later, but the churning sea brought it back up not long after, and she gave up trying after that. Even the thought of food made her ill, and she spewed up bile when her stomach was long since empty.

By evening Wyatt had damned servants and friends and propriety to hell and come to sit beside Cassandra as she groaned and tossed and turned in her bed. She didn't even open her eyes to look at him, but gratefully curled into the comfort of his embrace as he took her into his lap and placed her head against his shoulder.

She slept then, and Wyatt glared defiantly when Bertie appeared in the cabin door to serve as arbiter of the conventions. Seeing Cassandra peacefully asleep in the earl's arms, her colorful tresses spilling down Wyatt's shoulders, her face childish in slumber, Bertie backed away. He would sooner defy a wild lion protecting his young than Merrick at this moment.

They persuaded tea and toast down Cassandra when she woke, and Merrick left her in Lotta's care for the evening, but by morning the illness had returned again. This time Merrick was there to hold the basin, and he didn't leave her side for the rest of the day.

By the time the ferry docked, Bertie had resigned himself to what he had tried to deny before. He praised the heavens that he had somehow managed to persuade Thomas to stay behind. The sight of the Earl of Merrick carrying his lady off the boat to a waiting carriage would have driven his hotheaded younger brother to violence. He couldn't deny a tug of anguish of his own as Cassandra clung willingly to Wyatt's shoulders. It was much too late to stop whatever was happening between these two.

With Cassandra wan and ill throughout the journey to Paris, nothing improper could happen, Bertie observed. Since he and Wyatt had fought it out and got drunk together in Dover, they hadn't spoken of the relationship again. But only a blind man couldn't see the protective shadow on Wyatt's face as he lifted Cassandra from the carriage and carried her up the stairs to her room. And only an idiot wouldn't guess the reason that the earl paced up and down his own chambers every night instead of sleeping like a normal man. And Bertie was neither blind nor an idiot.

When Merrick installed them in the most expensive hotel in Paris, Cassandra was too tired and ill to notice. She curled up in the center of the massive feather bed with gratefulness and slept like the dead for a day and a night. Bertie closed his eyes and pretended he didn't see when Merrick slipped out of their shared room in the middle of the night and didn't return until dawn.

It wasn't until late the next morning that word came that Cassandra was awake and demanding breakfast. The look of relief on Wyatt's face was so blatantly obvious that Bertie was ashamed of himself for his earlier thoughts. Even smitten by love or lust, the Earl of Merrick was a proper gentleman. He wouldn't have forced his attentions on an ill woman. From the shadows under the earl's eyes, Bertie surmised Wyatt had merely sat beside Cassandra's bed and watched her sleep. Such devotion could not be motivated by lust alone.

Bertie was almost ready to commiserate with rather than condemn his friend when they went to join Cassandra for breakfast. Wyatt looked like hell, whereas Cassandra was her usual cheerful self again. She looked at Wyatt's drawn features with startlement, turned her gaze to Bertie and paled slightly, then nodded absently as a waiter poured her coffee.

"I did not expect such noble company, gentlemen." She hated coffee. She stared at it with distaste rather than meet the eyes of her company.

Merrick took a chair, removed the coffee from in front of her, and drank it himself. Bertie gaped at this rudeness and lowered himself carefully into a third chair. To his surprise, Cassandra threw Wyatt a look of gratitude and something more. The adoration in her eyes as she watched a bleary-eyed Wyatt drain the cup struck him forcibly. Wyatt was no Adonis, nor even a Byron, to be gazed upon with such open admiration. Women never looked at Wyatt like that. He gulped

blindly at his own drink as the waiter placed it in front
of him.

The obvious affection between these two made it
even harder to believe when they finally exchanged
words. Cassandra's was the opening shot.

"I am sorry to have put you to such trouble, gentlemen," she began innocuously enough, before launch-
ing her bombshell, "but you really must go home now.
I cannot expect my husband to take me back while I
am in the company of other men."

A muscle tightened over Wyatt's jaw, but he merely
signaled the waiter to fetch hot chocolate for Cassandra. When the man was gone, he answered without
any outward sign of emotion. "We'll talk to Rupert
together."

A white line appeared around Cassandra's lips as
she reached for her cup. Constrained by Bertie's presence, she did not give vent to her rage and fear. "You
cannot do that, Wyatt. I will not allow it. This is none
of your affair."

"Like hell, it isn't." The normally equable earl
glared at Cassandra, then at Bertie, wishing his friend
to blazes so he could beat sense into his mistress. He
gathered his defenses once more and tried to regain
his calm. "You are being childish, Cass. If you truly
wish to return to Rupert, I won't stand in your way. I
just insist on being there for the interview. If Rupert
becomes abusive, I'll not leave you there."

Cassandra caught her breath and forced back her
tears. Lud, how she wanted him with her when she
warned Rupert of Duncan's treachery. Perhaps . . .
Just maybe . . . She shook her head forcefully at the
thought. No, not Wyatt. She couldn't bring Wyatt into
this fantastic disaster she had made for herself. She
wanted Wyatt untouched and safe. It was all her fault
that this had happened. She would be the one punished
for it, not he. By whatever means it took, she had to
drive him away.

So she smiled brilliantly for Bertie's sake and

mouthed a few words of agreement and fled back to her room. She would have to leave now before anyone suspected anything. Wyatt would see Lotta and Jacob home. She could not afford to keep them any longer. The last few coins in Rupert's bag might feed her until she found a job as a governess or companion, but she was conscious of her own worth. Some cit with wealth seeking to better his daughter's position would surely be impressed with her lineage. If nothing else, she could resort to cards. She would survive once Wyatt left. She might die inside, but she would survive for the world to see.

Carefully concealing her coins from her concerned maid, Cassandra made some excuse about using the privy out back, and slipped out of the hotel. She had warned Merrick. He could not fault her for that. He just hadn't believed that she would do it. She just wished he hadn't looked so ill and worried when she left.

She wasn't certain that she believed that she was doing this either. Remembering the feel of Wyatt's strong arms around her, his body inside hers, she almost cried aloud with the pain of that loss. She recalled vividly the sun lighting his thick hair as he looked up over his coffee cup. She also recalled his masculine physique as he strode naked to her bed. Two Merricks she knew: the proper earl and the hungry man. She would carry them with her always.

She had difficulty explaining her destination to the sedan carriers. Her accent was miserable and they couldn't read the written address she held. A passerby straightened out the situation, and soon she was lurching through the streets in the direction of Rupert's apartment. The prospect made her more ill the closer they came.

When she finally stood in front of the impressive edifice, her stomach had churned into a return of nausea. She had to choke it back. She couldn't disgrace herself in the street right in front of her husband's home. She had to be calm and assertive.

She wished she had brought Jacob with her. He would in all probability have gone straight to Wyatt with warnings, but she should have taken the chance. Her terror of Rupert was overwhelming. Merrick had taught her the way it could be between a man and a woman, but she greatly suspected Rupert's efforts would be considerably more violent. She must not give him the opportunity to touch her.

It was midday. He certainly could not be drunk at this hour. She would give him the message and leave. Perhaps it wasn't too late to just write the message. Would he believe her? If she were in his place, she wouldn't. No, she would have to convince him, make him see reason. She could not bear the prospect of any man's death on her hands, not even Rupert's. She would give him the message about Duncan and leave, disappear from all she knew forever.

Bravely she stepped forward and lifted the knocker.

A servant efficiently swung open the door and accepted her card. She'd not had any engraved with her married name, but Rupert knew who she was. It served the purpose.

When a footman returned, she followed him through hollow, carpeted halls, their feet making no sound in the magnificence of this monument. She felt as if she were in some sacred tomb where she must speak in hushed tones. Her gaze followed the soaring ceiling upward to what very much appeared to be obscene cherubs on the cornices. She blushed at the positions she recognized, and looked back to the floor.

She almost didn't find Rupert in the room to which she was led. Towering stacks of books and enormous ancient furniture huddled in the gloom of the heavily draped windows. The books startled her. She hadn't thought Rupert a reader. Thinking herself alone, she cautiously approached the nearest shelf. Even though the titles were in French, she recognized the trick of hollow bindings to fill the shelves with the illusion of knowledge. That was the Rupert she knew.

"Well, wife, did you come to see me or my shelves?"

The voice came from so close behind her that she jumped, startled. Already she was at a disadvantage. She swung around and came face-to-face with her nemesis.

The signs of dissipation were a little more marked, but he was still a well-looking man. He was slender and not much taller than herself, but she had reason to remember the strength behind the padding of his coat. Cassandra edged away from the trap of the wall behind her.

"If I thought the shelves would show more sense and sympathy, I would speak to them. I am likely to receive more reward for my effort."

Rupert crossed his arms over his chest and leaned back against a medieval hand-carved chair. "If you have come to solicit my charity, you are quite likely right. You have already stolen all that you will get."

He was still closer than Cassandra liked, but she could not speak to the back of his head. She remained where she was. "Had you listened to me that night, I would have helped you get back all that you had given Duncan and seen him punished for his efforts. What I took scarcely compared to what you tried to take. That is not my reason for being here. I will not see another man die in my name, not even you, Rupert. I don't know what is necessary to obtain an annulment, but I suggest you seek one immediately, and be certain to let Duncan know when you have obtained it."

Rupert's fair brows lifted with cynical interest. "You are warning me? How very interesting. And what do you seek from this?"

"My freedom, that's all I ask. Duncan covets your wealth and will seek it through me. He could have hired assassins here already."

Rupert threw back his head and laughed. When he

calmed, he turned back to the glittering *objet d'art* illuminating the gloomy mausoleum around him. She was more beautiful than he remembered, more mature. The last few months had been good to her. He lowered a thoughtful gaze from her stubborn features to her full breasts and lower. When he looked up again, he grinned.

"And you are concerned for my health? How considerate of you. But I enjoy challenges, my dear, and you are worth the danger. We'll have no more talk of annulments. It is time we got to know each other. You may end up a wealthy widow, but I will have enjoyed every minute of our time together. Come, let us begin at once."

Rupert reached out to catch her arm, and Cassandra smacked his hand and moved swiftly toward the door. There was no use standing here arguing. She had given him the warning. If he wanted to make her a wealthy widow, that was fine with her. It would save Wyatt, leastways.

Rupert grabbed her from behind, jerking her around and crushing her close to his body. Cassandra caught the faint fumes of some strange liquor on his breath as he pressed his face close to hers.

"I'll not let you escape again, my dear. I paid well for you. Now I'll see what my coins have bought. Has someone else been teaching you what you should have learned in my bed?" His hand caught cruelly in her hair as she struggled to escape, and his eyes glittered as they met hers. "I do not feel the hysteria of innocence this time, Lady Cass. You know what I mean to do now, don't you?"

He chortled as one hand cupped her buttocks and pressed her hips against his arousal. Cassandra squirmed to evade him, but her movements only served to arouse him more and show her the mockery of the act to be performed. This would be no gentle lovemaking, but torture, pure and simple. It would not surprise her if he meant to kill her when he was done.

That would explain his reckless ignoring of her warning.

She had played the part of fool once more. Wyatt would come after her, and Rupert would kill him too. She had saved no one with this act of sheer willfulness. Once again, it would be all her fault.

Fighting for Wyatt's life as well as her own, Cassandra freed one arm from the trap of their bodies and swung her fist as low as she could. She only grazed his hard abdomen and made him laugh more.

Catching her hair tighter and pulling her head back, Rupert covered her mouth with his. When Cassandra refused him entrance, he jerked her hair harder and lifted her against him at the same time, causing her to gasp with surprise. His tongue took full advantage, filling her with his lust and the threat of what was to come.

Cassandra beat futilely at his shoulders, gagged and screamed, and kicked at him with her thin slippers. No one came to help. In all probability, no one could hear her in this dismal place. She bit at Rupert's tongue and scratched at his face, and he was forced to return her to the floor just to catch her hands.

She fought and struggled, bringing her knee up whenever a space opened between them, swinging her fist at him when he was forced to protect himself with his hands. He cursed and held on, knowing he was the stronger of the two and soon he would wear her down.

Already she was panting furiously as her screams rent the air. Rupert aimed a blow at her jaw, but she ducked and grabbed for a brass figurine on the shelf. The object nearly connected with his head and he had to drop his grip on her hair to avoid the blow.

Cassandra took that opportunity to lift her skirt and run. Rupert dashed after her, slamming her facefirst against the closed door and viciously tearing at the fastenings at the back of her gown, pressing her in a trap between the solid wood and himself.

As she felt his hands ripping at her clothing, Cassandra began to scream in earnest, unknowingly concealing the commotion in the hall.

Another door further down the room opened, but Cassandra didn't notice until Rupert was suddenly flung away from her and she felt herself sliding down the wooden panel, weeping.

The harsh crack of bone against bone and Rupert's furious growl forced Cassandra to find her reeling senses. She turned around, scraping her bare back against the carved wood as she took in the astonishing sight of Wyatt repeatedly plowing his fist into Rupert's stomach. Those sensitive fingers that played the pianoforte so magically had become weapons of destruction, and she could not bear the sight.

This was her fault. She had done this to him. She was a curse. She had never done anything right in her life, and now she was destroying the man she loved. With a groan, Cassandra climbed to her feet and sought some weapon.

Almost as if he read her mind, Wyatt brought his merciless punishment to a halt with one solid blow to Rupert's jaw. The smaller man crumpled and lay still where he fell.

The sound of a cheer drew Cassandra's gaze from Wyatt's furious face to the sight of the audience forming at the far end of the room. Bertie looked solemn and concerned, but Lotta and Jacob began hurrying toward her, grinning defiantly. Rupert's servants huddled uncertainly in the background.

"Get her out of here," Wyatt commanded, gesturing toward Cassandra's silent, tattered figure. "Tie her and lock her up if you must, but don't let her out of your sight until I get back."

Cassandra gaped in astonishment at this cruel command from her gentle lover, but Wyatt had already turned his attention to the man on the floor. Heart filled with pain, she didn't linger to watch what would happen now. She hastened out the door ahead of her bodyguards.

Chapter 23

Merrick signaled the servant with the basin to leave them alone. Rupert was starting to come around. The bastard could hold the cloth to his face himself. Wyatt didn't need an audience for what he had to say.

Rupert lifted a suspicious gaze to the furious tall man hovering over him. The Earl of Merrick had never been given to wearing fashionable clothing, and the lack of padding in his frock coat made him look less muscular than he actually was, as he had reason to know. Rubbing his jaw, Rupert frowned at the pain as he attempted to speak.

Merrick curtly gestured him to silence. "Just listen, and listen close. My solicitors will forward a petition for annulment to you. You will sign that petition as soon as it arrives and return it to the messenger, who will wait for it. If you do not, I will personally return with that paper, and you will be in no shape to do anything but sign it when I am done with you. Are you understanding this?"

The hatred glaring in Rupert's eyes answered that question. Merrick helped himself to a cloth brought by the servants, and wetting it, wrapped it around his injured knuckles. His aristocratic features had returned to their normally impassive expression as he gazed down upon his enemy.

"If you ever come near Cassandra again, I will shoot you, so there is no reason for you not to agree to the annulment. She is no longer under Duncan's protection, but mine. It would behoove you to note that there is a decided difference.''

So saying, Wyatt turned around and strode out. Cass would kill him if she knew what he had done, but the point was moot. He was going to strangle her for placing herself in such danger for no good reason at all.

But when he returned to the hotel, Cass was too busy being violently ill for him to do more than pace the floor outside her door. When Lotta finally assured him that her mistress was sleeping, Wyatt wearily made arrangements for their return journey.

He had known Cassandra would be a rare handful. She was willful, stubborn, temperamental, and wild to a fault. She did not know the meaning of restraint, and propriety was a synonym for prison to her. He had enjoyed the pleasures of her abandoned nature. Somehow, he had to learn to endure the consequences. Never in his life had he lashed out at anyone as he had Rupert. It would have given him great pleasure to kill the man. His own violence horrified him. Yet even as he favored his aching knuckles, Wyatt savored the moment when he heard Rupert's jaw crack.

He would become as heathen as Cassandra at this rate. Casting a glance at the door behind which she lay, he experienced a sharp pang of pleasure at the thought. For the first time in his life, he felt truly alive.

Coming face-to-face with his best friend produced another emotion entirely. Wyatt took the glass of port Bertie handed him in the private parlor outside Cassandra's room and waited for his friend to speak. He had no intention of defending his actions to anyone, but he hated to consider the loss of this one friend who had stood by his side throughout boyhood fights and adult differences. Wyatt sipped at his drink and scanned Bertie's face for the open expression of his disapproval or condemnation.

He found none. Bertie merely raised his glass in silent toast and sighed, ''She's a rare handful, ain't she?''

Wyatt felt a load lift from his shoulders, and a small smile of something approaching tenderness curved his lips as he pictured Cassandra's fierce passion in love and anger. " 'Rare' is as good a description as any. Luckily, Rupert is too crude to appreciate that. He's agreed to an annulment.''

Bertie's blond eyebrows rose, but he poured another drink in celebration. "By Jove, you're a lucky bastard, Merrick. How you going to explain that to Duncan?''

Looking decidedly grim, Wyatt set his glass aside and turned his attention to the now-quiet room where Cassandra rested. "No explanations are necessary. The deed will be done without him. Do you think I ought to send for a physician?''

Lotta emerged in time to hear this last, and she shook her head vehemently. "None of them Frenchie quacks, milord. Let us get her out of here as fast as we can, and she'll righten up, just see if she don't.''

Wyatt looked skeptical, but to Lotta's relief, he finally agreed. Bags were packed and preparations made to depart immediately.

The return journey was much more pleasant, the sun coming out long enough for them to bask in its warmth for the better part of the day. Cassandra found herself waited upon hand and foot while she rested in a chair fashioned for her on the ferry's deck. The livid bruise on the side of her face began to fade and the throbbing disappeared, but only in the evenings could she keep her food down long enough to enjoy the company.

Wyatt discreetly left her alone as he had promised, but Cassandra feared the questions in his eyes when he joined her on deck. She had left him, defied his wishes, and caused a great deal of grief. Bertie in all probability thought her a fallen woman and would no longer allow her to visit his family. She had created disaster and chaos all around her, and had not accomplished even one of her goals. Rupert was still in danger from Duncan, and Wyatt still seemed to feel responsible for her. He must hate her for the upheaval she had caused in his pleasant life. She could scarcely bear to face him. Perhaps she ought to return to London and Duncan.

But when they arrived in Dover, everyone was as solicitous as ever. All the decent rooms were taken. Bertie immediately ordered Thomas to surrender the room he had taken while waiting for them, and the two brothers agreed to travel ahead, leaving Wyatt and Cassandra to travel at a more leisurely pace. The shadows under Cassandra's eyes spoke of a need for rest and quiet, and Bertie gave a silent shake of his head as he caught Wyatt's hand in farewell. Grateful for his understanding, Wyatt watched as the brothers rode off, then turned back to the stairs and the room where Cassandra rested, the room they would share for the first time in over a week.

Cassandra had made no objection when he had led her to the room and had their luggage carried in. She had said she was leaving him. It was very probable that she no longer wished his attentions, but he couldn't allow her to lie ill and alone in a strange inn. They would have to settle this matter sometime. He would let her rest, and they could discuss it when she woke.

Wyatt found her sleeping soundly with Lotta at her side. He dismissed the maid to find Jacob in the servants' quarters, and began removing his travel-stained cravat. Cassandra looked so pale and still, he sat down beside her to be certain she was only sleeping. It was an odd feeling, this need to protect someone else, to know her life was in his keeping—odd, but somehow satisfying.

Wyatt touched her brow and Cassandra stirred. A murmur of protest passed her lovely lips and, satisfied, Wyatt smiled and began to remove the rest of his clothing. Even in sleep with the mark of Rupert's hand across her jaw, she was beautiful. Perhaps she would leave him come morning, but for now she was still his to care for.

When Cassandra woke, it was dawn and her stomach was churning, although there could not possibly be anything left in it. She reached wearily for the basin, as had become her habit these last few mornings. Only when a strong hand reached to hold her shoulder did she realize she was not alone.

Wyatt held her quietly as she heaved the meager contents of her stomach into the bowl. Then he rose and mixed a weak concoction of brandy and water to clear her mouth and sent for someone to bring warm water for washing and hot tea to drink.

Cassandra watched warily as Wyatt prowled the room wearing only his trousers as he waited for his orders to be carried out. Her gaze took in the raw scrapes on his knuckles, rested thoughtfully on the bare expanse of his chest and shoulders, but refused to lift to meet his eyes. They had discussed nothing since Paris. She understood instinctively that that lack was about to end. When Wyatt finally came to sit on the bed beside her, she was tense and nervous.

He leaned back against the headboard and drew Cassandra into the curve of his arm. She came reluctantly, red-gold hair spilling in a silken rainbow over her breasts and down his side. She rested her head against his shoulder, and he stroked the silken waterfall thoughtfully.

"How long have you been ill in the mornings?" Wyatt asked as casually as he could manage.

With all the things to be said between them, this was the least expected. Cassandra frowned and wrapped a curl from his chest around her finger. "The carriage ride made me sick coming down here, that is all. I'll be fine when we're home again."

Ignoring this remark, Wyatt forced himself to continue the interrogation. He had been abysmally blind for too long. It was time now for some home truths. "Cassandra, we have not slept together this past week. Have you been having your monthly courses?"

Shocked at the proper Merrick asking her such an

improper question, Cassandra finally glanced up at his face. What she saw there terrified her into answering. She didn't want to lose him through lack of honesty or stubborn willfulness. Crushing her embarrassment, she replied with curiosity, "No. Is that why you stayed away from me?"

Wyatt tipped her chin up so he could study the lovely curves of her bewildered face. He had a sinking feeling in the pit of his stomach as he contemplated all that innocence. How could he have ignored it for so long? "Has your mother explained nothing of what happens in a marriage bed?" he demanded.

Cassandra grew even more bewildered. "Only that it is unpleasant. But I thought that what we did . . ."

Her voice trailed off as a slow smile curved Wyatt's lips. He touched her cheek gently. "Yes, what we did is what happens between man and wife. For some, it is unpleasant. I can vouch for that. We are among the lucky ones. But did she not explain the results of our lovemaking? Come, Cass, you are a country girl. Surely you know what comes of coupling?"

She stared at him in confusion, waiting for him to explain. Wyatt sighed and pressed a kiss upon her forehead. His palm sought her breast beneath the linen nightshift. Was it his imagination, or did the firm swell already seem a little fuller?

"You have shared my bed for nigh on two months, my sweet. Not once have you refused me because of your courses. Can you remember the last time you suffered them?"

This was really too intimate a conversation to be having. Cassandra attempted to sit up and escape, but Wyatt bent to place a kiss upon her ear. At the same time, his hand insinuated itself beneath her gown, and she groaned with the pleasure they had not shared in a week. Desire flooded her veins, and she arched welcomingly against him, turning her lips to nibble at his throat.

"I'll have your answer, Cass. It is important."

"I don't remember, Wyatt. Why is it important?" She suddenly sat up when he withdrew his hand. "Am I ill? Is that what you're telling me?"

Flashing blue eyes dared him to confirm this outrageous statement. Wyatt chuckled, his concern evaporating at this return of her spirit. He continued unbuttoning the multitudinous seed pearls of her gown. "Not ill, my love, just increasing, I suspect. I would know better if you could bring yourself to remember some dates."

Increasing? Cassandra searched his face for some sign of a jest. "Increasing, like Christa? I don't look like that. I'm not married. I can't be increasing. That means carrying a baby, doesn't it? Only married ladies have babies. So I can't be increasing."

She sounded so very logical that she almost convinced herself. Wyatt continued smiling as he shook his head and began to push the voluminous gown down over her shoulders. "Married ladies and ladies who behave as married ladies. What we do here in bed is reserved for husbands and wives. That is why I have been trying to persuade you to marry me. You are in all probability carrying my child, Cass. You have no choice but to marry me now." The decision was made, the die was cast. He literally breathed relief as he continued undressing her.

Stunned, Cassandra scarcely noticed as the gown fell from her shoulders. She didn't look pregnant. He was making up that tale to persuade her to his thinking. Still, his questions bothered her, nagged at her mind even as Wyatt began to possess her body. She couldn't *think* when his kisses caressed her like that. They had denied each other for too long, and the need was stronger than thought. She gave herself up to his touch, reveled in the pleasure of his flesh against hers. Only somewhere in the back of her mind did she keep thinking: he could be putting his child inside me. The notion was a powerful one, more driving than the desire flooding between them. Cassandra rose up to meet his thrust with an eagerness and a fear unmatched in their previous experience. Wyatt's child. She could bear Wyatt's child. The phrases sang through Cassandra's mind as her body convulsed with the frantic urgency of his rhythm, and she opened wide to receive his seed.

She was pregnant. She understood it now. Somewhere deep inside where they had joined, a baby grew. It scarcely seemed credible. She, Cassandra Howard, carrying the Earl of Merrick's child. The scandal would be enormous. She didn't care. Turning on her side to keep him inside her when he rolled over afterward, she kissed his shoulder.

"When you first took me to see Thomas, that was the last time," she murmured sleepily.

Wyatt cuddled her closer, knowing what she meant. That was well over two months ago. They hadn't wasted any time. It had taken months to get his wife pregnant. It had taken Cass a mere week or two. His arm tightened around her, and he prayed feverishly to a God he had taken for granted too long. Blessings came in strange ways. He just hoped this wouldn't turn out to be worse than the plague of Job. He had to keep her from the scandal.

But as Cassandra lay relaxed and warm in his arms, Wyatt imagined a lifetime of nights like this, and he smiled. It was worth every bit of trouble she got him into.

When they finally set out for home, Merrick treated Cassandra with such care that Lotta and Jacob immediately became suspicious. Cassandra laughed and threatened to take his horse and leave him with the cushioned carriage. Later, she was grateful for Wyatt's concern when the corrugated roads left her stomach in her throat and he ordered an early rest.

They proceeded at a much slower pace than before, and Cassandra felt stronger at this end of the journey than the other. When the carriage drove past the drive to her house and continued on to Merrick's home, she leaned out the window in puzzlement, trying to find Wyatt for explanation.

It wasn't long in coming. When the carriage rumbled to a halt at the entrance stairs, Wyatt beat the footman to the door. Without a word of warning, he slid his arms beneath her legs and shoulders and lifted her clear of the carriage. Cassandra grabbed at his neck for support as she swayed in the air, and then she was resting comfortably against his chest while the Earl of Merrick carried her across the threshold.

Thoroughly bemused, she heard him announce to the waiting servants that his wife required tea and a hot bath. She still wasn't certain that this wasn't some sort of practical joke when he carried her up the stairs to the family rooms that she had never entered. But when she found herself in his obviously masculine chambers and heard the dowager's screams floating up from below, Cassandra knew she had been well and fully trapped.

As Wyatt set her down upon the bed, Cassandra stared at him accusingly. "You did this on purpose, didn't you? You have never forgiven me for locking you in my bedroom."

Wyatt's lips twitched as he met the gaze of his rumpled and irritated lover. "I have never forgiven you for refusing my offer, puss. Now you have no choice." He caught her shoulders and gently pushed her back to the bed when she rose to protest. "It will be only a matter of weeks before it is official. Do not deny me this time, Cass. There is the child to think of."

The child. Well and truly trapped. She continued to stare at him accusingly as the room filled with servants carrying buckets and tubs and tea and lighting the fire. Lotta came in with them, ordering the placement of the luggage and urging the maids to be careful with the unpacking, imperiously managing the operation without lifting a hand to help. At the sound of the dowager outside the door, Wyatt bowed regretfully in

Cassandra's direction and left her in Lotta's care, closing the door carefully behind him.

She ought to call his bluff. She ought to tell all and sundry that she was St. Wyatt's mistress, and he had installed her in his home under his mother's nose. It would serve him right for his high-handed methods. This was little better than abduction. He could never get away with this.

But Wyatt had a way of turning everything to his wishes. Against Cassandra's sound judgment he had taken her to his bed, given her a home, obviously browbeaten Rupert into an annulment, and even got her with child. She was beginning to believe there wasn't anything he couldn't do when he put his mind to it.

There was only one flaw in this picture. She wasn't a Howard. The child she carried had Merrick's noble blood and the ancestry of some unnamed commoner who had got her mother with Cassandra and disappeared. Merrick had to be told before he made a fool out of them both. As the room cleared of servants, Cassandra signaled for Lotta and sent her off to find the earl.

Lying in the tub that must have served many noble Mannerings, Cassandra gazed idly at her surroundings. This was how she could have lived had she been truly the daughter of a marquess. Her parentage had never bothered her overmuch before. Had it not been for Duncan, she would have thought twice before telling Wyatt now. But she had to make him see that this would never work, before Duncan blackmailed him into bankruptcy.

She looked longingly at the massive draped bed on the dais between the two bowed windows. The window draperies were pulled back only enough to allow in a sliver of sun and reveal the welcoming window seats within. She could easily live out all her days here, sleeping on those pillows, lifting her arms to Wyatt as he came to her during the night, bearing his children on that bed. She would be secure here, and her child would have a chance of happiness. Why couldn't she be granted this peace?

The door slipped open and closed and Wyatt was standing there, a ray of sun glinting off the rich chestnut highlights of his hair. He looked immensely weary, but a smile began to curve his lips as he gazed upon the creamy goddess emerging from the waters of his tub.

"Bubbles become you, my sweet. What is the urgent matter we must discuss before you even have your tea?"

Wyatt handed her a towel as Cassandra rose from the tub. Never had he admired her slender height more. She was the goddess he proclaimed her, from the stack of sun-touched tresses, the ripe curve of her generous breasts, to the well-turned length of her legs. He wanted those legs around him now. His loins swelled at just the thought, but he refrained from doing more than discarding his soiled riding jacket and cravat.

This was his bedroom and he was entitled to undress here. Cassandra bit back a protest as she reached for her robe. She felt no shyness in standing naked before him, but she wanted his thoughts on what she had to say, not on what she wasn't wearing. If he proceeded to undress, she would have great difficulty in forming the words.

"Wyatt, there are very good reasons why I can't be your wife. I do wish you would listen to reason."

Relieved of the nuisance of his coat, Wyatt undid the fastenings of his cuff. He caught the flicker of interest in her eyes and deliberately he shed his waistcoat while speaking with apparent disinterest. "Your marriage will shortly be ended, Cass. It was a mockery of a marriage and well you know it. I can see no other reason why you can't be my wife."

Cassandra held the robe tightly around her and stared at him pleadingly. For once, he had to listen to her. Perhaps he was older and wiser and better able to control the situations that sent Cassandra fleeing into the night, but this time the situation was beyond his control. He had to listen.

"Wyatt, sit still and hear me out. I am going to say this only once. I never thought to shame my mother by revealing her secrets, but I cannot shame you by keeping them. There was a time when I didn't care, but I do now. Will you listen?"

Wyatt was listening. He dropped his waistcoat to stare at her. In whatever roundabout way she went at it, Cassandra had just admitted that she cared. He had not thought the matter important before now. Suddenly it was very important. He wanted to know that he was doing the right thing. He wanted to know that she cared enough to stay with him for a lifetime.

"I am listening, Cass, but I doubt that there is anything you can say to change my mind."

Cassandra nodded and gathered her thoughts. She could not face him as she named herself bastard. She wandered to the window and looked out over the magnificent emerald park. A willow blew in the breeze over the shallow lake constructed just to look beautiful for the owner of this chamber. No Howard had ever considered manipulating nature to create beauty.

"I am not the daughter of the Marquess of Eddings, Wyatt. Look at me, then look at Duncan. He is the image of the late marquess. Have you ever seen so dark a parent breed so fair a child?" She mouthed the words that Duncan had once thrown at her. They had been meaningless then, but she understood them now. Her mind wandered, wondering what the child inside her would look like.

"Never have I seen so fair a child, nor woman." Wyatt came up behind Cassandra and circled her waist with his arm, sheltering her against his chest. "Actually, it is quite a relief to believe you are not of their tainted blood. I feared waking up one day to discover our child looked just like Duncan."

Cassandra smothered a nervous laugh at this bold

condemnation of her family. "You have no fear of that, perhaps, but what kind of person would have sired me and then left my mother to suffer the result? All I know is that he is not of the nobility. He could have been a footman for all I am aware."

Wyatt swung her around, pulled her into his arms, and kissed her thoroughly. While she was still breathless, he replied, "Then he was one handsome, talented footman, and I welcome him to the family. You can make up any tale you like, Cass. I still intend to marry you."

He didn't believe her. He wouldn't believe her about Duncan either. She wasn't even certain she believed Duncan for any length of time, but she knew him too well. Duncan would make Wyatt's life a misery until he had what he wanted, and he never ran out of wants. She couldn't do that to Wyatt. She couldn't.

But she couldn't leave either. Giving herself up to Wyatt's impassioned kisses, she vowed to think about it later.

Chapter 24

"I don't believe a word of it. He could not possibly have married you. It is not like Wyatt to behave so impulsively."

Cassandra moved a rose into closer proximity with some lovely branch of white flowers in the vase and wondered what the name of the plant might be she had stolen it from. Perhaps Wyatt had a picture book of flowers in his library. She liked to know the names of things.

To the dowager's spiteful remarks she replied, "Not at all impulsive, Mother." Cassandra grinned to herself at the dowager's furious intake of breath. "He has planned the annulment for months. Surely he told you." She really shouldn't torment the woman like that, but the countess had huffed and puffed and made Wyatt's life a misery. It was time someone took the wind out of her sails. The dowager countess, she amended to herself. Wyatt would have all the world believe that Cassandra was the new countess. The idea was patently ridiculous, of course, but the charade was certainly amusing.

"It is not right. I don't know what this world is coming to. Young people didn't used to be so ill-behaved. They respected their elders and married where told. I cannot like this."

The dowager sat on the sofa and fanned herself against the heat of the afternoon sun pouring in the salon windows. Cassandra had already won the battle of the draperies, pulling them open every time the dowager ordered a footman to close them.

At the monotony of this complaint that had been heard once an hour every day of the last week, Cassandra sighed and stepped back to admire her arrangement. "Perhaps arranged marriages like that of my parents are the reason we have decided to choose for ourselves. I can't see that Wyatt was particularly happy with the marriage you arranged for him."

There was certainly truth in that, but Lady Merrick refused to admit it to this willful chit. "You cannot mix meadowsweet with roses. It is vulgar."

Cassandra's smile brightened. "I like it." Defiantly she set the vase in the center of the Adam mantel.

Not having yet learned the danger signal of Cassandra's smile, the countess blundered on. "You have no talent for that sort of thing. I have supervised the flower gardens for decades. I ought to know."

The challenge was flung, and Cassandra rose to accept it. "The gardens are cold and formal and not at all as I would like. I think I shall ask Wyatt if I might have a corner to do as I wish."

As the dowager emitted a small scream of rage and began to turn purple, Cassandra donned a radiant smile and swept out, signaling a footman to fetch the smelling salts. At least once a day she succeeded in sending the dowager into the vapors. It was becoming quite tedious.

Restless, she hurried up to her chamber to change into a riding habit. Despite her outrageous words, she had not attempted to interfere in the day-to-day operations of the household. She felt an outsider, an impostor, and she did not assert what little authority she possessed. Lotta had reported that the servants were whispering among themselves about the hastiness of the marriage. They had little knowledge of the legality of annulments, but sensitive feelers for scandal. The earl's impromptu marriage reeked of scandal. She knew better than to upset the apple cart when it stood on such precarious grounds.

The brilliant blue riding habit Wyatt had ordered for her made her momentarily happy as Lotta helped her pull it on. The long train of the skirt swept elegantly about her feet, and the tailored jacket made her feel like a countess even if she were not. She had never owned clothes like this before, nor had a room like this to call her own.

Cassandra's gaze swept the lovely fragility of the Queen Anne furniture, the white eyelet and lace of the bed hangings, and the splashes of pale green on pillows and carpets that created this chamber next to Wyatt's. She had made few changes in the room, liking it just the way it was. Wyatt had insisted that she needed a room of her own to escape the activity of the household. She had not understood his insistence at first, but she was beginning to now. This was her haven. No one could intrude unless invited, even Wyatt.

Not that Wyatt needed any invitation. She smiled to herself as she remembered last night when he had swept her from the piano bench and carried her daringly into the elegant state bedchamber and made love to her on the gold-embroidered tapestry that covered the not-to-be-touched gilded bed. She had slept in his arms every night of this week. The nights were the happiest of her life.

The days presented a problem. Refusing to think about that, Cassandra pulled on her riding gloves and started down the stairs. Problems had a way of taking care of themselves after a while. Right now, all she needed was fresh air.

Wyatt had insisted that a groom accompany her whenever she went out. She knew he feared she would crack her head on another branch, but it was a dreadful nuisance to be followed all about. Still, he had been so thoughtful about everything else, she could afford to make this one concession.

The bars of the trap he had caught her in seemed

remarkably resilient. She did as she pleased, went where she pleased without incurring Wyatt's wrath in any form. She didn't know how long he would remain so complacent, but perhaps if they didn't go about much in society, she could learn to live this way. But could Wyatt?

It was another of those things that nagged at her conscience. Turning her mount to the apple orchard, Cassandra kicked her heels and drove the thought out of her head.

In the orchard, she surprised a handful of ragged village urchins seeking the young green apples among the branches. The few children on the ground squealed and ran away as she approached. With amusement, she noted the others pretended to blend in with the leaves. They weren't terribly successful.

The groom helpfully offered to pull the "little beggars" down, but Cassandra shook her head. Riding up under the branch where the smallest hid, she called up to her. "Those apples will make you sick. You'll have to wait until they're ripe. I know where there's a lovely cherry tree. Why don't we go see if the cherries are ripe yet? Then we can have Cook make us some pies."

The child looked terrified and clung to the branches, but a bigger boy leaned down from a higher roost and gave her a suspicious glance. "Who are you?"

"Lady Merrick," she answered promptly, without a qualm. "And these are my trees. I used to climb them when I was your age, but I waited until the apples were red. Bring your friends, and I'll show you the cherries. I've grown too big to climb up in the branches anymore."

They seemed to accept that ingenuous statement. With whoops and laughter they tumbled from the trees and ran in the direction that Cassandra led them. Judging by the pained look on the groom's face, Wyatt would raise an unholy ruckus when he discovered what she'd done, but it was time she tested the bars of her

cage more fully. If he didn't understand that she had
no concept of property rights by now, he never would.

By the time the afternoon ended, the entire household understood that the new regime had a wholly different vision of propriety than the old. The head
gardener nearly fainted at the sight of a horde of little
urchins scavenging his prized cherry trees. The cook,
a more prosaic lady with children of her own, merely
shook her head in bemusement as the kitchen filled
with dirty gremlins carrying pails of ripe and unripe
cherries.

The new countess herself looked disheveled and
windblown as she led the grubby crew through the
enormous kitchens to a basin, where she ordered tiny
hands to be washed. She failed to mention faces, and
juice-smeared mouths grinned when she had to fetch
a rag and wipe them herself.

The commotion inevitably reached the ears of the
dowager, who promptly sought her son in his study.
Wyatt lifted his brows questioningly at his mother's
incoherent tirade, and shrugging, followed her through
the corridors to the kitchens he seldom saw.

As the dowager glared defiantly at the scene within,
Wyatt halted in the doorway to fully absorb the magnificence of this chaos. His gaze found Cassandra first,
and his lips turned up at the corners at the sight of his
brilliant sun goddess with flour dotting her nose and
cherry juice smeared across her cheek. The neat pile
of tresses he had noted with approval at the breakfast
table now hung in tattered wisps about her face and
throat, and occasionally she brushed at them, account-
ing for the interesting pattern of food across her face.

She sang some foolish song he greatly suspected she
had invented on the spot, since it involved cherries and
cherry pies, but the children chanted the refrain with
delight. His brows lifted even higher at the sight of a
half-dozen village urchins patting at rounds of dough
and covering themselves in flour. His heart gave a
quiver at the thought of the kitchen tantrums he had

suffered in the past, but when his gaze swept to the temperamental staff, they were laughing and singing and nudging each other while pretending he wasn't there.

He didn't have to be told that his cherry trees had been stripped, that the cherry jam he so enjoyed would be in short supply this year, and that the cherry tarts meant for his table would be filling the bellies of these urchins before day's end. He ought to raise a fearful scold or Cassandra would think she was entitled to turn his household into an uproar at every whim and fancy.

But as he watched her carefully flute the pie crust, using the pudgy little fingers of the smallest tot, he could not bear to interrupt. He could not remember the last time he had seen a child run riot through the household, nor heard the sound of joyous laughter. He was just beginning to realize what his orderly life had been missing. His mother continued to glare at him, but Wyatt had the worst feeling that there was a silly grin spreading across his face.

"Wyatt! Do not stand there like a blithering idiot! We'll have no dinner tonight if this continues. Make them stop this commotion at once!"

The dowager's voice carried, and Cassandra glanced up to seek the source of complaint. At sight of Wyatt, her lips curved in a genuine smile of delight, illuminating the entire kitchen. The children instantly turned and silenced in awe at sight of the grand earl himself.

"I'm not certain I've quite got that melody." Wyatt advanced into the now quiet kitchen, humming lightly to himself. "How did it go? 'Cherries, lovely cherries, sweeter than sugar in the summertime'?" He sang the refrain he had heard earlier.

Cassandra's smile grew even brighter as she joined him. The children laughed uncontrollably when she plopped a fat fruit into the earl's mouth before he could finish the song, and juice dribbled down his chin before he could swallow it.

When Wyatt wreaked revenge by kissing Cassandra's cheek with his juicy mouth, the dowager gave a squeak of fury and departed in a huff. No one noticed her departure.

The fact that his dinners weren't served on time, that his mother suffered the megrims daily, and that the neighbors stared at him as if he were gone mad did not diminish Wyatt's enjoyment of Cassandra's vibrant presence in his life. She had the gardeners in a snit, the grooms in shock, and the kitchen in song. Lotta and Jacob had appointed themselves lady's maid and valet respectively, and upon occasion usurped the duties of head housekeeper and butler, causing these worthies to threaten to give notice. Merrick complacently heard their complaints and referred them to Cassandra, who cajoled them with promises he didn't care to investigate. He rather suspected that the wages of his staff were about to double, and he would be supporting them all into doddering old age, but he was too happy to care.

When his mother caught him singing one of Cassandra's nonsense songs as he threw the morning's post upon the fire, the dowager held her hand to her heart and stared at him as if he had truly taken leave of his senses.

"What has come over you, Wyatt?" she demanded when she gained her breath. "You go about as if you were a heedless child. You cannot discard letters as if they are of no importance. You have *always* answered your correspondence. What has she done to you?"

Wyatt flipped another invitation into the growing pyre as he considered his mother's question carefully. True, he was being blatantly irresponsible by ignoring his social obligations. And she was right, he was behaving like a child, singing silly songs and dreaming silly dreams and generally enjoying himself rather than facing the consequences of what he had done, and the consequences were truly enormous.

But as he considered what he had done, a happy grin began to form on his face. He had found a woman who made him want to sing. He had started a child after all these lonely years of craving one. He had kidnapped a wife, bedded a goddess, and decimated the desperate loneliness of these cold halls. He knew very well what Cassandra had done to him, and his grin grew wider as he replied, "She made me love her, Mother. Astonishing, wouldn't you say?"

And singing softly to himself, the elegant and proper Earl of Merrick went in search of his hoyden mistress.

"Wyatt, you must stop her at once!"

Wyatt choked as his cravat nearly strangled him with the slamming open of his bedroom door. Jacob swiftly removed the mangled linen but remained out of the line of fire as the earl swung around to face his furious wife.

"Normal people knock before they enter," he began calmly enough. It was obvious Cassandra had not even begun to dress for dinner, and he had invited the Scheffings to dine with them tonight.

Cassandra ignored his reprimand. Irate, she shoved a tumbling lock of hair from her face. "Your mother has ordered all my flower arrangements thrown out before the guests arrive. You know I have not come to you with complaints before, but I will not have this! I have worked so hard to make these rooms look lived in, and she is ordering it all thrown out! I will not have it, Wyatt!"

He thought she might follow this tirade by stamping her foot, but she apparently checked the impulse to do so. Stormy blue eyes awaited his reaction, and Wyatt held out his hand for his cravat. He had known Cassandra and his mother would never get on. He was well aware of the many altercations that had taken place this past week and more. He knew of only one solution to end them, but he hated to make that decision unless forced. It would be much better if they could learn to get along.

"Can we not have this argument later, Cass?" He lifted his chin and tried to arrange the folds of linen into some respectability, but he was unaccustomed to having an audience for this process. "The Scheffings will be arriving shortly."

Cassandra came across the room and brushed his fingers aside, assembling the linen with nimble fingers. "Did you not have a valet before Jacob arrived?" she inquired severely.

"Mother dismissed him for insubordination." Wyatt grinned at the fierce look forming on her face. "I gave him good references and found him a new position, so don't look at me like that. You will just have to learn that she is accustomed to having things her own way."

Cassandra patted the linen in place and turned to Jacob. "You are not dismissed unless I say you are, Jacob, is that understood?"

Wyatt caught her by the back of the neck. "Have I nothing to say in the matter?"

Crossly she walked away from his hold. "No. If your mother told you to dismiss him, you would. You are just much too nice, Wyatt. I shall go downstairs and tell her I'll set fire to her bed hangings one night when she's asleep if she touches one petal of those flowers."

She stormed out, slamming the door behind her. When Jacob turned a fearful look to see how his employer was taking this tantrum, he stared in wonder as the earl's shoulders shook in mirth.

Catching the servant's eyes, Wyatt refused to stifle a disgraceful grin. "I daresay she would, wouldn't she? Does anyone know how the old manse burned down?"

Jacob looked properly horrified but held his tongue. If anyone knew the answer to that question, it would be Lotta.

Merrick noted the flowers were still standing when

he arrived downstairs to greet his guests. Cassandra had an eye for color, but the arrangements reflected her rather capricious habits. Wildflowers mingled with cultivated roses and shrubbery to form airy but far-from-formal bouquets. The petals from one shrub were already making a snowfall on the polished foyer table. At one time, he would have ordered it removed. Now he rather approved of the splash of color in the dismal formality of this hall.

Cassandra came down to join him just as their guests arrived. She looked stunning in the shimmering pale green lutestring gown he had ordered for her. With her hair pulled severely back from her delicate face, she looked older, more mature, and not in the least rattled from the haste she must have used to get ready after her tantrum. The glance she gave him was still cold, but strangely enough, Wyatt felt warm inside. Had any other woman looked at him like that, he would have shied away from her company forevermore. With Cassandra, he was confident the spat would be settled in his bed a few hours hence. He had to turn his concentration on his guests and away from his "wife" to cool his stirring ardor.

The dowager did not come down to dinner. When Wyatt whispered a question in Cassandra's ear before they led their guests into the dining room, she answered blithely, "She has locked herself in her room and refused to come down. Shall I have dinner sent up to her?"

Wyatt didn't want to hear what had brought that on. He shook his head and sought out the quiet, pleasant Mrs. Scheffing. He could very well have made a major mistake in assuming Cassandra could be tamed to polite society. Remembering the disastrous episodes of Hampton Court, he shivered. He would make certain not to suggest billiards after dinner.

Still, as he accepted congratulations on his marriage and watched Cassandra charm the stout squire, Merrick felt the changes in himself. He had only to recognize that, pretend as he would, the woman sitting in the place of honor as his wife was actually his mistress, to realize he had come a long way from the staid man he once had been.

Cassandra looked up then and caught his eye, and the worried look she gave him sent a sharp pang through his middle. She had changed too. For all her heedless ways, she had developed a conscience and a concern for others—most others, he amended, his mother excluded.

Later that night, she came into his room without knocking, as usual. Wyatt gave a nod and sent Jacob away. As he proceeded to remove his waistcoat, Wyatt debated giving her the scold she deserved, but he couldn't do it. Her eyes seemed enormous in her pale face, and the clinging of her frail nightrail to her slender figure reminded him heavily of the child she carried, a child she hadn't wanted or asked for. He owed her much, and he lifted his arms in welcome and held her to his chest when she came to him.

"Are you very angry with me?" she whispered against his shirt.

"Very," he agreed.

"Shall I go away and leave you alone?"

That question held echoing chasms of the future, and Wyatt crushed her tighter. "Never. I'm tired of being alone."

She sighed. "So am I. Hold me, Wyatt, and don't be angry anymore. I can't bear it."

"No one could be angry with you for long, my sweet, most especially me." Gently Wyatt rode his hand down to the very small curve of her abdomen. "How does Junior fare today? Does he still trouble you?"

"Only in that I have never had a stomach before." She mocked a small pout and looked up to him. "What will you do with me when I am fat and ugly?"

"Make love to you," he answered promptly, earning himself a kick with bare toes. When he had her firmly in his hold again, he asked with curiosity, "Did you think Christa fat and ugly?"

"Just fat." Cassandra squirmed in his embrace. "She looked awfully uncomfortable. How will I be able to ride when I get like that?"

Wyatt picked her up and threw her on the bed, falling down beside her and holding her pinned when she tried to roll away. He gazed sternly down into her flushed face. "You will not, my lady, so you might as well begin practicing temperance now. No more wild gallops across the meadow like the one today. Understood?"

Cassandra gazed up into his frowning features and felt a softening inside as she read the worry and concern in his dark eyes. She lifted a hand to stroke his hair and smiled warmly. "The child is important to you, isn't it?"

He wanted to say, "Not as important as you," but she owned too much of him already. He would wait until he was certain his feelings were returned. He spread his hand over the nearly invisible thickening of her waist. "I want this child very much, Cassandra. I hope I have not asked too much of you."

"No more than you have asked of yourself, my lord." She smiled then and pulled his head down to meet her kiss.

Chapter 25

The warning that Rupert had returned from France came unexpectedly a week later.

Wyatt had grown anxious over the fact that his messengers had not returned with the annulment papers. The news that Rupert was no longer in Paris struck him with foreboding. He had hoped to have the papers signed before Rupert discovered that he had not actually murdered Thomas. It looked as if time had run against him.

He stared at the note in his hand, then crumpled it and flung it at the brass container beside his desk. His solicitors had assured him the annulment could be effected without Rupert's cooperation, but that meant Cass filing the petition. He wasn't at all certain he would receive any more cooperation from her than from Rupert.

But the fact that Rupert had returned to London without signing the papers meant he was prepared to fight for his wife. That did not bode well at all.

Wyatt paced the room, clenching and unclenching his fists. He was not a coward, but there had been no room in his life for the idle pursuits of other young gentlemen. While his peers were playing at fisticuffs and fencing, he had been learning the operations of his estates here in Kent, others in Sussex, and in the north. He had even inherited a small competence in Scotland. Although he had good managers, they were only as good as the supervision they received. At the age of twelve, when he had come into his inheritance, and even at twenty, when he had taken control of it, he had not had a minute to spare beyond the supervision of these responsibilities. He could challenge Rupert to a duel of adding figures or counting cows, but he greatly suspected that wouldn't settle the matter.

The thought of losing Cassandra and the child she carried to that brutal bastard could not be borne. He would have to remove her somewhere safe while he dealt with the problem. Perhaps now that she knew she carried a child, she could be more easily persuaded to begin annulment proceedings.

But then he would have to tell her that Rupert was back, and she might get another one of her notions to talk to him herself. It was impossible to anticipate the little witch. She might take it in her head to run away and hide, and this time he wouldn't be so lucky as to find her. He still didn't know why she had left him last time. If it was that nonsense about being a bastard, perhaps he had settled that fear, and she would be all right. And then again, perhaps not. Who knew?

The uproar in the downstairs hall came to Wyatt as a distant roar, but he ignored it. Cassandra was as easily capable of quelling a riot as causing it. He seldom found it necessary to intervene. Even his mother had given up any hope of his assistance. The running argument with Cassandra had become part of her routine. She certainly couldn't complain of boredom any longer.

Contemplating all the changes Cassandra had brought into his life ever since she had plummeted into his arms those many months ago, Merrick despaired at the thought of losing her. He couldn't go back to deadly dull dinners of discussing the length the grass should be allowed to grow in the lawn. He couldn't imagine climbing into his bed without Cassandra there warming the sheets for him. Life without her laughter and song, or even her tempest and fury, would not be a life at all. He was truly and thoroughly well smitten.

So, somehow, he would have to learn to manage

Cassandra and her mismanaged life as well as he did his estate. Obtaining an annulment and keeping Rupert at bay would be his first aim. He had used persuasion and brute force without any luck. The next step was trickery.

That thought came to Wyatt like a lightning bolt. Of course! Rupert and Duncan and their ilk swindled their way through life. Those were the only terms they knew. So he would have to beat them on their own terms. He wasn't at all certain that he knew the rules, but if he tried to think like Cassandra . . .

Jacob knocked at his open study door, and Wyatt looked up in surprise. The lanky ex-soldier knew his place very well and had never disturbed his privacy. As a former servant of Rupert's and a loyal supporter of Cassandra, his credentials were open to question, but Wyatt had found his service exemplary. He lifted a questioning brow and gestured for the man to enter.

"I wish to offer my resignation, my lord, effective immediately."

Surmising this had something to do with the uproar below, Wyatt sat on the edge of his desk and eyed the stoic valet with impatience. "Might I ask why?"

Jacob appeared to develop a slight red tinge around the ears. "Lotta and I work together, my lord. That's understood between us. If she is no longer welcome here, I must go with her."

"Cassandra dismissed Lotta?" Wyatt didn't try to hide his incredulity. The chit was like no lady's maid he had ever known. She was a wanton piece of goods if he had ever seen one. But the bonds between maid and mistress were strong, and he had no wish to sever them. He found it difficult to believe that Cass would do so.

"No, my lord. Lady Merrick did."

Wyatt nodded in understanding. Cass wouldn't come to him with this latest argument, and Jacob feared it was one she would lose. The charge must be serious indeed. He sent the man a piercing look. "For what reasons?"

The red tinge grew a little deeper. "She's with child, my lord."

Wyatt choked back a laugh that threatened to explode at the expression on the man's normally impassive features. Maintaining a straight face, he inquired, "Yours, I assume?" At Jacob's nod, he continued conversationally, "Do you mean to marry her?"

The valet visibly squirmed, then nodded reluctantly. "If it comes to that, my lord."

This was rich. He wished Cassandra were here to appreciate it with him. On second thought, perhaps it was better that she was not. Thinking quickly, Wyatt said, "I'd recommend it. How would you and Lotta like to come with me to London?"

Jacob almost managed a smile. "We would be honored, my lord. When shall we be ready?"

"As soon as you get yourselves to the vicar and make things proper. By the time the banns are cried, we'll be back here for the ceremony. You can assure yourselves that Lotta will not end up on the streets while in my employ."

The servant made a deep obeisance and hurried out. Knowing the working of his household well, Wyatt returned to his desk with pen and paper and waited for the next intrusion.

It came sooner than expected. His mother knew better than to interrupt him at his work. Cassandra had no such scruples. She burst through the door and hugged his neck and kissed his cheek before he could even rise from the chair. When he reached to pull her around where he could see her, she curled up in his lap and began pressing excited kisses along his jaw.

"Oh, thank you, Wyatt. You are a blessed man. Lotta is my only friend and it's too bad of your mother to scream at her like that just because Lotta got dizzy and spilled the tea over her new gown. Do you think she'll dismiss me when she finds out I'm having a baby too? Will you take me to London with you? I haven't seen my mother in months and I worry about her.''

That was too many difficult topics at once. Wyatt shifted Cassandra more comfortably against his shoulder and played his hand along her side as he pressed a kiss to her forehead. ''It is time we discussed plans for this child, since you will be showing shortly. I think it would be best if we removed to one of my other estates where our history isn't as well known, until we can make our marriage official. Then we can take an extended wedding journey. When we return with the child, no one will ever be able to pin down the exact date of our marriage or the child's birth, and although they may speculate as they wish, it will all appear proper, which is all that is necessary. Where would you like to go on our honeymoon?''

Cassandra grew still. The excitement she had entered with seemed to die and spill out of her. She pressed her hand against Wyatt's waistcoat and sought comfort in the beat of his heart beneath her fingers.

Burying her face against the linen of his neckcloth, she whispered, ''Don't send me away, Wyatt. Can't we go on as we are? Everyone believes we are married. Can we not leave it at that?''

Wyatt steeled himself for the tantrum that would follow the soft pleas. ''I'm not sending you away, Cass. I have to go to London for a short time. I think you would be happier away from my mother. I'll take you to Sussex and introduce you to my staff there. Then, when I come back from London, we can travel on to the Lake District. You will be much more comfortable there through the summer as the child grows bigger. The air is marvelous, and I know you will love the fells. I have no desire to leave you for any length of time at all.''

Cassandra sat up and slid off his lap. ''But I cannot leave until harvest, surely you must see that? The men would think I was deserting them. And I've made such promises—''

Wyatt stood and caught her arm. "Don't be nonsensical, Cass. MacGregor can manage your few acres along with my own. He can lend them the equipment they need. The crops can be stored in my barns. That is not the problem here."

"Oh, yes, it is, too! That is the whole problem here, Wyatt Mannering! Everything must be done *your* way. It is *your* concerns that must be put first. *Your* name must not be muddied by the presence of a pregnant mistress. What *I* want has nothing to do with it. I don't want to go to Sussex. I want to go to London. And I shall, even if you won't take me." Cassandra shook his hand off and flew out the door before Wyatt could stop her.

Her argument was specious, of course. Wyatt realized that. He had waited for the real reason to come out, but she had kept those words to herself. He could hear them anyway, even louder for being unsaid. "*You* are the one who wants to get married. *I* don't." Why hadn't she just come out and said them?

But she carried his child. That thought straightened his shoulders. She was young and heedless and had never been given an opportunity to spread her wings. He would have to give her that opportunity, but not until his child had a name. She would simply have to accept that fact.

Now all he had to do was figure out how to protect her while he went to London. He shouldn't have suggested that Jacob go with him. The ex-soldier would prove a more competent bodyguard than anyone else he knew. But he needed the loyalty of that pair and their knowledge of Duncan's and Rupert's households to carry off this scheme. Perhaps he should just abduct Cassandra and carry her off to Sussex against her will.

That would be tempting fate too far. He had managed to trick her into playing his wife, and it had amused her to keep up the charade. She would not be amused by a repeat of the situation. How else could he keep her out of trouble?

She wanted to see her mother. Her mother was something of an invalid. Could she be persuaded to travel? What if he sent Lady Eddings to Sussex? Surely Cassandra could be persuaded to a few weeks out of the way in that case. He should never have mentioned marriage in conjunction with travel.

Not that Sussex was the safest place in the world. It would just take a little while longer to trace her there. The Americas wouldn't be far enough if Rupert truly wanted to find her.

He would just have to act quickly. Rupert had to be brought in line. A man like that would seek his revenge on hapless females before seeking out his stronger opponents. There really was no point in asking that of Cassandra. The annulment would come from Rupert, and the villain would keep his distance from Cassandra forevermore when Wyatt was done with him.

Bolstering his sagging courage with these decisions, Wyatt sat down to start writing the notes to set the wheels of destruction in motion.

"It was too bad of me to lose my temper that way, Wyatt. I promise I shall never do it again. Will you truly take me with you?" Wearing only her chemise and stockings, Cassandra flung herself into Wyatt's arms after his first words.

"Do not make promises you cannot keep, sweetheart. You will curse me often enough in the years to come. Just be certain to apologize afterward just like this." Wyatt lifted her up in his arms and reveled in the pleasure of Cassandra's soft curves melting against him. She might be slender, but she was tall and graceful and her arms fitted perfectly around his neck as she stood on her toes and covered his face with kisses. He must always remember that Cassandra's tempers had their opposite in passion.

"I shall be a terrible burden to you. Duncan has said I am a miserable witch when I don't get my way.

I don't mean to be, Wyatt, really I don't. But it is just so very . . . *annoying* that I cannot control my own life, that I must always wait and rely on someone else. You cannot know how it is.''

"No, perhaps I cannot. I will try to be more understanding, Cass, but you must promise the same. I worry about you, and I want to make you safe and happy. You must let me muddle through this in the best way I know how.''

"Oh, you do very well, my lord." Cassandra wriggled in his arms, feeling the hard state of his arousal rubbing against her through the tight cloth of his pantaloons. "Very well indeed," she murmured as his mouth sought and claimed hers. She had wondered if Wyatt would tire of her as her father and brother so quickly tired of their mistresses. Each time he came to her like this was another moment stolen from time. It could not last. Nothing did. But she would make the most of every minute.

They slept in her room that night, unable to cross the distance to the larger master bedroom before their needs demanded satisfaction. Cassandra cried out her joy as Wyatt once more proved his desire for her, and when he came to her twice more before the dawn, ecstasy replaced rapture. Surely he would not leave her anytime soon if he still felt this strongly. Bliss wrapped her in tender tentacles as she lay in his arms and watched the sun rise. Perhaps, just perhaps, she had found a home.

The cotton padding of that night held her safe through the next few days as Wyatt made arrangements for their journey and seemed aloof and distant through much of the time. As long as he came to her at night, she would allow him his preoccupation. Wyatt was a busy man. He did not need to wait on her both night and day. She could visit Thomas, oversee her fields, search the library for gardening books, and pluck at the pianoforte. She rather missed their musical interludes before bedtime, but Wyatt stayed in his study

until the small hours, writing interminable letters and
instructions. One would think he was planning a war.
But he always came to her bed, so she did not complain.

When they finally set out, Lotta and Jacob traveled
with the baggage, and Wyatt made certain Cassandra
was ensconced in his most comfortable carriage. He
insisted that they travel slowly so the jolting did not
disturb her, but the sickness had passed as quickly as
it had come, and she was bouncing with eagerness to
see the countryside. She wanted to ride with Wyatt,
but he had not thought to bring a horse for her. She
hid her disappointment and made him laugh through
the alfresco luncheon from the basket that Cook had
prepared.

It was the only time Wyatt laughed that day. As the
sun drew low in the sky, Cassandra kept searching for
the cloud of smoke signaling London, but the countryside only became greener, and occasionally she imagined the scent of salt air. She wished Wyatt would ride
back to the carriage so she might question him, but he
rode ahead of the carriage, his gaze on something in
the distance.

When they turned through the arched gateway of
someone's country estate, she swallowed her disappointment. She hadn't remembered the journey to
London being so long, but Wyatt had been excessively
careful in his attentions. He probably feared to tire her
and wished to rest before continuing their journey in
the morning. She was impatient to go on, but she had
vowed to please him. The delay of a single night could
not be so very vexatious.

Wyatt opened the landau door before a footman
could, and his eyes scanned Cassandra's face as she
threw her arms around him most improperly to be
lifted from the carriage. Reassured, he kissed her
cheek and took her hand on his arm to escort her into
the house.

The door swung open as if they were expected, and

Cassandra gazed around with curiosity at the lovely oak floors polished and smelling of beeswax, the welcoming arrangement of flowers overwhelming the charming foyer dominated by a curved staircase to the upper floors. The house was much smaller and less impressive than Merrick, but it had a comfortable elegance Cassandra liked at once.

She smiled up to Wyatt as the servants formally lined up in the hall to greet him. "Whose house is this? I feel as if I am a princess," she whispered.

"To them, you are. This is one of my smaller estates." Before she could question, Wyatt introduced her to the upper servants, then sent the staff scurrying to prepare rooms and carry luggage. A discreet look to the butler received a nod, and the older man led the way to a small suite of rooms in a separate wing off the formal front rooms.

Expecting to be led upstairs to the bedchambers, Cassandra exclaimed with delight at the cozy warmth of the yellow silk-lined salon to which they were led. At a sound from a velvet fainting couch near the fire, Cassandra turned her gaze from the wide expanse of draped window to the room's occupant.

"Mother!" Nearly squealing with delight, she raced to the lovely invalid lying propped against the pillows, waiting for her.

Wyatt watched the reunion with growing trepidation. How long would Cassandra's delight last when she discovered they were on the Sussex shore, now two days' journey from London?

Chapter 26

"Why, Wyatt? Why can I not go with you?"

He gave her sleepy face a kiss. "Would you leave your mother here alone? Now, go back to sleep. I'll be back before you know it."

He was already dressed for traveling, wearing light dust-colored trousers and polished Hessians, his hat in his hand as he bent over the bed. Cassandra could smell the fresh scent of his shaving soap, and she ached to go with him, but deep in her heart she understood. He could present her as wife to his country friends, but not to the *ton*. Not that much of society would be about this time of year, but enough to start the gossip clucking. She sighed and sat up. "Be careful, Wyatt. I'll miss you dreadfully while you're gone."

"Will you?" He looked vaguely pleased by that notion. Then, bending, he pressed a kiss to the glorious tumble of her hair. "I'll buy you something pretty while I'm there. What would you like?"

She shook her head. There was nothing he could buy her. Security didn't come in a box wrapped in fancy ribbons. At his troubled look, she suddenly brightened. Eyes the color of summer skies turned up to him in brilliant delight. "Lace! The village has no lace for a christening gown. I should very much like to make the gown myself, if I might."

A flood of relief rushed over Wyatt at this ingenuous request. She meant to stay, then. He had feared she might have some mad scheme for running away before they could be married. But she wasn't even angry that he had misled her on their destination. He smiled at her sleep-flushed face and wished he could climb into bed beside her again.

"I shall find the most beautiful lace in all of London, then. You do not mind if I borrow Jacob?"

"Of course not, although why you would wish to take Lotta too is beyond my understanding. I know Jacob won't go without her, but that wagon cannot be comfortable in her condition."

"Spoken from experience, I realize. I believe it has something to do with some family matter. Perhaps they wish to invite guests to the wedding."

She nodded dubiously. "Just do not let them lead you into trouble, my lord. I realize they appear very proper when they wish, but they are not at all what they seem."

Wyatt grinned. "I am not so green as that, little goose. Now, give me a hug and I'll be off."

He was gone quickly, too quickly, Cassandra remarked glumly as she allowed the proper lady's maid Merrick had assigned to help her dress. All the servants thought them married, but Wyatt had not chosen to lie to her mother, nor did he tell her the truth. He left the decision up to her, and Cassandra wasn't at all certain she knew what to do with it.

She joined Lady Eddings in the first-floor wing far from the chamber where she and Merrick had spent the night. By choosing this wing, Wyatt had saved the invalid many steps, made her a part of the downstairs activities, and carefully arranged their own privacy. He always thought of everything.

Lady Eddings smiled up from a bed tray of delicious-smelling coffee, tea, and a basket of muffins, scones, and toast. "I have been very spoiled here. I may never leave. Has Lord Merrick taken that into account?" She hid her concern as she noted the shadows under her daughter's eyes. Cassandra normally blew into a room like a whirlwind. She had noticed last night that there was a decided lack of such energy

now, but she had ascribed it to the long journey. This
morning's less-than-enthusiastic greeting did not bode
well.

"He has been all that is kind, Mother. I should have
thought of your removing out here rather than my going to London to visit. It will be much more pleasant
this way. The air from the sea is so invigorating, do
you not agree?"

"It is always lovely anywhere that one can see clear
sky. I just do not understand why Lord Merrick has
been so considerate. I know that he has been all that
is proper, but it must cause talk if you travel in his
company. I cannot help but worry about you, Cassandra."

"Worry, Mother? What is there to worry over?"
She adjusted a chair near the breakfast tray and made
use of the spare cup provided by the ever-efficient servants.

Lady Eddings watched her with increased suspicion,
her fair brows pulling down in a slight frown. "Cassandra, I did not believe you ever lied to me. Would
you begin now? That wretched rogue that Duncan
married you to has returned, and you are not at all
worried?"

Cassandra went white as she froze with a partially
broken muffin in hand. "Rupert? Rupert is in London?"

Elizabeth Howard felt a brief pang of regret at having revealed what Lord Merrick had obviously kept
quiet. She knew he had been notified. Why had he not
passed the information to Cassandra?

Elizabeth waved her hand in casual dismissal. "But
he cannot disturb our peace here. It looks so pleasantly warm in the sun. Do you think I might attempt
a walk outside?"

Confined by the steep staircase in London, Lady Eddings had seldom set foot belowstairs, and therefore,
never outside. To venture on this journey and now ask
to walk in the sun was an improvement not to be ex-

pected. But the question flew right by Cassandra's head as she slowly crumbled the muffin.

At the questioning silence from her mother, Cassandra jerked her attention back to the prone woman on the couch. "What? I'm sorry, I didn't hear. I think . . . If you'll excuse me . . ." Cassandra started to rise, her mind awhirl. Merrick had known. That was why he had hidden her here. What was he going to do? The possibilities seemed limitless, but Rupert would allow only one. She could not allow Wyatt to challenge him. She could not.

"Cassandra!"

Her mother's voice raised in sharp rebuke startled Cassandra from her reverie. She glanced to the invalid in confusion.

"Sit down, Cassandra. It's time we talked."

Her mother speaking in clear, coherent sentences was one thing; ordering her about was quite another. Confused, Cassandra sat.

"Lord Merrick has gone to deal with your husband, has he not?"

Cassandra nodded numbly.

"Why?"

How could she answer that? Uncertainly, she threaded her fingers together and stared at them. "Rupert has not been a husband to me since we married." She halted there, unable to explain further.

Lady Eddings' blue eyes narrowed suspiciously. "But if I do not mistake, Lord Merrick has very much been behaving as one. It is in one of his houses that you have been living, is it not? Duncan said so. And this is another one of his estates. I am right, am I not, Cassandra?"

Cassandra rose abruptly and paced the room. It was a lovely room, shimmering in yellow silk in the morning sun now that the draperies had been pulled back. The park beyond rippled in emerald colors into a distant blue. The sea probably crashed against the shore somewhere beyond that line of lawn and shrubs. It was a beautiful setting for her mother. She could see her getting well here. If she could marry Wyatt . . . If this were the best of all possible worlds . . .

She shook her head impatiently and swung to face her mother. Defiant blue eyes met sad, curious ones. "Wyatt would have me for wife were it not for Rupert. I would have him for husband were it not for Duncan. As you can see, it is quite impossible."

Elizabeth continued to stare at her only daughter. "That is not all of it, is it? If what you say is true, your marriage can be annulled. For all he is my son, I cannot tell you how to control Duncan. He is too much like his father, and I never made any impression on him. But I cannot believe Duncan is the only reason that you find this marriage impossible. Has Merrick found out that you are not a Howard? Is that why he cried off earlier?"

She really could not stand another shock. Cassandra crumpled into the nearest chair and stared at her mother. How was it possible for a person to change so overnight? "Merrick did not cry off, I did," she managed to whisper.

Elizabeth frowned, an act not natural to her fragile skin and delicate bones. "Because of your father? Or because of Duncan?"

"Both. I could not wish him hurt, Mother. He is too good a man."

"And you think you do not deserve him? That is certainly not spoken like a Howard. What have I done to you, Cass? You are the best of us. You deserve whatever you can have. Merrick is no fool. I am not certain that he is right for you. I cannot imagine how he can be. But do not construct obstacles between you. There are enough as it is, without imagining that you are not good enough."

Cassandra's fingers bit into her palm as she faced her mother. "As long as we are opening my life, what about yours, Mother? Who is my father? Are you ashamed of him? Is that why you have never spoken of him?''

Lady Eddings smiled with satisfaction and patted the seat beside her. ''Do not sit across the room as if we are strangers. You always used to sit on the bed beside me.''

Cassandra hesitantly came forward and took the chair she had abandoned earlier. She did not know whether she felt dread or hope now that the moment was near. For so long she had heard of the greatness of the Howard family. She knew their ancient history better than her own. To finally and at long last be severed from it was a rather frightening prospect.

Elizabeth patted her hand, then took a sip of her cooling coffee. ''You have no blame for your parentage, Cassandra. That is my shame and my happiness. I married the man my family arranged for me to marry. We were not happy together. Neither of us expected to be. I brought him money. He gave me prestige. After I gave him his heir, I did not break his heart when I had an affair. Just one affair, Cassandra, in all my life with him. Can you forgive me for that?''

Thinking of what she herself had done, Cassandra could only marvel that her mother had the moral fortitude to surrender only once, while still remaining a proper wife. Then, trying to imagine an affair with anyone else but Wyatt, she began to understand, and her eyes widened.

''You loved him, didn't you? And he left you. How could he? How could any man leave you to a life like that? Did he not care at all?''

A brief flicker of sadness crossed Elizabeth's features, but then she donned a mask of determination and plunged on. ''He cared enough to risk two families for me. I was the one who was weak. You were not born yet. You cannot remember that time. There were debts. There were occasional drunken parties, the gambling all of society indulges in, but not the financial disaster of now. I was a marchioness. I had a young son, a place in society, respect. I was never very strong, but I had admirers. It wasn't an unpleasant life.''

Cassandra resisted the impulse to get up and walk away. She didn't want to hear that. She didn't want to hear any of it. She had always known her mother was weak, but she had thought it a physical weakness. She didn't want to know she had been condemned to a life of wretchedness because her mother enjoyed her title too well. She gritted her teeth and nodded, unable to speak.

Lady Eddings gave her a brief look to be certain she still listened, then continued. ''I met your father at one of the parties the marquess liked to indulge in. Your father had just bought the last of the Howard shipholdings, although I didn't know that at the time. He was here alone. His wife didn't like to travel. He is an American, you see.''

Cassandra gulped and her stomach tightened into unreasoning knots as she tried to assimilate this information. An American! That was so far outside society as she knew it that she couldn't even stretch her imagination to picture it. Her mother continued to speak as she struggled with her thoughts.

''He stayed longer than he intended. We had one lovely summer together. He wanted me to leave with him, but I could not. We would both have to petition for divorces. We would have been banned from society forever. And we would have lost our children. I couldn't do it. I couldn't give it all up, even for him. I didn't know about you until after he left. He left me the name of his London solicitors, but I never wrote to him. It was simply too late for us.''

The sorrow in her mother's voice brought tears to Cassandra's eyes, but she still couldn't grasp the entirety of the situation. Somewhere across the sea she had a father and half-brothers and half-sisters, a whole world of people she would never know. It seemed an enormous gap in her universe. She didn't know how to fill it.

"Why are you telling me this now, Mother?"

Lady Eddings nodded approvingly. "Because I wrote to your father when Duncan threatened to marry you off to Rupert. And because he replied."

The breath rushed out of her lungs as Cassandra stared at her mother. "He replied? How?"

Her mother shrugged carelessly. "Very curtly, actually. Just a note to say he was making arrangements to be here. He cannot be very pleased with me to discover after all these years that he has a child he knew nothing about. But since I received the reply a few weeks ago, I should think he would be on his way by now."

Cassandra couldn't remain seated any longer. Her mind boiled with all the possibilities. She had a father. He could take her away from here. He could hate her, disclaim her. He could settle a sum on her mother so she needn't worry about providing for her anymore. Anything was possible. But it was all too late.

She swung around and faced her mother with tears in her eyes. "Thank you for telling me, but I cannot wait for his rescue. It is too late in coming. Forgive me, Mother, but I must follow Wyatt. Rupert will kill him. I cannot allow that to happen, don't you see? I must do whatever is necessary to put an end to this. I will not allow the Howard taint to destroy his life as it destroyed yours."

She rushed from the room before Elizabeth could stop her.

"Where the hell is she, Eddings?" The slender man swung his ornate ebony cane against the fireplace pokers, causing the heavy iron to clang ominously. "And don't give me that faradiddle about not knowing! She's your bloody sister; you know damned well where she is."

Duncan rested his much larger frame against the

desk and crossed his arms over his chest. "I didn't even know she'd gone to Paris to see you. You don't know Cass very well if you think I have a chance of keeping up with her. Why did she go to see you?"

"To warn me about you." A malicious gleam lit the baronet's eye as he swung on his brother-in-law. "It seems my generosity isn't sufficient, you want my lifeless body as well. Not very sporting, old friend."

"Cass is a damned fool," Duncan muttered. He watched his unwanted visitor warily.

"My wife is a very resourceful lady. She has kept me in France by keeping the news of her lover's recovery quiet. She has demanded an annulment by assuring me that to do otherwise would mean my certain death. And she brought her latest lover with her to emphasize the point physically. Most resourceful, I must admit. But I don't intend to let her go just yet. And I certainly don't mean to otherwise enhance your coffers, old friend."

"Latest lover?" Duncan thought hurriedly, seeking some benefit for himself in these discoveries. "Cass is quite likely to lie about anything that aids her cause. I should like to hear a fuller version of this tale. Of just what do I stand accused?"

Rupert laughed, a sound that held little merriment but much experience. "I'm certain you would like to hear more, but I did not come to entertain you, only warn you. You will gain nothing by my death. Only by my continued existence will you and your heathen sister benefit. Now, I suggest it is in your best interest to remember where you misplaced her. I will be at my club when you come looking for me."

As he swung and stalked out, Duncan resisted the urge to spit on his shadow. Cass had a lot to answer for, but he'd be damned if he let that rutting scoundrel have the best of him. There had to be some way to win this game without giving up the cards.

Merrick's visit to the marquess's home a scant few hours later coincided with the arrival of a stranger garbed entirely in gray, with the exception of his immaculate linen and a diamond glittering in the folds of his neckcloth. Merrick bowed politely and allowed the older man to enter first. Both men presented cards to be carried away on a salver by a servant who appeared to have spent the better part of the day in the wine cellar.

Restless, Merrick was disinclined to converse with the stranger, but the man had a presence that could not easily be avoided. As the older man stood perfectly still, concentrating his attention on the stairway in the distance, Merrick paced and sent him surreptitious glances. The man was frighteningly familiar in some way, but Wyatt was certain he had never met him before in his life.

When the servant returned to inform the stranger that the marchioness was not at home and that the marquess was not available, the stranger merely made a polite bow and strode out. Merrick stared after him, then asked of the footman, "What name did he give?"

"'Is lordship said somethin' to the effect of Wyandott, milord. Can't rightly read, so don't know what was on the card. The marquess said as how he's too busy to see you."

Wyatt uttered a particularly filthy curse and brushed past the bewildered footman. He didn't know any Wyandott, but he knew a lying marquess when he heard one. And this particular species of mendacious nobleman was about to be brought to heel.

After a pungent argument with Cassandra's recalcitrant brother, Wyatt ordered his curricle toward the business district. He preferred handling the ribbons himself, but he needed someone to mind the horse while he carried out his errands, and his driver aped grave insult when not allowed to flaunt his expertise. After dealing with Jacob and Lotta these last days, he was in no humor for arguing with servants. He was in no humor for arguing with anyone. He had argued

more in these last days than he had in a lifetime, but
the results were about to pay off.

Merrick strode into his solicitor's office with the air
of a man about to demand satisfaction. "Well, what
have you found?"

The nervous man behind the desk rose and hastily
wiped his spectacles when confronted with the sudden
apparition of the tall, elegant earl. Wyatt's dark gaze
pierced the solicitor with increasing irritation as the
man wavered uncertainly.

"We have found out much, milord," the solicitor
murmured deferentially. "But there has been so little
time . . . He is an unsavory character. His reputation
is of the lowest in every endeavor, but he is immensely
wealthy, milord. He has covered his trail well. All of
your leads have been good ones. Your manservant has
been extremely helpful. We are on a trail of something
of great importance if I can only find the proof . . ."

Wyatt paced impatiently. "I need truths, not promises, and I need them now. Immediately. What have
you got that I can use without being labeled slander-
ous?"

The solicitor sucked in his breath and consulted his
file. The most promising issue would be not only slan-
derous if it couldn't be proved but also cataclysmic if
it were. Flipping over that page, he began with the
better documented details.

Chapter 27

Completely cloaked in a black domino, Wyatt commanded his troops. The Eddings' town house had already been stripped and cleaned by an army of servants and refurbished by what could only have been a tribe of imps from hell, under Merrick's orders. Walls and windows of the downstairs rooms were draped in black, pitching the rooms into complete darkness even before the sun set. Lanterns covered with thin red shades cast eerie glows in obscure corners. Only the tables scattered throughout the rooms held more than one candle. Merrick ignored the decor as he pointed at a masked devil.

"Bertie, you take this room. You have your story straight?"

The devil nodded. "Deuce take it, Merrick, I ain't no green schoolboy. I can remember lessons, not that I see where it will do any good."

"You've got a point there, Albert." A starkly garbed gentleman in flowing black cape, top hat, white gloves, and half-mask leaned arrogantly against a mantel festooned in henbane. "As a gambling hell, this is all very clever. I don't know why I didn't think of it myself. But you can be certain this is no more than an imaginative party to our prey. I see nothing in it for me."

"Your soul, Eddings. You'll have your soul. At the worst, you'll save your life. If you fail me in this, I'll skewer you to the wall." Wyatt made a gesture of irritation as he paced the room, waiting for the rest of his troops to appear.

Duncan gave an abrupt laugh. "You and who else, Merrick? My lovely sister? Hitting me over the head with a poker is more Cassandra's style. I'll believe it of her faster than of you, St. Wyatt."

Merrick swung around, his growing tension escalating into flaring anger. "We have an agreement, Eddings. It's too late to back out of it now. For once in your damned life, think of someone besides yourself."

Duncan shrugged and shut up as a tall Roman soldier entered, his visor concealing his face and the wide breastplate disguising his gaunt frame.

"Damn, it's about time." Merrick spun around to confront this newcomer. "Where's Lotta? The women are already gathering in the back room."

"She's with them now, milord," Jacob intoned formally.

"Good, then take your position." Merrick turned to a shadowed figure resting in a chair in a far corner. "Thomas, you are to take your place and not move. I need you for the final act, and I'll not have you giving out before then. Is that understood?"

An amused young voice responded, "Aye, aye, Captain." Rising, Thomas drifted out of the larger room to his appointed station.

As the door knocker sounded, Wyatt took a deep breath and sent a prayer winging to the heavens. He would feel more confident of the outcome of this charade were Cassandra at his side to help direct it, but he could not risk putting her in the same company with Rupert. The dangers were too great.

Checking his pocket for the papers crackling there, reassured, he blended into the darkness to take his own position.

Rupert arrived in the company of the tall distinguished man Merrick had met on the Eddings' doorstep, although the earl was not there to note it. Neither man had wasted much time in costume, although the invitation had specified this was a masquerade. Each wore a half-mask as a concession to the occasion.

A plump Cleopatra immediately brought drinks and led them to the first salon, where a crowd had already gathered around several faro tables. Rupert immediately joined in, while his companion idled in the background, watching his surroundings with hooded interest.

Rupert found his empty glass replaced with a full one as swiftly as he drank the contents. Mentally calculating the odds in favor of where Eddings had obtained such a quantity of liquor, the baronet threw his coins down upon the table and looked about for an interesting female.

He wasn't long in finding one. A heavily veiled Salome sidled up to him, snaking her hand about his waist as he raked in his winnings. He noted full breasts and a heavy scent of roses and smiled inwardly. Perhaps his wife rejected his favors, but there were any number of others eager for his company. Deciding Duncan had perfected the art of successful parties, Rupert pinched his consort's ripe bottom and eased from the table.

"Let me show you some of the other rooms," Salome whispered, clinging to his arm.

The heady scent of roses enveloped him, and Rupert eagerly followed, forgetting the friend with whom he had arrived. The encounter he had in mind did not require a third party, and he smiled in satisfaction when they entered a secluded alcove off the main rooms. A candle burned in the sconce over the velvet settee, and Rupert turned to the lady attending him.

She came willingly into his arms, pressing heated kisses to his mouth through the layer of veils. His body went rigid with desire, and he pushed her backward toward the settee.

"Ahh, my little man was always a hasty lover,"

Salome murmured mockingly as she sprawled back across the cushions and brought him down with her.

Intent on removing the voluminous cloth hindering his access to the flesh beneath, Rupert almost ignored her mutters, but something in the inflection warned him. Lying half across her, his hand halfway up her skirts, he halted and stared down into her covered face suspiciously.

"You know me?"

The laugh following this question was hollow. "I know you, my noble baronet. You were my first. With luck, you will be my last. Do you not remember me, Rupert? I have cause to remember you for the rest of my life."

She moved seductively beneath him, her hands disarranging his clothes with practiced gestures as her hips ground against him. Rupert jerked at her veils, swearing when one came loose to reveal another.

"Oh, no, you really wouldn't rather see," she admonished. "I am not what I once was. After what you did to me, I had no choice but to sell my favors elsewhere, you see. I was too green to avoid the dock taverns back then. I thought one man the same as any other. They didn't all have your polished manners, but some were much kinder, I discovered."

She ground herself tightly against his arousal as the last of the veils fell to the floor. At the sight suddenly revealed in the candlelight, Rupert gagged in disgust and swiftly gained his feet. The whore sat up and taunted him as he averted his eyes and arranged his clothes, rubbing his hands against the cloth with revulsion. Her ravaged face could still wear an expression of contempt as she watched.

"Some of those sailors carried the French pox, I fear. Does that disturb you, Rupert? I'm still a good lay, ain't I? I know a lot more than the day you raped me, Rupert. Don't you want to see what I've learned?"

He would swear he had never seen the creature before. No one could prove he had anything to do with it. She was in all likelihood quite mad. But the memory of a sunlit day in his sixteenth year and a buxom dairymaid flitted into memory as she spoke with the accents of his home. He refused to acknowledge the image.

He strode out without a second look back. He'd find Eddings and demand to know why poxed whores were on the premises. It was enough to turn a man's stomach. Why, he could have . . . It didn't bear thinking about. He'd escaped the creature's mad clutches in time. Remembering her impassioned kisses, he wiped his mouth with his sleeve and reached for another drink on the tray of a footman, his stomach churning with the foulness of the encounter.

The damned darkness made it difficult to discern faces. He wasn't even certain what disguise Eddings wore. Cursing, Rupert stumbled into a room of eager dice players. His drink was replaced as he stepped up to the table, and he indulged in a small wager while examining the company.

A heavyset devil eased into an opening at his side. Wheezing drunkenly, he pitched his coins on the table. "Never thought I'd do this again," he muttered to no one in particular. "Not since Teddy got taken that way. Demmed shame, that. Lost everything he owned at the tables, left his widowed mother and sister homeless. Saw them in the streets just the other day. I'll spit that fellow Percival if I ever find him. He ruined that family, and no need of it, I hear. Has guineas up his nostrils, they say. I say, don't know the fellow, do you?" The devil demanded this last as Rupert eased away.

"Never heard of him." Leaving his bet on the table, Rupert hurried from this company. Damn Eddings, anyway. He probably had every rumormonger in town in here. That story about Teddy Wilhoite wasn't common knowledge. It would be if that drunken devil kept on about it. He'd be ruined in what little society was still open to him. Wilhoite was little more than an encroaching cit. What difference could his ruination be to anyone? And what was Eddings up to with this charade? He wasn't a superstitious man, but a shiver of apprehension made his nerves jumpy, and he tried to hang on to his anger as he searched for his host.

Beginning to feel the effects of drink, Rupert finally stumbled into Duncan. Before he could take him to task for the rudeness of the company, the marquess caught his shoulder and steered him toward a private parlor.

"I've been looking for you. We've got a lively game going in here, more your sort than those others. Can't introduce you to the company, don't recognize them all myself, but I wager we'll figure them out by the way they play their cards."

Reassured by his friend's bluff heartiness, Rupert took a chair at the table. Duncan Howard was a fool, but he had friends in the right places who gained him access to a more exalted society than would otherwise welcome him. Once he had Cassandra in line, invitations to these affairs would start pouring in. The Howards might be a beggarly lot, but even Prinny recognized their stature. He glanced around surreptitiously to see if any of the company rated royal status.

Recognizing only the American who rose from the table to give up his place, Rupert picked up his cards. Gambling was merely a game he played in order to forward his acquaintance among the *ton*. In time, given the right connections, he might persuade a more noble title from the pockets of the perpetually bankrupt nobility. A small barony somewhere might be found in return for a large enough sum to the right party. Opportunities abounded if one knew the right people. He craved a "Lord" before his name. Who knew? Duncan was the last of the Howards, and he didn't appear ready to perpetuate the line. Married to Cassandra and willing to change his name to hers, it might be possible . . . In the event anything happened to Duncan, of course.

Rupert lost the first and second rounds but didn't count the sum. He gestured for another drink. He had already dropped a few hundred pounds at Duncan's tables, but his markers were good everywhere. The dwindling coins in front of him didn't concern him.

Rupert scanned the company again, trying to deduce their identities. The man in the black domino seemed familiar. He didn't speak, so he had no clue to judge by. He knew Duncan and Wyandott, the American, of course. The fourth player seemed rather young, but he was raking in quite a bundle. Whom did he know with that color blond hair who could wield cards like a professional? Not many that age were so proficient. He couldn't think of any, other than Cassandra.

Remembering the first time his treacherous wife had cheated him out of his purse, Rupert smirked. He knew where she was now. It would just be a matter of days before she graced his bed. He might have to kidnap her and tie her down until she became used to the idea, but she would break soon enough. He could almost vow that St. Wyatt didn't know any of the tricks he had learned to keep a wanton woman in line. The thought of what he could do to that haughty wife of his once she was strapped to the bed made his loins ache. He would set off on the morrow. She was his wife. No one could stop him. He chuckled at the thought of what Wyatt would do once he learned his red-haired mistress graced another man's bed. It almost made life worth living.

Cassandra beat furiously at the door knocker. There was only one lamp burning in Wyatt's town-house window, but she knew he had to be there. She couldn't conceive of him being anywhere else. She had to tell him once and for all that it was over. He would laugh if she said she feared Duncan would blackmail him dry. He would dismiss the fact that her father was some unknown American. His life would be destroyed before he knew what had happened if he persisted in this insane decision to marry her. She would save him as she had been unable to save anyone else.

The thought of confessing to loving another had come to her in the carriage on the way here. It wouldn't be easy. She didn't know many people, and he wasn't likely to believe she was enamored of Bertie or Thomas. But her mother's story had given her an idea. She could pretend her lover was an American who had left London when reading of her engagement in the paper. That would work.

The only obstacle was the babe. That a child of theirs was growing inside her did not seem quite real yet. She couldn't lie and say the child belonged to her American lover. Merrick knew she had been a virgin. Damn her innocence, anyway. Had it not been for that, he would never have gone off on this tangent of marriage. She could have easily remained his mistress for the rest of her life. Or until he tired of her.

Not willing to think those negative thoughts, Cassandra lifted the knocker to slam it again. The door swung open before it connected, nearly pulling her inside, so fierce was her grip.

The elderly butler looked at her with condescending inquiry. The London staff didn't know her. She daren't proclaim herself Wyatt's wife unless he were here to confirm it. She drew herself up haughtily and refused to give any name at all. "I must see Lord Merrick. Let me in."

The butler's unblinking expression did not change as he gazed at a spot somewhere above the tall cloaked figure standing in the drizzle. "His lordship has gone out for the evening."

Cassandra's hopes plunged into the blackest hole. He couldn't already be meeting Rupert. It had taken her days to slip away from Wyatt's watchful servants. It had taken her even longer to manage the chain of coaches and chaises necessary to reach London. She was exhausted, wet, and nearly ill from worry. She could not have come too late.

"It is a matter of life and death," she summoned the courage to say. "I am the Lady Cassandra Howard. You must tell me where I can find him."

This time the butler blinked. Jacob and Lotta had made their mistress's name known belowstairs. Since there had been no announcement in the paper, no ceremony to establish it, the London staff was skeptical of their claim that his lordship had married, but there was no doubt in anyone's mind that his lordship admired the lady. Her name was on his lips with every word spoken.

The servant drew the door wide and offered her entrance. "There was to be a masquerade this evening, my lady. His lordship did not know when he would return. He dismissed most of the staff for the evening."

A masquerade! She was worrying herself into a state of paralysis and he was out playing child's games! She knew about masquerades. Duncan had told her about them. Costumes gave shameless people the license to behave shamelessly in public. She would have his head on a platter for this.

"I must find him," she asserted. "Have you any idea where the masquerade is to be held?"

Helping her off with the dripping cloak, the butler stiffened. Suspiciously he intoned, "At Lord Eddings', I believe." Surely Lady Cassandra would know her brother held the masquerade.

Cassandra issued a curse that sent the servant's eyebrows into his hairline. Sweeping off her wet garment, she started for the stairs. "You must have some old costumes in this place. Where are the attics? Are Lotta and Jacob here? Send them to me."

There was no doubting that she was a Howard. With a sigh of resignation the butler followed in her path. "Lotta and Jacob have gone out for the evening, my lady. I will send a maid to you. If you will wait, I'll have the housekeeper prepare a room."

It was two hours later before the attics were suc-

cessfully rummaged for a costume and it could be
adapted for Cassandra's use. Some young Merrick
must once have disguised himself as Robin Hood. The
surtout was not meant for female wear, but it was loose
enough on her to almost disguise her breasts. Unfortunately, it was short, and if any tunic had been worn
beneath it, no evidence could be found of its remains.
The close-fitting tights that went under the costume
convinced Cassandra the costume was meant to be
worn without tunic, but on her the result was as
shameless as she imagined a masquerade ought to be.
She gazed at her long forest-green-clad legs beneath
the dark surtout and blanched. Wyatt would kill her.

Or Rupert would kill Wyatt. With that thought in
mind, Cassandra grasped the brown homespun cloak
the servant held out to complete the costume. If she
kept it pulled about her, she would pass. A hood effectively disguised her countenance, hiding her hair as
well as her features.

Merrick had left the landau in Sussex, but the curricle was available. It was uncomfortable in the rain,
but the distance to St. James wasn't great. Cassandra
suffered it in silence. The terror gripping her was very
real. The Howard town house had been the site of too
many emotional, anguished scenes for her to doubt
that another one was about to be enacted. Duncan and
Rupert must have set some trap, but she could not
fathom Wyatt walking into it. He was too intelligent
to let them trick him. So why would he attend what
he had to know would be one of Duncan's drunken
orgies?

There was only one way to find out. When the driver
let her out at her former home, Cassandra gazed up at
the draped windows in puzzlement, but she didn't hes-
itate. Without a qualm, she let herself in. No one came
to take her cloak, but that was scarcely unusual. What
was unusual was the hellish decor and the crowd of
people crushing the unused front rooms. Cassandra
gaped at the black-draped walls and flickering lanterns

and shivered. Duncan had never gone this far before. This was worse than some of the worst gambling hells she had seen.

It was damned difficult to make out her hand before her face, but she knew Merrick would be here somewhere. And Duncan. And Rupert. That name made her cringe inside, but Cassandra kept up her steady search. There would be an end to this, and soon.

She spotted a towering Roman soldier she would swear was Jacob, but he disappeared down a hallway to the private salon beyond. That seemed a better place to start than this mass confusion of the public rooms. Working her way around drunken monks and amorous Sir Walter Raleighs, Cassandra sought the quieter hall she had seen the Roman soldier enter.

In minutes she was in the shadows outside the candlelight of a table of card players. Several others leaned against the walls to watch the play, but her gaze focused on the players. She recognized Duncan and Rupert easily, since they made no attempt to disguise themselves. Despite his domino, Merrick was easily recognized by his height, at least to her eyes. From the talk or lack of it around the table, she wasn't certain that everyone knew him. The light was dim, after all, and Merrick sat far back in the shadows. The candles in the center of the table might make it difficult to see past the light, and Rupert was across the table from Merrick.

That didn't make sense. If Duncan and Rupert were creating some kind of trap, they should be the ones in disguise. Her gaze drifted to a fourth player. He seemed vaguely familiar, but his mask hid his features and the darkness hid all else. She would have suspected Bertie, but he seemed younger, perhaps a little taller. It was difficult to tell, but he didn't sit like Bertie.

How could she get Wyatt out of here without a commotion? None of the men had paid any attention to her entrance. They couldn't know she was here. There had to be some way of removing Wyatt before the trap was sprung. What devious plan could Duncan have devised now?

She instantly counted the winnings before each player, but did not feel relief even when she saw Wyatt's coins were as high as Duncan's. Duncan could be leading him on to bigger stakes. It was an old trick, but not one she had taught Wyatt. He could start gambling recklessly on the basis of this lucky streak, only to find it all lost on the turn of a well-placed card.

Rupert was the only one doing badly, but he did not seem to mind it. A number of empty glasses littered the table before him, and she knew he was drunk. He didn't have much of a head for liquor, but he was dangerous when he had had too much. She knew that much to her regret.

As Cassandra watched the cards go around, she realized they were wagering for incredibly high stakes. Duncan didn't have that kind of money to lose, although the sum in front of him might cover a round or two. Rupert didn't have that much on the table, but his wealth was such that in all probability he could afford to lose for the rest of the night. His markers would be good for it.

Cassandra glanced uneasily at Merrick. She knew he was wealthy, but she suspected much of his wealth lay in his lands. Should he lose steadily at these rates, he would have to put up some of his estate for collateral. It would break his heart to lose what he had worked so hard to keep. Why in the devil was he doing this?

The next round brought her answer. Cassandra blanched as Rupert laid his scribbled marker on the table and Merrick leaned over to shove it back. Rejecting a gentleman's marker just wasn't done.

The man in the domino spoke without inflection, breaking the eerie silence. "There is only one piece of paper with your signature on it that we'll accept from you."

Rupert glanced up in surprise as he recognized the voice. As a sheaf of papers appeared on the table before him, he stared at them in drunken amazement, not even picking them up to read them.

Not so backward, Cassandra leaned forward to read the large print at the top of the legal documents spread in front of her husband. She had to strain to pick out the letters in the candlelight, but she finally made them out: Petition for Annulment.

The urge to scream and overturn the table swept through her. She wanted to berate them all, to tell them just exactly what she thought of them for playing behind her back this way, and then she wanted to flee in the face of her overwhelming embarrassment. But those were the reactions of a much younger Cassandra. She was older than that now.

With casual aplomb, Cassandra drew her cloak closed and stepped forward into the candlelight. "Gentlemen, may anyone join this game?"

Chapter 28

They all looked up in startlement. The intruder's voice was muffled behind the heavy hood, but the diversion gave them time to gather their thoughts. Rupert glanced at the tall newcomer with disdain but no recognition. He shoved the paper back toward the coins mounting in the center of the table.

"My markers are good. I have no need of this far-adiddle." In truth, he was shaken. The encounters with the whore and the drunken devil had unnerved him, making him uncomfortably aware of how precarious his situation was. If either Eddings or Merrick had any notion of those incidents, his reputation could be ruined in every fashionable house in town. And if they had uncovered secrets that deep, they could be very close to the darkest secret of all. He shivered at the thought. His marriage to Cassandra could not save him then, far from it.

The knowledge that he had been playing with people who knew him but whom he hadn't recognized did not bode well for the evening's outcome. Rupert glanced suspiciously at the rest of the room's occupants, but they were mere shadows outside the candlelight. Remembering the American lounging against the wall, he relaxed. He had one friend here, even if newly made. Gathering up his scattered courage, he threw Duncan a shrewd glance. There was no telling which way that bird turned. The marquess had refused to reveal his sister's whereabouts, but neither had he been the one to produce the documents. He could be friend or foe, depending on the turn of the cards.

The cowled newcomer glanced at the sheaf of papers in the table's center and made a rude noise. "Worthless without a signature. Looks like good odds to me. Put up a worthless paper and win a fortune. Want me to take your cards?"

Cassandra! Merrick gritted his teeth and glared at the heavily cloaked figure near Rupert. She must be sweltering in this heat in that outfit. How the deuce had she found them? Or got here in the first place? She endangered herself as well as the child she carried by these tricks. He ought to shake her until her teeth rattled, but his first imperative was to remove her before she was recognized.

"The game's closed, sir. You'll have to wait your turn."

Rupert grinned. Now that he knew his opponent's identity, he felt safe in contradicting him. "What are you afraid of, Merrick? Thought I didn't know you, did you? Maybe it's time we let some fresh blood into this game. Let's keep it on the square, shall we? Duncan, why don't you remove yourself and let our medieval friend join in the play?"

That wouldn't work. Duncan's skill with the cards surpassed Merrick's. To allow Cassandra to enter the game would be disastrous, but at least she had the expertise needed to keep the cards out of Rupert's hands. What else she would do was anybody's guess, but Merrick had to act quickly. Catching Thomas' arm, he nodded toward the darkened corner.

Obediently, the less-skilled younger man rose from the table, carrying his winnings with him. "I'm comfortable for the night, and paper won't pay my bills. You're welcome to take my hand if you will."

Cassandra scowled as she recognized Thomas' hearty voice, but she gladly accepted his chair, keeping a careful distance from Wyatt's long arm. She felt certain he recognized her. The anger in the tense set of his shoulders revealed that much. But she was angry enough for both of them. She picked up Thomas' hand and threw the brooch holding her cloak onto the pile of coins.

"That's worth more than a bundle of papers," she announced scornfully to the table at large.

A tall man in a half-mask visibly started, then stepped closer, almost as if he would protest, but the players ignored him as, intent on their game, they drew their next cards.

The play went swiftly and viciously after that. Under Cassandra's and Duncan's dexterous hands, Rupert didn't have a chance. The original plan had called for the winnings to fall to Merrick, but Cassandra's interference made it a contest between brother and sister. Nothing Merrick could do could play the cards away from them if they chose to leave him out. This past week of practice had taught Wyatt only the rudimentary skills, and he had not yet learned to count the cards as Cassandra did. With resignation he tried to adopt a new scheme to force Rupert's hand in the event that the documents fell into other hands. Unsigned, they were worthless. He had to have Rupert's signature.

"My hand, I believe." The homespun cloak moved to reveal a slender arm in a tight sleeve as the winner raked in the pot.

The sheaf of papers lay on top, and Rupert smirked. "Have joy of your winnings, sir. The documents might be worth a few pounds in legal fees."

"You tendered them as markers, sir. I believe a gentleman signs his markers." Cassandra shoved a page toward him. "Your signature, please. These other gentlemen might act as witness."

Rupert shoved furiously from the table. "Don't be an ass, man. I'm not gambling my wife to her lover. Don't interfere where you're not known."

"Your signature, as a gentleman," Cassandra demanded more loudly. Her heart was in her throat. She hadn't meant to do this. She had only meant to keep Merrick out of her affairs, but the proximity of her husband's evil nature activated her instincts of self-preservation. She would be rid of the foul fiend once and for all.

"I will give you my marker," Rupert replied arrogantly.

"Your marker is worthless. You wagered your wife, and you lost. Sign." Cassandra stood at the same time as Rupert, forcing him to look her in the eye, daring him to see and defy her.

He was too blind from drink and anger to see. Reacting in his usual manner to the insult of having his marker refused, Rupert lifted the dregs of his drink and flung them at his antagonist's face. "I'll not be insulted by a young pup. Name your weapons."

A gasp ran around the room. Before the growing rumble could become a roar, Merrick shoved the table aside. "Cassandra, stop it. You need only sign those papers yourself and my solicitors will see them to court. You don't need him at all."

Rupert went white at the mention of his wife's name, but rage returned him rapidly to his senses as he reeled in recognition and jeered at the caped figure. "Try it, my darling, and I'll fight it through every court in the kingdom. All the world will know what a willing whore you've become."

Bertie leapt forward and shoved against Merrick's shoulder as the earl lifted his fist to swing furiously at the man offering this insult. Shorter but much heftier, the squire's son threw his weight into the maneuver, succeeding in pushing Merrick backward before the fist could connect with Rupert's jaw.

Chairs toppled and Duncan caught the brunt of Merrick's weight as the earl staggered backward from the force of Bertie's shove. Before Cassandra could decide whether to lunge at Rupert's throat or run to Merrick's side, the American stepped forward and silenced the growing chaos with a voice of command.

"Eddings, your sister has just been insulted. Is it not your place to see her name protected?"

As Merrick recovered his balance, Duncan glanced toward the arrogant older man in bewilderment. He didn't know the man from Adam, but he was being pierced by the sharpest pair of blue-green eyes he'd ever had the misfortune to encounter. They seemed startlingly familiar, but the rugged face behind them had no place in his memory, and the colonial accent was beyond his realm of acquaintance.

Cassandra's scream of protest interfered with Duncan's thought processes, and he shook his head to clear it. Rupert had insulted Cassandra. That point was quite arguable, since it seemed she had taken Merrick for lover. But if it took only Cass's signature on those papers for her to be free, he would lose his chance at claiming Rupert's thousands. When a clanking knight leaned over and whispered a few words in his ear, he felt a sudden reversal in his fortunes. Under the furious glare of the stranger, Duncan found himself dropping his head in agreement.

"You can't duel a female, Percival, even if she is your wife. I'll stand in her place. Somebody fetch some pistols. We'll settle this now, like gentlemen."

"No, you won't!" Cassandra screamed in fury. "I won't be fought over like a bone between two mangy dogs. I'll sign that wretched paper and Rupert can take it to every court in the damned world, but I'll not be his wife!"

Merrick caught her firmly by the shoulders and began shoving her toward the door. "It's too late now, Cass. It's not your affair any longer, it's theirs. If you'll get out of here, I'll try to talk them out of it."

"No! I won't leave! Why can't you see?" she cried in anguish. "It's my life they've ruined. It's my life they fight over. None of you have any business here. Let me have the pistol! I'd rather he shot me than see another fall in my place. Merrick, *let me go!*"

She was furious, near hysterical with rage. Tears

rolled down her cheeks even as she fought Wyatt's greater strength with every ounce of passion in her body. Fearing for her health as well as the child's safety, Merrick could do no more than hold her until she calmed.

The stranger again stepped forward, catching Cassandra's rigid shoulder and swinging her rage toward him. "It's no longer your fight, young lady. It's a point of honor between two gentlemen. Do not disgrace yourself further by these dramatics."

It was easier to turn her fury on this stranger than Merrick, and she did so with alacrity. Cassandra spit at his feet. "That to honor! They have no honor. Call the watch and have them thrown in Newgate to cool their heels awhile. They will be alive when they come out, and their nonexistent honor will not be one whit harmed. I'll not see another man struck in my name. I won't! I cannot live with the guilt anymore. I'll cut my hair and scar my cheeks so no man will ever look upon me again. Just make them stop!"

Her pleas were piercing, paralyzing every man in the room. Merrick moved as if to gather her into his arms, but the American held up his hand to stay him. He brushed back the hood and touched Cassandra's creamy cheek with a kind of wonder. A wild mane of red-gold fire fell loose from its binding, cascading in a glittering waterfall down her back.

"It's not your fault, little one. Believe me, you have nothing to do with this. They are men with their own lives, who make their choices based on their own greed and desires. You are an excuse, nothing more. Go home now, and let them settle their differences in their own way."

Feeling the fury seep out of her, Merrick quickly gestured for Jacob. The man looked reluctant, but Cassandra's sobs would tear him in two if she lingered longer. "Get Lotta and take them home," he ordered.

With a desperate lunge, Cassandra broke free. "No, I won't, I can't," she cried as she pushed past the stranger and ran for the freedom of the world beyond the door. No amount of words could ease the pain or cloud the knowledge of what was happening. They were all in this together, even Merrick, whom she had trusted.

"Follow her, dammit!" Merrick roared as Jacob hesitated.

The valet hovered uncertainly, holding the box of pistols he had produced from somewhere. Then, shoving the box at Duncan and muttering, "Not the diamond," he ran after Cassandra.

Relieved of their lone obstruction, the men remaining glanced uneasily at each other. Remembering Jacob's whispered words and his own resolution, Duncan straightened his shoulders and started for a door in the rear of the room.

"The back garden should be sufficient for our purposes, gentlemen. Merrick, do you stand with me?"

This had gone much farther than Wyatt had intended. Should anything happen to her brother, Cassandra would never forgive him. In all likelihood, she would never forgive him this night's disasters as it was. Trickery was not his style. He could see that right now. Wondering at the man who had seemed to instigate these proceedings, Wyatt threw the enigmatic American an uncertain look. Jacob had said he'd arrived with Rupert. Yet he did not behave in Rupert's best interests. Puzzled, Wyatt turned back to Duncan.

"As your second, I must seek some form of amelioration with Rupert's man. Rupert, who stands with you?"

As Merrick suspected, Rupert turned immediately to the American. "Wyandott, will you second me? It's a mere formality. We'll have this done in a trice."

The tall silver-haired stranger lifted his gaze briefly to Wyatt's hostile look, then nodded. "I'll act for you. Lord Merrick, shall we discuss the terms?"

Rupert waved his hand in dismissal of the ritual. "We have the pistols. The garden isn't large enough for more than ten paces. There's nothing to discuss. Let's get this over so I can find my wayward wife. It is past time that she learned her place.''

Every other man in the room tensed at these words. Bertie caught his younger brother's shoulder, pressing him into silence. Both Scheffings turned to the man who had set this masquerade into motion, but the earl's eyes had gone hard and cold and followed Rupert out. Whatever the outcome of this duel, Wyatt stood to lose. He would kill Rupert if Duncan didn't, and even an earl couldn't keep the law from hanging him.

Jacob caught up with Cassandra as she fled down the darkened city street in the wrong direction. A few more blocks and she would be in the slums by the river, fair prey to every thief, murderer, and rapist in the city. She wasn't thinking clearly, and this wasn't the time to indulge in female histrionics. He daren't grab her, but raced in front of her to hold her up.

''Don't, my lady! You've got to come back. Them pistols are rigged. Hurry, now. I ain't got time to linger.''

The proper valet's lapse into the vernacular brought Cassandra up short. She had run senselessly, simply avoiding what she didn't want to hear. Jacob's warning made too much sense of the world as she knew it, and she turned hastily to go back. Rigged! Of course they were rigged. Neither Duncan nor Rupert had done an honest act in his life. She would take the wretched pistols to their foul hearts herself. That was the only suitable ending to this affair.

Jacob sighed with relief at the sudden flare of fire in the lady's eyes. It might already be too late. His long legs carried him hastily back to the house at a lope Cassandra could scarcely emulate. Luckily, freed of her hampering skirts, she kept a pace close enough to arrive at the mews behind the house within seconds of him.

The men were already spreading out around the garden with the two duelists in the center. Jacob cursed as he noted they already held pistols in hand. Holding up his hand, he halted Cassandra before she could break through the bushes. It was too late now.

They stood back-to-back, pistols pointed upward as Bertie began the count. Duncan looked almost regal with his ebony hair gleaming in the moonlight, his broad shoulders in their elegant black evening coat thrown back as he counted out his steps. Rupert, the smaller man, seemed almost impatient as he moved forward jerkily, paying little attention to the pace.

Before anyone could shout a warning, Rupert swung around and lowered his pistol at the count of nine. Cassandra's scream had scarcely parted her lips when Duncan, too, swung before the final count. Her scream escaped as Duncan's slippered foot slid in the moist grass and he fell forward with the same instant that Rupert's shot fired.

The second gun went off even as Duncan spun sideways with the force of the first shot. Rupert staggered as Duncan's wild bullet struck home, but he did not fall. Even as the witnesses converged upon the two men, cursing their cowardice, Rupert reached in his coat pocket to produce a small gun that he aimed unwaveringly at his enemy.

Cassandra felt as if she were caught in a deadly nightmare. She saw but could not act. Her feet tried to move, but they seemed mired in quicksand. The scream was in her throat, but it couldn't escape in time. In horror she watched the gun aim—not on Duncan's kneeling figure, but on the man bending to help him up.

"Wyatt!" The scream split the air in the same instant as the gun's report.

Then still another shot echoed through the night, and Rupert crumpled, leaving the American standing alone, a smoking pistol in his hand.

Merrick felt the pain shoot through his side, and grabbing his ribs, he lifted anguished eyes to Cassandra's pale face against the shrubberies. Gad! How could this happen? It wasn't fair. He couldn't get to her in time. He glared accusingly at the older man approaching; then, too weak to stand longer, he lowered himself to one knee beside Cassandra's fallen brother. He could see Cassandra disappearing from view, and his mind sent futile cries of protest after her. Not now! Not when he couldn't go after her.

Bertie was tearing off his coat while Wyandott tended Duncan. Merrick tried to concentrate on what needed to be done, but he could see only the shock in Cassandra's eyes. He felt the sticky warmth running down his side, and the numbness began to wear off, the pain distracting him from even thoughts of Cassandra. It hurt like all the hinges of hell, but he was alive. And Cassandra was gone. Somehow, he had to go after her. He tried to struggle to his feet, but intruding fingers pressed him down.

"I have a ship that can carry you out of here tonight," Wyatt heard the American saying to the cursing marquess beside him. "You'll live, but I'll not recommend remaining here until the hue and cry blows over. If word of your cowardice gets out, you'll be cut from society anyway. Here, hold this cloth in place while I open the brandy."

Merrick listened in amazement as the older man bent to give Duncan a swig from his flask, then applied the strong spirits to a trouser torn from the marquess's satin breeches. Rupert's gun must have misfired to shoot Duncan so low as to hit his thigh, particularly with his unexpected fall. The more amazing thing was that the American now meant to pin Rupert's death on Duncan, who had done no more than wing his opponent.

Duncan, too, seemed to find this grossly unfair. "Wait a minute! I ain't going nowhere! You killed him. My sister's a widow now. She'll need me. Bigad, you killed him in cold blood! You'll be the one going to Newgate."

"I don't think so. I merely acted to prevent murder.

Lord Merrick, I apologize for being a little slow on the draw. Age has a habit of slowing the reflexes.'' Wyandott glanced briefly to the earl, being attended by two blond giants, then returned to his task. ''On the other hand, Lord Eddings, you behaved with despicable dishonor. Even if the law does not come after you, you are certain to be held in contempt. I recommend a long journey for many years to come.''

''With Rupert's wealth in my hands, I can withstand contempt.'' Duncan winced and uttered a groan as the brandy soaked his wound.

From out of the darkness Jacob appeared bearing a lantern and accompanying a portly gentleman with a familiar physician's satchel. At Duncan's words, Jacob snorted loudly enough to draw the attention of every man there. The cloaked figure behind him scarcely drew any notice as she blended into the shadows.

''You'll not get a bloody shilling out of the bastard unless you've got his signature on a piece of paper,'' Jacob announced. ''The whole lot goes to his wife. I already made certain of that.''

Duncan didn't even bother to look at the lanky ex-soldier. ''Cass won't know how to handle it. As her only male relative, I'll be appointed trustee, so don't set your bloody sights too high, lackey.''

Wyandott halted in his ministrations and surrendered his place to the physician. Gazing down at the haughty marquess with contempt, he replied, ''As her father, I rather think I'll object to that.''

Jacob's reply covered the hasty intake of breath behind him. ''That ain't to the point. Lady Cass ain't his widow. My sister is. They were wedded when she was but ten-and-six, and she's got the lines and the child to prove it.''

With a bellow of rage, Merrick shook off his caretakers and lurched toward Jacob, his fist balled in a deadly knot. ''You bastard! You let Cass go through hell and didn't tell her . . .''

His side ripped in half as he swung, and Jacob easily

dodged the blow, catching him by the arm to keep him from falling and handing him gently back to Bertie and Thomas. "Wasn't anything I could do about it, my lord. I didn't know the lady until she was wedded. And afterward, there weren't no sense in saying anything. She was determined not to marry you, to keep her brother from picking you clean. I'd only cause her more trouble by saying the marriage wasn't legal-like. My sister and her boy were living in the streets when I came home from the war. There wasn't no one else but me to see to their welfare. I did it the best I could. I had those pistols ready, thinking to use them the first opportunity. The mark would have gone wide had Lord Eddings not turned and slipped when he did. I would have called him out myself, but who would take notice of a batman? I'll make it up to the lady in any way I can."

Jacob turned to apologize to Cassandra, but the brown-cloaked figure in the shadows had already disappeared.

Catching Jacob's surprise, Merrick and Wyandott exchanged glances. Wyatt staggered toward the path she must have taken, but the American halted him.

"Let me go after her. If I am any judge, you have caused her enough pain as it is."

Merrick clamped his hand to his side and grimaced. "You don't know the half of it, sir. She's carrying my child. I'll have her back if I must turn the world sideways, but right now, I'd just see her safe. She's not well, and the traveling isn't good for her."

Wyandott's wide jaw set in a fierce frown as he glared at the earl. "You'll pay for this. You damned aristocrats . . . ." He cursed and swung hurriedly down the path Cassandra had taken.

Swaying on his feet, Merrick watched him go. He had lost her. His mind told him that, but his heart just wouldn't believe. She hadn't stayed. She didn't care. She was free now.

What would she do with her freedom?

Chapter 29

Wesley Wyandott carefully concealed his concern as
he gazed upon the drooping figure of his youngest
daughter on the carriage seat across from him. She had
come without protest when he had caught up with her,
but he was beginning to suspect that her lack of speech
now was unnatural. The fiery creature who had earlier
turned a room full of experienced men into chaos,
challenged her husband to a duel, and chastised her
lover in no uncertain terms could not be the same person as this weary creature sitting across from him with
head flung back and eyes closed.

He studied the unhealthy pallor of her cheeks, the
shadowed circles of the fragile skin beneath her eyes,
and remembered Merrick's words. Mentally he calculated the years since he had been here last, deciding
she could be no more than nineteen, wondering that a
girl of that age could behave as she had in these last
hours. He knew the British considered his homeland
less than civilized, but even in the States his other
daughters retired to dim salons and couches and were
treated as delicate porcelain after they announced they
were expecting. And his other daughters were well
into their twenties and thirties and long married with
husbands and servants to wait on them. How on earth
had it come about that his youngest and frailest daughter, the one brought up in the lap of the oldest aristoc-
racy in civilization, could be pregnant and unmarried
and garbed in outlandish stockings and little more
while entertaining a table of all-male card players?

It staggered the mind to consider it, but comparing her sunset hair, flashing eyes, and fiery temper to his memory of his younger self, Wyandott had to reflect that she came by it naturally. She should have been a male if she were not to inherit any of her mother's ladylike graces, but smiling at Cassandra's lovely features, he had to admit he was glad she was not.

"You will make Lord Merrick a good wife," her father announced, startling even himself when his thoughts came out aloud.

Long gilt-edged lashes lifted briefly from upward-slanted eyes, but the murky color beneath revealed none of the flash and fire of earlier. The lashes returned to ivory cheeks again, and the carriage fell into silence once more, except for the jerking creak of ropes and leather outside.

"The wound was not deep. He will be fine in a few weeks. I don't know how things are done over here, but I should think a quiet wedding in the country would be suitable."

This time, the lashes didn't even lift. Wyandott had the urge to shake her, but reasoning that the travel made her ill, as Merrick claimed, he kept his tongue. There would be time enough in the future to learn more of this daughter he had never known he had.

The next few weeks proved him wrong. Merrick's driver speedily returned them to the estate in Sussex, but even their ecstatic reception by Cassandra's mother did not return the life to her eyes. Scarcely acknowledging this reunion of lovers torn apart long ago, Cassandra drifted up the stairs to the bedchamber she had once shared with Merrick.

Worried eyes followed her as she continued to drift, unsmiling, through the days that followed. Questions met with silence. Angry pleas met with the turning of a cold shoulder. Only simple requests elicited any response, and that was only by silent action.

Elizabeth's nails bit into her palms as she watched this pale ghost of her daughter through the front window. Cassandra had taken to daily walks along the coast, staring for hours at the sea, and Elizabeth could not help but consider this a dangerous sign. Desperately she turned to the tall man beside her, who also stared at the lone waif being drawn to the cliffs.

"You must *do* something, Wesley. Write to Merrick. Tell him he must come. He will marry her, won't he? He hasn't set her aside?"

"Of course he hasn't. If I am any judge, he will do his duty. He's aware of his obligations. I daresay the scandal of the duel is enormous right now, and he must deal with that. I shouldn't think he would be able to travel for a while, either. I'll write and see how he fares."

Even to himself this sounded like cold reassurance. Words like "duty" and "obligation" were not ones a nineteen-year-old girl would care to hear. But Merrick was older, a man of the world. He had not taken a well-bred young lady to bed without expecting to pay the price. Except, at the time, he had thought her married.

That was no excuse. Wyandott fired off a letter that afternoon, demanding to know Merrick's intentions. He also included a brief description of Cassandra's withdrawal to spur her lover along.

The creamy vellum with the earl's frank appeared in the next post, addressed to Cassandra. She took the folded missive from her father's hand and drifted up the stairs with it. She held it a while longer as she stared at the spiky writing on the outside as if she could hear the contents without seeing the words. Then ever so gently she laid the thick package in the center of her small writing desk, then left it unopened.

A second letter arrived promptly a week later. When Cassandra returned from taking it upstairs and once more headed for her silent walk along the coast, her father took the liberty of invading her empty chamber. There, in quiet companionship with the first, lay the second letter, still unopened.

He swore. He cursed. He contemplated ripping both letters open to scan the contents, but just the idea of tearing into those perfectly arranged elegant packages seemed to shatter the brittle silence of this darkened room. Instead of slamming the door as he strode out, he nudged it gently. He felt as if he left a house of mourning.

Out on the cliff, Cassandra found her favorite perch overlooking the ocean's hypnotic undulations. The sea gulls' cries overhead seemed piercingly lonely, and she felt content in their company. The wind lifted her hair from her face, since she made no attempt to conceal it with bonnet or hat. Freckles had begun to frame the bridge of her nose, but she had little concern for her appearance. The weather was growing cooler now. She supposed it must be mid-September. As she often did when she considered the lateness of the season, she raised her hand to the curving plane of her abdomen. She felt nothing there, no sign of the life within, and she removed her hand, disappointed. There ought to be something, some signal to indicate the truth. What if Wyatt were wrong? What if she did not carry his child?

She didn't know whether she would be relieved or not. She didn't know if Wyatt would be relieved or not.

So she sat there waiting for some sign from beyond to tell her what to do.

"Dashitall! I cannot lie here a moment longer." Merrick threw the sheaf of papers in his hands to the floor as the physician examined his side and shook his head. He winced as probing fingers found the infection, sending fiery spirals of pain through his chest.

"If you do not lie here a week longer until the inflammation goes away, you will be lying forever in a cold grave," the young physician informed him sternly.

"By Jove, man, if you only knew . . ." Merrick

leaned back against the pillows piled at the head of his bed, closed his eyes, and groaned. The pain in his side was as nothing to the pain of the words on those pages cluttering the floor. The blasted American was threatening to take Cassandra away. What in hell was the matter with her? Why didn't she answer his letters?

He probably didn't want to know the answer to that. With Cassandra, words were useless. Only actions counted. And he was laid up here in bed with a damned physician telling him it would be a week or more before he could even rise from the mattress. He gritted his teeth and cursed a particularly vivid phrase.

"I haven't heard that one before." The physician finished taping the fresh bandage in place, his fingers gentle and competent despite the invective from his patient's lips scurrilizing the ancestry of all physicians and dogs. "A man as inventive as you should be able to write a book of curses in a week. It will keep you occupied."

"I'd be better occupied tarring and feathering the drunken sot who leeched me and left me to fester like a two-week-old pox. I'll carve his eyeballs out of his head so he can never mistreat some other poor unfortunate again."

The doctor, who had heard all this before, began to pack his bag. "You would do better to use your influence to improve licensing laws. Write letters to your peers describing the quacks allowed to roam the streets under the questionable title of doctor. Medicine is a science. It is time society recognized it as such."

Merrick growled something incomprehensible. The sound of footsteps pounding up the stairs brought his head up, however, and he waited impatiently for the door to open. At the sight of Bertie's fair head, he grimaced with relief and began to maneuver himself from the bed.

"It's about time you got here, bigawd! This devil has threatened the servants into disobedience, Jacob's deserted me, and I'm too damned helpless to find a shirt. Find me some clothes, Bertie. I've got to get out of here.''

Thomas followed his brother in and both fair heads turned to the young physician they had brought to the house a week ago. The man had worked wonders to bring the earl out of his raging fever. They awaited his reply with a respect bordering on religious fervor.

''If that wound opens again, the inflammation will flare up all over and he is too weak to fight it any longer. Just the act of going down the stairs could kill him until the infection is gone.'' The physician jerked on his gloves, picked up his bag, and gave a curt nod to the Scheffings. Without a further reprimand to the fuming earl behind him, he strode out.

''Devil take it, Bertie, I might as well be dead as to lie here and let Cass get away! Help me, damn you. I've got to find out why she doesn't answer my letters.'' Wyatt struggled to tip himself out of bed without moving the muscles over his ribs. He had no grand desire to reopen the wound and be set back another two weeks or end up in a grave, but he could not bear to do nothing.

Bertie sent his younger brother a look and they converged as one upon the bed, pushing the protesting earl back to the pillows and holding him there.

''You're a damned fine fellow and all that, Merrick, but you ain't worth a shilling to no one in your casket. Now, what's this about Cass? Why ain't she here, anyway? What happened to that fellow who went after her? Claimed he was her father, didn't he?'Fess up, old boy, and we'll do your walking for you.''

Wyatt groaned and leaned back against the pillows. He couldn't claim illness to avoid these questions any longer, not if he wanted to get up. But he'd be damned if he could answer any of them coherently.

''She's in Sussex with her mother.'' He thought rapidly, trying to remember the scraps of identity thrown around that fateful night and to arrange them in some respectable lie. ''Wyandott's an old friend of her father's. He thought it better to get her away after what she went through that night.'' He wanted to mention the child, his fears for Cassandra's health, but he realized he had no right to. He choked back the anxiety uppermost in his mind. ''I've not told her I've been ill. I didn't want her to worry, what with Duncan and all . . .'' He allowed his voice to trail off vaguely.

The Scheffing brothers nodded understandingly. Under the direction of the American, Duncan had been bandaged up and hauled off protesting to a ship waiting in the Thames. His health and whereabouts wouldn't be known for months. That was more than enough for a gentle female to worry over. The fact that Merrick had been injured and Rupert killed would be sufficient to send any lady to her bed. It was for the best that Cass stayed away now.

''She'll be right as rain soon enough. You ain't got to worry over Cass. Her name ain't even been mentioned at the club, so you don't need to fret yourself over that either. Didn't nothing get out that we didn't want to.'' Bertie settled comfortably in a wing chair beside the bed and propped his new Hessians against the bedcovers. ''That valet or batman or whatever he is of yours did a bang-up job of explaining the dustup. Somehow, everybody's thinking Duncan challenged Rupert over wedding his sister without getting shed of his first wife. Your reputation stands you in good stead. You come out the hero for chasing Rupert off the continent and marrying Cassandra posthaste, without a word of the merry dance she led you. So you ain't got nothing to do but lie there and rest and get better.''

And worry if his child would ever have a name or if it would be born across an ocean or if he would ever see her again, Wyatt amended gloomily to himself, leaning back against the pillow with a pained expression. His boredom with the dull routine of his life had led him to seek a little magic, but the damned sorceress was too unpredictable to know whether he had become toad or prince.

Before Bertie could sneak out thinking he was asleep, Wyatt spoke aloud. "Go get her, Bertie. Take her back to Merrick. I don't care how you do it, but pry her away from that damned arrogant American and bring her back where she belongs."

Scheffing looked startled, then amused by this flight of fancy in his practical friend. Thinking the fever was returning, he agreed wholeheartedly. "Of course, old boy. Didn't that Jacob of yours mention wedding his Lotta? We'll all go down and see the happy couple joined. It would be better could you wait to travel with us, but we'll tell you all about it later."

Wyatt nodded in uneasy relief. He trusted Bertie. He wished to hell he could trust Cass. The image of her laughing eyes, sunset hair, and lithe figure taunted his senses, but the cloaked shadow in men's tights haunted his thoughts. Witch or woman? Would he ever know?

Cassandra didn't have time to run and hide when Bertie and company exploded into her secluded life. She was in the foyer, garbed for her walk, when the knock came at the door. Before she could flee, Lotta was racing forward to grab her hands, Jacob was towering over her dressed to the nines in a gentleman's coat and trousers, and Bertie and Thomas were beaming and making polite noises to her parents when they appeared.

Her parents. It seemed a very odd notion, but as Cassandra watched the two of them while Lotta chattered, she could see that her mother and the American were very much a pair, even after all these years. From scraps of conversation, she knew Wyandott was a widower now, and her mother's cheeks held the first flush of color she had seen in them in years. Each day she was up and about more, and there was no doubt in

anyone's mind that the American's affectionate bully-
ing and badgering had much to do with it.

As she watched them now, Cassandra felt a painful
ache grow wide within her. Wyatt had been by turns
tender and withdrawn. His cold authority could wither
the flowers in a bouquet, and she knew that part of
him was more natural to the life he had lived before
she entered it. The gentle man who loved music and
touched her with both passion and reverence was a late
arrival and could disappear with just a brush of wind.
Perhaps he had already disappeared. The events of
these last weeks were more than enough to drive any
rational man into flight. But still she longed for the
same love her father expressed to her mother as they
whispered between them, and she grew jealous of the
unspoken words in their gazes when they looked upon
each other.

Unwilling to watch any longer, she pulled on her
gloves and continued out the door as if guests hadn't
arrived. Lotta and Jacob exchanged looks but, still
dressed in their traveling clothes, they hurried out after her. Thinking this another of Cassandra's whimsi-
cal escapades, Bertie and Thomas willingly did the
same.

"And we're to be married in the church with flowers
and everything," Lotta chattered as if their conversation hadn't been abruptly interrupted. "We don't know
where we'll be staying as yet. There's so many lawyers
and solicitors and all and Jacob's sister is still in shock
and can't decide nothing for herself, so we'll wait to see
what happens. But, Cass, you've got to promise to stand
up with me or I'll be scared to death up there in front of
a whole church. I ain't been inside a church . . ." She
took a deep breath and tried to remember when.

Thomas took advantage of the pause to add his eager
messages. "And Christa's had her baby! She and Cunningham are acting perfect asses, as if theirs was the
first heir ever born, but Christa insists you and Merrick must grace the christening. She says the place is

much too dull without another woman to talk to, and she's waiting impatiently for your return. Actually, she just wants to show off the squalling brat, but he is handsome in his own way. You will return with us, won't you, Cass? Merrick said you might.''

The energy swirling around her buffeted all her senses, catching her up and jerking her this way and that. Caught up in the excitement of their plans, carried away on their eager friendliness, Cassandra was instantly jarred to the ground by the sound of Merrick's name. She found herself staring into four happy, familiar faces awaiting her answer, and before the clouds of despair had time to descend again, she heard herself saying, ''Of course.''

Chapter 30

"And Lord Merrick said we might stay in the cottage until we decide where to go. Just like gentry, imagine that, Cass! I can't believe it myself. I keep pinching myself, waiting to wake up."

That effectively closed that option, Cassandra decided immediately as the carriage lumbered ever closer to Kent. She wondered if Wyatt had intentionally created this obstacle or if he had just magnanimously offered the little cottage to Lotta and Jacob out of some misplaced gratitude for their interference. She couldn't intrude her presence on the happy couple. They would feel as if they had to serve her as before. Now her only choices were the ruins at Eddings and Merrick's home. And without Lotta and Jacob, she couldn't face those haunting ruins.

"Well, I've quite decided your father had to be one of the Scheffings, so you are gentry, Lotta. Just stick your nose in the air with the best of them and no one will know the difference."

Lotta smiled to herself at this sign of her lady's returning spirit. The gray, listless Cass they had found in Sussex had been worrisome indeed, but the closer they came to home, the more like herself she became. Lotta wasn't certain if it was the prospect of seeing the earl again or the challenge of coming to cuffs with the dowager countess that brought out the fight in her, but either possibility was welcome. It would be a few days yet before the earl could travel. His mother would give Cass something to do until then.

Alighting from Wyatt's carriage in front of the sprawling Merrick mansion for all the world as if she were the reigning countess, Cassandra swept up the stairs on Bertie's arm, greeted the smiling butler with charm, and encountered Lady Merrick in the front hall.

"Where is Wyatt?" Startled that her son hadn't stepped out of the carriage too, Lady Merrick spoke the first words that came into her head.

"You don't know?" Cassandra answered sweetly, her tone carrying a plethora of implications.

Knowing the earl had gone out of his way to conceal his injuries from everyone, Bertie hastily intruded. "There's still business in London for him to see to. There's solicitors crawling up the walls, what with Eddings' hasty departure and this business with Jacob's sister and all. You know how he is, a finger in every pie. He promises to be back soon enough."

"I should certainly hope so. MacGregor is entirely out of line. It is time he is brought down a peg or two. I shall write and tell Wyatt he must be home at once." She scarcely gave Cassandra a second glance as she nodded a hasty farewell to Bertie and started to retreat.

Joyous anger swept through Cassandra at thus being ignored. She had once determined that Merrick's mother must be conquered if she were ever to win his affections. Now was her opportunity. In dulcet tones, she sent her challenge zinging after that broad back. "You may also write and tell him his wife requests fabric samples for the draperies in the second salon. Those abominations are coming down."

The air should have exploded with the electric tensions colliding in that towering hall as Lady Merrick swung around to confront her nemesis. Cassandra was certain lightning would strike her for naming herself what she was not. She waited for the storm to break, but the dowager merely glared and said, "Tell him yourself."

Cassandra grinned and kissed a frozen Bertie's cheek. "It's good to be home again."

* * *

"Open the draperies, James," Cassandra ordered idly as she held up a measuring stick to the far wall and guessed at the measurements.

"Close the draperies, James," Lady Merrick commanded as she swept into the room a moment later.

The harassed footman pulled the rod back toward the center of the window.

Cassandra looked up in annoyance. "Madam, I require the light to work. If you won't do this, then I needs must. Has MacGregor come in yet? I need to talk with him about my fields."

Lady Merrick gestured for the draperies to be opened again. The footman sighed and began pulling the heavy brocade open, spilling in the late-morning sunlight.

"Indeed, you ought to speak with him. He and those feebleminded field hands of yours have taken it into their heads to practice some kind of experimental harvesting. You will no doubt lose half your crop, or what those men don't steal. Someone must keep watch over them every minute."

"Well, I cannot be in two places at one time. If you will not order these draperies replaced, I must. And that means the entire room must be refurbished. Just look at the discoloration where that painting has been removed."

Lady Merrick glared at the bright square on the wall, then back at the slender woman balancing precariously on a chair arm to reach the top of the window. "Order the servants to do it. That's what they're here for. I'll have the carriage brought around, and I'll show you what I mean about those fields."

Cassandra nearly toppled from her perch. She turned and stared at the dowager and found the footman staring too. Such condescension from the haughty woman was unheard of. Hastily, she scrambled down and handed her pad to the startled James. "Here, find someone to help you. Mrs. Marlow might be able to write the dimensions if you'll measure."

Lady Merrick nodded imperiously and sailed off to seek her bonnet. Catching her breath, Cassandra hurried to do the same. A fluttering in her stomach bespoke her nervousness, but she ignored it. Winning Wyatt's mother would be half the battle. He couldn't put her out if his mother approved her as his wife.

Later that night, after spending a day of inspecting the crops and arguing over the best methods of handling them, Cassandra retired to the lovely ivory-and-green room that Wyatt had assigned to her. She cast a longing gaze to the connecting door to Wyatt's chamber after her maid left her alone. It had been weeks since they shared a bed. They had not been apart that long all summer. Would she ever be allowed to enter that chamber again, or had he finally realized how thoroughly unsuitable she was to be his countess?

Misery welled up in her, overwhelming her as it had those first weeks since the duel. She should never have run away. She should have stayed by Wyatt's side, nursed him to health, helped him deal with Duncan and Jacob and Rupert's estate and all. She had only herself to blame that he had developed a disgust of her and refused ever to see her again.

She didn't know why she had run away. It had all happened so quickly, so horrifyingly. There had been nothing she could do. The feelings of helplessness were new to her, terrifying her beyond all control. She had never imagined what it would be like to lose someone close to her. The death of the marquess hadn't been real. He had been dead to her long before the actuality. There had been times she wished Duncan dead, but when she had seen him fall, it had been much, much worse than she had thought possible. To have it followed by Wyatt's cry of pain . . . She shuddered, refusing to think of that terrible anguish.

Walking to the window overlooking the park, she stared out at the dusk-covered landscape. The moon was trying to rise just over the hill. The silhouettes of trees tossed restlessly in the breeze, and Cassandra momentarily contemplated rushing out to join them. The pain inside her needed some release, and she knew no other solution but to run until it dissipated or she left it behind.

She didn't know how else to deal with it. Dropping the curtain, she turned back to face the bed. She had lost Wyatt that night as certainly as if he had died. She had humiliated him by interfering where she wasn't wanted. She had lost her temper and her courage and behaved like a wicked child. And then she had run away.

She had done what little she could before running away. She knew nothing of nursing wounds. There were men there better qualified to deal with them than she. So she had found a physician to do what she couldn't. That was all she had known to do. It had been such a nightmare. She had wanted to run and cry and have Wyatt take her in his arms, but he hadn't even known she was there, or even seemed to care. He hadn't seemed in much pain. A dying man wouldn't rise up and try to kill Jacob. None of it had made a bit of sense. And she couldn't face the fact that a man had died because of her. She hadn't wanted to face it.

Then, discovering that the distinguished man directing the proceedings was her father . . . Well, that had been the finish of what remained of her equilibrium. Her own father had stood there and pulled the trigger that killed her husband. Or her false husband. She still couldn't believe any of it. Her father hadn't seemed a violent man. Her marriage had seemed very real. She could no longer believe her own senses. These last weeks her father had tried hard to be kind to her. Her mother evidently still idolized him. But he had killed Rupert.

Not that Rupert didn't deserve to be killed. Restless, Cassandra couldn't climb into her empty bed, but sought the comfort of the small fire smoldering in the grate. Pulling her bare feet under her, she curled up in the chair beside the fire and stared at the dying

embers. From all she'd heard, Rupert had been a worse
bastard than she had ever imagined. Jacob's sister and
nephew would still be starving on the streets if Rupert
hadn't died. And he would have haunted her the rest
of her life had he lived. She knew that, but it was
difficult to accept the concept of death.

She wished Wyatt were here to explain these things
to her. She knew she wasn't the sort to think things
through and make sense of them. That night, she would
gladly have killed Rupert herself and considered the
consequences later. But once a man lay sprawled on
the ground, his life's blood seeping out of him, it was
too late to consider consequences.

Leaning her head back against the chair, she tried
to imagine how her father had felt when he had seen
Rupert shoot one man and aim at another. He must
have known then what kind of husband she had been
given to. He had done the same thing she would have
done in his place. She knew now where she had inherited her impulsiveness.

Her hand spread tentatively across the slight swelling of her abdomen. Would Merrick's child be the
same way? Would he act without thinking, never fearing the consequences? Or would he be sensible and
reason things out in advance and try to control a situation so it didn't get out of hand? Smiling to herself,
Cassandra realized even Merrick hadn't been able to
control the situation with unpredictable heathens such
as herself and her brother and her father. Poor Wyatt.

Not poor Wyatt. Rich Wyatt. He had everything:
family, wealth, power, a happy home, friends, intel-
ligence, security—everything she had always dreamed
of. And with all that, there wasn't an arrogant bone in
his body. He was the kindest, gentlest, most generous
man she'd ever had the fortune to meet. And she had
thrown him away.

Pain rose up and engulfed her, carrying her off on
tides of anguish. She couldn't bear even the thought of
losing him, she needed him too much. Had she been

wise, she would have accepted her father's offer and fled to another country and started all over again. But she couldn't be wise. She could only sit here and love a man who probably despised her by now. She would grovel at his feet if necessary, but she'd much rather fight to win him back. She could challenge his mother, refurbish his home, watch over his estate, amuse his friends, but could she ever make him love her?

She didn't even know if he still wanted the child. He must, if he had insisted that she be returned here. That gave her something to dwell on. If he wanted the child, he couldn't cast her off so easily. Merrick couldn't be so cruel as to separate her from her child.

That gave her a toehold of sorts. Would that be enough? He was so very good at ignoring the people around him, at going his own way and pretending the world outside didn't exist. She understood how that could be, given his background and inclinations, but did she have what it took to break through that barrier and make him notice her?

She couldn't lose faith now. For the sake of the child growing inside her, she had to make him recognize her. No matter that she was the most unsuitable countess the Merrick title might ever know, she would overcome all obstacles. She would be Wyatt's wife, whether he liked it or not.

The day of the wedding began with a steady drizzle, but it didn't dampen the spirits of the happy couple. Cassandra stood up with Lotta, and Bertie was impressed in Merrick's place as Jacob's best man. The company was an interesting assemblage of Merrick servants and townspeople eager for the pomp and ceremony as well as to exchange gossip and wonder at the couple rising from the ranks to the place of near-gentry by dint of an unscrupulous rake's wealth. Even Jacob's sister, the new widow, and her son were there to bless the proceedings and to add spice to the gossip that flowed like fine wine through the congregation.

Afterward, much to the dowager's horror, Cassandra invited the assemblage to a gala reception at the mansion. As the clouds cleared away, fiddlers played on the lawn, lanterns were lit, and ale kegs were breached. The village might have been deprived of viewing the earl's marriage to his new countess, but this celebration substituted rather better, since everyone could take part. Cassandra viewed the crowd with proud success as Jacob led Lotta onto the back lawn to begin the dancing.

Arriving unnoticed in the confusion, Wyatt signaled the footman who opened the door to silence and watched the gaiety from the conservatory window. Still clutching the extravagantly expensive bundle of Alençon lace he had searched all of London to locate, he focused his attention on the festivity. His gaze immediately sought and found Cassandra, and hungrily he drank in the sight he had dreamed of these many weeks.

She wore her glorious hair wound in primrose ribbons that accented fiery hues and spun in tantalizing whirls around her face and throat. Her high-necked gown was all that was proper, but the gauzy material filling her neckline could not conceal the womanly curves beneath. Eagerly he sought the changes the child she carried would make, but the distance and the growing dark were too great. Still, he watched as she threw back her head in laughter, kissed Jacob on the cheek, and lifted a mug in toast to the new couple. She was alive and well and here. He could scarcely ask for more.

When he saw Thomas approach and beg her for a dance, Wyatt's eyes narrowed jealously, and he started for the door. To his surprise, Cassandra laughed and shook her head and linked her arm with the boy's and led him to one of the village girls standing wistfully on the edges of the crowd. Wyatt felt so proud of her that he near burst with the pleasure, and his hand halted on the door latch.

He was overweary from the reckless pace he'd made

to get here as soon as the physicians had released him for travel. He was covered with the filth of the road, and he knew he looked more ghost than human. It wouldn't do to terrify them all by his appearance. Bertie had assured him they didn't know he had been ill. Cassandra seemed content for the moment. Before he destroyed everyone's joy, he would prepare himself.

Sending commands for a bath, Wyatt wearily climbed the stairs to his chambers. He had made some decisions in these weeks confined to bed. For one thing, he knew he wasn't made for a life of deceit and trickery. Perhaps honesty had its boring moments, but it didn't end up in duels and death. Cassandra was just going to have to learn to endure his propriety, and the first step toward that was to make an honest woman of her.

He fully expected a vociferous argument. She would rail and shout and throw things at him. He wasn't in any condition to throw her over his shoulder and carry her to the nearest preacher with the special license crackling in his pocket. But he would prevail. He had to.

The invitation and her father's permission rested in the same pocket with the license. The only document missing was Cassandra's consent. She had never answered his letters. He hadn't heard one word in reply to his passionate pleas. He knew he had hurt her. He knew the duel had probably been as fatal to Cass's capricious emotions as it had been for Rupert, but he still couldn't believe she would deny the child she carried a name. Now that the world knew her marriage to Rupert was null, it was even more imperative that she be legally bound to him, for the child's sake. What imp of Hades had entered her now?

Mulling over Cassandra's odd behavior, Wyatt undressed and soaked in the bath brought to him. He knew little about women. He had no sisters or female cousins to teach him how their minds worked. His mother had more or less taken the place of his father, and he seldom thought of her as female. So he could not compare

Cass's behavior to very many examples and try to determine why she hadn't answered his letters. Her father had said she was so blue-deviled that he feared for her health, yet she had seemed right enough outside a few minutes ago. Would she have come back here if she meant to run away from him again?

Wyatt stepped out of the bath and dried himself off. He wanted to confront Cass and work this out, but he couldn't ruin her festivities by putting in an appearance now. He would rest for a while, until everyone had gone home. Then he would seek her out and demand explanations. He reached for his dressing gown.

Below, a footman whispered to a maid, who reported to the kitchen staff, who carried the tale outside with trays of meat pies and pitchers of lemonade. Within the half-hour the tale had reached Cassandra's ears. Forgetting her surroundings, she dropped her glass, lifted her skirts, and ran for the nearest door.

Having just heard the word themselves, the newlyweds exchanged glances and grinned.

"I wager she boxes his ears roundly." Jacob set his mug aside and slipped his arm around his new wife's enticingly plump waist.

Lotta gave him a scornful look. "And I say they'll be in their bed before we reach ours."

Jacob leered. "I can find a way to prevent that."

As he lifted her squealing into his arms and started for the beribboned carriage waiting for them, their guests laughed and waved and made way.

One good celebration deserves another. Those closest to the couple began counting months and laying wagers as to the date of the christening.

The lanky ex-soldier and his vivacious bride didn't seem to notice.

Chapter 31

"Wyatt, how could you? Why did you do it?"

The chamber door slammed open, rattling a rather ancient Chinese vase on the mantel. Wyatt jerked abruptly awake and stared into the gloom of his chambers. He didn't need a lamp to see the glowing incandescence of Cassandra as she flew into the room. Whether she were angry phantom or fairy, he did not care to consider. Gingerly he sat up.

"How could you set up such a treacherous scheme? He could have killed you! I'll never forgive you. Never! You're an odious, odious man! I thought I could trust you. I thought you would be reasonable and proper and I would never have to worry about such absurdities again. Must I begin worrying about carrying a fatherless child too? I hate you for doing this to me, Wyatt Mannering! How could you?"

She flew up and down the room like a vengeful wraith, her primrose ribbons bouncing and swirling against the darkness. Wyatt stared after her in bemusement, trying desperately to make sense of her complaint. But for the first time in his life he truly listened instead of letting the words fly around him, and what he heard and what she said seemed strangely at odds. To his shock, as she ranted and raved, Wyatt realized that he was hearing what she didn't say more clearly than what she shouted. Her cries of outrage hid a flood of emotions that were left to him to interpret.

In growing wonderment he listened as she shouted, "You could have been killed!" and he heard, "You terrified me!'' ''How could you leave me to do such a thing?'' became ''I needed you beside me in this.'' Wyatt shook his head as the words ''I hate you'' thundered through the air again. Cass had never hated anyone in her life. His eyes opened wider.

A man might have said, ''Sorry about the dust-up, old boy. We missed you.'' He wouldn't bury the language in a deluge of emotions and histrionics. That's where women had led him astray all these years. He wasn't supposed to listen to the words, but the feelings behind them. Extremely odd, but the discovery delighted him. Wyatt had to admit saying ''We missed you'' or ''I was worried'' didn't have quite the same effect as this fiery explosion all over his carpet. With fascination, Wyatt listened as Cassandra berated him with growing tears in her voice. He wasn't quite certain he was awake, after all. This was the stuff of dreams.

''I don't mind when you go all stiff and proper. And I try not to intrude when you're thinking and ignoring me. And I really do want to be just as you want. But when you do this . . .'' Cassandra threw her arms up in a bewailing gesture, her voice choking on sobs. ''I thought he'd killed you! And it would have been all my fault, and I could never live with myself, and I don't know how you could expect me to go on living like that. I'll not do it, Wyatt! I won't. Living with Duncan was horrible enough, but I knew I could live without him if he went too far. I'll go to America with my father. I don't have to live like this. I know you don't care about my feelings. It doesn't matter. I'm just tired of feeling guilty. All my life—''

The shock was beginning to wear off. Merrick rose from the bed, and before she could launch another attack, he trapped her in his arms. It was a bit like capturing a whirlwind, particularly since he was still weak from his illness. She wiggled and squirmed and protested and ducked her head out of his reach, but he held firm, pulling her close and running his hands up and down her back until the tension began to flow out of her and she was sobbing against his shoulder.

"Hush, Cass. I'm alive and you're here and there is no reason to feel guilty about anything. You're going to have to learn that what I do is my choice, not yours. I made a mistake. I may make many mistakes in the years to come, but they'll be my mistakes, not yours. Your feeling guilty will not make me feel better. Feeling guilty about anything won't make anyone feel better. You may admit to as many errors as you wish, Cass, and I shall never blame you for them. You may be as beautiful as a goddess, but I certainly don't expect you to behave as one. All I want from you is to say you will stay with me."

Cassandra looked up with tears wetting her lashes, but Wyatt didn't give her time for reply. He had been waiting for weeks to have her back in his arms again. Perhaps she hadn't exactly come to him with the words he wanted to hear, but he didn't need the words when he heard the emotions and felt her need. She was a chaotic mixture of grace and beauty and the fierceness of an elemental storm, but she needed him. He heard the melody of her desire behind the crashing fugues of her anger. Filled with elation at thus recognizing what she had long denied him, Wyatt bent and silenced her protests with a kiss.

Such a kiss! Cassandra's lips clung to Wyatt's as if parched and offered sweet water. She couldn't get close enough. Her lips parted eagerly to give him entrance, and her tongue twined with his in hungry desperation. She buried her fingers in the velvet folds of his robe and stood on her toes to press closer into his enveloping embrace. The masculine scent of his beard-stubbled jaw filled her senses. She closed her eyes and threw her head back and melted in sweet ecstasy as his lips softened and gentled and caressed as Wyatt stroked and nibbled and came back for more, always more, more than lips could offer.

She shuddered as his hands found the ties to her

bodice and shredded the fragile tucker beneath until his flesh held hers. The magic of just that touch transferred fury into passion. Hands shaking with the desperation of her need, Cassandra slid her fingers beneath Wyatt's robe and clung to his muscular shoulders while he bent to taste the ripe curves he had uncovered.

He lifted her and held her against him so he could kiss and caress the aroused peaks of her breasts until Cassandra cried out with the pleasure and need for more. She struggled to free herself from the confines of the gauzy material of her gown, but Wyatt was too impatient to wait. He pulled bodice and chemise down to her waist so he might more fully explore the white curves beneath, and she leaned back against the bed to give him full access to what he sought.

In the next instant, she was shrieking with horror and pulling Wyatt's robe from his shoulder to uncover the wide white bandage wrapped across the broad swath of dark hairs on his chest.

"Wyatt! What is this? You've been hurt. They said it was naught but a scratch! Wyatt, stop that! You'll hurt yourself. Oh, my word, I cannot . . ."

The words were smothered by Wyatt's kiss, the fears crushed by his pressuring fingers. "Don't distract me now, Cass," he murmured against her cheek as his hands rode down over her hips and buttocks and filled with the fine fabric of her gown. "I'm going to make love to you first. Then you may weep over my crippled body."

"Crippled, indeed," she gasped as he brought her up against his hardness. Then his kiss found her mouth again, and her next words slipped into oblivion while the passion swirled around them.

Riding her gown upward until it crushed in mangled folds at her waist, Wyatt cupped her soft buttocks in his palms and groaned as she lifted herself to rub against his aching maleness. Without the strength to hold her up, he leaned her against the bed, as he had once dreamed of doing. "Let me love you, Cass," he murmured into her hair, spreading his kisses downward until the fire of their breaths meshed and held.

He didn't have to ask. Cassandra's long legs lifted to twine around his narrow hips, and in the instant that it took to feel her openness and vulnerability, he came into her.

The swiftness and thoroughness of his entry left Cassandra breathless. She had him now, deep inside her, and she would never let him go again. With triumph, she gave herself to the staid Earl of Merrick, and knew the gift to be returned threefold by the hungry man in her arms.

Later, they lay naked, wrapped in each other's arms, a sheen of moisture glistening over their bodies as they touched and caressed and renewed the sensations that they had been so long missing. Cassandra's fingers swept gently, curiously over the wide bandage on Wyatt's chest, and blue eyes lifted in confusion to warm, dark ones.

"Why did everyone lie to me? I should have been there with you. But when I saw you swing at Jacob, I thought surely . . . I could not believe you had been seriously hurt."

Wyatt brushed a kiss across her brow. "You had quite enough to deal with in Rupert's death and Duncan's cowardice. I'd not add to your burdens. Besides, it was not the wound that caused my trouble, but the incompetence of the physician who did his best to murder me. There was nothing you could have done but fret, and that would have made me feel worse."

Cassandra kissed the bare expanse of skin above the bandage, exulting in the warmth and strength of him beneath her fingers. "I could have murdered the physician for you. I could have brought you flowers and sung to you. I don't want you to lie to me, Wyatt. I never want you to lie to me. Please, I've lived with lies too long. If you have any feelings for me at all, you will always be truthful with me."

"Any feelings at all?" Wyatt chuckled and lifted himself up on one elbow to run his fingers through her hair and stare down into the delicious cream and rose of her face. "Do you have any idea of the fantasies a man carries in his mind? The dreams, the wishes, the desires that can make his every waking moment a delight or a torment? Can you even begin to imagine the fantasies I have created ever since you leaned over that stairway and kissed my cheek at Roxbury's ball? Cassandra, my sweet, you are my dream come true, and I'll lie, cheat, steal, and commit murder to hold on to you. I fear you have a very exalted notion of my character."

"Me?" Cassandra stared at him in amazement. "You dream about me? Why ever would you? You could have any woman you want. Just because I have shamelessly pursued you . . ."

Wyatt's laughter rolled up from his chest as he rolled her into his arms and snuggled her against his chest. "You are an awful innocent, my love. After what we just did, do you still have doubts about what I see in my fantasies? I used to think there was something wrong with me when I imagined taking a beautiful woman as I just did with you now. When I suggested to my first wife that we make love elsewhere than in the bed, in the dark, with our nightclothes on, she became hysterical and called me a perverted monster. Is it any wonder when you kissed me on the cheek in a public room, lured me into your bedroom and let me do as I willed in daylight, that I began dreaming all sorts of impossible dreams?"

Cassandra tweaked a hair on his chest. "You have led me astray, my lord. I thought what we did was perfectly proper, since you aided in it, and you are never improper. Now I find you only wished to make a lewd woman of me. What shall you do when I grow as big and round as Christa and you cannot get near me? Will you find another innocent maid to lead astray?"

The smile fled Wyatt's lips as he lifted Cassandra's chin so their eyes met. "Yes, I have led you astray, and I am not proud of the pain I have caused you, but believe me, Cass, when I tell you that it is not only what we do in these chambers that binds me to you. You are the magic in my life, the song that fills my days. I'll be quite content to do naught but hold you and watch the child grow, if you will let me."

Cassandra choked on the words filling her throat as she stared down into Wyatt's serious face. A lock of rumpled chestnut hair fell across his forehead, and in the lamplight his dark eyes held a mysterious luster that held her bound. She traced a finger across the sharp angle of his cheek down into the hollow beside his lips, caressing the thin and wholly masculine curve of his lip.

"You will grow bored with me," she whispered unhappily. "I am immensely ignorant. I will shame you before your friends. My impulsiveness will grow to irritate you. We cannot suit in any way but this."

Wyatt glared up at her. "You did not even read my letters, did you? Why, Cass? I poured my damned heart out to you in those letters. I all but got down on my knees and begged. And you didn't even read them. You have made my life a misery these last weeks, Cassandra Howard, and you seem determined to go on doing so. Why could you not at least read what I had to say? You can read, can't you?"

Cassandra bit her bottom lip and slid back to the pillow beside him, where she didn't have to meet his accusing gaze. She heard the harshness in his voice and knew she deserved it. Now was the time for all truths to be known, but she hated to think of what would happen then. Surely he would not cast her off, but could she live with the knowledge that he despised her for her ignorance?

Defiantly she replied, "Of course I can read." Staring at the canopy overhead, she added in a less certain voice, "I just can't read your writing, or almost any other's."

Wyatt frowned, wondering if she had set out on some new ploy to make a cake of him. "Let me understand you. You can read, but you cannot read writing. I know my penmanship is not of the best, and perhaps in haste I did not make myself clear, but surely you could pick out a word or two, enough to take my meaning."

Cassandra kicked the sheet away and started to swing from the bed. "I'd rather hear the words," she announced mutinously. "Why should I sit and decipher scribbles when you have a tongue in your head and have never used it?"

Wyatt sat up and jerked her back before she could escape. "Stop talking in circles, Cass. Either you could not read the words or you refused to read them. Which is it?"

When he would not let her go, Cassandra crossed her legs on the bed's edge, folded her arms across her chest, and glared at him. Red-gold hair fell in wanton abundance across creamy skin, catching the lamplight and sparkling in glittering highlights with every breath she took. Wyatt took a deep breath and resisted pulling her back to the bed and making wild love to her again. His gaze traveled downward to the barely detectable curve of her abdomen, strengthening his resolve.

Shaking his head at her mute defiance, he tried again. "If you will bring me the letters, I will read them to you. But first, tell me what you can read so I'll know how to address myself to you in the future."

Cassandra watched him warily, and her resolution began to falter. He was going to find her abysmally ignorant. She didn't want him to despise her. But if he meant to make it a practice to write her letters, he would have to know sooner or later.

She caught the sheet and pulled it up to her neck. "My tutors said I was quite impossible and too willful to learn." Defiance still tinged her voice.

"They were undoubtedly correct," Wyatt agreed with alacrity. "But you are intelligent, and you can learn. You said you learned to read."

Cassandra's lips set in a straight line. "Print. I can read books with pictures and those nice straight letters. One governess taught me how to read them from a slate. But I cannot look at books with all those words in them. They give me a headache."

Wyatt sat up with the sheet covering his lap. He knew Cassandra had a sharp mind, sharper than most. Few could count cards as well as she, and her perception of other people's thoughts and actions was precise and accurate. The arrangement she had made with her workers to recover the Eddings estate was nothing short of brilliant for one so young and totally inexperienced in the field. Willful she might be but not stupid.

Remembering a maiden aunt of his, Wyatt had a glimmer of understanding as he examined her words carefully. "You can read block letters but not written. You can read letters written large on a slate, but not the fine print in a book." A sudden inspiration took him. "Can you see the notes on a page of music?"

Cassandra turned and stared at him suspiciously. "Of course I can see them. But they're just like reading cobwebs. I'm just too dumb to make anything of them. I've been trying to tell you, I'm totally unsuitable. I could not even help you keep the household accounts. All the spidery writing on the invoices makes my head whirl with fatigue. My tutors gave up on me long ago. You cannot help where they have failed."

Wyatt grinned in relief and reached over to capture a thick lock of her hair. "I will write you love letters in block print and hire a secretary to keep accounts. And if we cannot find magnifying glasses that will let you see the music clearly, I'll have a printer make them large for you. You're not dumb, little witch, you are only just half-blind."

Cassandra glared at him. "I am not blind. I can see you perfectly well."

"Even better from a distance, I wager," he agreed cheerfully. "And I do not have particularly fine features to confuse you when you are up close. It's no wonder that you can look blissfully upon this dull visage of mine. You do not see it as others do. And I wager you do not know how rare your beauty is because you cannot see the flaws in others. Ah, Cass, you are a miracle to behold. Come here and kiss me and tell me you'll be mine."

She went to him uncertainly. He seemed quite pleased with himself and not at all shocked at her ignorance. She knew perfectly well that she had quit trying to read those endless books her tutors had given her at an early age. Her mother had finally given up in despair when they had moved to London. It had little bothered her to never look at a book. Her father kept no library and she had not felt called upon to visit one. But Wyatt had a vast library and she knew he spent many hours a day poring over pages of fine print. Surely he must think her lazy, if naught else.

"You mistake me, Wyatt," she murmured against his shoulder as he cradled her against his side. "I am not at all like you. I simply do not have the patience to study over a book. And I really can see you quite well. You have lovely thick hair, and dark eyes, and lips that curve up ever so nicely when you laugh at me, like now."

"And can you tell me where the freckle is that I hate so much?"

Cassandra tilted her head up and stared at him with suspicion. "What freckle? Is this some ploy to make me search you all over? I shall, if you like."

Wyatt laughed. "Yes, I should like that. Perhaps you can find other freckles of which I'm not aware. However, if you have not seen this one, I doubt that you'll find more." He took her hand and placed one finger on a spot just in front of his ear. "There, my sweet. There is a quite noticeable brown speckle just there. Shall I fetch a candle for you to see it?''

Cassandra squinted and supposed there was some darker spot there if one looked closely. But that was scarcely to the point. ''Who is to notice such a thing?'' she demanded. ''If everyone were to go about looking for speckles on people's faces, we'd appear very strange indeed. I do not spend my time staring at people's faces to see if they've got spots.''

''But you see, Cass, other people don't have to stare to see them. They notice them right off. You have a whole different view of the world from most of us. You can't see the details, so you concentrate on the whole. Your lovely bouquets, for instance. You don't see that the petals of some of your choices scatter all over the furniture. And it doesn't occur to you that one flower doesn't suit with another because you are seeing only this lovely haze of color. You need spectacles, my love, but I love you just as dearly the way you are.''

Cassandra stared up at him in confusion. She didn't know whether to argue over her blindness or kiss him for his words of love. He had never said he loved her before. Did he mean it, or were they just pretty words like the endearments he showered upon her? Gentlemen were supposed to scatter gallant flattery at a lady's feet. She had taken all his words of praise with a grain of salt, but this was Wyatt, not just any gentleman. Might he truly mean it?

''You are just saying that for fear you have hurt my feelings,'' she murmured. ''You needn't, you know. I have been told often enough that I'm stubborn, willful, and stupid. Being told I'm blind can scarcely compare.''

Wyatt caught both her shoulders and pressed her back against the pillows. Leaning over her, he interspersed his words with kisses. ''Stubborn and willful, I'll not deny. Impetuous, occasionally wrongheaded, and decidedly argumentative, of a certainty. But not

stupid. Never stupid. You are generous, lovely, talented, and the solace of my soul. And if you cannot
love me in return, I will understand, but I shall never
stop trying to make you love me. Isn't that enough to
base a marriage on? Say you'll marry me, Cassandra.
Tell me you'll stay and be my wife. I really don't intend to give you any choice, but I'd like to hear the
words. Say them, Cass. Say you won't ever leave me
again.''

Cassandra was breathless from his kisses and the
ardor with which Wyatt wooed her. It was a most improper marriage proposal, indeed, but she would not
have it any other way.

Wrapping her slender arms around his shoulders and
arching brazenly against him, she complied with his
heated demands.

"I'll never leave you, I'll always love you, and we
shall make beautiful music together for the rest of our
lives. Now, will you make love to me?''

Wyatt crowed in happiness and triumph, and Cassandra didn't have to ask him twice. With gentle care,
he joined their bodies, and in passion he took her to
that world they shared alone, a magic kingdom for
those who love.

Chapter 32

"Cassandra's mother requests a private wedding, Mother. There will only be the two of us. There is no need for you to accompany us." Wyatt returned his cup to the saucer and lowered his paper to stare at his mother after her unusual demand.

"But you have only just returned and now you must go jaunting off again! It is not like you, Wyatt. It is nearly harvest. You must supervise the fields. You have neglected all your other properties this summer. You cannot neglect Merrick too. It is just not done."

Cassandra scooped a spoonful of eggs from the platter on the sideboard to her plate. She wore her hair in a discreet chignon with only a few ribbons to flutter down her back, and the modest muslin morning gown she had chosen flattered her figure without revealing it. Despite being showered in lace and indulging in passionate love play not more than an hour ago, which Wyatt's admiring gaze reminded her of forcefully as she approached the table, she felt quite proper and sure of herself as she sat down.

"But, my lady, Wyatt has you and MacGregor to keep sharp eyes on everything. The estate runs so very smoothly, it cannot need more than an occasional word or two from Wyatt to keep it running steady while we are gone. The biggest problem will be my dowry."

The dowager sniffed haughtily. "That is another subject I find very odd. Why should the Marquess of Eddings leave his lands to his daughter instead of his son? It is all very peculiar, to be sure, and I am not at all certain that that dreadful American isn't somehow behind it. How can your mother marry a man who for all intents and purposes sent her son into exile? It is a dreadful scandal.''

Cassandra and Wyatt exchanged meaningful glances. When Wyatt had ridden to Sussex to inform Cassandra's parents of their intention to marry, Cassandra's father had offered the former lands of the Marquess of Eddings as dowry. Wyatt had been thunderstruck, but the explanation, when it came, had been simple. The estate was never entailed. When the house had burned and the marquess found himself up the River Tick, he had offered the lands for private sale. Wyandott's British solicitors had written him of it, and surmising that his former lover might be in a precarious situation, he had purchased the lands, never knowing that one day he would discover a daughter who loved them.

But the fact that Cassandra was not the daughter of the Marquess of Eddings had never been imparted to the dowager, and neither saw any reason to do so now. Wyatt merely picked up his paper and coffee and spoke from behind the newssheet. ''Wyandott sent a dissipated bankrupt out of the country to learn better manners. Since he and Cassandra's mother will be returning to New York shortly, Duncan will have family with him, so it isn't complete exile. This man Wyandott is a very firm character. If anyone can straighten out Eddings, it will be him. I hope so, for Lady Eddings' sake, but it is scarce any of our affair.''

''Well, that doesn't mean you must condone it. There is considerable work to be done before that property can be profitable. I should think you would need stay here to see to it.''

Cassandra smiled at her plate of eggs. There were many things the dowager didn't know and, luck prevailing, would never know. Wyatt had not seen fit to inform her that their ''marriage'' was all a hum, and she was no more Lady Merrick than the man in the moon. The special license in his pocket would repair

that quickly enough, as soon as they got away from
Kent, where they were so well known.

The matter of her pregnancy had not yet been presented. Everyone thought they had been married at the
beginning of August, in France, only two months ago.
Yet she was nearly four months gone with child and
could not hope to conceal it much longer. Now was
the time for Wyatt to announce their plans, but he
seemed strangely reluctant to do so. She threw him a
thoughtful look as she waited for his reply to his mother's latest demand.

Behind his newssheet, Wyatt turned and gave his
"wife" a wink. Then, lowering it firmly, he met his
mother's glare with equanimity. "As a matter of fact,
Mother, it will in all likelihood be next spring before
I see to Cassandra's property. You and MacGregor
might discuss possibilities this winter if you like. Just
remember, he's my steward and you can't discharge
him without my permission."

Lady Merrick glared in outrage at her only son.
"Next spring? Whatever are you talking about? What
can occupy you the whole of the winter that you cannot see to it yourself?"

Setting aside his paper, Wyatt rose and proudly set
his hands on Cassandra's shoulders. To his amusement, her cheeks flooded with color, and he lifted a
hand to stroke the velvet softness gently. "I am saying
that Cassandra and I have never had our wedding journey, Mother. And since we have just discovered that
she is already with child, we have decided to take it
now, before she is burdened with the difficulties of
motherhood. You would not deny us a few months'
privacy, would you?"

A child! The dowager's mouth gaped open, then
closed as she grasped this announcement. Years she
had been waiting for this, years of desperation when
she thought her only son had given up any thought of
heirs. Joy was her first reaction; then practicality set
in. Of course, this should have been expected. Wyatt

had been behaving like a besotted schoolboy for months, and men had only one reason for behaving as such. And with a wanton handful like the Howard child . . .

Her eyes narrowed shrewdly as she cast a gaze on Cassandra's demure blush and Wyatt's proudly possessive grasp. One didn't take extended journeys when with child. It just wasn't done. Except . . .

Resignedly she set aside her napkin and rose from the table. "Of course, Wyatt. I can see that you must be right. Motherhood is a most strenuous and demanding occupation. You would do right to enjoy yourselves now. I trust you will take a reliable physician with you? You cannot be too careful with Cassandra's health. She may be carrying the next Earl of Merrick."

"Let us not rush things, Mother," Wyatt replied wickedly. "I plan to be around for quite a long time. We shall look for a Viscount Swansea first, shall we? But I'll settle for a lady this first time around. Females are very refreshing to the soul, and I intend for my sons to have some around to teach them what's important."

As his mother hastily departed, Cassandra sent Wyatt a startled look, but he gave her a reassuring kiss, and she relaxed, smiling. More than one child. It astounded the mind. She would be but twenty when this one was born. There would be time for several sons and daughters. There was a whole lifetime ahead of her to share with Wyatt and his children. It sounded too wonderful to be true. A real home, a real family, and someone to love. . . .

Wyatt caught her misty look and bent to press a kiss upon her cheek. "We're not married yet, sweet," he whispered. "Does the thought of young Mannerings make you wish to cry off?"

"No, that wasn't at all what I thought of," she murmured with a mischievous gleam in her eye. "It was how all those young Mannerings would get here that crossed my mind.''

Wyatt grinned as his loins responded to her sultry look. There would be many nights ahead to explore his fantasies as well as hers. The breakfast table was tempting, but perhaps, just this once, he would resist. Feeling noble, he kissed her cheek and stepped out of temptation's reach.

''Once the house is overrun with little creatures, you'll lose interest quickly enough. I'll just make certain I take my fill while I can. Lunch at the oak grove?''

Wyatt knew from her smile that she understood. They had not yet made love outside. It gave him something to think about as he waded through the morning's chores.

Sunlight filtered through the arched windows of the old church, casting a rainbow of color across the dark hewn pews. Dust motes floated in the beams, but there was none to notice, for the pews were bare of inhabitants.

In the nave, four people stood before the vicar, more elegant people than the ancient country church had known in many a year. The two men were tall and well-built, their wide-shouldered frames elegantly encased in tight-fitting frock coats, one of gray, the other of a rich navy. Since this was not an evening affair, both had disdained knee breeches, but their uncreased trousers fitted neatly to strong legs, revealing the expensive tailoring. Gleaming white linen accented their throats and hands, and the subtle gleam of a gold watch fob on one and the sparkle of a jeweled stud on the other bespoke not only wealth but also aristocratic wealth. Neither man had the need for ostentatious display.

Beside them, the women made a fascinating portrait in contrasts. The younger, taller lady stood proudly beside the gentleman in blue, her head held at a tilt that held more curiosity than arrogance. Dancing eyes watched the vicar's stiff stance with a gleam much akin to amusement before they strayed on to the dusty candelabra at the altar and the sparrow fluttering near the vaulted oak ceiling. Through the delicate web of fine lace covering her hair, a glimmer of red-gold caught in a stray sunbeam. A gown of silk so fine that its pale silver-blue changed color with every movement molded a figure of exquisite proportions, clinging to a slim waist one moment, brushing a rounded hip the next. Blue ribbons fluttered beneath her high breasts, and a tantalizing wisp of gathered lace blew in some draft, giving haunting glimpses of the creamy swell beneath. The gentleman at her side had difficulty keeping his attention on the vicar.

The lady standing beside the man in gray was more petite. She rested frequently on the arm of her companion, but the look on her face as she occasionally looked up to him gave her features a serene glow. She wore a darker blue more suited to her pale coloring. She wore no lace or ribbons, but a rope of pearls caught the light and gleamed with a soft luster. Her gloved hand came up occasionally to touch them, as if in pride and disbelief.

"Will you, Wyatt Avery Charles Swansea Mannering, Lord Merrick, take this woman to wife, to have and to hold . . ."

The time-honored words drifted past them, as much a part of the setting as the vicar and the windows and the pews. To the couple speaking them, they were mere formalities. The real vows had already been said and sealed with hearts, minds, and bodies. This ceremony only made public what they had known privately for a long time. Whatever their differences, they were meant to share their lives together. The groom smiled at his bride as he placed the ring on her finger, and the smile she gave him in return illuminated the altar as well as the sunbeam had the pews. The vicar coughed nervously at the passion flaring in that exchange of gazes.

When the final words were said, Wyatt had to satisfy himself with a brief promise of a kiss before turning to shake the hands of Cassandra's parents directly behind them. There were hugs and kisses all around, and then the older couple stepped before the altar. Cassandra and Wyatt exchanged conspiratorial glances, and after standing witness to this second ceremony, they fled from the altar and up into the crumbling organ loft.

A thunderous wheeze startled the three remaining occupants of the nave as they bent over the register to sign their names. They glanced nervously to the towering pipes filling the whole of the loft balcony. Since the death of the last village musician in the middle of the last century, the small parish had not been blessed with anyone talented enough to bring sound from the ancient instrument. When another wheeze followed the first, the company raised questioning eyebrows, but this wheeze was more whisper than thunder. The vicar hurriedly made out the wedding papers to the occasional rattle and hiss of the enormous pipes.

Above, Merrick issued a mild curse as Cassandra leaned anxiously over his shoulder. They had chosen this church not only for its privacy but also for this magnificent organ. The temptation to make the kind of joyful noise that would have the heavens singing had been too much for either of them to resist when they had discovered the instrument. Only now, it seemed as if the only noise they would make was the kind to drive mice from the pipes.

"One more time, Wyatt. Try it one more time. I know it will work," Cassandra whispered coaxingly. From habit, her fingers slid into the back of his hair above the crisp linen of his cravat, deriving hope as well as pleasure from this touch.

Wyatt glanced up to his bride's shining face, and catching her hand, he brought it to his lips for a kiss where his ring now rested on her finger. "If I could

ut touch the organ with the same magic as you touch
ne, it would sing forever, my sweet.''

Heart spilling over with love and eyes brimming with
moisture, Cassandra dared not let the tears spill too,
or fear she would never stop weeping in happiness.
She kissed Wyatt's ear lingeringly, then gently ran her
ingers over the scale of notes he was attempting to
persuade from the instrument. ''There, I bestow my
magic upon yon machine. Make it sing, Sir Wyatt.''

Wyatt pumped once more, then applied his skillful
ingers to the keyboard.

As the final papers were being signed below, the
irst recognizable notes began to escape the ancient
instrument. The vicar nearly dropped the book he was
holding, and the look of disbelief on his face would
have given credence to the legend of ghosts in the up-
er loft. More notes followed the first, and as the vicar
handed the newly wedded couple their marriage lines,
he notes became a haunting melody echoing through
he upper lofts in joyous approval.

In ghostly accompaniment to the organ, an angel's
voice began on the refrain. The couple below nearly
orgot to thank the vicar as they stared in proud awe
o the loft as the music lifted and soared and filled the
oly chapel with stirring sound. With tears of joy, the
icar dropped instantly to his knees and bowed his
ead as the glorious music poured down from above
or the first time in decades, startling even the spar-
ows into silence.

Moisture bathed the cheeks of the petite bride as her
ew husband kissed her gently, and hand in hand they
valked down the aisle to the door. A better wedding
ift could not have been purchased with all the wealth
1 the world, and they halted at the doorway to hear
he song's end. The resounding organ rattled ancient
les and shook centuries-old dust from the rafters, but
he sweet song of a magical nightingale wrapped in
nd around the mellow notes, bringing tears to the

eyes and raising goose bumps on the flesh that lingered well after the last note died.

The new Mr. and Mrs. Wyandott waited for the musical Lord and Lady Merrick to join them, and together the two couples walked out into the brilliant autumn sunshine.

It had been planned as a private ceremony, with none but themselves in attendance. Yet as they stepped onto the church steps, a shower of wheat chaff dusted their hats and hair and covered their shoulders before blowing into the breeze, and laughter marked their entrance into the world as couples.

Wyatt and Cassandra looked up to find Lotta and Jacob perched in the bell tower, dumping the first of the season's harvest from burlap bags. Laughing, the earl and his bride clasped hands and ran for the waiting carriage, leaving the bemused older couple standing on the church steps, waving farewell.